SHERWOOD

Also by
MEAGAN SPOONER:

Hunted

MEAGAN SPOONER

SHERWOOD

HARPER TEEN
An Imprint of HarperCollinsPublishers

HarperTeen is an imprint of HarperCollins Publishers.

Sherwood
Copyright © 2019 by Meagan Spooner

ISBN 978-0-06-242231-6

Typography by Torborg Davern
19 20 21 22 23   PC/LSCH   10 9 8 7 6 5 4 3 2 1
❖
First Edition

To the tall girls who wish they were dainty
To the short girls who wish they were elegant
To the girls who've always been too much
And the girls who are never enough

To those who persist
This is for you.

PROLOGUE

He wakes to the sounds of steel and fire, and the distant wailing of a Saracen woman. His sword is in his hand before he's on his feet. He'd been dreaming of rain on leaves, of the sound and feel of a wet day in Sherwood. When he lurches out of his tent in the English-occupied part of the city, the heat hits him full in the face, dazzling him as he tries to escape the lingering memory of green and damp and earth. Sand stings his eyes as a riderless horse gallops past, panicked, a long red line across its flanks spilling a crimson curtain down its hide.

Before he can begin to tell friend from foe, a blade swings out of the red-hot midnight toward his face. His sword hand lifts to deflect the blow automatically, his shoulder taking the brunt of the impact. It's the battle that brings him back to himself, banishing the last hints of his dream of home—the frantic staccato of panting and grunting and steel scraping bone and arrows whistling past. A second or two more and his opponent falls, screaming and trying to hold himself together with both hands across his stomach.

There's no time to dispatch the Saracen. Robin is forced to leave the man there and fend off another blow from another assailant, knocking him back with an elbow to the stomach.

He is surrounded by the enemy. There are far too few English blades around him. He catches sight of a familiar man, recognizable more for his style of battle than anything else. By now they are all so burned by the sun and rubbed raw by wind that at first glance they seem no different from the infidels they're fighting. In the dark they might as well have been fighting amongst themselves.

"Where is the King?" shouts Robin, his voice breaking.

The other man screams a reply, but over the sounds of battle Robin cannot hear. The other man's sword sticks in his opponent's rib cage, and he's forced to plant a boot against the man's chest to pull it free. He gestures with his sword, then turns to reengage.

Robin sees a crowd in the distance, at the edge of the safe part of the city. Or what has been the safe part—the enemy has penetrated their defenses in the night, bypassing the fortifications. They must have killed the sentries in silence. The distant commotion is a cluster of a dozen English soldiers using a narrow alley to hold off a horde of Saracens one hundred strong. They're making for the edge of the city, guarding something.

The King.

Something thuds into Robin's shoulder, sending him off balance, and he whirls, searching for the blade he knows is coming. There is no one there. It's then that he feels the fiery lance of pain racing down his biceps and he gasps, sword dangling uselessly at his side. He cranes his neck and sees the fletching sprouting from his shoulder. He reaches up, bracing himself as he curls his fingers around the long arrow shaft buried in the muscle there. He breathes in, out, and in again, and then snaps the shaft off with a deft twist.

Robin sways to one side, dizzy, concentrating on the spots that swarm his vision for the space of a breath. Then he passes his sword to his left hand and slings his bow over his shoulder with the wounded arm and gets moving.

He heads for a set of stone steps leading up to one of the roofs, hoping for a better vantage point. It's the route the women take in the mornings when they bring up their laundry to dry in the sun, and Robin clears the draped fabrics away with a swipe of his sword as he sprints up the steps. The city is lost. He can see it in the way the others are fighting, in the way most of the soldiers have gathered around to ensure the King's safe retreat through the postern gate. But there is too much distance to travel to reach safety. Too many enemies, and not enough blades.

He reaches the rooftop, but before he can scan the city, a shadow darts from a corner across his path. With a roar he raises his sword, momentum already bringing it down before his eyes focus on the figure running past. A child. A girl, which he knows only because of the way her head is covered. She cannot be more than twelve, and for a burning moment her huge black eyes meet his and she freezes. His sword won't stop. His left hand is too clumsy, too weak to divert it.

He throws himself to the side with a cry, his sword striking stone. The tip shatters and the sword leaps from his hand, skidding away. He can hear the girl screaming, speaking too quickly for him to understand any of the few words of Arabic he's learned. He looks up and sees her scrambling away from him to press her back against the half wall surrounding the rooftop. She's unharmed.

Robin pushes himself back up on his left hand, then staggers to the edge of the rooftop. He can still see the men defending the King. There are fewer attackers now, but there are fewer allies as well. Robin reaches for his bow.

Drawing it is an agony, and he can feel the wounded muscle tearing around the arrowhead still lodged in his shoulder. But his aim is true, and from this height he can reach the front line. An attacker goes down, replaced by another behind him. Robin looses another arrow and another man falls.

He sucks in air through his nose, the hot dust scorching his lungs. He can feel the weakness coming, can feel blood pouring past his armpit, down his rib cage. His aim is faltering. But he can see the King now, his crowned helmet gleaming in the light of a blazing fire engulfing one of the gatehouses. They are on the edge of the city. There are horses waiting—they need only to make it another few paces to the gates, which stand open.

Robin draws his bow again. One of the King's defenders goes down, and the firelight glints off a curved blade as its wielder races at the King. Robin draws in a long breath, willing his shaking arm to steady, begging his muscles to hold for one more shot, one last arrow.

Out of the corner of his eye: movement. The glint of light on a blade, the whisper of a soft sole against the sandstone. Robin could turn, could loose his arrow into the man creeping up behind him. His muscles quiver, and with a snarl of pain and focus, Robin narrows his eyes and lets the arrow fly. It courses straight and true through the air, inscribing a gentle arc down, down onto the battlefield, and buries itself in the brain of the King's attacker. Robin takes a breath—the King is away, galloping into the desert.

And then a blade crunches into Robin's side and he's knocked down against the stone with the force of the blow. He cannot move, cannot feel anything below his rib cage—there is no pain. Robin's eyes move slowly, lazily, sweeping across the rooftop. He sees the girl, pressed back into the corner as far as she can, everything covered except her eyes. They fix on his, wide and black. She is silent now.

"Marian," Robin whispers to her. "Don't be afraid."

There are voices above him, but he does not hear them. Instead he can hear rain, a gentle patter against broad green leaves. The smell of wet earth rises all around him, and the world is wrapped in fog. From beneath the padded armor under his mail, he withdraws a chain; on the end of it is a small gold ring set with a bloodred stone. He curls his fist around it, enclosing the little ring in the shelter of his fingers to shield it from the world.

"Marian, I'm sorry."

ONE

"MY LADY." THE VOICE was urgent. "My Lady, please—
please wake up."

Marian swam up out of a dreamless sleep, her mind groggy
and confused. It was dark, but as her eyes adjusted, the light of
a candle came into view. Behind it she could see a familiar face,
drawn and frightened.

"Elena," she croaked, dragging herself upright. "What is it?"

Her maid swallowed, the candlelight bobbing and sway-
ing with the trembling of her hand. "It's my brother, my Lady.
They've got him—they've arrested him and they're going to kill
him at dawn. Please, my Lady, I don't know what to do."

Marian was on her feet before she could think, reaching for
yesterday's dress hanging over her changing screen. She threw it
on over her shift, ignoring the trailing laces at its back. "Where
is my cloak?" she demanded, quick and curt.

"Here, my Lady." Elena was shaking, terrified, but still competent. She thrust the cloak at Marian and then stepped back.

"What are you going to do?"

"I'm going to stop them." She wasn't thinking, just acting. She didn't know what Elena's brother had been accused of or who had arrested him. But Elena's family was from Locksley—Robin was the one who'd suggested Elena for a lady's maid and companion when Marian's mother died. *And I won't let Robin come home to find his people being slaughtered on his own lands.*

Marian flew down the stairs and into the courtyard, where a few torches had lit the way for her. Midge had Jonquille ready and was holding her by the reins. No sign of her father awake yet, for which she was grateful—she didn't have time to argue about whether she should or shouldn't go. Several servants were standing around in their nightclothes, candles transforming their drawn faces into waxy masks. A lad stood by the stables doubled over, red-faced and gasping. She recognized him as the son of one of the farmers from beyond Robin's manor house—he must have run all the way from Locksley town to bring Elena the news. At a dead sprint it was an hour's journey on foot.

Marian ignored them all and bunched her skirts up around her thighs, mounting the dappled mare and taking the reins from Midge.

Jonquille had picked up on her mistress's urgency, and as soon as Marian let her grip on the reins loosen, the mare leaped into a run. The glow of the torches in her manor courtyard fell away behind her, and she was left to race through the darkness.

Edwinstowe was quiet—her father's lands were small, and the town at their center even smaller, and his people all farmers. They'd stir soon, to feed and water their animals and work the land, but they'd sleep until sunrise.

Marian leaned to the side and cut through the finger of the forest that stretched across Edwinstowe lands, aiming for the

King's Road. Branches whipped past, and she dropped her head, burying her face in Jonquille's mane. Jonquille knew the way. Locksley was her home, too.

The sound of Jonquille's hooves striking the earth changed, and Marian lifted her head. They were on the road. Not long now. Marian raised her eyes to the glimpses of sky she could see overhead as the branches passed. A terrible lightness painted the sky to the east the color of bloody ink.

"Hurry, love," Marian whispered, leaning low across her horse's neck, trying to lessen the resistance of her body in the wind.

The road forked. The road to the right would take her into the heart of Sherwood, while the road to the left passed through a hedgerow and then on to Locksley town, and beyond it, Locksley Manor. Jonquille knew which way to go without being told, and together they burst through the undergrowth bordering the fields with a gust of honeysuckle and heather on the wind. The landscape was awash in blue-gray light, the cold harbinger of the dawn.

There were torches burning in the center of town. Marian aimed Jonquille at the light, not bothering to slow her down. Men in chain mail stood in a semicircle around the town center, and a figure in dark gray armor and a black tabard stood at the head of the crowd. The Sheriff's men. Beyond them the townsfolk watched, pale faced and silent.

In the center of the firelight was a young man on his knees in the stocks, a hood of rough-spun canvas over his head and tied around his neck. The soldier nearest him held an ax.

Jonquille broke into the crowd, people scattering left and right and hens fleeing in a startled wave. Marian threw herself off the horse before the mare came to a full halt—all the better for no one to have time to see her with her skirts hiked up above her knees.

"I demand to know what's going on," she gasped, gripping Jonquille's reins more to support her shaking legs than to control the horse.

The man in the tabard was staring, and with a jolt, Marian recognized him. His eyes raked her over, from her wild hair to her muddy, day-old dress. "My Lady Marian," he said quietly, inclining his torso. "Good morning. Are you all right? You seem . . . distressed."

"Good morning, Sir Guy." Marian smoothed down her hair, abruptly aware that she wasn't wearing the modest veil she ought to have donned. "This man. What is his crime?"

Guy of Gisborne pulled off his horsehair helmet and ran a gloved hand over his hair. He was older than Robin by a few years, but had none of his boyish good looks. Scars marked the right side of his face, ugly welts of purple that traveled down and vanished under his high collar. "He has been accused and convicted of highway robbery and poaching, my Lady. This is no place for you—allow my men to escort you back to Edwinstowe Manor and I will visit you when I have finished here."

He was already turning and gesturing to the two men on the end, and Marian stepped forward swiftly. "Sir Guy," she said firmly, "I know this man. He is the brother of my own maid. There has been a mistake. Who have you been sent to arrest?"

Gisborne strode over to the young man in the stocks, his stiff-legged gait giving the sound of his steps an uneven quality. He ripped the hood away, ignoring the grunt of pain that emerged when the ties caught against his captive's jaw. "You are William Scarlet, are you not?"

Marian was unprepared for the shock of hearing his name.

There'd been no mistake. Gisborne *had* been sent for Elena's brother. Will lifted his head, and Marian's heart sank. He'd been badly beaten, and his eyes were swollen shut. He turned his face toward her, but Marian couldn't tell if he could actually see anything through the bloody ruin of his face.

He didn't answer Gisborne but spat a mouthful of blood and saliva into the dirt at his feet. Gisborne stepped back, glancing down in distaste.

"You see, my Lady," said Gisborne, "he has no respect for the laws of this land."

Marian wanted to shout at Will—his disregard for Gisborne's authority wasn't going to make her job any easier. But she calmed her thoughts, imagining Robin standing there instead, imagining how he'd handle this situation. *If he were here, this situation wouldn't exist.* She inhaled sharply. "And so you are to execute him? There is no room for leniency? What evidence do you have?"

"My Lady," Gisborne replied patiently, "please leave this to me. These matters are too upsetting for someone of your gentle upbringing."

"Sir Guy." Marian took another step forward. If nothing else, they wouldn't behead Will while she was standing near enough to be spattered by his blood. "Please. I am begging you to spare this man's life."

Gisborne gazed back at her, expressionless. The moment stretched, and then abruptly he turned away and signaled to the man with the ax. "Unlock him."

"Oh, Sir Guy—thank you. I will not forget your mercy." Marian moved forward as the executioner dropped his ax and unlocked the stocks. Elena's brother staggered to his feet.

"We will only take his hand." With a cold, metallic scrape, Gisborne drew his sword. He still carried the sword he'd worn in

the Holy Land, as a soldier in the King's army, before he'd managed to get injured enough to be sent home to England.

Marian's heart froze. Before she could think, she was running
forward, putting herself between Gisborne and Will Scarlet. She
took Will's arm, lending him her support. They were almost
of a height, and he was battered enough that he leaned heavily
against her.

"Sir Guy!" she barked, summoning every ounce of command
she could. "I demand that you release this man into *my* custody,
pending a fair trial. He will be punished, but on *my* terms."

Gisborne lowered his sword, but his grip stayed firm. He
was backing down only in deference to her presence, and Marian knew that the second she moved, Gisborne would exact his
punishment.

"By what right do you lay claim to this man's fate?" Gisborne
asked.

"He is from Locksley town, has lived here his whole life. He
cannot have traveled far—the crimes will have been committed on Locksley lands. Though the new laws place these crimes
under the Sheriff's jurisdiction, traditionally he must concede
to a lord's right to try his own men." Marian tried to keep her
voice from shaking. She knew it was improper for a landown-
er's daughter to have studied such things, but she'd learned some
from Robin when they were children, and then from her father,
who had never tried to convince her she didn't need to know
about the law.

Gisborne frowned, but to Marian's relief, his face bore none
of the shock that most gentlemen would display at a lady's familiarity with matters of jurisprudence. "Lady Marian—"

"I will be Lady Locksley," she continued, speaking over him
and pitching her voice to carry, "the day Robin returns from the

Holy War. In his absence, I demand the right to preserve the spirit of his governance over these lands."

Gisborne was silent for a long moment, watching her. The tip of his sword dropped, resting against the ground. Beside her, Will lifted his head again, and this time Marian could see the flash of his eyes set deep in the puffy skin around them. His breath caught, but he didn't speak.

"Then no one has told you," Gisborne murmured.

"Told me what?"

Before Gisborne could speak, Will jerked forward, shoving Marian hard toward Gisborne. She wasn't ready for his strength—was his unsteadiness as he leaned on her an act?—and she would've gone sprawling in the dirt were it not for Gisborne's quick reflexes, grabbing at her shoulders and hauling her up.

Marian twisted in his grasp to see Will sprinting through the fields, making for the line of trees marking the edge of Sherwood Forest.

Gisborne stopped long enough to make sure Marian's feet were under her, then jerked his head toward his men. "Shoot him," he ordered calmly, then reached for Marian's hand. "Are you unharmed?"

"No—stop!" Marian lunged for the nearest man, the quickest one to draw his bow. She banged into his shoulder hard enough to send pain shooting down her own arm, but more importantly sending his arrow corkscrewing harmlessly into the thatch of a nearby house. "He is *Robin's man*, do you understand?"

She could feel control slipping away. Something was wrong. The townspeople weren't even looking at Will as he disappeared into the trees, safe under their cover. They were watching her. They were silent.

Gisborne muttered something tense and cold under his breath, his eyes on the trees. "Stand down," he blurted finally, striding a few steps away and then turning. "Lady Marian," he said tensely, struggling with his temper. "That man is an outlaw, and there is no telling what crimes he will be willing to commit against the innocent now to stay alive."

"He's Robin's man," Marian repeated through clenched teeth, resisting the urge to massage the shoulder that had banged into the armored bowman.

Gisborne sucked a breath in through his nose, then snapped, "Robin is *dead*."

Marian's brow furrowed, her mind slowing to a halt. The world grew strangely hot and dry, a roaring like wind rising in her ears. "What?"

Gisborne rubbed one gloved hand over his mouth, regret bringing a hint of color to his features. "I am sorry, my Lady. I did not intend to—but it is true. Robin of Locksley is dead; he died three months ago in Jerusalem. We have only just had word of the latest casualties of note."

It's not true. Lies, plots against Locksley lands. The Sheriff's planning to take over, control the taxes, drive these lands into dust to line his coffers.

But she could not speak any of the words. She could only stare at Gisborne, taking in the details of his face as though they'd provide some relief, some hint that he was speaking false. The deep scar on his jaw and neck, suddenly different now, no longer the mark of a traitor—now she could not help but imagine such scars on her Robin. Except that his wounds would never heal, never scar over. She knew Gisborne could tell she was staring at his disfigurement, but she could not look away.

But he just gazed at her, a surprising sympathy in the grim set of his mouth. "I was going to come to you after I dealt with

William Scarlet of Locksley town. As Robin is the last in his line, the Sheriff has appointed me to take over the governance and ownership of his lands."

Gisborne reached out for Marian's hand, but she pulled away with a jerk, stumbling backward. "No," she said finally. "No. Robin cannot die."

He paused, taking a careful step forward, approaching her like a man would approach a skittish horse. A detached part of Marian's mind wanted to laugh at his antics, scoffing at the idea that she was some fragile lady about to shatter.

I am the Lady Marian. I am a free woman and I am loved by Robin of Locksley. I don't shatter for someone like Guy of Gisborne.

This time when Gisborne reached out, he managed to take gentle custody of Marian's hand, turning it over so he could drop something small and cold into her palm. "Nevertheless, it is true."

Brow still furrowed, Marian looked down at her palm. The sun had risen while they debated Will's fate, and she could see the object clearly.

It was Robin's mother's ring. Tiny, understated, a simple band of braided gold set with a single tear-shaped ruby. Marian knew it well. She'd worn it every day after he gave it to her, until the day Robin left for the Holy Land wearing it on a chain around his neck.

"I am sorry, my Lady." Gisborne was still cradling her hand in his.

TWO

GISBORNE HAD TWO OF his men escort Marian back to her father's estate. He remained behind—Marian had foggy memories of his voice as he began to organize search parties for Will. A detached part of her told her she ought to refuse the escort, to stay and hinder Gisborne's efforts as much as possible, but she found she had little control over her body. She was as biddable as a frightened child.

Though the ride back, at a sedate walk, must have taken over an hour, she remembered none of it. She was abruptly at home, being thrust into her father's arms. He'd been awakened—by Elena, no doubt, after Marian was safely away—and dressed, and Marian dimly heard him talking with the men who'd delivered her. Through the soles of her feet she felt the thudding of their horses' hooves as they galloped back out of the courtyard and back to their commander.

Then she was inside, and being eased into a chair before a roaring fire. Her father was holding her hands, down on his creaking knees before her and peering into her eyes. The heat from the hearth brought her back to herself, and she blinked, focusing on her father's face.

It was like waking from a dream. A nightmare—a hellish gallop through a dark wood, a man's life she held in her hands, the unbearable weight of a tiny ring dropping into her palm. A ring adorned with blood that flowed across her palm and trick-led down toward her elbow.

She was crying. Hot tears fell on her arm. "Father?" she whis-pered, confused.

"Oh, my Marian." Her father rose up on his knees and pulled her in against him, holding her as he hadn't done since she was a little girl. His eyes were wet too, and his breath shaking. "They told me. I'm so sorry. I'm—I would give anything to spare you this."

"Robin cannot die," Marian whispered. And it was true. In that moment she would have believed her horse could fly and that time could flow backward and forward and in circles more readily than that Robin of Locksley had fallen in the Holy Land. The world, her world, no longer made sense.

"I've sent for the physician from Locksley town," her father said. "He'll bring something to help you sleep."

She couldn't think why her father wanted her to sleep when she'd only just woken, and more than anything she wanted to avoid slipping back into that nightmare where a ring fell, over and over, into her palm. Then she realized her father had let her go and was offering her a draught that smelled of sweet wine and something else, bitter and herby, and that another man was there too now. The physician from Locksley—how had he come so quickly? She drank, and her eyes were on the window, where the sun was slanting through—but these windows faced the southwest and only saw sun in the afternoon.

The fire, which had been burning so brightly a moment ago, was down to embers.

She'd believe time could flow in circles more readily than that Robin could ever die. . . .

Her thoughts, already foggy, grew sluggish and thick. Her father was plucking at her hand, which was curled into a fist. She found as she tried to open it that her muscles had all but solidified that way, a grip she'd held so tight and so long she could not remember how to uncurl her fingers. But as her vision darkened, as she felt the bitter wine bringing its false warmth buzzing through her limbs and numbing her lips, her hand relaxed too. And her father slipped the tiny ring from her palm as she fell into darkness.

Marian was kept asleep much of the next few days. She'd wake to eat, to relieve herself, to let Elena untangle the leaves and twigs from her hair and brush it before the fire. But it wouldn't take long before her world would start to swirl again, as if all natural laws were sliding away—her heart would begin to pound, her breath would start to gasp in and out of her chest, and her body would surge as though she were running for her life when all she was doing was sitting on the rug by the hearth in her room.

The physician explained very carefully to Marian that she was having hysterical episodes of fear now that she'd lost the stability promised by her betrothal, that it was common for some women, especially those particularly dependent upon their husbands, to experience similar terrors in the wake of such a loss.

Marian didn't see him again after that and knew her father

had sent him away. She might have been foggy and confused from the sleeping draughts, but she'd seen the way her father's face grew tighter and grimmer with each word the man spoke. She felt like laughing. Instead she began to weep, and soon she was asleep again.

She lost track of the days, but it was some time later that she sat with Elena, leaning against her knee as her maid brushed her hair—it was tangle-free, but the touch of her maid's hands and the feel of the brush were soothing. And it was with a jolt of her heart that she remembered what had brought her to Locksley that day, and she sat bolt upright. "Elena!" Marian gasped, ashamed she hadn't thought of it sooner, that she'd been so buried in her own grief while her maid attended her tirelessly. "Your brother—Will—"

Elena had tensed at Marian's sudden shift, reaching for the bottle of herb-laced wine in case Marian was about to have another of her "episodes," as the physician had called them. But she paused, swallowing. "No word, my Lady," she said softly. But Marian could see the hope in her eyes. No word was good. No word meant they hadn't found him. No word meant he might still be alive.

The jolt of realization had made Marian's heart flip over, but she was able to take a few quick, sharp breaths, and the fear that usually came surging in after such a jolt faded. Though her shame at having forgotten her maid's own woes burned, it was the first time she'd felt something other than panic or numbness.

After that Marian only took the draught to sleep at night, but for a few occasions when the panic returned. It always came from something innocuous, like working at her loom or visiting Jonquille in the stables. Only later would she realize that she'd been weaving foliage of the type of tree by which Robin had first kissed her; or that Jonquille had stamped her urgency to be ridden, for Marian usually took her at least once a week to Locksley town.

Marian tried to practice her archery, for—with the exception of Robin—standing before a target with a bow in her hands was the only thing that ever made her feel *real*, and alive, and herself. But her hands shook when they gripped her bow, and her thoughts could not settle. To shoot with abandon and precision required surrender, and she could not force her mind to quiet. Her arrows went wide of the mark most days and sometimes missed the target altogether, and she added one more fear to the sea of countless, nameless terrors in her heart: *Have I lost this, too?*

She joined her father at dinner but kept to herself and to Elena most days, and her father let her. But one afternoon she sought him out in his study, where he was poring over a stack of documents and muttering under his breath as he squinted and frowned.

"Father?" She hovered in the doorway.

"Marian, my dear." He lifted his head, blinking at her.

"Am I interrupting?"

"You are," he said, and closed his sheaf of papers with a hefty slam. "Please continue."

Marian slipped through the doorway, feeling strangely awkward in his study. As a child she'd learned numbers by watching him wrestle with his accounts. Her father had not been born with a head for numbers and was often frustrated with the mathematical side of running his lands. Marian remembered her mother used to come into the study with a mug of watered ale and a kiss for his receding hairline, and soon he'd be relaxed again, his accounts in order, the tension gone from his brow.

But she wasn't a child anymore, and her mother had been

gone for some years now. And she hadn't thought to bring him something to drink.

"What is it, my dear?" Her father was leaning back in his heavy carven chair, watching her with patient concern.

Marian went to the window. The view overlooked the eastern pastures, and she could see Jonquille and a few of the other mares grazing, tails flicking the flies away and sun warming their flanks. "I need a task," she blurted finally, turning from the window and gripping the stone sill. "I cannot sit at my loom or walk through the pastures or ride to Locksley without thinking of—and I cannot sit idle in my room all day. Give me something to do, Father, please."

Her father's lips twitched, and he muttered, "You're welcome to settle my accounts for me."

Marian, however, was desperate enough to take him at his word. "Show me where you're stuck and I'll—"

"Marian," her father interrupted, chuckling. "That was a joke. I suspect you'd have my accounts in order far more quickly than I, but it's not proper." He spoke the words with regret.

"Who would know?"

"Gisborne, for one." Her father grimaced at her. "Sir Guy has called here twice asking for you. I told him you were indisposed. Eventually you'll have to receive him, though, and if he asks after your days, what will you tell him?"

Marian felt like scowling. "Lie and say I spend all day embroidering daisies on handkerchiefs."

Her father laughed, covering it up after half a second too late by pressing his knuckles to his lips. "And when he asks you to embroider him a token to wear on his sleeve? What will you do then, when the last thing you ever embroidered was that pillow there, which I had to rescue from the midden?"

Marian glanced at the chair in her father's reading nook, which had on it a cushion she'd tried to decorate for him when she was eleven or twelve. The stitches looked like a child's drawing of a chicken, and the tail feathers ended in an angry snarl of thread. She'd been trying to embroider a dove. She vividly remembered tearing at the knotted snarl of thread and then hurling it violently, pillow and all, onto the trash heap.

Her father's eyes were still merry, but there was a sadness behind them, a weariness he couldn't hide. "My dear, I can't tell you how to spend your days. I can't tell you what will fill your time, your heart, the void he's left behind."

Marian blinked, feeling the hot sting of tears behind her eyes. She so desperately wanted her father to tell her what to do, even if it was correcting the figures in his accounts. "What did you do when we lost Mother?" Marian had been so young when her mother died that she scarcely remembered her except for a misty impression of beauty and stately elegance and a reserve Marian could never hope to emulate.

Her father set his quill into its holder and leaned back in his chair again, closing his eyes. "That was different. You and Robin were lucky—you were born to be together, in love since you were children. Your mother and I—we met only a week before our marriage, you know. It was arranged by our parents. That's not to say I didn't love her," he said quickly, seeing Marian's face. "I did, terribly. But it took time. And we had a whole life together before she became ill, and then she was ill a long time. In some ways that makes it harder. But in others—I had time to say goodbye. Time to understand I would have to carry on without her."

"But *how*?" Marian felt like hurling his account books through the heavy-paned window. She wanted to go to that chair, pick up that pillow, and start unpicking every uneven stitch of the chicken-dove. She wanted to shout at someone, anyone. She closed her eyes, trying not to let the pounding of her own heart frighten her.

Her father's chair creaked, and she pictured him rising to his feet. "Oh, Marian. For me, that answer is easy. I had you." She felt his hands wrap around hers, and the destructive urge in her fingertips eased.

Marian's eyes filled and she leaned forward so her father could wrap his arms around her shoulders. They were almost of a height. She was unusually tall for a woman, taller than Robin himself. There'd been a period when they were children when she'd started to grow taller and he hadn't, and she'd towered over him. He'd alternate between complaint and boast: crowing when he could outshoot or outrun her with his shorter limbs, then throwing tantrums when she could easily wrestle him to the ground hand-to-hand.

But she had come to resent it, this gangly height that so set her apart. She resented her own strength, the fact that she could best the future Lord of Locksley in combat at twelve years old but that she could not stand next to other girls without drawing attention. Though Robin seemed oblivious, the other young ladies of Nottinghamshire were all so dainty that she felt rather like a troll or an ogre out of legend, lumbering around and banging into doorways and accidentally knocking over half the dishes at supper when an uncontrollably long leg kicked the table. And she'd begun to resent Robin, too, for being entirely unbothered by their height difference, for the rough-and-tumble nature of their friendship. She couldn't have explained why she was upset, not then—she only knew that he didn't seem to *see* her, not the way he ought to.

But then he hit his own growth spurt, though he never did

catch up to her in height. Their wrestling matches became evenings spent by a fire after long rides through the wood. And archery competitions became excuses to sneak away into the field, where the long stalks of wheat concealed their conversations from the world. And he saw her, as she was, as she wanted him to.

She'd asked him, once, if it bothered him that she was taller than he, and he'd lifted his head from his fletching and eyed her through the firelight as though she'd asked him to sprout wings and fly.

"That," he'd said finally, "is ridiculous. If you were shorter, who would keep me on my toes? Come hold this arrow for me—the glue keeps smearing while I'm stitching."

The memory was so vivid Marian's breath caught, and her father let his arms relax enough that he could pull back and scan her face. "You lost Robin so quickly," he said quietly, "and so unjustly, that of course you feel lost. Of course your heart panics. That physician"—and his lip curled a little with distaste—"attributes these floods of fear you've been suffering to some feminine weakness. But one thing you have never been, my dear, is weak."

Or feminine.

It was Robin's voice, and so real that Marian's heart thumped with fear and longing both, and she almost turned to search for Robin standing somewhere behind her. Confusion momentarily robbed her of sense.

Her father continued, stroking a piece of hair from his daughter's eyes. "I was able to talk to your mother, before she—before she left us. I was able to listen to her, know what she wanted for me, for us. You never had that with Robin, but that doesn't mean he's not still with you. It doesn't mean he can't still help you in that way."

Still with me. As a voice in her mind? Her father had not heard, had not noticed the stiffening of his daughter's frame. Marian swallowed hard, vision blurry as she tried to focus on her father's face. "How?"

"You know him better than you know yourself, my dear. Ask yourself what Robin would want for you, and you'll find your way."

"*Stop fussing at* your tunic, Robert," chides his mother, her face calm but her eyes sparking as she tugs Robin's hand away from his collar. Her ring glints in the light reflected off the emerald leaves of the forest outside.

"But it's too tight," he protests, the lacings digging into his neck. "I don't want to go live in a castle."

"It's not a castle, it's a manor house. Your father writes that you will have your own grand suite of rooms, and you can choose any of the horses for your own—won't that be fun? And look around us—you will have all of Sherwood Forest to explore."

Robin glances at the leaves passing the window of their carriage. "I guess."

Abruptly the leaves give way to fields, and the house is there, with figures arrayed in front like an army of tiny wooden knights. Robin leans out of the carriage window and his mother catches hold of his tunic to keep him from toppling out, protests spilling from her lips.

"Who's that?" Robin asks, watching as one of the gathered people—even tinier than the other distant figures—makes a break for freedom, reaching as far as the edge of the drive before someone chases it down and hauls it back.

His mother is leaning out of the carriage window now too, forgetting that she was chastising her son moments before for the same behavior. "Those will be the manor servants—oh, and some of the other families from this part of Nottinghamshire. Your uncle was much liked, before he went to be with God."

"No, that one." The tiny figure breaks free again, and this time three of the gathered servants go after it. Over the clopping of the horses' hooves and the wind stirring the leaves of the great forest they've been riding through, Robin hears a delighted shriek as one of the figure's pursuers makes a grab for the escapee and trips instead.

His mother looks at him, and then at the distant child struggling now to break out of the grasp of a man in stable livery. "That's Edwinstowe's daughter. She's just about your age."

"She's a girl?" Robin slumps back in his seat, crossing his arms over his chest and chafing at the ties of his tunic.

"Daughters usually are," says his mother, amused, eyes on the house. "Edwinstowe has some lovely land, Robin, and you'll be a man before you can blink, and looking for a wife."

Robin makes a choking sound in his throat and slumps lower. The sound of distant laughter comes again, and after glancing at his mother to make sure she's not watching, Robin lifts his chin enough to look over the edge of the carriage window again. The girl's being carried off into the house, slung over the stableman's shoulder, a handful of other well-dressed children watching in horror at their parents' sides.

"Do you think she can ride a horse?" asks Robin cautiously.

THREE

MARIAN HADN'T QUITE MADE up her mind to ride to Locksley when she swung herself up into Jonquille's saddle. Her poor horse had been suffering during Marian's mourning, for Jonquille was a gift from Robin, and the mare had been left to graze and grow fat in the fields while Marian fought off her terrors and her grief. For all Jonquille was a sweet-tempered mount for Marian, she had a stallion's ferocity whenever anyone else came too near. Only Midge, the head of her father's stables, could approach, and only to saddle and occasionally groom her if Marian had been neglecting her care.

Elena was the only other person whose presence the dapple gray tolerated. In fair weather Elena often took her mending—or Marian's mending, as Marian's attempts to darn stockings were shockingly inept—outside and leaned against the paddock fence. She had a tendency to hum while she worked, and Jonquille liked the sound of her voice. Marian would often emerge from the manor house to find Elena bent over a hemline with Jonquille just behind her, head dipping over the edge of the fence, as if about to lip at Elena's immaculate braids.

Marian, having seen the stable boys' attempts to entice Jonquille with apples and oatcakes, rather thought Jonquille preferred Elena's company because she *didn't* try to win the mare over.

Her horse had a mind of her own, and Marian preferred it that way. Like the barn cats, Jonquille could not be bidden except in extreme circumstances, when her mistress's urgency convinced her it was necessary. So when Marian mounted her outside the stables, some weeks after the news of Robin's death, a part of Marian's mind must have known where Jonquille would want to go.

Jonquille wanted to run, and Marian let her, for a little while. But the few weeks she'd been indoors had weakened Marian's muscles, and her legs grew tired quickly, and she eased Jonquille—with some difficulty, for the mare still wanted to gallop—back down into a brisk trot, and then a walk. When they reached the fork in the road, the turning that would take them either toward Locksley town or deeper into the forest toward the King's Road to Nottingham Castle, Jonquille paused.

How many times had Marian met Robin here, at this fork, to let their horses wander deeper and deeper still into Sherwood Forest, so close that their riders' legs would sometimes touch? How many times had her father begged her to keep to the paths close to Edwinstowe, citing bandits and adders and the deceptive nature of Sherwood's winding paths?

What would Robin want for me?

Marian nudged at Jonquille with her right knee. Jonquille disliked the bit of her reins, and Marian had learned early that guiding her horse with her legs was easier for them both. She'd never seen anyone else ride in quite the same way, but it left her hands free for her bow when she practiced archery on horseback.

Her eyes stung and she gasped a breath. Robin had taught her archery. Or else, she had taught him—they were well matched, and though he was the only one to receive formal lessons, he passed along every tidbit he learned. She had mastered each new skill a tiny bit faster than he had, and not once had he resented her for it. She could not imagine drawing a bow again without fear and grief choking her.

How could she fulfill her duty to the people of Locksley? It wasn't a legal duty, not anymore—she was no longer their future Lady. But she'd been Robin's betrothed for so long that she felt Locksley was a part of her soul as much as her father's own lands. And Robin would want her to make sure all was well until he came ho—She caught herself and made her thoughts cold and still.

The town was as bustling as ever, gray wisps rising from a few chimneys despite the warm day. The smell of wood smoke mixed with the smell of burning coal in the smithy, almost masking the aroma of blackberries and baking dough coming from Gisla's house. Laurie, whose difficult birth Marian had assisted in years ago, when she was little more than a child herself, was a lad of seven now—she spied him chasing a cluster of chickens down one of the laneways, trying to herd them back toward his parents' house. A herd of cows lowed in the distance, gently stirring their comments into the hum of the summer insects in the air.

Everything was as it ought to be, as it ever was. Except that it wasn't. It could never be again, because Robin was dead.

Marian tugged on Jonquille's reins and veered away from the town, taking the long way around toward the Locksley manor house. She could not quite bear to face the townspeople, not yet. She knew they'd want comfort from her, assurances despite the death of their Lord—or, worse, they'd want to give her sympathy. She wanted none, and had none to offer.

Guilt slid like rancid oil into her stomach, for Robin would want her to help them. But she could not make herself go.

During Robin's absence, the private side of the manor house lay mostly empty. Most of the servants had families in town who they lived with when their services weren't required, though a few lived at the house full-time. There was the groundskeeper, who lived in a cottage behind the house, and the steward, Bellden, who had quarters belowstairs and oversaw the rest of the staff when the house was fully occupied. She shrank from the idea of confronting them. The door would be barred, Marian knew, but she'd snuck in and out of Robin's house so many times in her life that she automatically made for the first-floor dining room, where one of the shutters that allowed air to circulate during the heat of evening meals was loose. Robin knew of the problem but had never mentioned it to Bellden or to any of his staff. It was the easiest, quickest route for Marian to enter undetected. She left Jonquille to lip at the dandelion and meadowsweet growing in the lee of the manor walls and continued on foot.

Marian had only gone once or twice to the house since Robin had left to fight at the King's side. While much of it still bustled with life, too much a fixture of the town to be abandoned completely, she hated to see any of the rooms dark and empty, for it had been a second home to her as a child, and her mind painted the walls with the glow of beeswax candles. It made her long to rip the dust covers off the furniture to let it breathe and live again.

But as she shimmied her way through the low, broad cutout into the hall, she felt a sense of calm and quiet settle over her. She replaced the shutter behind her and rose to her feet, breathing the still air and the smell of dust. The long table and its chairs were all stacked in the corners, the tapestries missing from the walls. She drifted from the hall into the gallery, passing the suit of armor worn by Robin's grandfather, feeling it watch her, ghost-like, through the ethereal drape of its shroud of linen.

The whole house watched her, unmoved, until Marian began to feel she was the ghost—no more than a restless spirit, glancing from room to room, the veil between worlds too thick for her to see the life and vitality that ought to be here in this house she'd loved since she was a little girl. She could see only pallor, and stillness, and the blanched ivory of linen. Everything was covered, concealed—it was her own eyes, her own shroud, that stood between her and this world.

Marian's feet took her to the main staircase, and she mounted the broad oaken steps. It had taken years of cajoling from Bellden before Robin would move into the master suite—it was his father's room, Robin insisted. He had no need of its wide oak bed and view of the valley. His boyhood room overlooked the stables, and he could not sleep without the soft sounds of dozing horses in their stalls, the muffled pawing of their hooves. But he'd finally given in to Bellden, some four years after his father's death. He'd only slept in the room for a few months before he decided to join King Richard in his crusade.

So it felt strange to Marian to stand in Robin's father's room and see Robin's things there. There his record book, his ink and quill. There his clothes chest, slightly ajar where he'd left the corner of a tunic or jerkin to dangle and keep the lid from closing properly. And there his old wooden knight, once a constant companion, now a keepsake on a shelf, still bearing the shiny polish of his young hands on the horse's nose, its flanks, the ripple of its tail with a piece missing from the time Marian had thrown it off the banister in the main hall in a fit of pique. She could not remember now why she'd been angry with him. But there it was, the chipped tail, the edges of the break worn round and smooth with time.

His sword and belt, which usually stood in the corner by his desk, were gone, and his bow and quiver too. *He'll need them to fight the infidels,* Marian thought, glad that Robin would be fighting with his own weapons, the ones that had grown to fit his hand, the ones his hands had grown to fit.

Then she remembered. And she wondered if Robin's killer had taken up his sword after he died, if English steel was even now being used to cut down more of the King's men.

Grief, thought Marian, was not the melancholy mourning of a loss, not the long and dwindling ache that ballads sang of. It was forgetting, and remembering, again and again, an endless series of slashes, each as violent and sharp as the last. It was execution by a thousand different wounds, it was bleeding to death so slowly that you are certain it will never end, that you will suffer this torture for eternity, long after your natural life has ended. You are Prometheus, and instead of your liver, the eagle is tearing out your heart.

Marian stood at the foot of Robin's bed, eyes on the linens protecting the mattress beneath, her fingers tracing the woodwork of the clothes chest. The red oak gave under her fingertips, and she remembered the corner of fabric keeping the lid from closing. She stooped to correct it, and she found herself holding the edge of Robin's old cloak. He hadn't brought it with him to the Holy Land, for he'd be wearing the King's colors. Marian lifted the lid of the chest and pulled the cloak out, sinking onto the floor and letting the cloth pool in her lap.

It was heavy, a thick, coarse wool weave dyed again and again with woad and turmeric and verdigris until it was the deep, dark color of a shady summer day in Sherwood. Robin's armor was in the chest too—not his chain mail, but his leather breastplate, his armguards, his archer's glove. The chest smelled like him—or, perhaps, he smelled like his gear—and for the space of too many heartbeats Marian couldn't move, just breathing.

I'm here, said Robin.

Marian's fingertips tingled where they rested on the wool, and her breath caught painfully. So familiar was Robin's voice, surrounded by his belongings and his scent, that she knew she was imagining his voice to comfort herself. Or else punish herself, for hearing him speak to her was a searing torture—it warmed her heart and made it bleed.

A distant thud jarred her from her stupor. Bellden was in the house, making his rounds or else repairing this or that. His tasks would lead him to the upstairs eventually, and if he found her there, she'd have to talk. Marian didn't know if her heart could take it.

She couldn't leave Robin's clothes strewn about. Bellden would assume there had been a break-in. So Marian rose, her arms full of green wool, and hurried to the clothes chest. She rummaged among the discarded clothes and belongings covering its bottom—*for heaven's sake, Robin, tidying your room doesn't mean throwing all your things into your closet*—until she found a pack. Robin's armguards went in first, and his glove. Her exploration of the chest's contents had left everything so jumbled the lid wouldn't close at all, so she shoved his leather tunic into the pack too, and a few other bits and pieces of clothing she didn't stop to examine. The cloak wouldn't fit, but neither could her shaking hands get it back into the chest unfolded. So she bundled it together and rolled it up like a camp bed, and tied it to the stolen pack with its trailing laces.

She moved toward the door, first pressing her ear to the thick oak and then opening it a crack to listen. When the pounding of her heart quieted enough, she made out footsteps, quiet at first, then changing to sharp clicks. Shallower steps, then longer strides against stone. Bellden had climbed the stairs. Marian eased the door closed again and stood, heart pounding, sweat forming along her brow, on the small of her back, between her breasts.

No, she thought, trying to ignore the longing in her mind for the physician's numbing drink. It was so easy to fall into that stupor, so effortless to simply let the draught sweep her from the turbulent currents of her own thoughts.

Some distant part of her mind told her to open the door, to walk out, to greet Bellden, to simply explain she was taking some of Robin's things to remind her of him. But the thought of facing another human being—of being forced to recall *him*—brought only a further sweep of terror, one that made her want to gag. She turned blindly for the window and shoved it open, seeking fresh air. But the air only smelled like Locksley town, carrying the scents of Gisla's baking bread and the wild crisp of clear-eye sage and boneset from the midwife's garden.

Though she could no longer distinguish between the sound of Bellden's footsteps and the thrashing of her own heart, Marian felt sure he'd open the door at any moment. She slung the pack over her shoulders and slipped through the window onto the stone ledge beyond, shutting the pane behind her.

She crept sideways so she'd be invisible from within the room, then crouched there, trying to steady herself as she shook and gasped. She cursed herself for traveling without the physician's tonic; true, it made her sleepy and slow-witted, but without it she had no way to stop this racing heart, the seizing of her every muscle. All she wanted was to run, but she was stuck a full story above the ground, clinging with one hand to the window frame and pressing her stolen gear between her back and the stone.

This isn't me, she thought, closing her eyes, shutting out the vista she usually loved, the fields and distant trees marking the edge of the wood. Marian struggled to suppress the urge to jam a stone into her leg or strike herself to snap her thoughts from this cycle of fear. *This cannot be me. I fight. I don't fear.*

Robin would know how to beat this. . . .

A memory flashed by, so quickly Marian almost dismissed it. Robin, passing along what his archery tutor had told him. *Breathe from here,* Robin told her, his hands at her waist. They were young then, and Marian remembered trying to do as he said, then shouting an epithet when the stiff fabric of her dress wouldn't allow her ribs to move where his hands rested. She'd stripped off her kirtle, there in the field, and practiced wearing only her shift. It was the first time she'd outshot him.

Marian's shaking fingers went to the ties at either side of her ribs. One settled into a knot at her inexpert fumbling, but the other loosened and then fell free, and Marian threw her head back until it rested against the stone.

Breathe from here.

It was Robin's voice again, but she was too frightened, too overwhelmed, to question whether it was conjured by her own memory or whispered by some lingering fragment of Robin's spirit.

Her ribs expanded, contracted. Her belly rose, fell. She felt a rush of dizziness, tightened her grip on the window frame, adjusted the positioning of her feet on the ledge. Slowly, she registered the smells around her: the clear-eye sage, the stables on the other side of the house, old stone and the scraps of greenery clinging to it, the worn leather of the pack she'd unearthed from Robin's wardrobe.

With her eyes closed, she could almost feel the gentle curve of the bow in her palm, see the clarity of the target ahead. Her shoulders drew back as she breathed again, and on the exhale she let go of the tension in her frame. In her mind's eye she saw the arrow fly, and with it went her fear, vanishing into the fog of her imagination.

The sun was drying the sweat on her brow, and as Marian took another experimental breath, a part of her felt like laughing, shaky with relief.

Go back inside, she told herself, stern. But her body wouldn't move. After all, she'd climbed this way before. True, she usually crept out of Robin's house by safer means, but every now and then they lost track of time and she'd had to sneak out of his old bedroom, which was only a few windows down from where she crouched now. They'd never lain together, both too conscious of the laws of God and man, both too sure it would only be a matter of time before they were properly wed. But that wouldn't stop the ruin of Marian's reputation were she to be seen creeping from his house after dark.

Marian started the climb down, finding after only moments that she felt as exhausted as if she'd been climbing from a tower and not the second floor. Her terror could not have lasted more than a few minutes, but it felt as though she'd been toiling for hours. When she reached the ground, she landed with a thud and a much harder jarring of her bones than she'd intended. She could barely summon the breath to whistle for Jonquille. By the time the horse trotted up with half a dandelion plant and its dirt-covered roots still hanging from her lips, Marian had managed to find her feet again.

FOUR

IT WASN'T UNTIL MARIAN handed her cloak to her father's steward that she remembered her bodice, remembered how disheveled she must appear—but her father was there an instant later, before she had time to pull herself together again. He blinked at her, eyebrows drawing together in concern. He had never been one to lecture her—most of Marian's knowledge of the expectations placed on her by birth and by betrothal had come from other ladies her age. Her mother, who rarely lectured but was the perfect model of a lady to the public, had died when Marian was still a child. Most of the time, Marian felt it quite possible her father wouldn't notice if she wandered around Edwinstowe in her shift and a dressing gown. But just now, he stared at her dangling bodice with obvious agitation.

"I went for a ride," Marian said, crossing her arms over her belly, pressing the fabric of her dress back into place. She'd been gone for hours—dusk had nearly arrived.

"Get upstairs," her father hissed, urgent. "Sir Guy is here."

Marian went cold. Her shift was still damp where it had collected the sweat from the small of her back, and she wanted to shiver. "Here? Now? Why?"

"Go get yourself—you know." Her father waved a vague, helpless hand in her direction.

Marian eyed the cloakroom, watching the steward hang her cloak—there was a third cloak there, black, oddly bulky, looking heavy enough to rip the iron hooks from their settings. She glanced at her father's stricken face one more time, then hurried toward the staircase.

Uncertainty and alarm quickened her pace, but as if her earlier attack of "hysterics," as the physician would've called it, had inured her to fear for a time, her hands stayed steady as she combed them through her hair and started working at the knot on the other side of her bodice. She wouldn't have time to change her shift, but she could throw on a different dress.

"Elena!" she hissed, hurrying through her room toward her maid's adjoining chamber. She came to a skidding halt, however, when she found Elena's room still and dark. Marian drifted back into her own room and saw there was no fire, that the lamps hadn't been lit. Venturing closer to the hearth, she found it cold—the fire had been out for hours.

In near darkness, Marian fumbled with the knots on the other side of her dress until her heartbeat did start to quicken. "Elena!" she tried again, sticking her head out into the hall—but there was no answer.

Giving up, Marian reached for the trailing laces on the open side of her dress. She'd have to hope the fabric hadn't been stained by grass when she fell, or smell too much of horse and sweat. She did up the ties as quickly as she could, ignoring whenever she missed an eyelet. She smoothed down her hair and then slipped a net over the crown of her head, wishing she had time to light a lamp. She'd have to hope Gisborne had no eye for women's fashion—which, given his common ancestry and the fact that he'd been given his title only upon returning from the Holy Land, wasn't an impossible hope.

She skidded to a halt outside the entrance to the main hall, pausing to gather her breath and her courage. She hadn't seen Gisborne since the morning he'd told her of Robin's death.

She stepped inside, hoping to slip in unnoticed. Her father was at the fireplace, one hand on the mantel, back to the archway. But Gisborne was seated at the low table, and his eyes found her as soon as she appeared. He rose to his feet, looming in that stiff way he had—Marian could not think of a better example of someone who'd sought nobility all his life only to wear it like an ill-fitting costume once it was his. He wore black, perhaps to detract from the darkened, scarred flesh at the right side of his chin and throat—his unfashionably high collar was certainly an effort to diminish the signs of the wounds that had sent him home from the war.

"My Lady Marian," he said, with a stiff, wooden bow. His eyes followed her as she gave up her attempts to enter without ceremony—they followed her still as she entered the glow of the firelight, until she tore her gaze away.

Her father had turned, and when she looked at him, he flashed her a brief, wide-eyed look and scrabbled at his side with his hand. Marion looked down and saw a fist-sized bunch of fabric poking through her dress—she'd managed to get part of her shift tangled up in her ties. She caught her breath and turned, hoping Gisborne hadn't seen, and tried to shove as much of the fabric as she could back through the openings between the ties.

A heavy silence fell, broken only when Gisborne cleared his

throat and said stiffly, "Ah—are you unwell?"

Only belatedly did Marian realize she hadn't returned the man's greeting. "Just a—a passing ill humor." Her shift was tied into the laces at one point—she couldn't remedy it without undoing the ties. So she let her arm fall, concealing the seam of her bodice, and hugged it against her body.

"Your father tells me you were visiting the people of Locksley town," Gisborne said, after another slightly too long pause. "You ought to bring an escort with you—these are desperate times, my Lady. There are thieves and brigands in these woods, not to mention the townspeople themselves."

Marian felt herself bristling at the thought that any of her beloved people would harm her, but she forced the feeling down. "Thank you for your concern," she said instead, too annoyed to keep the chill from her voice. "But I've been riding alone to Locksley and back since I was a child. There's much to do there to assist the town in this 'desperate time,' as you call it, and I do not intend to abandon them now."

Gisborne gave a minute bow. "Your dedication is admirable," he said in that slow, wooden way he had. "I am glad to find you still so attached to those lands. Nothing would please me more than for you to go on caring for those people, as you were once intended to do." He had a sharp, hawkish nose, and his expressionless lips were always pressed into a tight line. His eyes were so dark a shade of brown as to look black, indistinguishable from his pupils.

Marian could only gape at him, confused. Of course she would continue to watch over Locksley—it was what Robin would want, if nothing else.

Gisborne shifted his weight from one foot to the other, the leather of his tunic creaking in the silence. "I have been governing

Locksley lands in the absence of their lord, and the Prince has seen fit to grant me permanent stewardship. I believe you might help ease the transition in the hearts of the people, and perhaps ease your own transition as well."

Marian's confusion drained away, leaving her cold, empty, a shell of herself. "Are—are you asking me to marry you?"

Gisborne inclined his head. "Indeed. I am aware my familial background is a mark against me, but the length and . . . ah . . . intensity of your connection with the previous Lord of Locksley may make other offers for your hand scarce. The marriage would benefit us both."

Marian managed to turn her head enough to look at her father, who met her gaze with a grim, but unsurprised, look of his own. Gisborne must have discussed his offer with Marian's father already—perhaps on one of his many visits during her so-called hysterical convalescence. Her father must have been keeping it from her, trying to spare her the reminder that she'd have to eventually marry someone, that she couldn't mourn Robin forever.

The instant she looked back at Gisborne—standing there unmoved, his face still, his stance awkward in his nobleman's attire—fury, hot and blinding, rose up to fill the emptiness in her heart. "Sir Guy," she said, voice shaking, all sense fled. "You'll find I do not respond well to extor—"

"My daughter is still in mourning." Her father's voice strained to drown hers out, words tangling together in his rush to interrupt. "Perhaps you might call on us another time."

Gisborne arched an eyebrow, attention shifting from Marian to her father. "Your pardon, sir, but my understanding was that she was merely betrothed—she cannot mourn a husband she did not have."

"Nevertheless," said her father, mastering his own emotions far better than Marian was. "She's still—ah—fragile."

Marian felt like screaming, if only to remind the two men that she was standing not three yards from them, and fully capable of explaining her own mind and heart.

Gisborne frowned, glancing back over at Marian. "I was informed by the physician that the lady was suffering from some emotional ailment, a hysterical terror at the loss of her future status. I thought perhaps she might be receptive to an offer that would restore that future, that it might ease her unhappiness." And, if Marian were to marry Gisborne, then ownership of Edwinstowe would pass to Gisborne upon her father's death, as it was intended to pass to Robin.

Marian reached for the back of the long bench in front of her, gripping it so hard her fingers turned white.

"You are a generous and thoughtful man," said Marian's father. "But I believe my daughter is not well just now—you see she is struck dumb."

Gisborne grunted in agreement before remembering himself enough to bow. "Then perhaps I will call another time. In the meanwhile, consider my offer. My Lord," he continued, bowing to Marian's father. "My Lady." He turned that bow in her direction, head lifting so he could look at her. He paused there, as though considering approaching her for a more direct address—then straightened. "My regards, and wishes for your speedy recovery."

He turned to make his way out with his stiff-legged gait. How this power-hungry lackey of the Sheriff's could ever presume to take Robin's place in her affections—Marian choked back the urge to put an end to his hopes once and for all. Just now she didn't care about her own reputation, her own future;

but her father was there, suddenly, at her elbow, wrapping his arm around her shoulders and squeezing.

She had to play the game, at least for this moment. For her father, if not for herself.

But as Gisborne moved, she heard again the creak of leather, and she blinked, and focused again on his attire. He wore black— Marian had never seen him in anything else—but she hadn't taken notice of the clothes themselves. He was not dressed for a social call, and he wore no belt. Abruptly she remembered the weight and bulk of his cloak by the door. No man, even the lowest of peasants, would wear a sword belt to a marriage proposal.

"Sir Guy—" Marian left the protective circle of her father's arm to go after her would-be suitor. "What business brought you here?"

Gisborne straightened, expression grim once more. Displeasure seemed to be his natural state. "I am in pursuit of a fugitive we believe may be hiding in this part of Sherwood, my Lady. Perhaps this knowledge will encourage you to be more cautious when you leave the safety of your father's home." With a nod to her father and then to her, Gisborne retrieved his cloak— without waiting for the steward to fetch it for him—and the sword belt that had been hanging beneath it, lending bulk to its outline on the hook.

Marian waited until the door had closed behind Gisborne, then turned to find her father there, his face grave and weary.

"Oh, Marian—I should have warned you." He scrubbed a hand over his face. "I've been keeping him at bay, but I had no idea he would—"

"Where's Elena?" Marian interrupted with a shake of her head.

Her father blinked at her. "Elena? Your maid?"

"Has she been gone since before Gisborne arrived?" The pieces were still coming together in Marian's mind, the explanation for the dread in the pit of her belly.

Her father was frowning. "I . . . I'm not sure. But Marian, what does your maid have to do with Gisborne? I'm not sure you're—"

"It's Will." Marian whirled and ran for her cloak. "Will Scarlet—he's Elena's brother. Gisborne was about to execute him the morning I . . ." The morning her world fell apart. She pushed that from her mind, thinking instead of the memory of that badly beaten face, so swollen she barely recognized the boy she'd known from childhood. "If Gisborne knew that Elena was his little sister, he could have planned to use her to draw him out."

A hand came down over hers as she grasped her cloak on its hook. She turned to meet her father's gaze, his confusion supplanted by genuine fear. "Marian, you cannot go after them. It's one thing to ride to Locksley and ask for mercy, but this—a manhunt, at night, in Sherwood Forest? You cannot go, you cannot be seen there. We have time for you to decide what to do about Gisborne's offer, but if he catches you prowling around the forest at night trying to warn or rescue an outlaw . . ." Her father's hand squeezed her fingers in a wordless plea. "There are some things we cannot explain away by grief or hysteria or feminine weakness."

The wry set of her father's lips was what brought Marian back to herself. He was right—and perhaps if it were only her reputation, only her own neck at risk, Marian would feel differently. But it was her father's status, lands, home—and life—that could be forfeit were his daughter to be caught aligning herself with outlaws. And the people of Edwinstowe would suffer for having lost him as their lord.

"I must at least go out and look for Elena. She could be lost—she doesn't know the forest like Robin and I do. She could be hurt." She took a breath, using the pause to think. In her daze as she'd returned to the house, she'd left the pack with Robin's cloak on Jonquille's saddle. No doubt Midge, the stable master, had discovered it—she would have to hope it hadn't been brought up to her chambers. "I won't approach Gisborne—I'll just look for my maid."

"If he sees you—"

"I promise you, Father." Marian draped her cloak over one arm. "Gisborne won't have any reason to think I'm not exactly where I'm supposed to be: here, thinking about marriage, discussing terms with my father."

Her father scrubbed at his face again. He had a knack for knowing when she was being less than honest, and he had that look now. But she wasn't lying—the cut of Robin's cloak clearly denoted its wearer as a man, and her height ought to reinforce the disguise.

If she kept her hood up, and made sure no one saw her face, Gisborne couldn't recognize her as a woman, much less herself.

"Be careful," her father said finally.

Marian kissed his cheek, then slipped out the servants' exit toward the stables.

The girl is supremely disinterested in him. Their parents leave them together under the watchful eye of a hateful old maid, him in his best tunic again, her in a dress that looks almost as uncomfortable. Robin greets her, reciting the words he's been taught. She returns his greeting, sounding even more bored than he is. She gives him a nosegay of wildflowers and he gives her an ivory comb his mother pushed into his hand. His mother gave his hand a squeeze, the press of her ring a familiar comfort, but now he's nervous and antsy again.

Then the girl looks out the window and tugs at the neck of her dress. "Do you know how to shoot?" she asks.

Robin stares at her. "Like a bow?"

She eyes him critically. "Yes, like a bow. Father says I'm too little, and anyway they want to teach me to shoot like a lady and I want to learn for real. Can you teach me?"

Robin has never had much luck with a bow in his hand, despite the best efforts of his tutor. "Yes," he says instantly. "Yes, I can teach you."

FIVE

THE NIGHT WAS HEAVY and thick with the threat of rain, making the air smell like wet earth and bark. The dull pounding of the gelding's hooves against the packed dirt and leaves of the road reverberated in Marian's head, thudding against her temples. Lungs aching, heart thrumming, Marian struggled to keep panic at bay, trying to shove the inner voices of logic and worry aside.

God, what am I doing? It's Robin—Robin's the one who should be here.

She thought of Will, of the swollen and bloodied features beneath the executioner's hood; she thought of Elena, her maid's devotion to her Lady despite knowing word of her brother's death could come at any hour. *Don't think of Robin,* she told herself. *Think of—*

She hadn't dared bring Jonquille, for the mare was too recognizable. The gelding she'd taken instead gave a sudden lurch to the side, momentum preventing him from stopping altogether. Marian barely kept her seat, ducking low and clamping her legs around the gelding's flanks—a tree branch had cracked under the weight of an earlier rain, and dangled from the break so that its leaves draped like a curtain across the road. She leaned right, trying to urge the gelding back around the branch, and the horse swerved so close to the tree that Marian's shoulder slammed into the bark.

Half-stunned, left arm starting to throb, Marian fought to take a full breath. Her legs ached—she'd been neglecting her riding, and after her climb down from Robin's bedroom, her muscles were exhausted. She should have brought Jonquille after all; this horse lacked her quick reflexes and familiarity with Marian's style of riding.

She could not afford to stop and inspect her arm—she could move it, and though it hurt, the pain was not sharp enough for a broken bone. She tightened her legs against the gelding's ribs until he settled, and this time she kept her eyes fixed on the road ahead, for all she could not see more than a few paces in front of her.

Robin's wool cloak concealed the shift and kirtle she wore beneath—Marian had to hope that the mist and the shadows would do the rest of the work of concealing her identity and her gender.

She'd brought her bow and archer's glove, and her sword. The gear had been sitting neatly by Jonquille's saddle—Midge had seen it but not packed it away. She was keenly aware of the weight of the weapons as she rode, and could not budge the heavy dread in her stomach at the thought of arming herself against men instead of game. The little ruby ring that had belonged to Robin's mother rested between her breasts, strung on a lacing from her bodice. She'd taken it off to don the archer's glove, and it had lain in her palm like a drop of blood—like an omen.

She hadn't dared leave it behind.

The mist thickened, turning the trees and branches into slate-gray specters sweeping out of the fog toward her. An owl, startled from its hunt, hooted irritably—Marian caught a glimpse of pale feathers vanishing into the mist. She could not be far behind Gisborne's men; only a fool would ride at such a breakneck gallop through Sherwood Forest in the dead of night.

Only a fool, Marian's thoughts echoed. But this time she didn't have to smother the voice or the fear. Her instincts took over: her mind calmed, her muscles focused, her breath steadied into the rhythmic in-in-out, in-in-out, matching the triplet drumming of the horse's hoofbeats. Marian's body knew this—the ride, the chase—and her battered heart was too tired to do anything but be swept along.

Up ahead a swirl of fog hinted at a thinning of the trees, the intersection of the path from her father's house with the King's Road. The riding would be easier there, but she'd be exposed. She could not catch up to Gisborne in the open—if he hadn't found and caught Will yet, there'd be no one to rescue, and if he *had* found Will . . .

Marian swallowed, her throat raw with the effort of breathing the chilly night air so harshly. Gisborne had already shown his hand: he'd intended to execute Will in Locksley town. He was a commoner, after all, and not worth the effort and expense of a public execution in Nottingham. If Gisborne found Will before Marian caught up to them, then Will would die.

Marian burst out onto the King's Road and reined the gelding in sharply, eliciting a high squeal of protest from the creature. Her heart wrenched at the sound, and she paused, stroking the horse's neck as she scanned the ground, breath slicing at her lungs.

The moon was only a sliver and cast the palest of glows through the fog. It had rained only a few days before, and the ground was still wet. Though the road was pockmarked with hoofprints and wagon ruts in both directions, the sweep of five—no, six—sets of prints all leading from the road Marian had taken revealed Gisborne's path.

North. Deeper into the forest.

She hesitated then, reins gathered in her right hand while she flexed her left wrist, testing how much her bruised shoulder would hamper her abilities.

Before she could plan her next move, a distant sound slipped through the quiet. For a breath, Marian thought it some bird, a jay or a rook, waking long enough to cry a protest against the dark. But the gelding's ears pricked, and Marian's breath caught. She recognized that sound: a shout.

She urged the gelding back into a run but veered off the road, under the cover of the trees. Her ears strained to listen over the sound of her own horse—from somewhere ahead, she heard the answering echoes of other hooves against the ground. Marian slowed, listening. The fog scattered the sound as utterly as it did the moonlight, but after a few heartbeats she could tell they were moving east from the road. They wouldn't break from the road unless they had reason—some sign that Will had gone that way, or else some other outlaw hiding in these woods.

Marian paused, her mind's eye replaying the trail that had brought her here. Six sets of tracks. Gisborne, a battle-scarred veteran who'd survived a war that had killed Robin, plus five of the Sheriff's men—in a forest that sheltered murderers, thieves, and highwaymen.

Another shout echoed from the mist, louder this time.

Marian could cut through the forest and catch up to them. They were still on the chase—she could follow them, using the sounds of their pursuit to hide her own, until they found Will. And then . . .

But there her plan faded, vanishing as if into the mist ahead of her. She was no weakling, no fumbler with a blade, and her aim was better than Robin's when it came to the bow. But even Robin would hesitate to take on six armed men in the dark of Sherwood Forest with a wounded arm and an unfamiliar horse.

She'd have to hope a solution would come, taking shape out of the fog ahead, in time for her to save Will.

Gisborne's men rode mostly in silence, a sign of discipline that brought Marian no comfort. Their occasional shout served only to warn the others of some telltale sign, some track that pointed toward their quarry. Marian drew closer, a boulder-studded overhang looming out of the night and offering a place to hide. From the sounds of Gisborne's party, they would pass close to the overhang—she'd be able to get a glimpse of them, their arms, be certain of their number. She'd never had Robin's head for tactics—though she could often best him when it came to combat, he beat her every time when it came to war games.

Knowledge is the only ally you need against superior numbers, said Robin's voice in her ear. And though the warmth of it was a comfort, suddenly Marian wasn't so sure.

Eyes straining, she peered into the fog to the northeast as she edged the gelding toward the overhang. Every time she thought she saw a shape emerging, it turned out to be a billow of mist, a trick of the faint moonlight, a failure of her own eyesight. Marian's head pounded with strain, her aching thighs throbbing from the unfamiliar saddle. She wound the reins around the pommel and reached for her bow. She'd still not regained the skill with the bow she'd had before Robin's death, but on her worst day she was still a better shot than most. If she could pick off a few of Gisborne's men as they approached, she might stand a chance.

She saw the ruby ring in her mind's eye, resting in her palm like a drop of blood collected there—like an omen. *I am no soldier . . . I cannot kill a man.*

Not even to save another man's life? asked Robin, as if he stood at her elbow, surveying the same treacherous tableau of mist and shadow.

So focused was she on the impenetrable curtain of fog beyond the overhang that when something rushed out of the leaf mold with a roar, she could only let out a ragged gasp as the gelding reared, shrieking his fear. Marian's stomach slammed downward, and despite how tightly she clamped her legs against the gelding's flanks, the violence of his response threw her from the saddle. She hit the ground with a sickening thud, driving all the air from her lungs. Groaning, gasping, she heard the patter of the horse's hooves as he galloped away—she struggled to rise, but the horse was already lost in the mist before she could see.

Instead, she saw a thick, blunt branch swinging out of the darkness toward her face. She moved without thought, instincts slamming into place, overtaking the panic she felt at having lost her horse. She dropped back flat to the ground, abandoning her bow and rolling away from her assailant—rolling until she could use her momentum to find her feet. The cudgel came at her again, its wielder a shadowy, wild shape that danced in her half-stunned vision. She threw up her arm to deflect the blow and swung out with her leg—her attacker reeled back with a grunt, buying Marian enough time to draw her sword.

The scrape of steel made her opponent step back, and Marian caught a faint glitter of eyes in the darkness, a flash of fear, a streak of blood on skin. He wore no armor—he bore no crest.

And he was afraid.

Marian staggered with relief, her sword point dropping. She tried to speak, but her lungs were still in spasm from her fall, breath so tightly bound that she couldn't so much as squeak.

Will.

SIX

WILL RUSHED HER, CHOOSING the likelihood of death fighting one armed opponent over the absolute certainty of dying fighting six. Her instincts told her to raise her sword, defend herself—but this was no friendly bout, no lesson in swordplay. In near-total darkness, knee-deep in wet leaves and mud, with Gisborne's men moments away, one wrong move with the blade could end Will's life—or hers.

She dropped the weapon as his body collided with hers, and her world narrowed to a frantic staccato of gasps and grunts. Will wasn't without skill, but he fought like the village boys, all bravado and brute strength. Marian was far quicker, though hindered by her attempts to gather enough breath to speak—he landed a blow to her side, and another to her hip, never noticing in his desperation that Marian wasn't fighting back but only trying to avoid his blows. She hooked her foot around his leg, intending to send him crashing to the ground, but she dropped her guard checking to make sure she wasn't sending him headlong into a boulder, and Will's elbow struck her in the throat.

Gurgling, Marian staggered back as Will fell, flailing in the leaves to find his footing. Lungs still spasming, throat in agony, she felt she might burst trying to utter his name, some clue to tell him in the melee that she was friend, not foe. In the distance, Marian heard hoofbeats.

Gisborne.

And then Will got to his feet, and in his hand was Marian's sword.

The sight hit her like a plunge into icy water. She still could not speak, but the world straightened itself out, and she ducked easily when he rushed her, twisting so that she could land a jab of her elbow into his arm below the shoulder. Will gave a muffled cry, the sword dangling from half-nerveless fingers; Marian, ears straining to hear Gisborne's approach, heard his voice like a scream.

For God's sake, Will. Before he could turn and recover his grip on the sword's hilt, Marian struck out at the back of his head, momentum half spinning him so she could ready a second blow. But before she could strike, his knees crumpled and he dropped to the ground. She remembered the sight of his face when Gisborne pulled the hood away, bloodied—he'd been beaten already, and she'd seen men whose wits had flown after repeated blows to the head. Will might not have recovered entirely from his first encounter with Gisborne.

Marian ignored the pang of guilt and dropped into the leaves after him. Will was still half-conscious and struggled vaguely as she grabbed his arm. She ignored him, dragging him farther beneath the overhang, then pulled his body in against hers so she could twist his arm behind his back and wrap her left arm, throbbing from the shoulder down, around his neck. She covered his mouth with her hand.

He tried again to break free, his efforts increasing as he recovered from her blow to his head—and then a sharp whistle from the fog-shrouded wood made him go still.

The pounding hoofbeats of pursuit had stopped. Marian could not tell from her vantage point what sign had prompted Gisborne or his men to halt—perhaps her horse had left a visible trail as it fled—but they were close enough now that she could hear the crunch of leaves as someone dismounted.

She wanted to speak, to tell Will to be quiet, to trust her. But a whisper would cut through the stillness like a knife, and if she spoke, even beneath her breath, it would give her away. She might have the height of a man, the skills of a fighter, but she could not hope to change her voice—her higher timbre would carry in the quiet.

She could feel the violent thrashing of Will's heart against her stomach, where she held him still. He had gone almost limp—recognizing, perhaps, that whoever he thought he was fighting, it wasn't one of Gisborne's men.

Marian resisted the urge to shrink back farther into the recesses of the hollow, her every nerve raw and tingling. Wet leaves had invaded the tops of her boots, and somewhere in the leaf mold an old, decomposing carcass made the air stink of death and decay. Something wriggled against the back of her neck, stirring her hair and crawling beneath the fabric of her shift.

Marian made herself stone.

Voices, indistinct, told her that the rest of Gisborne's party had dismounted. They were moving away, but slowly—searching, not chasing.

Marian felt a touch against the arm around Will's neck and

looked down to find him tapping at her wrist. *Let me go,* the touch said. Marian hesitated—if he made a move, either against her or to flee, Gisborne's men would hear it and find them. And they would kill Will.

The touch came again, and she could see the edge of Will's face, no more than a silhouette in the blackness, as he strained to look up at his captor.

Marian took a few breaths, readying herself—and then eased her arm away from Will's neck.

To her relief, he barely moved when released. His fighting instinct having faded, he seemed every bit as aware of the danger beyond the overhang as Marian was. He turned a little to look at her.

She could not see his face, only the dark outline of where he lay against her, his other arm still held behind him, against Marian's stomach. But she could see the silhouette of his head move—his eyes went first to her face, as unidentifiable in the darkness as his, then slid downward. And caught.

For a moment, Marian wondered wildly if her clothing had torn in the struggle, if he could see that she was a woman. But when she looked down, she saw that the little ruby ring had slipped free of her kirtle during their fight and lay dangling from its lacing against the soft sweep of her cloak. It glinted, shifting as she breathed, in a spectral fragment of moonlight dripping through a gap in the rock.

She felt Will tense. She heard his breath suck in, tremble out, shudder in again.

"Robin?" he exhaled.

The sound of his name hit her harder than any of Will's blows, harder than the tree roots against her shoulder, harder than her fall from the flighty gelding. She could not move, could not speak. *If only,* she thought. *If I were Robin, we would both of us be safe.*

And then a voice, deep and resonant and harsh, split the air.

"Surrender yourself," the voice shouted, "and your death will be swift. Continue to flee, and your feet will be the first thing I remove when I find you." The sound of Gisborne's sword scraping against its sheath was like a gravedigger's shovel striking bone.

SEVEN

"TRACKS," CALLED ONE OF Gisborne's men, the voice accompanied by the crunch of boots on leaves. "Fresh hoofprints—leading east."

Marian's breath caught. The cursed gelding, long gone now—perhaps he would be their salvation after all, leading the men away.

"Hold," snapped Gisborne as a horse's bridle jingled impatiently. More footsteps. Then a pair of boots appeared over the lip of the hollow—Will saw them too, his body tensing where he lay against Marian.

"But sir, if he's found a horse, he could be—"

"The boy is not without wits, to have eluded us so far." Gisborne's voice was as calm and collected as it had been when he spoke to Marian of marriage, hours before. "If I were a clever criminal, I would use whatever resources I could find to mislead my pursuers. If I found a horse, and the law was so close on my heels, I would use the beast for distraction."

Marian longed to close her eyes but would not dare. Gisborne was so close she could have lunged forward and pulled him down into the hollow, were there not five other men with whom to contend.

Gisborne halted, boots turning against the leaves. "Fan out."

Marian gulped air, trying to make no sound, certain her every breath sounded like a death rattle. Her throat throbbed and ached where Will had hit her, and her muscles were quivering with prolonged strain.

Damn Gisborne. Her thoughts were scattered, fractured, useless—exhaustion kept focus at bay, mind circling again and again, pacing like a cornered animal.

Mislead your pursuers. Robin's voice echoed Gisborne in Marian's mind, overtaking the frantic slivers of thought. *Be clever. Use distraction. . . .*

She did not question the voice this time, only listened, recognizing the wisdom in his words.

Marian lifted her head, steeling herself against the skittering thing still crawling down her neck, drawn to the warmth of her skin. *Gisborne's not wrong,* she thought, taking a bracing, deep breath of the damp, chilly air. *If they light torches, if they conduct a true search, they'll find us immediately. Will is wounded—confused from the head wound, most likely—and I'm in no shape to fight. He cannot run, and I cannot stay hidden. . . .*

She could not know where Gisborne's men were—she could only see Gisborne himself, his boots and the tip of his sword. She could not know where their horses were, or how spread out they'd become. But while a man on horseback can easily outpace one on foot over a long distance, it takes time to mount, to turn the beast in the right direction, to get up to speed. . . .

She hesitated, playing out the scene in her head. If all of

Gisborne's men had dismounted, she'd have twenty, maybe thirty seconds of a head start even if they were standing by their mounts.

Enough to disappear into the fog—if nothing goes wrong.

Marian glanced down at Will, who was shaking and shooting glances at the ring hanging a finger's breadth from his eyes. She moved, squeezing his shoulder and slowly, very slowly, releasing his arm from behind his back. She could tell what he was thinking—that Robin was alive, certainly, and that he had come to Will's rescue.

And he has, Marian thought grimly. She wouldn't be here if it weren't for his voice urging her on. Except that Robin would never have gotten on the wrong side of the Sheriff's forces, never would have found himself in a position that would earn him the hangman's noose. Robin would have stopped all this somehow.

Marian squeezed again and felt Will shift in response. She eased away from him, first pressing her finger to her lips and then holding up her hand, palm outward. *Stay.*

Will hesitated but nodded, the dark silhouette of him barely more than a shadow.

Marian retrieved the makeshift club Will had been using, a rotten branch he must've picked up from the forest floor. She watched Gisborne, waited for his boots to turn as he oversaw his men searching for his quarry—then heaved the cudgel as hard as she could.

The crash it made in the undergrowth was a cacophony, and Gisborne's boots jerked toward it, then started to run.

Marian wasted no time and took up her bow. She left her sword, for it would only hamper her as she ran, and slipped out of the hollow on the far edge, opposite the direction she'd thrown the branch. She spared one backward glance—long enough to see Will still crouched in the shadows, Gisborne striding toward a dense thicket, sword raised, his men converging upon it—and then broke into a sprint.

She made no effort to quiet the noise she made as shouts erupted behind her. Just now, she needed speed, not stealth. She needed them to follow her, so that Will could escape once she'd led them away. Her lungs were already on fire, still shredded from her hard ride, her fall, Will's blows. Her hip where he'd slammed into her screamed with every step. She tripped, going face-first into a blackberry bush, stifling a moan as thorns ripped at her scalp.

Marian pulled herself back up to her feet. She couldn't stop to see if the fog had closed between her and her pursuers, but she'd have to run an unpredictable path if she was going to lose them in the mist. She could hear horses now—they'd remounted faster than she'd hoped.

She turned again, and then again, moving with greater and greater care each time she changed direction. The sounds of pursuit began to fade, and as Marian's vision began to spark with lack of air, she took a long enough pause to look behind her, half expecting to see Gisborne loom up out of the night like some cursed spirit, sword raised for a fatal swing.

But there was nothing. She could see only mist, and trees, and overhead, a glimpse of a shrouded moon. The weather was shifting—the fog was beginning to clear. Marian stifled a sob of relief and crept away into the night.

By the time Marian woke, her father had left for Lord Owen's manor in Clifton to consult about the rising taxes on their lands. Elena was nowhere to be found, and Marian drifted through the house half-waking, ghostlike. Her whole body ached, and when she splashed her face with water from the rain barrel outside the kitchen, lines of icy fire raked across her cheeks and along her hairline.

She'd crept in silently the night before, collapsing into her bed fully dressed, still bleeding sluggishly from a few of the scratches from the blackberry thorns. She hadn't paused to think, to process—exhaustion, not fear, had won out. But now, gazing at the translucent reflection of her battered face in the rain barrel, the image stirring gently in the breeze, she felt as though the blood in her veins was slowly turning to lead.

Oh God, Robin—what have I done?

Memory came in fragments, as detailed as paintings and as empty of life—the gelding slamming her shoulder into the branch, Gisborne's boots grinding the leaf litter into dust, the flash of Will's panicked face, the glimmer of his eyes as he recognized her ring.

She had no way of knowing if Will had escaped—no way of knowing if he was still alive. If Gisborne's entire force had followed her headlong dash, then Will could have slipped away, injured and befuddled though he was. But if any of his men had stayed behind . . . Will was unarmed, untrained, and—

Marian's breath caught. Will wasn't unarmed—he had her sword. Her sword, which Robin had had made for her in Nottingham, as long as a man's but with a narrower grip to fit her hands. *Her* sword, which, if traced to the blacksmith who'd forged it, would give her away.

The fog had cleared altogether, the morning bright and clear and crisp with the promise of autumn. Unless she waited until nightfall, Marian could not simply don Robin's cloak again and steal away into the forest—she'd be recognized before she'd traveled half a league. And by nightfall, any of a thousand things could happen to betray Marian's identity.

Her muscles screaming a litany of protests, Marian moved into the pantry, glad that she'd managed to sleep through the household's fast-breaking, and that the storerooms were unguarded. Will would be hungry and thirsty, and he was wounded. Marian gathered up the heel of yesterday's bread, a few dried apples from last year's harvest, some hard cheese, and salted venison into a cloth. The storeroom also had a stock of feverfew and comfrey, and strings of sage hanging from the shelves—she took a few leaves here and there, trying to avoid leaving an obvious bare patch among the herbs, and some boiled cloth for bandages.

She didn't bother to change but left Robin's cloak concealed below her mattress, and exchanged it for her own pale blue wool. If anyone saw her, she could claim to be out for a day ride through the outskirts of the forest, the supplies for her own luncheon. It was an excuse she'd given a thousand times with Robin at her side—and the thought caused her to feel his absence keenly.

At least she'd be able to ride Jonquille this time. She couldn't help but wonder what would've happened if she'd taken her own mare to find Will the night before—if the gelding hadn't thrown her, she wouldn't have ended up cornered under an overhang, surrounded by the Sheriff's men.

Oh God. The gelding.

Marian stopped dead in the entrance to the stables, heart pounding. Half a dozen excuses appeared in her mind, dismissed half a second later. The theft of a horse was punishable by imprisonment—the theft of a horse belonging to a nobleman like her father was punishable by execution.

Though did it count as theft if it was her own father's horse?

"Seems it was an eventful night," said a voice from the recesses of the stables.

Marian jumped, running into the edge of the door and

grimacing as the impact jarred her injured shoulder. She stepped inside, leaving the daylight behind and letting her eyes adjust to the gloom. Midge, her father's stable master, stood a few paces from the gelding's empty stall, its door ajar.

Marian groped for a response but was saved when the old man sighed, winding the leather of a worn halter around his palm.

"I suppose if a thief were to choose any of our stock, that jumpy rouncy would be the one I'm least sad to lose." Midge strode forward, his lined face grim.

"L-lose?" Marian repeated, focusing on the open stall door beyond Midge, in the hope that her face would not betray her guilt.

"I know I shut everything up tight last night," Midge replied. "No way any of our steeds run off unless taken. Don't worry, my Lady, I'm sure the thief will turn up. Or the horse will. Or the gear he stole, for there were a few things—a cloak, a bow— missing this morning as well. Will you be riding Jonqu—" He'd drawn close enough to see Marian in the light. "Good God, my Lady—you're injured."

Marian forced herself to stand her ground, though she wanted to turn away or retreat into the shadows. "A-a-a night terror, Midge, nothing more."

The old man had been like an uncle to Marian, despite their class difference—her love of horses and of riding meant that she'd spent far more time in the stables than other noble chil- dren. Midge's brow was creased with concern, and he reached out to grasp her chin, turning her face to the light. Marian could feel the sun gleaming hotter against the scratches there.

"A dream marked you so?" Midge's voice betrayed none of his skepticism—Marian had gone through a period when she was six where every other word out of her mouth was a lie, and Midge had always accepted her untruths as though he believed her. Or had pretended to.

"I woke still dreaming and became tangled in my bedclothes. I must have scratched my face while trying to free myself."

Oh, my love, you're going to have to get better at lying. Robin's voice in her head was choked, thin, on the verge of laughter. Marian felt anything but amused—that little voice could not be her own mind summoning his memory.

Midge frowned, but he seemed to be inspecting the scratches, not her expression. After a few long seconds, he released her chin and turned away, headed toward the tack shelves. He returned with a pot of salve and a nod, saying, "This works well enough for bramble scratches on horseflesh—I'd wager it works on noblewomen too."

Bramble scratches.

Marian could not keep the suspicion from her gaze as she regarded Midge—he was an outdoorsman, a woodsman, an expert in the forest and its realm. Did he recognize the look of thorn scratches? But he just smiled back at her, his pale blue eyes gently creased at the corners.

She took the salve with a mumble of thanks, slipping it into the satchel along with the food and herbs she'd taken from the storerooms.

"Keep your head about you if you're after a ride in the forest," Midge warned, turning for Jonquille's saddle. Marian heard her whickering from her stall a few doors down. "If there's thieves about bold enough to steal a horse from a lord's stables, they'll be bold enough to harry you."

Marian could not help but remember Gisborne's warnings the night before, his surprise that a woman could mind herself well enough to be safe in Sherwood without an escort. "I have boldness enough myself, Midge."

Midge's faint smile broke into a true grin, flashing for a moment before he turned away to lead Jonquille from her stall. "Aye, my Lady, there's no need to tell me of that."

A bit of the tension in Marian's chest eased at the familiarity of the conversation. She'd neglected Midge, too, while neglecting Jonquille in her grief. She let him saddle her horse, though she was used to doing it herself—it was a ritual of sorts, a confirmation of the old bond between them. She stood by Jonquille's head, eyes closed, feeling the mare's warm, wet breath on her neck.

"Take care, Lady," Midge said finally, as Marian mounted. "Times like these forge desperate men."

EIGHT

THE OVERHANG WHERE SHE'D grappled with Will the night before was empty. Marian had worried she wouldn't be able to find it again, but the area was well trampled by boots and hooves alike, tightening rings of a target centered on the bull's-eye where Gisborne had dismounted to find his quarry.

She saw no signs of bloodshed, which suggested Will was still alive, but she could not tell whether they'd captured him or he'd escaped. *Robin would know,* Marian thought bitterly. He had a way with tracking, an imagination that let him re-create the events of the forest as if he'd been watching from the shadows.

Marian left Jonquille nibbling at a blackberry patch and crouched, inspecting the crushed leaf litter. She crept closer to the overhang, scanning for signs of her own boots. If she could find hers, perhaps she could find Will's, and see if he'd run across the tracks left by Gisborne's posse. The trees above still held most of their summer leaves, though they'd begun to turn apple red and gold. Most of what lay underfoot was debris from the previous year, creating a thicker, denser soil to hold on to last night's footprints.

Jonquille whickered anxiously behind her, and Marian hid a smile—no doubt her horse had gotten a thorn in the lip for her eagerness. She shifted her weight, ready to rise and go to her horse.

"By all means," said a deep, unfamiliar voice, as something hard and blunt pressed in between her shoulder blades. "Keep looking for whatever it is you lost. An earring, perhaps, or some other bauble? We'll add that to your ransom."

Marian froze, mind racing. *You've every right to be here,* she told herself. *A picnic, a ride through the wood, even a secret tryst—scandalous, but hardly illegal. The Sheriff's men have no reason to place you here last night, and no proof if they do.*

"Turn, my Lady," said the voice. "Let us see those fair features." The thing poking into her spine, too blunt to be a sword, prodded at the shoulder she'd wrenched the night before. Unprepared, Marian let out a groan and tipped forward a little, catching herself on her palms. The sound prompted laughter from the man behind her, and her fear flickered over into a sharp glint of anger.

Marian stepped forward and rose to her feet, half-ready for the man to grab her for moving away. She turned—and nearly leaped back in surprise. The man was easily two heads taller than she, taller than any man ought to be. And he was no Sheriff's man either, dressed as he was in worn linens and leather bindings and boots split front and back to accommodate his large feet. He had brown-black hair but for the bramble thicket of a bright copper beard concealing most of his face. He held no weapons except a long, crooked staff worn shiny with use.

Seeing her shock, the man grinned, teeth appearing briefly in the rat's nest of hair on his face. "I think we've scared her, John," he called.

From somewhere beyond him, hidden in the foliage, another man's voice called back, "That's rather the point, John."

Marian scanned the trees but could see nothing—she glanced back at her assailant, still reeling. She'd been so focused on finding Will, so afraid of Gisborne's men spotting her, that she'd let herself be caught by common thieves.

The huge man tucked one hand through his belt, the other gripping the staff. "Calm your fears, little bird," he said, still grinning. "We're for gold, not anything more precious. Pay us our due, and we'll escort you to the edge of the forest before we take your horse."

Marian had to stifle a snort at the idea of anyone, even this giant of a man, forcing Jonquille anywhere she didn't wish to go. She could not be certain how many other men this "John" had with him, but he could have easily taken anything of value by assaulting her from the outset. Sherwood was haven to dozens of outlaws, and though they were all sentenced to the gallows if caught, the Sheriff rarely wasted manpower hunting for them unless they perpetrated crimes far worse than highway robbery. Either this man enjoyed toying with his victims or he was being truthful about having no intention to harm her.

Mistaking her silence for terror, the big man's voice shifted, gentling. "Tell me, my Lady—what's your name?"

Marian hesitated. If these men were arrested, they might trade information for leniency. Depending on Gisborne's determination to find Will Scarlet, he might ask about any strange encounters they might have had in this area. "Elena," she said finally. "I am a lady's maid in a household not far from here."

The large man's eyebrows shot up. He looked her over, head

to toe. "Elena," he echoed. "A lovely name. But you aren't dressed as a peasant."

"My Lady is ill. I borrowed her cloak and her horse, thinking to have a picnic in the fresh air while she slept."

The man snickered. "Imagining yourself a lady for the day?" He looked her over again, and Marian couldn't help but think he suspected she was lying. "Very well. Elena, I'm Little John, and my good friend back there is Big John." He paused, waiting for her reaction—no doubt she was intended to imagine with great terror someone even larger than the giant before her. "If you do as we say, you'll be back to your Lady in a few hours. Now, your valuables."

"Very well," Marian said slowly. "I have some food and medicines in my saddlebags. You are welcome to all you can carry."

"Fetch them," said Little John. He stood still, staff in hand, watching her carefully.

Marian had hoped he'd turn his back to rifle through her belongings. Trying to look frightened and cowed, she crept over toward Jonquille. Her horse was tense, ears flicked forward and alert, eyes rolling toward the large man a few paces away. Marian suppressed the urge to calm her and went instead to the saddlebags, pulling out the supplies she'd hoped to bring to Will Scarlet. She dropped each parcel to the ground one by one until the bags were empty.

"And now your coin," said John—although Marian knew it was unlikely to be his real name, or the real name of his comrade hidden in the trees. Half the outlaws in Sherwood were listed only as "John of the Hood" in the Sheriff's records, their names unknown, only that they'd someday see the inside of the executioner's hood.

"I carry none," Marian replied—the truth. She'd brought nothing with her of any value.

"Your jewels, then," said Little John, shifting his massive weight.

"I wear none—I would not have dared to steal my Lady's jewels, even on a lark. I would offer you my Lady's cloak, for it's of fine craftsmanship and warm, but you are neither a lady nor small enough to wear it."

The man laughed, the eyes just visible over his unkempt beard glinting. "She has wit, John. A shame we can't rob her of that; we could use the extra."

"Best hurry," his comrade shot back. This time his voice was deeper, tinged with concern, and Marian thought perhaps he was somewhere to the northeast, maybe forty paces.

"Patience." The big man lifted his staff to gesture at her. "I see that's a very fine ring upon your finger, my Lady."

Marian's breath caught, and she almost shoved her hand into the folds of her skirts. She'd forgotten Robin's ring. Swallowing, she said slowly, "I cannot give you the ring, sir. Please—there is value in the medicines there, and my Lady's horse will fetch you far more than a trinket like this—"

"The ring, Elena." Little John's voice grew harder.

Marian's pulse sped, and her hand tightened on Jonquille's gear. "It was given to me by my sweetheart. It has little value to anyone but me."

"Such a lucky lady's maid," said Little John, amused, "to have an admirer wealthy enough to give you jewels. I'm sure he will give you another."

Marian could not hide the flinch of her features. "He is dead."

Little John paused, the amusement in his features vanished. His weight shifted again. "My sympathies, Lady. But this is Sherwood Forest, where the only law is that those men who are strongest, fastest, fiercest, are the ones who get to eat. And that ring will buy me and my friend many meals."

"That is your law?" Marian's voice hardened. She would have left them the food, the medicine, even Jonquille's tack, had they thought to remove it before trying to steal her horse. But she would not give them Robin's ring. "Then if I am stronger, faster, and fiercer than you, by rights I should keep my ring and my food, and take yours as well."

This seemed to delight Little John, for he threw his head back and laughed, the booming sound of it making Jonquille sidestep nervously. Marian kept her hold on the mare's bridle, shifting her own weight.

"We don't have time for this, John," called the big man's compatriot in the forest. "Take the food and the horse and let's go."

Marian ignored him. "Well?" she asked Little John. "Are we agreed?"

John grinned. "Agreed. Come then, little bird. I don't doubt you have fierceness to spare, but when it comes to speed and strength, there are few who—"

Marian didn't wait for him to finish posturing. She swung one foot into Jonquille's stirrup, pulled herself up against her mare's side using her grip on her saddle, and urged the horse to bolt with a quick jab of her elbow. Already on edge, Jonquille broke into a run, and Marian hauled on her reins to aim her toward the man with the staff.

He had only time to splutter an oath and throw himself to the side before the horse was upon him. Marian let go, letting Jonquille sprint off into the woods, and rolled to soften her

landing. Jonquille knew her home well—if she could not find
Marian again, she'd make her way back to Midge.

John, now flailing in the leaves, had dropped his staff—
Marian threw herself down and snatched it up. She could not
wrap her whole hand around its diameter, but she shifted it until
she had a decent grip and rolled to her feet again. She had the
staff's tip against Little John's throat before he could stand.

"Well?" she asked, fighting hard to keep her breath steady,
singing in and out through her nose.

Little John's face was lax with surprise, and instinctively he
lifted his hands, palms up, to show they were empty. He was
struggling to speak, and Marian raised the staff a fraction so that
he could swallow.

"Drop the staff." His ally—Big John, he was called—spoke,
and when Marian lifted her head, he was standing thirty paces
away. He was scarcely taller than she, and certainly no bigger
than Little John, but he stood with bow drawn and arrow nocked
and eyes fixed on her.

At her feet, Little John coughed and called, "No, Alan, I gave
my word. This Elena, whoever she is, may keep her ring."

Big John—or Alan, as his comrade had named him—
hesitated a brief second but then lowered the bow. The arrow
stayed nocked to the string, though, and while John spluttered
and chuckled, Alan watched her with hard, suspicious eyes. "Her
name isn't Elena," he said.

John started to rise, but Marian could not afford to trust
John's word—or Alan's obvious antipathy—and kept the staff
in place, keeping him down. John made an exasperated sound.
"God's bones, Alan, you don't think there might be more than
one woman in England named Elena? Let me up, girl—you've
won your point."

"Forgive me if I don't take the word of an outlaw," Marian replied through gritted teeth.

"I swear upon my own grave, upon the executioner's rope, no harm will come to you, girl, not while you're in our forest."

"Drop the bow," Marian insisted, eyes on Alan.

"Drop the staff," he countered, voice tightening.

"Christ," muttered Little John. "Alan, put the bow down. You're as like to shoot me as her. He couldn't hit a tree in the middle of Sherwood," he added, an aside to Marian.

Marian took a breath, and as Alan stooped to place his bow down amongst the leaves, she withdrew the end of the staff and stepped back.

"I'm looking for someone," she said finally, glancing between the two men as Little John clambered to his feet. "A man, an outlaw like yourselves. He's most likely to have been on foot, a few fingers taller than I, bearing a quality blade but dressed low, like you. Recently beaten."

"We've seen no one," said Alan, still glaring at her as though he itched to retrieve his bow.

"Why?" John asked, brushing leaves from his filthy clothes and picking a twig out of his beard. "What reason could a lady's maid have for seeking an outlaw?"

Marian hesitated. "He's—my brother. The food and medicines were for him. He's being pursued by one of the Sheriff's lieutenants, a man named Guy of Gisborne, and I hoped that if he had supplies enough, he could hide until the law tired of seeking him."

Little John glanced at Alan, whose face was turning red, eyes narrowed as he spoke. "You're speaking of Will Scarlet. Which would make you Elena Scarlet?"

"God's knees, Alan." John's merry eyes had gone still and wide. "It's not Elena—"

"I know *that*," Alan snapped.

"Shut up, man, and let me finish. It's not Elena—it's *Marian*."

God's knees, Marian's thoughts echoed.

Alan's anger faded, then dropped away altogether. "Elena's Lady, Marian? Locksley's Lady?"

Marian let her breath out slowly. No point in trying to hide her identity anymore. "You seem to know Will," she said finally. "Have you seen him, then?"

The two men exchanged a glance. Little John took a step toward her but stopped when Marian jolted backward, lifting the staff. He raised his hands. "Easy, my Lady. Aye, we've seen the lad. But why are you here, alone, seeking him?"

"He's my maid's brother. And he grew up on Rob—on Lord Locksley's lands. I don't believe he is guilty of the crimes laid on him, and I wish to help him." She glanced at Alan, whose expressive features bore signs of grief now. "How . . . how do you know Will?"

Little John followed Marian's gaze, then rolled his eyes when he saw Alan's face. "He is betrothed to Will's sister. I suppose that makes him your maid's fiancé."

"Wh—Elena?" Marian's startled eyes first found Little John, then Alan, who now looked off into the forest, jaw clenched. "But . . . she never . . ."

Marian felt as though her head was full of chaff, thick and muffled—her thoughts dragged. Her maid had never mentioned so much as a sweetheart, let alone a fiancé, and certainly nothing about having had any ties to outlaws before the morning she found out Will was arrested.

Little John sighed, rubbing at his tailbone, which he had no doubt bruised while dodging Jonquille's charge. "We've a camp a league south. Perhaps you'd do us the honor of being our guest this afternoon, Lady Marian, and we'll tell you what we know of Will Scarlet. And then we can try to help you find your horse."

NINE

"WE WERE CHILDREN, ELENA and I." Alan leaned against a stout tree, fiddling with the pegs of an ancient and battered lute he'd retrieved after they'd brought Marian to their camp. "We loved each other from the moment we met. We were destined for each other, the greatest of loves, like Pyramus and Thisbe, like Orpheus and his Eurydice. . . ."

"Shut up, Alan." Little John tossed a clump of leaves at the other man's leg, earning him a scowl and a twang of strings. "Forgive him, my Lady. He was a minstrel at one point in his life—Alan-a-Dale he was called in the towns he visited—and sometimes the romance of it all gets to be a bit much for him."

"I am a minstrel still," Alan protested. "Once a man hears the call of the muses, he cannot turn away any more than a bird can leave the endless ocean of the sky."

"Uh-huh." John removed his cloak and spread it on a crumbling log, then gestured toward Marian. She would rather have sat upon the rotting log itself—the cloak had seen far too many seasons, and had a somewhat ripe stench—but she sat anyway, with a nod of thanks for John.

"Elena has been my maid for years," she said, eyeing Alan curiously. He was handsome, in a fine-boned, willowy way, underneath the filth and grime from living in the wilderness. "She's never mentioned you."

"Many trials, and the laws of men, have kept us apart," Alan said woefully. "But true love and destiny will triumph, my Lady—do not weep for us."

Marian eyed Little John, who was snickering as he dropped to the ground beside a stone-ringed fire pit. "I'll try not to," she said. John was definitely *not* handsome, with a nose that had been broken more than once, pockmarked cheeks, and an unkempt reddish beard. And yet his eyes were merry, and kind, and despite his massive size, there was a care to his movements like that of a craftsman. *Or,* thought Marian wryly, with the experience of her own life, *like someone who has had to learn to pay attention to keep his long arms and legs from knocking over every bit of furniture in the house.*

"They were childhood sweethearts," John said, leaning back on his elbows. "Till Alan was caught poaching, and gave up the life of an entertainer for a life of petty theft."

"Noble theft," Alan corrected him. "Someday I'll amass a fortune great enough to provide for my Elena again, someday when the King has returned and pardoned those good Englishmen whose only treason was deciding not to starve beneath the cruel laws and taxes of his brother the Prince."

"Enough, Alan." Little John was eyeing Marian curiously. "Begging your pardon, Lady, but there's not many noblewomen who'd come into Sherwood alone to help a peasant's brother."

"Elena's important to me. And her brother was important to Rob—to Lord Locksley. His parents died of the pox when he and Elena were young, and the previous Lord Locksley forgave their debts so they could stay in their parents' house rather than being turned out to fend for themselves. When the old Lord passed, his son found Elena a position as my maid, and Will a place with the miller in Locksley town. Rob—he wouldn't sit by and let Will be arrested. If he were here."

"I see." Little John picked up a charred stick by the fire pit and stirred the leaves. Their camp was barely more than a place to store their few belongings under a rock—no real shelter, and nothing but the depth of the fire pit to hide the flames from patrols.

"You said you would tell me what you knew of Will," Marian said, trying not to sound as impatient as she felt. "Have you seen him?"

John looked over at Alan, who stopped fiddling with the strings on his lute. He looked up, meeting Marian's gaze, and sighed. "Aye. We saw him. We started searching not long after midnight and found him half-delirious by a stream."

"Searching? How did you know to search for him?"

Little John started to respond, but Alan cut him off. "We heard him. Crashing through the underbrush like a herd of cattle."

John shut his mouth, and Marian glanced between the two men and thought of Elena—her maid had been missing since the night before. Her maid, who'd served her for years and never let slip she had ties to an outlaw.

She would not press them. Not about their sources, at any rate. "Delirious, you said—was he ill?"

"Only in his head," said Little John. "Battered and bruised, but not ill, no fever or chills. But mad, my Lady, quite mad."

"It wasn't madness," Alan argued. "The lad was walking in

circles, barely knew which way was north. And yet he escaped half a dozen of the Sheriff's men with nothing but a sword and his wits? Someone helped him, John."

"But a ghost?" Little John snorted. "Spirits and specters and spider's webs, Alan."

The ex-minstrel shrugged, shaking his head. "There's far more in this world than you or I will ever understand."

"Yes, but Robin of Locksley, risen from his grave among the infidels, returned to save Will Scarlet from the hangman's noose?" John snorted again, but the breath turned into a cough as he turned and saw Marian. "God's teeth. Forgive me, my Lady. I didn't mean to—Lord Locksley's your—uh."

Marian had no attention to spare for his misstep. "Will . . . Will says that Robin's spirit saved him from Gisborne's men?" The hairs lifted along the back of her neck, the ring on her finger burning her skin as she suppressed a shiver. The voice in her mind was silent now, but she felt its presence nonetheless. She would have been inclined to argue John's side, but for the vivid reality of Robin's voice lingering to guide her.

Little John scrubbed a hand through the long hair at the nape of his neck. "Aye, Lady. But there's no need to fear. I'm certain the lad's merely had one too many bumps on the head. No spirits here."

"Spirits have never frightened me," Marian replied. "Did Will say anything else about this . . . apparition?"

"Only that he appeared out of the rock itself and wrestled him down before Gisborne arrived to capture him, then led the soldiers on a merry chase through the woods before vanishing again. Said he was made of darkness and shadow, but he recognized the spirit by the ring he wore around his . . ."

Little John's eyes had dropped, and when his voice trailed off,

Marian remembered—too late—the ring. She tried to tuck her hand beneath her skirts, but John careened to his feet.

"My Lady," he said, voice hushed. "That ring—did it belong to Locksley?"

Marian's mind raced. She could not risk anyone knowing she'd been in the forest last night, much less a pair of outlaws who would trade information in a heartbeat to spare their own lives. "It was his mother's," she said haltingly. "He gave it to me—wore it around his neck as a token of our betrothal when he went to fight in the Holy War, and Gisborne returned it to me when he brought news of Robin's death—" Her throat closed.

"Christ," whispered John, gaze rising to meet Marian's.

"Please," said Marian, "if you have any loyalty or love for—"

"He was wearing it around his neck when he died," Alan interrupted, voice pointed and aimed at John. "As he was when he saved Will. And it cannot have been an impostor having stolen the original ring, as you believed, because there it sits, on his Lady's finger, where it belongs."

"Christ," John whispered again. Though most of his face hid behind that massive beard, what Marian could see of him had gone pale.

Marian waited, glancing between them, until a pressure in her chest made her realize she was holding her breath. It gasped out of her when she opened her lips, and the noise shattered the quiet.

"Oh, Lady," said Alan, abandoning his tree and stooping to one knee before Marian. "Do not weep. Your love is here, protecting you, protecting his people." He took her hand and cupped it in his.

"Shut up, Alan," said Little John, though the command held little fire, and the big man still looked shaken.

Marian still felt shaken herself. But if these men had found some other explanation for Will's escape than Marian's interference, she would not be the one to shatter their delusion.

"Will," she said, voice a little hoarse. "After Will saw—saw Robin—and after you found him, what happened then? Where is he?"

Alan released her hand and sat back, gaze falling. She glanced at John, who looked rather grim himself. "Captured," he said quietly. "He went off before dawn to find a tree to take a . . . to . . . um." His ruddy face grew a few shades ruddier, clashing horribly with the orange of his beard, and he cleared his throat.

"To relieve himself," Alan suggested.

"Yeah. Walked right into one of the Sheriff's patrols. Had him tied down and ass up—er, pardon, Lady—over the back of one of their horses before we'd woken up."

Marian lurched to her feet. "And you didn't go after him?"

Little John blinked at her—and even Alan was eyeing her, taken aback. "What," said John, "go after six soldiers with my stick and Alan's old lute and say, 'Pardon me, hand over that outlaw if you please'?"

"It's what Robin would've done," Marian said, stubborn.

"Maybe." John's voice was heavy and stern. "But if his spirit was in Sherwood last night, he wasn't there this morning when they took Will. And no use getting our necks stretched because Will pisses too loudly."

"Have to stay alive for Elena," muttered Alan, his eyes on the ground now.

"And I've got to keep Alan out of trouble." John's eyes were scowling beneath his bushy eyebrows.

Marian turned, pacing away from the little clearing. She wanted to be furious that all her efforts, all the risk of death and disgrace she'd taken to help Elena's brother, had come to nothing because these men had cowered in the bushes while the Sheriff's men took Will. And yet she'd barely been able to help him at all, and she'd been armed, trained—albeit informally—and prepared for danger.

It was only a few hours by horseback to Nottingham, and Will had been taken before dawn. Marian looked up, letting the sunlight scattered by the leaves half blind her. Nearly midday. Will had been dead for hours—dead before she woke this morning.

Her eyes stung, even after she shut them against the glaring noon sun.

"Let us see you safely to the edge of the forest." Alan's voice, behind her, was gentle.

"My horse will not have gone far," said Marian. "And she'll be more likely to come back to me if I'm alone—you scared her, after all."

"Robin of Locksley would not want us to let his love wander in these woods."

"If Robin's come back to save Will, then surely he's protecting me, too," Marian snapped. "Stay—keep your necks unstretched."

She heard John get to his feet, imagined his great bulk unfolding from the ground. "The food you brought, Lady—"

"Keep it." Marian took a breath, then looked over her shoulder. The two outlaws stood not far away, both looking at her with the same mix of guilt and . . . what? Marian gazed at them, trying to decipher their expressions.

"But—"

"Will has no need of it now." She twisted the ring on her finger, and abruptly she recognized what she saw in their faces: hope. *Robin*, she thought. *Back from the dead, and come to save his people.*

She could not bear the thought of shattering that, not for these two broken men with their strange sense of honor and their lives of fear and shame. "Keep it," she repeated, voice softening.

She hurried away, and from behind her came John's voice, echoing off the trees: "Sing if you ever need us, little bird."

Jonquille was not far from the overhang where she'd met Will, and where she'd found John and Alan. She was trained to come to Marian's whistle, and came trotting out of the trees, muzzle stained purple from blackberries, about an hour after Marian set off back in the direction of her father's lands.

Midge made no comment about Jonquille's purple war paint, nor Marian's attire, significantly dirtier than when she'd left. Her father had not returned from Owen's manor yet, and Marian hurried into the house through the side door, hoping to avoid seeing any of the servants. She could clean up the worst of the leaf grime and dirt on her skin with her morning wash water, and shake out and brush her cloak and skirts, and no one would know where she'd been.

She made it up the back stairs without incident, aiming to duck into her room before anyone could see her—and in her haste ran full tilt into Elena coming out of her own room.

Her maid yelped and fell back. She was half-dressed in her shift, with her plain wool kirtle laid out on her cot. Slung over the clothes press was a pair of man's leggings, and Elena's face was flushed, her hair in disarray.

Marian stared at her—lovely Elena, so sweet and gentle, diligent and kind and proper.

"Oh, my Lady, forgive me—I was . . . I was . . ." Her maid's eyes roved over the tiny room, seeing the leggings, searching for an explanation.

Marian was quicker to recover, all too aware of her own disarray and haste to cover it up. "Elena—stop, breathe. It's all right."

"Taking in laundry!" Elena burst out, seizing upon an excuse. "To make a little extra coin, to help my friends back in Locksley town—that's why I have men's clothes in my room."

Marian felt an irrational surge of giddiness. "Elena—stop, there's no need for excuses, I'm not—"

"Please, my Lady, don't mention it to your father. I'd hate for him to think I'm ungrateful for my position here, or that room and board and a station isn't kindness enough in exchange for my service, or—"

"Elena, I met Alan!"

"Or that I'm . . . I'm not . . ." Elena's voice petered to a gradual stop like a horse coming down out of a gallop. "You what?"

"I went to look for Will." The name made Marian's heart seize—how could she tell Elena what she knew of her brother's fate? "Instead I found Alan and another man. You were there last night, weren't you? To ask them to help find him?"

Elena's blue eyes were round and full. "Oh, my Lady—I'm sorry, I couldn't sit here knowing that he was out there, alone, without anyone to—"

"Me neither." Marian stepped closer and took her maid's hands. "How long have you been sneaking out to see Alan?"

"A few months," Elena whispered. "But only twice before last night, and only to tell him not to come for me. It's too dangerous—he's not a bad man, my Lady, he was only hungry, and a poor hunter, and he loves me so that it makes him foolish."

"Wearing men's clothing—you're far cleverer than I."

"My Lady?"

"Never mind—Elena, you don't have to worry. I have no

intention of mentioning any of this to my father, or to anyone else."

Elena's eyes brimmed, and she took a deep breath, squeezing Marian's hands. "Thank you." She leaned forward abruptly. "If you met Alan, then you know—you know what happened to Will?"

Marian nodded, finding it difficult to speak. "I'm so sorry. I tried, I swear to you that—"

"Have you seen him?"

"Who—Will?"

Elena's eyes darkened, her voice losing some of its urgency but gaining in intensity. "Lord Locksley," she whispered. "Or whoever . . . whoever is pretending to be Lord Locksley."

Marian released Elena's hands. "You know about Robin?"

"I went to town on my way back from the forest, hoping for news. There's word of a reward for information about a man claiming to be Robin of Locksley who was seen last night in Sherwood Forest, wearing his cloak and hood."

"Reward?"

"From Gisborne's own coffers. And also—my Lady—Will's life."

Marian stepped backward, shoulders hitting the wall behind her. "Will's alive?"

Elena nodded. "The Sheriff will sign a pardon for Will," she whispered, eyes filling again, hope etched in every line of her features, "as soon as the man in Lord Locksley's cloak and hood turns himself in."

Marian's brow furrowed. "Why? Why pardon Will for Robin?"

"He must believe Will knows something, and that fear for his life will make him betray Lord Locksley. Or that Lord Locksley must care enough about Will to turn himself in, if he'd risk his life and his lands to come to Will's aid in Sherwood."

Hoofbeats echoed up from the courtyard below, and a swift glance out the tiny window told Marian that her father had returned. She exchanged a swift glance with Elena, then hurried into her own room so that they could both finish erasing the signs of their adventures.

The man in Locksley's cloak and hood, Marian thought, lightheaded and reeling. If Will told Gisborne he'd seen Robin—if he'd told him with witnesses around, others who could testify to hearing reports that Locksley's Lord was alive—then Gisborne's claim to Locksley lands would not be so certain as he thought.

Or his claim to Locksley's Lady.

Marian's fingers shook as she unbuttoned her earth-stained dress and splashed cold water over her face. She could not turn herself in—she'd be killed or imprisoned, and her father too, and either way her father's lands would be forfeit, for to aid an outlaw was to commit treason in its own right. And though her father didn't know what she'd been doing, the Sheriff would never believe she'd done it on her own.

The "man" in Robin's hood couldn't come forward—but if Marian could keep the rumor alive, it might buy her enough time to find a way to free Will. And if enough people believed Robin was alive, she could refuse Gisborne's offer of marriage, stay with her father, help the people of Locksley and Edwin-stowe alike—and perhaps hold out until the war ended and the King returned.

A corner of green wool protruded from under Marian's mat-tress, a glaring mistake she'd been too weary to notice when she woke. If Elena had not been searching for aid for her brother, she would have uncovered it, and Marian's subterfuge, immediately. She would have to be careful.

Much, much more careful, said Robin's voice in her mind, grave.

Masquerading as Robin . . . the idea was mad—madder than Will and his ghosts.

Marian steadied her fingers and tucked the edge of Robin's cloak out of sight.

Madness, then, she thought with a grin. And then, missing the feel of wool on her fingertips, she thought, *Robin would have loved it.*

"*I thought you* were getting along," says Robin's mother from the daybed. "Many children your age have never met the people they're going to marry."

Robin kicks at a stone in the mortared wall that protrudes a little farther into the room than its neighbors. "She's not going to like it."

"She knows her duty," his mother says, exhaling weariness. She is tired often, these days, and Robin is allowed to see her only when she's not sleepy. "As do you, Robert."

"But . . ." Robin kicks at the stone again, not wanting to look at his mother.

Her voice softens. "But what, Robin?"

He hesitates. "What if it makes her start acting like a girl at me?" he blurts finally.

His mother laughs, the sound cut short by a torrent of coughing that brings a servant scurrying in from the next room. His mother waves the woman away, her eyes still amused, dabbing at her mouth with her handkerchief. "The combined efforts of an army of nurses, maids, tutors, and my own considerable abilities have done nothing to make Marian start acting like a girl, Robin. She acts like nothing—she acts like Marian."

Robin watches his mother through his lashes. "I guess," he mumbles. He's wondering if it's too late in the day to ride to Edwinstowe.

"Robin, will you come here?" His mother's voice is gentle, and he abandons his post by the window to cross to the daybed. She's slipping something from her hand. "I want to give you something."

"But that's your ring," says Robin, frowning, a deep alarm somewhere in the pit of his stomach. He sees a flicker of red in his mother's hand and thinks it's the ruby ring until he realizes that it's a droplet of blood on the handkerchief.

"It is," his mother replies, her smile buried at the corners of her mouth. "I'd like you to give it to Marian."

Robin reels back a step. "But——"

His mother presses her lips together, eyes dancing with amusement—and, nearly hidden, a touch of grief. "You don't have to give it to her today," she says, sinking back onto her cushions. "But someday you may want to."

Robin looks up at his mother's face. "But don't you want it still?" he whispers.

His mother smiles and folds his fingers around the little ruby ring. "I want your wife to have it."

TEN

"WHY IN HEAVEN'S NAME would you want to come with me?" Marian's father eyed her suspiciously from beneath his wiry gray eyebrows. "My God, when you were a child, I had to all but drag you with me when I went to Nottingham."

Marian schooled her features. The less her father knew, the better, for them both—he had little knack for deception. "I don't know—a change of pace, something other than these walls, these fields." She hesitated, hating the move she was about to make. "I see Robin everywhere here."

Her father's surprise softened, and he heaved a sigh. "All right, my dear. Come then, if you wish. But you know that Sir Guy will most likely be there, unless he's out chasing bounties for the Sheriff."

Marian didn't have to hide her expression at that—distaste curled her lip, and she shook her head. "I know. But I suspect we'd be seeing him anyway."

"He doesn't strike me as one to give up easily," her father

agreed. His face was neutral—unnaturally so—whenever Marian's suitor came up in conversation.

"At least his appearance won't be a surprise. And in Nottingham, I can claim other social obligations for part of the time."

Her father chuckled. "True. All right, tell Elena and pack what you need, and I'll have Midge saddle Jonquille."

Elena said nothing when Marian informed her of the trip, but her eyes grew round and wet, and Marian knew why—her brother was being held somewhere in Nottingham Castle, facing the gallows. How long the Sheriff would wait for Gisborne to extract information about the Locksley impostor, Marian did not know. But traveling with the family might give Elena a chance to see Will before his execution.

What Marian didn't share with Elena was that she had no intention of letting Will hang. Her plan was still hazy at best—she wished, again, for Robin's knack with strategy—but they'd be in Nottingham for at least a fortnight while her father attended the Sheriff. He and a dozen other lords from across the land had decided to converge upon Nottingham together in the hope of convincing the Sheriff to show more leniency in his taxation policies.

Two weeks. Plenty of time to help Will.

Marian kept scanning the trees as they rode through Sherwood, half expecting to see John and Alan there in the shadows. She tried to stop herself, for fear of giving something away to her father or Midge, who was traveling with them as horse handler and squire for her father—but every time she let her mind drift, her gaze swung back toward the forest.

Elena, at her side, kept her gaze ahead, her expression as calm and composed as ever.

You're far better at this than I, Marian thought.

Nottingham was only a few hours from Edwinstowe on horseback, but the ride felt interminable. By the time the King's Road finally emerged from the trees and into the green fields surrounding Nottingham, Marian was ready to bolt—and Jonquille, picking up on her rider's nerves, made a halfhearted attempt to break into a run.

The approach to the city was crowded with people, and beggars lined the roadsides as merchants and peasants dragged carts in and out of the gates. There had always been beggars in Nottingham, a handful of ragged people turned out of homes overcrowded or seized by the crown—but Marian had never seen so many in one place. Her father's presence and obvious importance kept most of the beggars away, though Marian could not ignore the way their hungry eyes followed the travelers. She did not carry coin. Her father would have some somewhere in his saddlebags. But a couple of coins to the few outstretched hands nearest them would be like a single twig bobbing in the open sea—it would not keep these people from drowning. And she could not look at them, sympathy and guilt weaving together like chain mail around her battered heart.

Far worse than the people calling out for coins or food were those who'd given up begging altogether. Clusters of weary, dirty, thin-lipped people dotted the slopes on either side of the city gates, barely registering the arrival of new nobility. They seemed to Marian like they were waiting—but not anxiously, not hopefully. They were waiting for some change they knew would not come, marking the hours and days and years only to pass the time.

Marian, chest tight and aching, tried to keep her eyes on Jonquille's mane. But she could not close her ears to their voices, and in the midst of the cries for alms, she heard her name. She glanced over and saw two boys—brothers, by their identical long noses and straw-colored hair—watching her. One was whispering to the other, and her ears picked out another name: Robin. The younger boy's eyes went wide, and when he saw her looking, he drew closer to his brother.

It seemed Will's story about Robin's return from the grave had spread. And they recognized her as his Lady.

Despite the fear in the smaller boy's eyes at the notion of ghosts and spirits, the older brother's gaze held something else, something Marian recognized.

Hope.

Marian pulled her eyes away, uncomfortable, unsettled. It was the same look she'd seen on the faces of the men she'd met in Sherwood—a look that made her deception, unintentional though it had been, feel like a crime. Robin hadn't returned—he never would, except in the hidden turmoil of Marian's thoughts. No one was coming to save them.

Guards met their party in the courtyard of Nottingham Castle, and Midge took his leave to see to the horses while a scullery girl led Marian and her father into the keep and brought them to their rooms. Elena followed close behind.

Marian sighed and went to the window, a narrow slit in the wall barely wide enough to see out. *Just as well the windows are tiny,* she thought, gazing down at the gray stone city and its sluggish market and huddled masses. Their rooms were selected for their indoor comforts—a hearth, a raised and canopied bed, tapestries on the walls—and not for their views outside.

In the corridor, booted feet arrived to fetch her father for the first of his meetings with the other nobles. Their bags arrived moments later, brought up by a pair of stable hands. Elena began unpacking Marian's things, but her hands were shaking so that when she pulled out the cloth brush for Marian's dresses, it clattered to the stone.

"I'll do that," Marian said gently. The odds of a servant gaining access to the castle's jail were slim, but Elena wouldn't rest easy until she'd tried.

Her maid flashed her a wide-eyed look of gratitude and fled.

Marian let her breath out, reaching for the saddlebags. If nothing else, she could not let Elena see what lay concealed beneath the dresses she'd brought.

She tossed a gown of burgundy wool onto the bed, and two shifts alongside it, until she saw a flash of green beneath her blue kirtle. She'd slipped away the day before to retrieve more of Robin's clothing from his room, dodging the steward—now she had leggings, a shirt and tunic, and his belt. The night Will mistook her for Robin, she hadn't had time to disguise herself completely. This time, she would not rely on darkness and luck.

Marian was pulling the cloak out from underneath the rest of the clothes when the latch on her door grated. She threw the bag to the floor, kicking it up against the edge of the bed as a maid—not Elena—stepped inside and curtsied. "Begging your pardon, my Lady. The Lady Seild invites you to join her and the other visiting ladies in the southern solar for music and conversation once you are recovered from your journey."

Lady Seild—that was Lord Owen's wife. She'd always been kind to Marian, though rather baffled as to what to do with her—she was well-meaning, with her invitations to long afternoons of sewing, chess, and gardening. Closer to Marian's age than her husband's, she nonetheless treated Marian with a maternal air, as if Marian were some wayward child, growing up motherless.

Marian hadn't thought about the fact that she wouldn't be

the only woman traveling to Nottingham—while the men had their council, their ladies would have their own.

"I'm—I'm unwell," said Marian, though she could feel her face flushing. "Please send Lady Seild my apologies and thank her for inviting me."

"As you wish, my Lady." The maid dipped into another curtsy and then scurried off.

Marian sagged against the edge of the bed. *You'd think you'd never told a lie in your life,* said Robin in her thoughts, laughing and gentle.

"Lies, yes," murmured Marian in reply. "But none that carried the weight of so many lives."

She scanned the room, searching for someplace to conceal Robin's clothes—she couldn't simply stuff them under the mattress, for the servants here would spot them easily while changing the bedclothes. Elena would be opening and closing the clothes chest to help her dress. The washstand was an oak frame only, no closed storage space beneath the basin. And the floor was stone, solid, no wooden boards or packed earth.

Her eyes went to the tapestries lining the walls, intended to ward off the autumn chill permeating the stone. After pressing her ear to her door, listening for approaching footsteps, Marian hurried to push the dressing stool over to a tapestry in the corner that depicted a genteel hunt, noblemen on rouncies and a lady riding a dainty palfrey, with a pair of dogs frolicking ahead of them.

She climbed up on top of the stool and pulled the tapestry back, peering up at the hanger to see if she could tuck the edge of Robin's cloak into it and let it hang concealed between the tapestry and the wall. But instead of the iron rods in her father's house and in Locksley Manor, the tapestry was bolted to the wall by means

of iron nails drilled into the stone. One might be able to conceal
something up there, but nothing so bulky as the woolen cloak.

A knock at the door made Marian jump and nearly fall
off the stool. "I am unwell," she called, unable to conceal her
irritation. Hiding anything in this castle was going to be more
complicated than she'd anticipated.

"I do not require much of your time, my Lady," came a man's
voice, muffled by the thick oak of the door. Marian froze, for she
recognized the voice.

"A moment, Sir Guy." She dropped down from the stool and
dove for the pile of Robin's clothing by the bed. Hands shaking,
she tried to stuff it all back into the saddlebag, but she couldn't
make the cloak fit without taking the time to fold and roll the
cloth with care. She scanned the room again, feeling panic try to
take hold as she searched for someplace to hide Robin's things—
this time she forced her fears down, and her eyes fell on the
canopy bed. With an effort that left her arms aching, she flung
the heavy wool up on top of the canopy. The canvas sagged under
the weight of the cloak, but it held.

Marian smoothed her hair down, settled the fabric of her
dress, and took a breath, willing the racing of her heart to calm
as she went to the door.

Gisborne stood outside, wearing his customary black, and
gave a stiff bow as Marian opened the door. "Forgive me for
interrupting your rest, my Lady. One of the servants said you
were ill." He didn't sound apologetic—if anything, he sounded
irritated, as if visiting Marian were simply one on a long list of
tasks keeping him preoccupied.

"I haven't had a chance to rest yet," Marian replied. Despite
her best efforts, she sounded irritated too.

"I will be brief." He made no effort to enter her room, to

Marian's relief. "I came to welcome you to Nottingham, and to ask if there was anything I could do to make your stay more comfortable."

"Thank you, Sir Guy." Marian hunted for a smile and pinned it in place. "I am very comfortable and have all I need."

Gisborne nodded, clearly expecting to be sent away without a task. "Then let me say that I look forward to seeing you at dinner tonight."

"And I you," Marian replied. Then, curiosity rising before she could stop it: "You aren't attending the Sheriff with the visiting nobles?"

Gisborne's face twitched, the scar tissue on his cheek jumping. A minute shift, but there was so little to see in his cold, wooden expression that it read like a smoke signal of frustration. "I am not a nobleman, my Lady. Not yet."

"I shouldn't have asked. I apologize." The Sheriff could invite Gisborne to participate, if only to observe—but evidently, he'd chosen not to.

"There is no need for apology." Gisborne shifted his weight and glanced down the corridor, the obvious body language of a man who wished he was elsewhere. When he looked back, his gaze went past Marian's shoulder. He frowned. "What were you doing, if I may ask?"

Marian's heart leaped as she turned, half expecting to see a corner of green wool dangling from the canopy. But there was no sign of her hidden cache, and it took her a while to see what was amiss: the dressing stool was still by the wall, part of the hunting tapestry caught and draped on top of it.

"I was—admiring the tapestry," she said, turning back to Gisborne and praying her face didn't betray her sudden panic.

"Ah." Gisborne's face settled into chilly blankness again. "It is of fine craftsmanship. You enjoy weaving and sewing?"

Marian let out a quick huff of a laugh before she could stop herself. Seeing Gisborne's raised eyebrow, she said hastily, "I—no, Sir Guy. I have never been skilled with a needle, or a loom. I was admiring the tableau."

Gisborne's eyebrows rose a fraction higher. "You enjoy hunting?"

"I enjoy any pursuit that takes me outdoors."

Gisborne's weight shifted again, but this time there was a flicker of interest in his face, a gleam in his eye. "Then perhaps, Lady Marian, while you are visiting Nottingham, you will honor me by accompanying me on a ride."

The stiff manner, the stilted speech, his attempt to paint himself a nobleman by language and demeanor—it all rankled. Not to mention that he was the most difficult and direct obstacle between her and Will. Marian could think of no one whose company she'd enjoy less. But neither could she think of a polite way to object. "Happily, Sir Guy. If my stomach ever settles," she added, remembering she was meant to be ill.

"Of course, my Lady." Gisborne took a step back, then paused. "Permit me another moment of your time—Lady Marian, has anyone . . . approached you?"

Marian didn't bother to hide her confusion. "Approached, Sir Guy?"

"A man, perhaps dressed as . . ." Gisborne paused again, eyes growing chillier. "A man claiming some familiarity with you."

Marian carefully held on to her puzzled expression, carefully waited so she wouldn't answer too quickly, carefully kept her eyes from sliding away from Gisborne's. He was talking about Robin—or the man he believed was impersonating him. "No,

Sir Guy. I don't know what you mean."

Gisborne glanced past her again, into the room, making Marian fight not to check again that Robin's gear hadn't somehow become visible while they spoke. "Very well, my Lady. If anyone does approach you, please report it to me."

"Of course." Marian kept her eyes wide, unshadowed. Guileless.

Gisborne was expressionless once more for a few long, empty heartbeats. "Good day, then, my Lady," he said finally. Another bow, this one somewhat hurried, and he stepped back.

Marian bade him farewell and eased the door shut. She turned and leaned against the oak, eyes on the sagging canopy over the bed. Gisborne had seen her in Robin's cloak for a few seconds at most, and only in darkness, as she ran from his men in the woods. With only Will's word of what had happened, it wouldn't take long for the law to dismiss his story as a futile, albeit clever, attempt to prolong his life.

Will would die unless Robin was seen again, and this time by someone whose word could not be denied, and whose own life— whose own future—hinged upon the truth of whether Robin was alive or dead.

Marian waited until she could no longer hear the clatter of Gisborne's boots against the stone as they retreated from her door.

ELEVEN

NOTTINGHAM CASTLE'S GREAT HALL was crowded for dinner, those lesser nobles and city officials who usually occupied the tables banished to hover around the edges of the room while the visiting lords took the high chairs. Marian would have happily continued feigning illness and skipped the whole affair, but with luck, Robin would be walking the halls of the castle tonight, and Marian wanted to make sure she wasn't noticeably absent.

Marian was waylaid near the door by a woman with soft eyes and long, shining copper hair braided into a net—Lady Seild. "Marian, dear," she said, reaching out to take her arm, "we missed you this afternoon. Are you feeling any better?"

Marian tucked Seild's arm close. "A little, I think."

Seild gave her arm a squeeze, eyebrows drawing in. "Is something bothering you? You can always speak to me. Your illness might well be catching—perhaps I'll need to join you in seclusion tomorrow."

Marian glanced back at the woman, whose mouth was carefully set in an expression of concern—the only sign of amusement was in her eyes. Seild had known her for years, since Marian was still barely more than a child. In spite of herself, Marian laughed, and felt a little of the restlessness quickening her blood ease.

Another squeeze, and Seild reached out to take Marian's chin in her fingers and inspect her. Seild was a tall woman, too—though not as tall as Marian—and her company always made Marian feel a little less uncomfortable in her own body. "You look tired," Seild murmured, amusement fading. "My husband told me of Robin's death. And the rumors—they're saying . . ." Seild shook her head. "Never mind what they're saying. I'm so sorry, Marian. If there's anything I can do, any way I can help . . ." Her sad smile finished the sentence for her.

Most people avoided the subject of Robin, as if she might forget about her grief if no one spoke of it. But Seild's gaze was gentle, and her touch warm, and her sympathy all too real. Marian's eyes stung, and she whispered, "Thank you, Seild."

Seild released her chin but held on to her arm a moment longer. "I should rejoin my husband, but may I visit you in the morning to see how you are? I'll leave the other ladies behind if you like." That came with another little smile, one that made it easier for Marian to smile back.

"I'll look forward to it." Marian laid her hand on Seild's for a moment, then took her leave to join her father by the tables.

Her father's face was uncharacteristically grim as they sat, and he gestured for a nearby server to fill his cup.

"Father?" Marian kept her voice low and waited for the server to retreat again. "What happened with the Sheriff today?"

He took a long swallow of wine, then sighed as he set his cup back down. "A lot of talk."

"I suppose if there's one thing to draw such thunderclouds to your face . . ."

At home, he would've laughed. Now, he only smiled a little, a brief flicker. "More taxes," he said, voice short. "Stricter laws and fewer watchmen for the towns—less ability to prevent crime and more power to punish it. Less relief for the poor. And more taxes."

Thoughts of Robin and her planned midnight escapade slipped away. Marian leaned closer, trying to keep her voice even. "More taxes? Father, half the people of Locksley town are already in debt. And our fields barely feed Edwinstowe as it is."

"Don't frown," her father said lightly, despite his own grim face. "I don't imagine most other lords are telling their wives and daughters and sisters about the conversations they're having with the Sheriff. I tell you only because Locksley will suffer, and by extension so will you."

Marian took a bit of mutton to buy herself a moment to school her features. "The Sheriff has only what he sees here in the city by which to judge the state of Nottinghamshire. Surely if he saw how low the people have become, he would—"

"The decree comes from the crown, not the Sheriff." Her father set upon his dinner methodically, a sign he had no appetite but was forcing himself to eat. "A portion of all livestock, feed, and grain now go to the crown each fortnight."

"Each—" Marian had to stop and adjust the volume of her voice. "Each fortnight? Most are lucky to have a new calf or lamb once a year. But for the big herds in the highlands, the Sheriff will have stripped the land of livestock before the season is over."

"A man may keep his animals each fortnight if he pays their value in coin instead." Her father speared a chunk of meat on his knife and glared at it. "Or if his Lord does."

Marian lifted her head, glancing around the great hall at the other visiting noblemen. Some were quiet, like her father—but others were laughing, making requests of the minstrels circling the tables, signaling for more wine, more meat. She could not imagine that every noble would consider it his duty to bleed for his people's livelihoods. "That's absurd," Marian whispered. "In a year's time we'll be standing with those beggars on the streets of Nottingham."

Her father swallowed the hunk of mutton with a grimace and muttered, "Midge makes a better roast than this, and he's a stableman." Then he laid down his knife and turned, finally, to look at his daughter. The lines about his eyes and mouth seemed deeper in the harsh light of the torches set at intervals around the hall, and he looked tired. "It's the first of many discussions, Marian. Don't trouble yourself with it yet."

Marian pushed a slab of bread around in the drippings on her plate and gazed toward the far end of the hall. The Sheriff sat there with two of the northern nobles and a man in royal livery, who Marian assumed was a representative of Prince John. The Sheriff was saluting the Prince's man with his cup, grinning, his beard glistening with fat from the meal. Gisborne stood nearby, almost vanishing into the shadows by the wall in his black garb; he scowled out at the rest of the diners, as though trying to offset his master's genial air.

Marian could not dismiss the image from her mind of Edwinstowe stripped of its meager wealth, its good people evicted and turned from farmers and bakers and herdsmen to thieves and beggars. Her vision seemed to blur as she watched the Sheriff signal for more food, and the pounding of her heart roared in her ears.

Abruptly she shoved away from the table and rose to her feet. Her father dropped his cup, splashing wine over the remains of his meal—across the table from her, a nobleman she didn't know got halfway to his feet in alarm.

"Pardon me," Marian said stiffly. "I'm still feeling ill."

Her father flicked wine from his fingertips and sighed. "Marian, please—"

"Father, may I go back to my room and rest?" She spoke loudly so as to be easily overheard by those nearby.

Her father eyed her with something like suspicion—she rarely asked permission to do anything. "Of course," he said finally, sighing a second time and gesturing for the man across the table to sit back down.

Marian turned before she could glance toward Seild, or worse, toward Gisborne, to see if they were watching her undignified retreat. Instead, she slipped out into the corridor.

The chill of the castle stone returned only a few paces away from the overcrowded great hall, but Marian welcomed it. It cooled her cheeks and helped her order her thoughts. She nodded to the guard at the corridor's end and strode off toward her quarters. Once out of sight, though, she located a winding staircase that took her down toward the lower levels of the castle.

She would have preferred to walk outside, but the stench of a city in summer still hung in the air of Nottingham, and the thought of facing the destitute crowds again made Marian stick to the gloomy corridors of the castle.

Footsteps made her slow her pace—a pair of guards passed through the hall before her, complaining about the extra hours they were forced to work as a result of all the visitors to Nottingham. They had not seen her, but the clink of their chain mail and creak of their sword belts gave her pause.

She hadn't been able to bring her bow with her, or any weapons at all, for fear of alerting her father or their servants to her masquerade. She didn't intend for anyone to get close enough for her to need a weapon, but as her first outing as Robin had proved, events didn't always go according to plan. But while she might not have been able to bring her own weapons to the castle, the castle itself had steel to spare.

She couldn't know for sure exactly where or how Will had been arrested—but she'd left her sword behind when she ran to distract Gisborne and his men, and there was a good chance he'd still had it when they captured him. Which meant there was an equally good chance that it was now sitting in the castle's armory. If she was going to let "Robin" be seen tonight, she might as well accomplish two tasks at once. If she couldn't find her own sword, any blade would be a welcome deterrent to keep anyone from interfering with her.

Marian made her way through the lower floors of the castle, avoiding the occasional servant or guard hurrying this way or that. She'd been to Nottingham Castle countless times but was only familiar with the upper floors. Her only reference point was that the jail was on the far eastern side of the castle—for that was where the doors opened onto the gallows.

The armory for the castle guard would not be far from the jail, so Marian headed that way and tried not to think of Will, and the gallows. She kept a running tally in her head of the turns she made, noting the stairways and corridors that led back toward the rest of the castle.

She found the armory by accident—a thick oaken door opened as she turned the corner, and before she could retreat, her momentum carried her headlong into the man exiting.

"My Lady?" A pair of hands reached out to steady her as she reeled back.

Marian looked up, and relief washed over her. "Midge!"

Her father's stable master blinked slowly, the only outward sign of his own surprise. He released her once she was on her feet again and stepped back with a hint of a frown.

"Midge—what are you doing here?" Marian regretted the question the instant her ears caught up with her tongue—Midge had far more reason to be here than she did.

But the stable master only gazed at her thoughtfully for a few seconds, then hooked his thumbs through his belt and puffed out his cheeks in a sigh. "I was thinking about our horse thief," he said finally. "A few other things were missing that morning, gear I'd seen the night before. If he'd been caught robbing someone else, then he—and his loot—would've ended up in Nottingham's armory."

Marian caught her breath. Midge hadn't said that her sword was missing along with Robin's gear, but it didn't mean he hadn't noticed. "And?" she prompted.

Midge seemed to consider her all over again, squinting in the gloom to better make out her features. "I've nothing to report."

Disappointment and relief together made Marian shiver. "The gear isn't there?"

Midge's head tilted to the side. "The bow and cloak that vanished from the stables? No, my Lady."

Marian hesitated. She didn't want to reveal to Midge that her sword was missing, but she needed to know if it was there. The sword could be traced back to her eventually, if anyone thought to put together the pieces.

When she didn't speak, Midge rubbed a hand through his

short-cropped hair. "I'd suggest you take a look—perhaps you'd recognize something I didn't—except that I suspect your father would not want you to be seen poking around the castle's weaponry. Not to mention being seen by the unsavory handful of men in there playing at dice."

Marian blinked and scanned Midge's features. Could he have guessed why she was here? Urging her to look, but warning her of the men inside . . . But his face was as grave and bland as ever, revealing nothing but polite interest and the habitual fond crinkle of his eyes when he spoke to Marian.

She swallowed. "All . . . right. Thank you, Midge."

"Of course, my Lady. If you've gotten turned around, there are stairs leading back up just down the hallway. You'll find yourself not far from your and your father's rooms."

Marian peered at him more closely but still could find nothing in his face to suggest anything other than geniality. "Um. Thank you, Midge," she repeated, and hurried away from the armory toward the stairs he'd mentioned.

TWELVE

"ARE YOU WELL?" ELENA was waiting for her when Marian reached her room after leaving the armory. Her maid was carefully transferring embers from the fire into a warming pan. "I heard from the other servants that you were ill this afternoon."

Marian shook her head. "Weary from the ride," she said finally, though guilt at the deception tightened her throat. Elena could keep a secret—after all, she'd kept Alan a secret from everyone for years. But Marian couldn't bear to heap more danger upon her maid—the more people who knew Marian's secret, the more she risked discovery. And to reveal that Robin hadn't come back after all would only dash her maid's hopes that Will would be saved. After all, Marian fully intended that he would be—she just hadn't figured out how to do it yet.

"Did you find out anything about Will?" Marian asked gently.

Elena shook her head, eyes on the bed as she placed the warming pan beneath the covers and smoothed them. "Only that he's still alive. And that news is two days old, from one of the cooks whose sweetheart is a guard." She kept smoothing, chasing down every last wrinkle and crease in the cloth under her hands.

Marian left her spot by the door and went to her maid's side. She'd never been a terribly affectionate person, even with Robin—but she took Elena's hand and gave it a squeeze. "We'll help him," she promised.

And in her mind, Robin said, *Don't make promises that you cannot keep.*

When Elena had gone, she dragged the dressing stool back to the side of the bed to retrieve the clothes belonging to Robin that she'd gone back to stash with the cloak on the bed's canopy.

They smelled mostly of dust and lye, but as she climbed off the stool with her arms full of cloth, she caught the faintest hint of a familiar scent. Instantly her mind flooded with memories. She was fourteen, and Robin was wrapping his cloak around her shoulders in the rain; she was eleven, looking at his face after disarming him for the first time during a swordplay bout; she was in his arms, feeling the scrape of his beard against her cheek; she was riding at his side, listening to his laugh.

Marian sank down onto the stool, clutching the soft white linen of Robin's shirt. She tried to turn off the memories, to think of something else—anything else—and keep at bay the wrenching pain of remembering Robin. She could not afford to weep.

Let yourself cry, said Robin. *There's no shame in it.*

She buried her face in the shirt and imagined what Robin would think of her now, impersonating him to buy Will more time. They'd broken the rules as children all the time—sneaking out at night, riding out unsupervised. But she could not think of a time when Robin had broken the law.

It's mad, Marian thought, lifting her head and staring down at the clothing now scattered around her. *I'll be caught, Father will lose his lands, I'll be jailed. Masquerading as Robin might buy Will time, but it won't set him free. And Gisborne will not let ghost stories stop his rise to power for long, no matter how many people claim to have seen Robin.*

She wiped at her eyes and stood, crossing the room to the window and pushing its thick shutter open. From the city below she heard a distant cry, a young child somewhere clamoring to eat. And suddenly she saw in her mind the two brothers standing there, the ones who had heard Will's tale, the ones who had recognized her as the beloved of the man who'd come back from the dead to help his people.

Robin's voice in her thoughts was gentle. *Will you take away their hope because you have none?*

Perhaps Will had been right. Robin's spirit was not at rest, but it wasn't Sherwood Forest he haunted—it was Marian. She carried him in her thoughts, and she would carry out his will with her own hands.

Marian pulled off her shoes, fingers going to the laces of her kirtle. *At least this time*, she thought as she reached for the slate-gray leggings, *I won't have to fight in skirts.*

Marian slipped into the corridor, pulling the hood of the cloak up over her head. She felt half-naked without fabric swirling about her ankles, and even more so without the weight of a sword at her side or a bow at her hand. And though the castle was quieter this late in the night, it was never truly silent—it never slept, not completely. Somewhere in the distance something metal clanged to the floor, and when she paused, she heard a woman's muffled laugh from the hallway behind her. The occasional opening or closing of a door somewhere in the castle made a fitful breeze sweep down the halls and tug at Marian's clothing, giving her the unsettling feeling that someone was just behind her.

Next time, she thought, pausing in an alcove to listen for signs of life ahead, *you need to do this outside.*

Next time? Robin echoed, amused.

She caught her breath and leaned back against the stone for a moment. *I don't know if you are real,* she thought, closing her fingers around the ring that hung from her neck. *Or if I simply want you to be.*

Robin replied, *Does it matter?*

She traced her way back down the staircase Midge had told her about, each soft step resounding in her ears, until she reached the corridor that led to the armory. The door was closed, and Marian pressed her ear to its surface, listening for sounds that might warn her that someone was inside. The dice game Midge had mentioned had surely been over for hours, and if she was unlucky enough to venture here at the moment the guards changed, she'd hear them in all their chain mail and heavy boots.

The air was utterly still, and after a few breaths to calm her heart, Marian lifted the latch and slipped inside.

The dice players had left a torch behind, and it burned low in its sconce. It cast barely enough light for Marian to avoid tripping over the racks and tables of equipment. The nearest tables held chain-mail vests and shoulder plates, the shelves above them full of helmets. Marian paused by the chain mail, reaching out to run a fingertip along the woven links. Perhaps with armor, she would feel less naked. But the vests were cheaply made—the sleeves were separate, attached to the shoulders by leather bindings. Mail might fend off an arrow or two, but it would slow her down, and if Marian ended up in combat, she couldn't afford to be sluggish.

She started searching in earnest, keeping half her attention on the midnight sounds of the castle, listening for approaching boots. Two racks, blade by blade, and there was no sign of her own. She turned to cross to the other side of the armory and stopped.

Slumped at one of the tables, the chain mail on it shoved aside to make a clear space, was one of the castle guards. He wore only his canvas undershirt, no chain mail or helmet, and he had no sword belt. He was still, unmoving. One of the dice players, Marian guessed—drunk, and out of his head.

Marian started to back toward the door, scanning the gloom for any other guards she'd missed. Instead, her eyes fell on a sword hanging at the end of the rack behind the guard's table. Her heart tripped. Her blade, the one made to fit her smaller hands.

Robin, I wouldn't mind a share of your luck at some point.

She let her breath out soundlessly, steeling herself, and then crept toward the sleeping man. He didn't stir as she slipped around his chair toward the rack on the wall. She hefted the sword up and out of the rack, grimacing when it scraped against the metal.

The guard didn't stir.

Marian made for the exit, skin prickling, certain that at any moment she'd feel the point of a sword at the small of her back, or a voice demanding that she halt and declare herself. Each step was a torment, and by the time she reached the door, she'd begun to sweat despite the chill of the stone all around her.

She fumbled with the latch in her haste, each clank of iron shattering her nerves, and half fell out into the hallway. She stopped long enough to look over her shoulder, shivering with disbelief—the guard was still asleep. While she watched, he shifted with a thud of skull on tabletop and began to snore.

Marian let the door close, stifling the sudden urge to laugh. She'd been so certain she'd be caught, so sure that she could not possibly best a castle's entire garrison—and she had not even been challenged. She shifted her grip on the sword, fitting the hilt into her palm and testing its familiar heft, then headed toward the back stair. She'd actually have to try to find at least a few guards, at a distance, to spot her and spread more reports of the man in the hood in Locksley's colors. Still giddy, she adjusted the hood of the cloak low over her features, quickened her steps, rounded the corner—

—and ran full tilt into a tall, broad man in black from head to toe.

Marian looked up and found her own surprise mirrored in Gisborne's features for a long moment, the sword dangling from her hand.

But then something kindled in Gisborne's dark eyes, a flash of decision or ferocity, and her instincts took over. She swung her blade up in time to deflect his blow, the clang of steel on steel bringing her back to herself. She skipped back and used the space to whirl around and press the attack, hoping to knock Gisborne off center with her added momentum—but he was already moving, ducking, faster than she'd anticipated. His sword came swinging at her rib cage before she could move to parry it, and she threw herself to the ground to roll away.

He's a better swordsman than I.

The thought was clear, quick, without fear, a calm realization. She was on her feet the next instant, every muscle taut and singing, ready for action—but Gisborne had stood his ground, and the hallway stretched between them. The hood still hung low over her face, but Robin's cloak was that uniquely rich, emerald-earth green, and Gisborne's eyes swept over her, cold and analytical.

"Locksley." Gisborne could summon more guards with a shout, and yet his voice was quiet, a deep rumble across the echoing stone. "And yet not Locksley, for he is dead. Who are you?"

Marian stayed silent, unable to answer him even had she known what to say. She shifted her grip on her sword, hyperaware of the sweat gathering on her palms and beneath her breasts and creeping down between her shoulder blades.

Gisborne's features grew colder, a shade of stone she'd never seen on any man's face. "Speak, man. Your crimes are still few—impersonating a nobleman is a forgivable offense. But disdain the authority of Nottingham and you will hang."

Hang.

He stood between Marian and her route back to her room—not that she could go there now, with Gisborne on her heels. She could not match his swordsmanship, but she was lighter on her feet. Marian straightened a little, moving slowly—Gisborne's eyes tracked her every shift, the point of his sword following.

"If you run," Gisborne said softly, "know that I will find you. I will not let any man make a mockery of the law, or my claim—I am Locksley now."

Marian's anger flickered, low and deep, constant beneath her fear. *You will never be Lord of Locksley*—and in the moment those words seared themselves in her mind, she could not tell whether it was Robin's voice or her own. Her sword arm ached with the need to strike.

You won't win. Not like this. Robin's voice was tight and urgent, impossible to ignore. *You have to choose your battlefield.*

Marian turned before pride could change her mind and fled, ignoring Gisborne's shout and the clamor of his boots as he took off after her. She narrowed her focus, not bothering to look for a path yet, thinking only of speed. She turned right and left and burst through doors—she ran up against one that was locked and whirled around, and made it to the next corridor before Gisborne appeared at the end of it. Her hood slipped back, and she tugged it down into place again as she sprinted through a group of servants pushing a barrow of linens out to be washed.

Marian ignored their shrieks of alarm and confusion—she counted, instead, how long it took them to cry out again when Gisborne passed through.

She was moving faster than he.

She slid to a halt as she passed one of the storerooms, and ducked inside. She shut the door and went still, ear pressed to the wood—in the distance she could still hear one of the servants chattering, but in a moment the clatter of running boots drowned it out. More than one set, by the sound. Gisborne kept running, his breath heaving, and Marian tightened her grip on her sword. He moved on past. More boots followed seconds later, guards drawn to the commotion or else summoned by Gisborne as he ran.

Marian waited, trying to silence her own aching lungs, letting the door take some of her weight. She kept still until she could no longer hear boots, then straightened and passed her sword to her other hand so she could shake out the arm that had been carrying it.

A small sound behind her had Marian whirling, passing the sword back and lifting it, all her tension snapping back into place.

"No, please!" The words were gasped—the gloom revealed no one at first glance, only a few tables and bulging burlap sacks in piles about the room. Marian heard the scrape of cloth on stone and saw a flicker in the shadows beneath one of the tables.

Marian hesitated. She was free to leave now, but she had no idea where she was in the castle—she'd as easily find a castle guard as a stair back to the upper floors. She sucked in a few more breaths, trying to imagine her father's voice, Robin's voice, even Gisborne's cold sneer. "Come out," she whispered, voice harsh in her throat, making it ache. "Slowly."

The shadows under the table moaned, but a few seconds later a worn-looking man crawled out. He clambered to his feet, both hands raised to show they were empty. "Please, gent, I've got nothing to steal. I'm a tally man. I won't tell no one I saw you, gent."

Tally man. Marian glanced around the room again. "What is all this?" She swung the sword down and dug its tip into one of the burlap bags—when she withdrew it, a pale gold stream came pouring out to pool on the stone. "Grain?"

"Yes, gent."

"But this is enough to feed every man in the castle for a season."

"It's not for us, gent—it's for port, for trade."

Marian pulled her eyes from the little pile of wheat, her body still alive from the brief clash of swords and the flight through the castle. She tried to focus on the tally man, but all she could see were the scattered crowds of people outside Nottingham, like herds of empty-eyed cattle, waiting and hungry. And ignorant of the wealth of food lying behind the castle's stone walls.

"When do you give the Sheriff your account?" She put gravel in her voice.

"By month's end."

Marian could not very well push barrows of stolen wheat through the castle, either as herself or as Robin—but neither could she let such a cache of food go to fill the Sheriff's coffers while his people starved. She'd figure out later how to rob him of his ill-gotten stores.

Later? said Robin in her mind. *Before or after you escape, and save Will, and somehow avoid marrying Gisborne . . . ?*

"How does the Sheriff transport his goods?" she whispered, cutting Robin off before he could change her mind.

But the man wasn't listening, the tremble coming back into his body as he stared at her. He was only a decade or so older than she, though labor and poor lighting had left his face lined around eyes and mouth. "You're—you're the ghost. The one they say came back from the Holy War, from fighting with the King."

Marian took a breath to fend off frustration. "Will you help me?"

The man swallowed nervously, eyes going from her face—hidden beneath the shadow of her hood—to the sword in her hand. "What need have ghosts of grain and coin, Lord?"

"It's not my need," Marian whispered. "Have you family in Nottingham?"

The man nodded, throat bobbing. "Two lads and a wee girl."

"Then sell the Sheriff out for *them*, for this grain should go to feed the hungry, and not to line the Sheriff's pockets with more gold."

"Caravan," the man said finally. Then, after looking at the sword in her hand again, he added, "The carts are well guarded on the road, Lord."

Marian felt a grim smile touch her face, though under her hood the tally man wouldn't be able to see it. "I am well warned." She drew back toward the door again, leaning close to listen for footsteps outside. "Where is the nearest stair up?"

"That way, Lord." The man pointed, hand still shaking, back the way Marian had come.

"My thanks." Marian lifted the latch.

"You don't—you don't seem like no spirit." The man had taken a step forward, fear making way for a sliver of curiosity.

Marian paused. "How many spirits have you met?" She left him there, staring after her and rubbing the cold from his joints.

To her relief, the tally man's word was true: the stair was where he'd said it would be. She hurried up, stopping this time to peer around the corner to check that the hall was empty. This part of the castle she knew—she'd walked this way countless times. A few minutes and she'd be back in the safety of her room, which lay beyond the next intersection.

She was halfway down the corridor when the sound of booted feet told her of a patrol approaching. She caught her breath, turning to flee back toward the stairwell, but it was too far behind her now; the patrol would spot her before she reached the shadows of the stairs. Her eyes darted around the hall for any means of escape and fell upon one of the heavy oaken doors. Ordinarily this part of the castle held few people, but now, with every nobleman in Nottingham visiting . . .

Marian uttered a curse and slipped inside the nearest room. She eased the door closed seconds before the sound of boots passed—only to hear a gasp and a scurry of fabric behind her. She turned to see a woman in the high canopied bed, bedsheets clutched to her, long copper braid shining pale in the moonlight coming from the slit window.

Seild.

THIRTEEN

MARIAN FROZE, TOO STUNNED by her poor luck to think. Seild gave a little cry upon seeing the sword in her hand, drawing back against the headboard.

Marian raised her empty hand to her lips—a signal for quiet. Seild obeyed, her gaze shifting from the shadows beneath Marian's hood to the sword's point. Marian listened at the door for signs that anyone had seen her enter, but instead she heard a voice, distorted by the echoing stone but nonetheless recognizable: Gisborne.

"Guards at each stairwell and intersection," he was saying. "No man gets through unsearched, servant or Lord."

Marian squeezed her eyes closed a moment. She must have betrayed something in her manner, her step, for Gisborne suspected that "Locksley" might be a nobleman and not a common thief. He'd anticipated her, blocked off her retreat. He must have come straight here after losing sight of her.

Marian looked back over at the bed, noticing abruptly that

Seild was alone. There was no sign of Owen, her husband, not even a second dimple in the sheets. She didn't stop to thank her good fortune, for Owen was no stranger to the sword, and crossed toward the bed.

"I won't harm you," she breathed, when Seild scrambled back. "Be still, and do as I say." Marian wished she could sound more sympathetic, but she had to disguise, however poorly, her true voice. Seild's eyes rolled toward the door, and Marian stepped to the side, blocking that escape. "You have my word, my Lady."

Seild shifted her grip on the sheets pulled up around herself. Her knuckles were white, her jaw tense. But she breathed out again, lifting her chin and fixing her eyes once more on Marian.

Marian scanned the darkened room. Her eyes fell on Seild's dressing gown, hanging by her washbasin.

No man gets through without being searched. . . .

But Marian wasn't a man. And Gisborne could hardly expect his future wife, as he hoped, to submit to being searched.

Marian strode across the room, glancing at Seild to make sure she wasn't about to run, and then set her sword aside so she could reach for the gown.

"It's fine quality," Seild said, voice halting and rough with sleep and fear. "Take it. Sell it for coin."

Marian paused. A thief, breaking into a noblewoman's bedchamber to steal a single gown? Too strange to escape notice. "Your jewels," she said abruptly, turning to Seild. "Where are they kept?"

Seild was trembling, and the fear in her expression made Marian's heart ache. If only she'd broken into the room of a stranger. "The box there by the washbasin."

Marian dug through the little box—it held a tiny wealth of jewelry, a few rings, a hairnet seeded with pearls, a gold rope of a necklace, and a few jars of precious cosmetics—charcoal for lashes, powdered angelica for the cheeks and lips, crushed lily root to whiten the face. Marian pushed them aside and scooped up a few of the rings.

A sound from the bed made her pause—Seild's fear had gone, making way for something else. "The turquoise," she whispered when Marian looked back at her. "It belonged to my mother."

Marian opened her fist, but she could think only of her own ring, and the panic she'd felt when John had asked her to surrender it. She glanced back at Seild, who looked so very small in the large bed, alone, huddled against the headboard.

She wanted to tell her again that she had nothing to fear, but she was afraid to speak any more than she had to. Marian hesitated, then drew herself up so she could bow toward the bed. The motion felt strange, stilted—she'd seen it countless times, a gesture as familiar as a smile or a wave, and yet her legs wanted to fold into a curtsy. She held herself straight with an effort and dropped the rings back into the box. She took the hairnet instead, and slipped it inside her tunic.

She could wear the dressing gown to hide her man's clothing, but it would not hide her cloak and sword, and she could not leave them here. She strode back toward the bed, Seild's eyes following her.

"Your sheet," she whispered.

Seild's face had cleared a little, her tears drying—but now she went rigid, her fear crystallizing like frost on the surface of a pond. "C-c-compassion, sir," she managed. "My husband—"

"I won't touch you," Marian interrupted, haste shortening her voice. "I only want your linens."

Seild hesitated, staring at Marian. She gazed so long Marian feared she could see through the shadows cast by her hood, see enough of Marian's chin or mouth to recognize the girl she'd known for so many years. "Why are you here?"

Marian paused, mind freezing. "To save a life," she whispered finally. Whose life she meant—Will's, hers, the starving boys' outside Nottingham's gates—she didn't know.

Seild said softly, "Thank you for leaving my ring." She tugged the blanket free of the linens beneath, pulling the heavier fabric toward herself so Marian could reach the sheets. Her fear was fading, and she watched Marian now with something like curiosity.

"Thank *you*, my Lady." Marian bundled up the fabric in her arms and headed for the door. She could hear nothing on the other side of it, and when she pushed it open a fraction, the hall looked empty.

She was about to leave when Seild's voice came again from the bed. "Robin?"

Marian froze. When she looked back at the bed, Seild was sitting upright, watching her, unafraid now.

Still reeling, heart pounding, Marian had no reply. Her throat felt thick, her tongue heavy. Seild's face held such hope— for an instant, Marian was envious of what Seild believed.

Robin . . . still alive.

Before she could do anything to betray herself, she slipped out into the hall.

After a quick scan, Marian dropped the sheet and spread it out on the stone. She stripped off her cloak, bundling it around her sword and then wrapping both in the sheet, shifting the folds and drapes until it looked more or less like an armful of fabric. Then she pulled the dressing gown over her clothes, cinching it tightly and drawing it up so that its folds would hide the neck of her tunic. She yanked the ties from her hair and pulled it forward, the chestnut waves crimped from confinement. She took a deep, steadying breath—and then headed toward her room, and the guards.

They startled when she turned the corner, and one half drew his sword—there were two of them, both in the shoddy chain mail and helmets of the Nottingham guard. "My Lady," said the taller of the two, gesturing for the other to sheathe his blade. "Why are you—"

"Lady Marian!"

She froze. Gisborne's gravelly voice had been recognizable before—now it was becoming horribly familiar. She turned to see him striding down the other hall toward her. "Sir Guy," she said weakly, as he drew near.

"Are you well?" Gisborne looked as collected as ever, his sharp nose and stern mouth grave. He had not a hair out of place, only a hint of color in his face to tell of his pursuit. "What are you doing in the halls at this hour?" One hand rested on his sword, making Marian itch to draw her own— less than an hour ago, she was fighting this man. Now, she forced her face to smile.

"I . . . was cold," she said. "Elena, my maid—she forgot to fill the warming pan for my bed, and I could not sleep for the chill. I wanted to ask for my maid to come attend me, but she's in the servants' barracks and I could not find my way."

Voices echoed down from the hall, and Gisborne glanced toward them, clearly eager to rejoin the chase for his fugitive. He stayed with obvious effort, nodding vaguely—but then he frowned, eyes going to the armful of cloth Marian carried. "You brought your bedclothes?"

Marian blinked. "I . . . tried to transfer the embers myself and I—I singed my covers."

Gisborne's frown stayed in place, but his eyes flicked up to Marian's face. "You singed your covers with a bed warmer."

Marian could see the disdain in his features. *What a silly girl,* she thought, imagining the words in Gisborne's cold voice. *So helpless she cannot look after herself for one night.* Her blood warmed, her pride objecting, demanding she think of some other excuse than one that made her seem so foolish. But then—what matter, if Gisborne thought her a fool? All the better. No one would suspect someone so inept of being the cloaked figure stalking Nottingham at night. So she made herself giggle, and dropped her eyes in seeming embarrassment, and hugged the bundled linen closer to her. The cross guard of her sword jabbed into her chest.

"Go back to your room, my Lady," Gisborne said finally. "I will assign a guard to your door."

"A guard?" Marian widened her eyes. "What's happening?"

"Nothing to concern yourself with, my Lady," Gisborne replied. "I will make certain no harm will come to you tonight. I will have someone fetch your maid." He stepped aside, gesturing to the hall beyond him. "And new linens for your bed."

He was dismissing her. Perfect. Marian lowered her eyes, nodded, and slipped past Gisborne.

"Wait—Lady Marian." Gisborne was gazing at her face when she turned, his brow furrowed, frown deepened. "You are perspiring. I can carry that for you. Allow me to walk you back to your room."

Marian's arms tightened around the sheet that held her cloak and sword. "You would perspire too, Sir Guy, if you had just accidentally set your bed on fire." She smiled.

Gisborne coughed, head turning a little for a moment.

He was laughing at her. Marian swallowed the sting of her

pride. *Silly girl.* But Gisborne recovered his civility, looked up, and inclined his shoulders in a minute bow. "Very well, my Lady. Good night."

Marian turned, feeling Gisborne's eyes on her all the way to her room—when she reached her door and glanced back, he was gone.

He is in the woods, kicking at acorns and strips of birch bark. The sun is high, but only slivers of it slip through the blanket of leaves whispering overhead. His head is ringing with voices—his father's, the priest's, his tutors'. Dozens of old men telling him what to think, how to feel, where to go, how to look.

He wants to scream.

"They're saying your mother died."

Robin looks up, and there's the Edwinstowe girl up in the branches of a massive oak, peering down at him over a freckled nose.

"Mm-hmm," he says. "She did."

"I'm sorry."

Robin waits for her to say more, to tell him how he's going to feel in a few days or weeks or months, or what he should do to feel better. But she just keeps staring at him, chewing at her bottom lip. Her feet dangle over empty space.

"Thanks," he says finally. Then, the words bubbling up despite his attempts to push them down, he blurts, "Everyone keeps pretending it didn't happen."

"My mother died when I was little," says Marian, glancing aside to pick at a patch of loose bark beside her. "People kept saying I should be happy she was with God."

Robin's anger makes him kick out again, and the acorn goes shooting across the forest floor like a stone skipping across the surface of a lake. "I'm so sick of people telling me what I should be."

Marian's heels swing to and fro, and she balances herself as she ducks her head. "Well, I'll promise never to tell you what to be . . . or how to feel about things."

Robin squints up at her through the fractured sunlight. Mousy brown hair haloes her face, and her feet are filthy. Robin tries to imagine wanting to marry this creature someday—tries to imagine her wearing the ruby ring, and instead all his imagination can conjure is his mother's hand, pale and still, her handkerchief lying where she dropped it. His eyes burn and he looks away, jaw clenched tight.

"Or I could be like Father Gerolt and give you a sermon about God's plan," Marian offers from overhead. "Don't despair, my child, for it is not for us to know the will of heaven. . . ."

Her voice is so like that of the nasal, overbearing priest at his mother's bedside that for a moment Robin almost laughs, and when he looks back up at the girl in the tree, he sees her smile for a second.

"I won't tell you what to be either," he says.

Marian's smile vanishes, and she rolls her eyes skyward, still half imitating the holy man. "Everyone always does, when you're a girl."

"Not me. I promise."

Marian looks back down at him, her gaze measuring. It holds him, and he doesn't move away. Then she bows her head, a strangely genteel gesture from someone perched high above in the branches of a tree. "It's a promise, then."

FOURTEEN

"MARIAN, DO COME IN!"

Marian hesitated in the doorway of Seild's chamber, then entered. Her heart was pounding—what if, in the light of day, Seild recognized something about her from the night before? Her height, her gait, the sound of her breath . . . Seild was not a stupid woman, and not given to superstition, no matter what she seemed to believe in the night. But Elena had brought a summons from Lady Seild before Marian had broken her fast, and Marian could not refuse without seeming suspicious.

Marian crossed toward the bed, where Seild sat clad in a dressing gown—borrowed, no doubt, for hers was in Marian's room, hidden atop the bed's canopy—with a shawl wrapped around her shoulders.

"Have you heard what happened last night?" Seild's eyes were big and anxious and fixed on Marian's face. Marian could only glance up and shake her head. "The hooded man was *here*! You've heard, someone must have told you . . . the rumors about Robin?"

Marian hesitated, but nodded. "They aren't true," she mumbled.

"But he was *here*," said Seild, leaning forward, her eyes lighting. "I saw him with my own eyes, Marian!"

Marian allowed a bit of her fear to show. "Someone broke into your bedchamber last night?" She sounded almost as horrified as she felt.

"Not just someone—someone wearing Robin's cloak, speaking in his voice. He didn't harm me or threaten me as an ordinary thief might have done."

"He spoke in Robin's voice?" Marian felt her brow furrowing.

"Whispered, but it sounded like him. That same . . . passion." Seild drew a breath and reached out for Marian's hands, folding them between hers. "I know it wasn't *him*, it couldn't have been. But . . . the resemblance was uncanny, Marian. I wanted to tell you before you heard it elsewhere, or before—God forbid—you saw him yourself." Her voice was animated, her face shining—if she'd been afraid the night before, Seild had recovered well.

Marian had underestimated the effect of the darkness, the shadowed face, the whisper—

If Robin's spirit truly haunted her, Marian thought, perhaps some of his seeming or aspect showed through when she took his guise.

"You are . . . sure it wasn't *really* him?" Marian asked cautiously. "How?"

"Because he's—" Seild paused and gave Marian's hands a squeeze. "He was too tall, for one thing—longer legs, and quicker than Robin ever was. But mostly because Robin . . . Robin is . . ."

"Dead," whispered Marian. "I know."

"I'm sorry," Seild murmured, her flushed face falling a little. "I didn't mean to make you hope."

Marian shook her head, dropping her eyes to the floor so that Seild could not see her fighting not to smile.

It had *worked*. Even Seild, a woman who'd known Robin for years, nearly believed it was him.

With Seild's enthusiasm and wonder echoing in her ears, Marian could not help but feel a rush of something through her body, a liveliness she hadn't felt since before she'd learned of Robin's death.

A tap at the door gave her the opportunity to look away and school her expression. Seild called out and Elena opened the door before curtsying. "Pardon me, ladies, but—Lady Marian—Sir Guy has requested that you be ready to ride out on the hour."

Marian frowned, staring blankly at her maid. "Excuse me? Ride where?"

Elena glanced from her to Seild, who was eyeing Marian sidelong now. "I don't know, my Lady. The servant he sent said only that you were to join him today for a ride and he'd like to depart as soon as you are dressed."

With a jolt, Marian remembered feigning interest in the hunting tapestry the day before. She resisted the urge to groan. "Thank you, Elena."

She was taking her leave of Seild when a pair of other ladies arrived, fully dressed, urgent and anxious. They inched their way around Marian in the doorway, casting sidelong glances her way before rushing to Seild's side. Someone had told them of the lady's midnight visitor, no doubt.

Marian could hear them whispering as she left, assuring themselves that Seild was unharmed. One of them said, as

Marian closed the door, "If he's caught, they'll hang him for a deserter. Faking his death and abandoning the King . . ."

Marian's legs felt unsteady, and she leaned against the stone outside Seild's room.

Deserter. The word rang in Marian's ears like a death knell. A few moments ago she'd been delighted by the success of her masquerade—but if all Nottingham believed Robin was truly returned, then they'd also have to believe he'd left the King's side in the middle of a war.

His honor would be ruined.

She longed for Robin to speak in her mind, tell her what he thought of her turning him into a villain. But no words of comfort or accusation came, and she took a deep breath and moved on down the corridor.

Gisborne would be waiting.

Gisborne glanced her way as she strode out into the courtyard toward the stables. He was holding the bridle of a big black horse and speaking to a pair of guards, but he dismissed them once Marian was within earshot. Two more armed men sat on horseback, ready to accompany them—chaperone, as much as bodyguard.

"You look well, my Lady," Gisborne said coolly, inclining his torso in a rigid bow. "I took the liberty of having your horse saddled for you, but she . . . declined to leave the stables with me."

Marian suppressed a sudden urge to laugh—the man was so stiff, so formal, that he couldn't bring himself to admit that Jonquille had bested him. "Thank you, Sir Guy," she said instead, certain he'd hear the laughter in her voice. But he only regarded her calmly, a muscle in his cheek making his scar twitch.

She offered him a quick curtsy, then went to the stables to

fetch her horse. The mare rolled her eyes toward her mistress in obvious protest, and Marian murmured, "I know. We just have to be polite for a few hours."

Gisborne came toward her as she led Jonquille from the stables, but Marian turned and mounted before he could assist her. The man paused, eyeing her coolly with one gloved hand half-extended. His jaw flexed, and he turned back to his own horse. "You have eaten?" he asked, swinging up into his saddle.

Marian had gone to call on Seild before breaking her fast, and her stomach was painfully empty after the night's exertions. But one look at Gisborne's face told Marian that all he needed was an excuse to prolong their outing into a picnic. "Yes, Sir Guy." She settled herself in her saddle and urged Jonquille into a brisk walk.

Silence spread out behind her, broken eventually by a muttered oath and a clatter of hooves. Gisborne's horse caught up with Jonquille. "You ride ahead without knowing where we are bound." The pair of guards accompanying them settled into pace some distance behind them.

Marian summoned a smile. "I knew you would catch up and direct us." She forced herself to meet the man's eyes, every heartbeat a battle not to look away. She could not shake the fear that he'd recognize her from the night before. His eyes were so shrewd, so coldly calculating, that she finally broke away with a shiver.

Gisborne cleared his throat. "You are well, after your . . . your interrupted night?"

Marian tightened her hands around Jonquille's reins to make sure they wouldn't shake. "The bedclothes, you mean?" She laughed, or tried to. "It was foolish of me. I'm quite well today."

Gisborne shifted, the leather of his saddle creaking noisily. The silence stretched again until he said abruptly, "Your rooms are satisfactory?"

Marian glanced askance at the man, who was staring dead ahead, impassive. "They're fine. Quite comfortable."

Gisborne's head nodded a bit, the cold eyes a bit distant—he looked, for a moment, very much the way her father did when checking his accounts: going through a list, item by item, placing a tick by each one. "Do you enjoy visiting Nottingham?"

Marian felt, for an incredulous instant, like laughing. She'd been so preoccupied with her own horror at the prospect of marrying the Sheriff's stiff, blank-faced lackey that she hadn't stopped to consider the obvious—that since his motivation for seeking her hand was to secure his claim to Locksley and Edwinstowe, he might have as little interest in spending time with her as she did with him.

Her failure to respond made him glance her way, and when he found her looking at him, he jerked his eyes ahead again. "Have I said something to offend you, my Lady?" His voice had grown a few degrees colder.

"I was thinking I would like to ride a little faster, once we're past the gates," Marian answered. Biting down on the inside of her cheek, she added, "May I?"

She'd turned her gaze forward again, but she felt Gisborne's eyes on her, a chilly presence that made her want to squirm away. "Of course," he said.

Once they were clear of Nottingham's walls, and the crowd of beggars surrounding the gate, Marian sat a little taller and eased her weight onto her heels in the stirrups—she'd barely started to shift her grip on the reins when Jonquille broke into a trot, anticipating her. Her mare was anxious to move, unused to being asked to walk sedately, and it was all Marian could do to keep her from breaking into an all-out run. By the time Gisborne and the guards caught up, they'd settled on a slow canter.

Too quick a pace to talk.

They rode in relative silence for a time, Marian timing her breathing to match Jonquille's strides. Gisborne's horse displayed none of her own mount's irritability, as disciplined and calm as his rider. Though the air was crisp with autumn, the sun was still high and bright, and beat down upon Marian's dark riding kirtle. They reached the edge of the cultivation, where the ring road curved right to encircle the town's outskirts. The King's Road through Sherwood forked off beneath the trees, and without thinking, Marian leaned left. The cool of the shady leaves washed over her, and she let her breath out.

Behind her, she heard a muffled utterance of surprise and a clatter of hooves. She turned in time to see Gisborne hurriedly wheeling his mount around at the fork, the guards milling in confusion. She was half-tempted to let Jonquille run, but she sat back heavily, keeping a tight hand on the reins. She had a smile on her face by the time Gisborne reached her, but instead of falling into step beside hers, his horse galloped on until Gisborne wheeled him around in front of Marian, forcing Jonquille to stop with an abrupt snort of protest.

"My Lady," he said, as coolly as if he were passing her in the castle hall—only a rebellious bit of black hair curling at his temple showed any hint of disarray. "The forest is not safe."

"Nonsense," said Marian lightly. "I've lived in Sherwood Forest all my life and have never come to any grief." She leaned forward, but Gisborne cut in before she could signal to Jonquille to continue.

"My Lady." This time, the words were not a request.

When Marian looked up, Gisborne was watching her intently, one hand on his reins, the other at his belt, where he wore his sword. For a moment she saw double—Gisborne there on his horse, duty bound to protect her from outlaws and brigands—and Gisborne in the bowels of Nottingham Castle, ready to draw his sword and kill her in the name of the law.

"Sherwood is not safe," he echoed. "We shall return to the ring road. And, perhaps, we ought to let the horses walk."

Jonquille danced beneath her, uncertain, responding to the tension in Marian's legs. "Perhaps," she agreed.

After they'd emerged back into the sunlight, and the guards were behind them once more, Gisborne glanced her way. "You ride well, my Lady."

"My horse was a gift from Robin—we rode together often."

Gisborne's eyes left her. "I see." He ran his glove over his hair, that untidy curl restored to its place. "My Lady, I must ask. Has anyone come to you regarding the man seen in the forest and in Nottingham Castle?"

"Man?" Marian echoed.

"My Lady, please do not insult my intelligence by pretending to have none of your own."

Marian shot a glance at Gisborne in surprise. His marred features twisted in a grimace.

"Forgive me," he muttered. "I had a trying night, but that is no excuse to abandon manners. I am certain, though, that you know of whom I speak."

"I have heard the rumors," she said slowly. "They are too painful to consider. I dismiss them."

She could feel his eyes on her again. "He has never spoken with you. Are you certain?" he said quietly.

"It would hardly be logical for a man impersonating Robin

of Locksley to visit *me*, would it?" Marian gazed ahead, at the curve of trees beside the road, stretching away across the fields. "I'd know him instantly for a fraud."

Gisborne was slow to respond. "I suppose so."

"And why should he? If he's some common thief, there are far richer targets than I for him to seek."

Gisborne made a sound in his throat, rather like a suppressed cough. "I cannot admit to any intimate knowledge of the motives of someone who masquerades as a dead man by night."

Jonquille was creeping out ahead of Gisborne's mount, and Marian pulled her in a fraction. "What do you mean?"

But Gisborne only shrugged, and they walked on, sinking once more into that dreadful stiff silence as punishing as the sun overhead.

It was as much to break that silence as anything else that Marian spoke. "Will Scarlet—the man you arrested in Locksley. He is in the dungeon at Nottingham, isn't he?"

Gisborne grimaced again. "You should not think about men like him, my Lady."

"He's Robin's man, Sir Guy. I'm only doing what Robin would, if he were here."

Gisborne exhaled audibly. This time, when his eyes flicked over toward Marian, there was a hint of annoyance. "The man is guilty, my Lady. Even if Locksley had returned, there would be no recourse for him. No man is above the law."

He spoke with such finality that Marian felt a chill, as though an errant cloud had leached away the sun's warmth. "Still," she said, voice quiet but steady. "I would . . . I would speak with him, if I could."

Gisborne's jaw worked a moment. "Why?"

"He's brother to my personal maid. If nothing else, I would

give him her love, and bring his sister whatever regards and words he might have for her." *And see where, and in what manner, he's being held. Surely no prison is unbreakable.*

Gisborne was quiet so long, Marian half feared that he would never reply, that he would let silence itself be her answer. "Your loyalty is admirable, Lady."

"She's been with me for years, I'm fond of—"

"Your loyalty to Robert of Locksley."

Marian's words stuck in her throat. "I'm not—that is to say, I don't know what Will—"

"Demur if you must," Gisborne said, and though his voice was calm, the chill in it overrode her own voice easily. "But as I said, it is an admirable quality, Lady Marian. If you wish to visit Scarlet, I will arrange it. And accompany you, for your safety."

Marian wanted to protest, but something in the set of Gisborne's face—the sharply angled profile and lowered brow, the distant eyes—made her halt. There was suspicion in that face, Marian thought. And while he might only be thinking of her lingering loyalty to his dead rival, she could not shake the thread of fear that he suspected her of more than loyalty.

If Gisborne was not convinced the hooded man was a thief, then he might believe he had some connection—beyond his masquerade—to Robin himself. Which connected him to Marian. Gisborne might not readily jump to the conclusion that Marian *was* the hooded man, but he might watch her closely, track who she spoke to. Use her sympathy for Robin to catch the man wearing his colors.

"You are tired." Gisborne reined in his mount, and Jonquille stopped a few paces ahead. "I will ride with you back to the castle." He started to turn his horse, the guards moving to make way for them both.

"Wait." Marian spoke before she knew what to say. Whatever direction Gisborne's ideas were headed, she had to waylay them.

Then Robin's voice came, certain and soft: *Flatter him. Make him think he's smarter—make him think he's winning.*

She smoothed the veil covering her hair, feeling its sheer hem flutter beneath her fingertips. "I'd rather keep riding with you a little longer," she said softly. She couldn't make herself meet his gaze—but then, lowering her eyes would probably be more ladylike anyway. "If you don't mind."

She could feel him watching her, those cold eyes scanning her features like a clammy caress. She wanted to tell Jonquille to run, gallop away at her fastest pace, bolt into the forest with no intention of returning.

"Very well." Gisborne's voice, for once, held something other than ice: a note, however tiny, of surprise. "We can keep riding."

FIFTEEN

WHEN THE THICK STONE walls of Nottingham town rose into view upon their return, Marian could have cried with relief. It was hard enough to decide to play the role Gisborne expected of her, but carrying it out made her want to scream. For all Gisborne had stated his intentions toward her, he showed so little interest in her person as to seem utterly indifferent. Flirtation was already outside Marian's expertise, but trying to appear receptive to his advances was all the harder when he made none. Marian told herself that his disregard was a blessing. But being ignored—even by a joyless sycophant like Gisborne—took its toll on her nerves.

Marian gathered Jonquille's reins and shifted forward, ready to demand a bit more speed from her horse, when Gisborne called for her to stop.

"My Lady," he said. "Consider me at your disposal from now on—should there be anything you require during your stay at

Nottingham, send a servant with your requests and I will see them granted."

Marian pulled her smile into place. "Thank you, Sir Guy." She was about to turn Jonquille's head back toward the road when she stopped, an idea flashing into existence. "Sir Guy— there is something you could help me with."

Gisborne's brows rose a fraction, and his grim-set lips relaxed. "Name it, my Lady."

"It occurred to me that since the man masquerading as Robin helped him escape, Will Scarlet might know something about him. Something you could use to catch the impostor."

Gisborne's face was stone, but his eyes were keen. "A clever thought, my Lady. But we have interrogated him at length without result."

Interrogated, thought Marian, the taste of bile rising in her throat at the half-formed images that rose to her mind. "You represent the Sheriff," she countered gently. "Will has no reason to confide in you. But I . . . I knew him before he broke the law, and I was Robin's . . ." Her voice choked on the word "betrothed." Grief still lurked in her heart, ready to throttle her.

Cold Gisborne might be, but he was no fool. She didn't have to finish the sentence. He lifted his head and glowered at the city walls. "I have no desire to involve you in any of this," he said finally.

"I'm already involved," Marian protested, unable to keep her frustration from her voice. When Gisborne's eyes fell on her face, she forced herself to meet his gaze. "Sir Guy, forgive me—but the sooner you discover the identity of this man, the sooner my torment will be ended, and all this will be over with."

The sooner we can be wedded, Marian thought bitterly, *and you can become Lord of Locksley.*

Gisborne considered this, eyes scanning her features—for signs of duplicity. "Very well. I will arrange for you to see the prisoner this afternoon. I'll remain out of sight so that he believes you are there alone."

Can he not give me a moment's victory? She glanced over her shoulder as if to watch the waving wheat in the fields, trying to hide her frustration. But this time, Gisborne anticipated her.

"My Lady," he said, voice softening a fraction, "I cannot let you see him alone. You would not be safe, and your reputation . . . you must have an escort in that part of the castle, around so many guards and low men. I give you my word he will not know I'm there. You need not entice me with the promise of gathering secrets. If you earnestly wish to convey to him his sister's regards, I will not interfere."

Marian blinked at him, utterly taken aback by the compassion in Gisborne's assumption.

Better and better, she thought, mastering her surprise. *If he feels sorry for me . . . I can use that.*

Marian smiled shyly and murmured, "You see right through me. Still, I shall try to earn Scarlet's confidence, my Lord."

Gisborne's lips eased again—*it must be his version of a smile,* Marian thought—and he corrected her carefully, "Sir Guy, my Lady. I am not yet Lord of anything."

"Of course," Marian said, blinking as though surprised at her own mistake. "Sir Guy. Forgive me."

Her attempt at flattery did not have exactly the effect she'd hoped—he didn't swell with ego or straighten in his saddle, and his gaze was no more fond. But he regarded her evenly for a few long moments, heedless of the guards some distance behind, who watched them with interest.

They rode side by side through the gates of the town toward

the castle. Marian closed her eyes, not wanting to see if the two boys who had recognized her the day before were there among the masses of supplicants in the streets. Instead, she thought of Robin, and imagined it was he who rode at her side, until the sound of Jonquille's hooves striking the stone cobbles of the castle courtyard shattered the daydream.

The under castle was dark even at midday, without windows to light the corridors. The guard who had come to fetch Marian was a short, stocky man who oozed disinterest. He smelled of days-old sweat and sour ale, and she kept a few paces behind him to avoid the stench.

He didn't try to converse with her—he was clearly one of the jailers, not a guard used to being stationed where he'd be near the nobility. But Marian was distracted anyway, and relieved not to have to assume a pleasant, ladylike facade for his benefit.

Elena had all but dropped to her knees when Marian took her aside and explained that she'd found a way to see Will. Marian had guided her to a chair and waited while the maid mastered her emotions, squeezing her hand. It was a breach of protocol, to be sure, but then, Elena was hardly an average maid.

Or maybe all lady's maids have secret adventures while their charges are governing their lands and attending high dinners, Marian thought, giddy and bemused.

Elena had given her a few words to pass along to her brother, dictated to Marian and jotted on some scrap from the library. Will had never learned his letters, but Marian could read to him—and it was something, however small, of his family that he could hold on to until Marian could think of a way to free him.

The guard led her down a dimly lighted stair, the air growing thicker and danker. Gisborne was waiting at the bottom, and

146

while Marian could not be sure it wasn't the unsteady torchlight, she thought he looked grimmer than usual. There was certainly no sign on his features of the lighter expression she'd seen that morning.

Gisborne nodded at the guard, who took his leave and moved on down the corridor. Gisborne watched him go until he'd turned a corner, and the sound of clinking chain mail began to fade. Then he turned that stern look on Marian, who fought the urge to draw back.

"My Lady," he greeted her, with that flawless veneer of politeness.

"Sir Guy." She waited, and when he didn't move, she added, "Is everything all right?"

He blinked and unfolded his hands from behind his back. "Indeed. Apologies, Lady Marian. I have been in council with the Sheriff since our ride. This way."

She fell into step behind him, thoughtful, mind turning over. "You seem distressed."

Gisborne's stride faltered, and he disguised the misstep as a pause to let her catch him up and walk at his side. "I beg your pardon," he said finally, but made no effort to explain his behavior.

He led them past the armory, which seemed to double as a break room for the guards during daytime hours, for a burst of raucous laughter muffled by the thick door trailed them as they passed. "You've known the Sheriff since you were children, haven't you?" Marian asked over the laughter.

"The Sheriff's father raised me after my own father died," Gisborne answered after the sounds of revelry from the armory had faded behind them. His voice was cool—Marian could not imagine speaking of her own father's death so calmly.

"I should think it would be nice to have a brother," Marian commented.

Gisborne turned a corner, his profile visible long enough for Marian to see his jaw tighten. "Indeed. This way."

Marian gave up, listening to the sounds of their steps. The air felt chill and damp, yielding only to the heat of the torches they passed. The only people present were other guardsmen, and as a few of them turned to watch their progress, Marian began to understand why Gisborne had insisted on accompanying her.

She wasn't the only woman present, though. Another turn revealed the stooped, ragged form of a servant on her knees, scrubbing at the stone beneath her. The floors were sloped down to one side, and the woman was moving watery sludge down the corridor with long strokes of a bristled scrubbing brush. The stench of rot and excrement assailed Marian's nose—she must have made some sound, for Gisborne paused as they reached a heavy, iron-bound door at the end of the hall.

"I can bring you back," he offered, unaffected by the smell. "If you wish, I will pass along a message to the prisoner."

Marian drew up her chin. "It's worth it, if he will tell us anything about the man who helped him."

Gisborne inclined his head. "As you wish," he replied, and opened the door.

Marian had never been in the caves beneath Nottingham Castle, though stories about their dark, labyrinthine tunnels ran rampant through the nobility and commoners alike. They were said to be endless, that if a man didn't know where he was headed, he could wander through the stone passageways until he died of thirst and cold. The very air in the caves was different, carrying an empty, bone-deep chill that seemed to slither straight through Marian's cloak and gown to her skin.

Passages broke off right and left as they walked, some lit by torches, others no more than gaping maws of darkness. It was down a lighted passage that Gisborne led her before coming to a halt as they reached a sharply sloping section of sandstone worn smooth by the traffic of booted feet.

"The cells are just beyond." Gisborne spoke quietly. "Scarlet will not know I am listening, but I will be within earshot if you require my assistance. You are certain you wish to continue?"

Marian forced herself to meet his eyes but could not suppress a shiver. In such darkness, so far from any source of comfort or safety, with nothing but stone above and below and all around, the effect of his cold stare was potent.

When she didn't answer immediately, Gisborne took a step toward her. "My Lady, I can—"

"No," said Marian quickly, stepping back in response, wrapping her arms around herself. "I will do as I promised. Thank you, Sir Guy."

She turned and hurried down the slope, half sliding on the slick stone. She'd intended to come up with some way to require privacy with Will, if only for a few moments, but her courage had failed her in that dark, cold atmosphere.

Marian reached the bottom of the slope and paused to shake herself, the gesture as much a shudder as anything else. She would hear Gisborne if he tried to follow her. And despite the overwhelming isolation the caves forced on the senses, there were guards and soldiers and any number of others down here who would hear her if she screamed.

She drove Gisborne's cold, invasive eyes out of her thoughts. Ahead the corridor swelled wider, with roughly hewn rectangles at uneven intervals on either side. Iron grates covered most of the openings, and only one torch was lit, burning unsteadily.

Intermittent sounds—scratching, gnawing, rustling—echoed like shouts in the quiet, and Marian could not tell if the sounds came from men or rats.

She took a breath through her mouth, trying to avoid the stench of human waste, but the odor was so pervasive she felt she could taste it on her lips. She stepped forward.

Will was not the Sheriff's only prisoner, although most of the cells were empty. Ordinarily criminals either served their sentences in the stocks in the town proper, or were hanged—neither fate demanded a lengthy stay in a dungeon. It seemed clear to Marian that only Will's usefulness in unmasking and capturing the Locksley impostor had kept him alive.

Marian crept quietly past several unoccupied holes before she heard a rustle of fabric to her left. She paused, peering through the gloom, until the shadows moved and a paler oval appeared from the darkness.

For a moment, Marian could not speak—he was so changed. She'd seen him beaten and bloody, but his time in captivity had reduced Will to something else entirely. His cheeks were gaunt and his eyes crusted and puffy; his lips were cracked with thirst, and one side of his jaw was purple and yellow and swollen.

"Good morning" came a voice, dusty and thin, and bitter as the astringent smell of urine in the air. "Or is it afternoon?"

Marian tried to regather her wits. "Will," she said softly.

He didn't rise, or come nearer the grate that blocked off his cave from the others. His eyes glowed balefully in the reflected torchlight. "Most of him," he answered.

"Will, I'm sorry." Marian stepped closer, glancing over her shoulder toward the corridor where Gisborne waited, listening. "Is there anything I can do?"

He eyed her for a long moment, eyes bitter. His expression

carried a desperate kind of insolence, as though the bars between them had stripped away the barriers of class and gender and civility. No one of the peasant class would look at any nobleman like that, and certainly not a noblewoman.

"Elena—" Marian's voice cracked, and she fumbled for the slit in her kirtle that would allow her to access her pocket. "Elena sends her love. She wrote a message—"

"I'll take it." The sullenness of Will's face eased a fraction, and he extended one dirty hand through the bars, palm up.

"You're sure you don't want me to read it to you?" She pulled the bit of parchment from the folds of fabric, hating the way her hand shook. Will was the one facing his death—why then did she want nothing more than to flee as fast as her feet would carry her?

His expression hardened. "I can read enough," he said shortly. "My Lord was always generous with any of his men who wanted to learn."

Robin. Marian hadn't known that he'd taught some of the peasants to read. It had certainly never occurred to her to teach Elena or Midge or any of the commoners who served her father—it had never occurred to her that they'd have any desire to learn. Cheeks burning with shame and disquiet, she placed the scrap of a page into Will's palm. The holes in the iron grille were large enough that he could've stuck his whole arm through up to the shoulder, but too small for anything larger. The lock on the door was massive and crude, a battered, rusty thing with a large keyhole.

It wouldn't be hard to pick, she thought, if she had something narrow enough and strong enough, but opening the lock itself would be the easiest part of getting Will out. How long would an emaciated outlaw last, trying to make his way up from the very bottom of Nottingham Castle?

A tiny sound prickled at Marian's instincts. How quickly her senses had adjusted to the atmosphere of the jail—this sound wasn't one of the rats, or a prisoner stirring. It was the tiny scrape of leather against limestone. Gisborne, in the corridor, shifting his weight from his bad leg.

"Will," she said, raising her voice a little. "The man who helped you escape before you were arrested. What can you tell me about him?"

Will had been staring down at the scrap of paper, frowning, and Marian wondered if he was regretting turning down her offer to read his sister's message for him. Now, his head snapped up, and the eyes she remembered as merry and full of humor narrowed with the same sullen ire with which he'd greeted her. "You mean your beloved. Pardon, Lady—your *former* beloved."

Marian had to force herself to speak, against the desire to clench her teeth. "It wasn't Robin, Will—it couldn't have been. Someone is pretending to be him."

"And your new lord and protector sent you here to see if sweet words and a pretty face would pull from me what his jailer's fists and firebrands wouldn't?"

Marian blinked hard, mind racing. Her retort—*he is not my Lord and never will be*—was on her tongue, her lips already parted, but the remembered feel of Gisborne's cold eyes on her kept it there. "I came because I care about your welfare. And if I didn't, I would care for Elena's happiness. If there's anything you can tell me, perhaps Sir Guy might find some measure of leniency for you."

Another scrape from the hallway. Gisborne had promised

no such thing to Marian, and she knew he would not feel obligated because she'd promised it to Will. *It doesn't matter*, Marian thought, *because leniency or not, I will save you*. She could not help wishing she could show the man in the cell her true self, just for a moment, to win his trust.

Will's eyes had gone colder than Gisborne's. "Your words are not as sweet as you imagine, Lady. And your face nowhere near as pretty as you think it is."

A flicker of answering ire made Marian's skin warm. She'd never been a vain creature—oh, she'd had moments, certainly, when she'd wished for the slight, graceful form that so many men found pleasing. She'd had more moments of envy than she cared to admit. But it was an old scar, and Will's assumption that insulting her appearance would hurt her was the far greater wound.

"Listen," she said, lowering her voice a little, but not so much that it might summon Gisborne from hiding. "I *am* here at Sir Guy's request. To speak to you. Appeal to you." She made herself gaze directly into Will's eyes, intent, then deliberately tilted her head toward the corridor.

Will scowled at her, but when she made the gesture again, his eyebrows drew in and his gaze darted toward the corridor.

Stay with me, Will. "Sir Guy," she said carefully, indicating the corridor with her hand, "would never want me to be here alone. He probably thinks I have the same loyalty to this impostor that you feel." And at that, she pressed her hand against her heart, so that the ring she wore—the ring that had identified "Robin" to Will that fog-riddled night when they'd fought and escaped together—glinted in the torchlight.

Will's eyes widened, and when he lifted those eyes from the

ring to Marian's face, he looked a little like his old self, beneath the grime. "Did he give—"

"Permission for me to visit you?" Marian interrupted, before Will could ask about the ring. "Sir Guy? Don't worry, I won't get into trouble for being here."

Will was silent, gaze moving between her face and the corridor.

Marian took a deep breath. The knife's edge she walked cut at every step, and her mind raced. She wasn't likely to get this concession from Gisborne a second time. This could be the only opportunity she'd have to speak to Will before effecting his escape—she'd been assuming a plan would come to her if she saw where he was being kept, or if she could somehow make Gisborne fall madly, blindly in love with her, or . . . but there was no convenient window with crumbling mortar in his cell, no key hanging just out of reach by the entrance to the jail, and with every moment she spent with Gisborne, the more certain she became that he felt as little for her as she did for him.

She had to give Gisborne something. She had to seem, to him, like an asset.

"It isn't Robin," she said finally. "I swear to you. Anything you can tell us can only help you, and betrays no one. He said nothing to you?" Will started to open his mouth, and Marian hurried to add, "Nothing about his plans, where he's hiding in Sherwood, other outlaws working with him? Anything that might help Sir Guy intercept him?"

Will stared at her as though she'd gone mad in front of his eyes. Marian gave an exaggerated nod, catching his eye and then tapping her ear, pointing again toward the corridor. She felt like one of the troubadours performing for the Sheriff's dinners, pantomiming and trying desperately to win some sort of reaction from her audience.

Her throat tightened and she swept her hand across her brow, weariness and despair urging her to give up. She was about to turn away when Will's voice finally broke in, slow and unsteady.

"Ye-es," he said, watching her with a faint frown. "Yes. He did say . . ."

Marian's breath caught, and she looked up. She nodded again, stepping closer to the bars. *Tomorrow*, she mouthed, and when Will blinked at her, she did it again, exaggeratedly.

"Tomorrow," Will said slowly. "He did say he would . . . meet the other outlaws working with him? Yes. Working with him. Tomorrow. In the forest. Sherwood Forest." He was watching her gestures and her lips with outright bemused confusion now.

Marian wanted to gasp for breath. She gave him an encouraging smile. "Do you know where?" She drew a line in the air, painted trees on either side with her fingertips, mouthed the words.

"The King's Road," Will blurted, then watched her more closely. "Off the King's Road. In the forest, by . . . by a river." He spoke more quickly, warming to the deception, elaborating. "There's a bend in the river that cuts close to the King's Road, where a series of granite shelves make a hollow in the wood. That's where he'll be. Tomorrow."

Marian let out her breath, gazing at Will, who gazed back with something altogether different from that despairing hatred his eyes had held at the start. Now there was light in them. Hope.

"Thank you," she said softly. "I know the man helped you, but it wasn't Robin, Will—I would have heard from him, if it was, and you know that. Whoever it was—you owe him nothing. The important thing is to think of yourself and your sister. I'll speak to Sir Guy. There must be room for mercy, if he knows the only reason you held your tongue was out of loyalty to your Lord."

Will reached back out through the grate barring him inside the rock-cut cell. Marian took his hand, ignoring the patina of slime and dirt on his skin, and squeezed.

"Well met, my Lady," he murmured just as softly, running his thumb over the little ruby ring on her finger, and bowed his head.

SIXTEEN

MARIAN WAS SHAKING BY the time she reached the corridor where she'd left Gisborne. He was waiting for her, his face more unreadable than ever. He made a quick, stifling gesture when she lifted her eyes to his, and reached out to grasp her arm.

She bit her lip, a bright, hot flash of fear making her want to tear herself away—but he wasn't embracing her, but rather pulling her along the corridor, away from the cells. The heavy door slammed behind them, and still Gisborne went on. His grip was tight but not painful, his movements taut with agitation.

It wasn't until they'd emerged from the caves altogether, the weighty air lifting, the torches brighter, the hewn stone walls rising around them once more, that he released her.

Marian gaped at him, reeling from the rough treatment—and even more so from the aftermath of her double conversation with Will. She wanted to fall to the stone floor, let every muscle go, abandon the white-knuckled grip she had on the reins and let her mind break into a run.

"How did you make him speak to you?" Gisborne asked, his face close to hers, the ordinarily cold eyes suddenly burning, intent, penetrating.

Marian opened her mouth but found she'd already lost her grip on herself enough that she couldn't regain it. Mind empty, consumed with an overwhelming desire to flee, she did the only thing left to her in that moment: she burst into tears.

She was dimly aware of Gisborne taking a step back with a muffled exclamation, and she sagged against the wall for a moment before her knees gave way and she dropped to the floor. The emptiness of her mind filled abruptly, overflowed, spilling thoughts in every direction: Will had trusted her; she'd figured out a way to get Gisborne and his men out of the castle; she could breathe again, the smells of rot and urine and death barred again behind the door to the jail; she was, perhaps for the first time in her life, acting as she was expected to act, crumpled in a ladylike heap. She buried her face in her hands, not sure if she was hiding her tears or the fact that she wanted to laugh.

A hand brushed her arm. She lowered her hands and saw a blurry shape before her. When she blinked, sending another few tears down her wet cheeks, the shape transformed into Gisborne's face.

"Forgive me," he said quietly, and for once the words didn't sound as if he were reciting them from a list of things one says to a well-bred lady. "I should not have touched you—but what the boy said is too . . . Curse it. I should not have let you do this."

Marian coughed and brushed at her eyes. "No," she managed, voice rather tremulous. "I'm glad you did, Sir Guy. You heard?"

Gisborne nodded, his face grim. Had it been her father, or Robin, or anyone in all England other than Gisborne, he would have smiled and tried to distract her and offered her a handkerchief. But Gisborne merely glowered at her. "I cannot say I trust what I heard. He sounded uncertain himself. But you, my Lady, did in a few moments what none of us could do in days of interrogation."

"I think," said Marian carefully, sniffing delicately to buy herself a moment to build the lie, "that you can trust him. He looked like he might weep, Sir Guy—he believed he was betraying Robin. Or if not Robin, then at least a man who'd tried to save his life."

"Do not concern yourself any further with it. You have done more to help the Sheriff and the crown than I had any right to expect. What comes after is my duty, not yours. My Lady, you must stop weeping." His tone actually held a note of frustration.

Marian could have laughed, there on the stone floor, with Gisborne crouching awkwardly beside her.

Oh, yes, said Robin, mirth making his voice dance, *she hears your command, sir. She will stop weeping this instant.*

Marian was caught between exhaustion and giddiness, and she wasn't entirely sure she could stop herself from answering, so she covered her face again.

Gisborne muttered something, and as the leather of his clothing creaked, Marian risked a glance between her fingers. He'd looked away, scanning the corridors as if looking for someone he could hand her off to, someone better suited to dealing with a hysterical lady. In that moment he looked so unlike himself, the stony facade giving way to a baffled helplessness that made him look oddly youthful.

Then the world reasserted itself, and Marian found her tears had stopped abruptly. Gisborne's hand was on his sword, and his fingers gripped the hilt, and he wasn't so much helpless as urgent. He might not wholly believe Will's—Marian's—story about a clandestine meeting in Sherwood Forest between the man in the hood and his unknown cohorts, but he was fixated on it regardless, desperate to act on anything that might bring him closer to dispatching his quarry.

By the time he looked back down at Marian, she was calm again. She smiled at him, and let him help her to her feet, and leaned on his arm as he walked her back through the castle halls. She bade him farewell, and wished him luck, and told him he need not apologize for being unavailable the rest of the day and the next. She didn't shrink when he bowed over her hand, and she made herself remain in her doorway as he retreated down the corridor so that, in case he looked back, he'd see her watching him go, like a damsel in an old tale gazing at her knight.

He didn't look back.

SEVENTEEN

MARIAN STOOD BY A window overlooking the stables, head down, listening to the rise and fall of voices and footsteps in the castle corridors. The overlapping rhythms of each separate life held no obvious pattern, for the various nobles and guards and servants who occupied Nottingham Castle were like bits of wheat chaff tumbling about on a fitfully breezy day, all scurrying in different directions, unpredictable. But the longer she listened, the more it seemed she could feel a general rise and fall to the sounds of castle life, ripples of activity that spread from a shout in the great hall or a clatter of dishes in the kitchen.

To anyone passing, she'd look pensive, ladylike, gazing idly out over the long slope down to Nottingham town. So she hoped, at any rate. Beneath her cool expression, she felt like she might burst into flames with the effort of inactivity.

Always in the past, her excursions as "Robin" had been entirely of her own making, dependent only on her own skill and timing and planning. But to rescue a prisoner from the heart of Nottingham Castle without being seen . . . not even the real Robin could have managed that alone. And so, for the first time, Marian had to put her trust in other players—and she had to wait.

Gisborne had ridden out before daybreak with a dozen of his men. That much of her plan, at least, had gone off without trouble. Marian had entertained the brief but unlikely hope that the Sheriff's second-in-command would bring half the castle's garrison with him in his zeal to capture the hooded impostor who stood between him and Locksley. Still, there were far more guards left manning Nottingham Castle's entrances, exits, and corridors than had gone to Sherwood Forest.

The next step of Marian's plan had not gone entirely as she'd expected.

The previous day, when Gisborne had escorted Marian back to her quarters after her visit to Will, she'd found Elena waiting for her. Her maid was brushing at Marian's riding kirtle with such vigor that she didn't hear the door open, didn't notice Marian's approach, didn't so much as pause until Marian laid a hand on the girl's shoulder.

Elena had gasped and dropped the brush, and as soon as her eyes fixed on Marian's face, they grew wet with unshed tears. "My Lady," she greeted her in a shaking voice. There was a question in her gaze.

Marian found what she hoped was an encouraging smile. "I spoke with Will. He's alive, he's not badly hurt. He—"

But Elena grasped at Marian's hands, the tears overflowing, and Marian had to give the rest of her account in bits and pieces. By the time she told Elena that she had a plan to free her brother, the tears had slowed. That statement made them stop altogether.

Marian interrupted Elena's questions by squeezing her hands and saying, "It's best if you don't know. If I'm caught, they're sure to interrogate you. I do need your help, though, with one thing."

"Anything, my Lady."

"The washwomen who scrub the floors—do they live here in the servants' quarters, or do they live in town?"

Elena frowned at her, puzzled. "Some live here," she said slowly. "Those who are unmarried, or who have outlived their husbands. What do they have to do with Will?"

"I need to . . . to borrow a set of work clothes from one of them. Do you know when they have duties that would keep them away from their belongings?"

"No, my Lady, but I could ask them." Elena's eyes were keen, though, and she hesitated only a moment before saying quietly, "I can get what you need."

"You can't be involved," Marian said gently. "Like I said—"

"You can't go sweeping down into the servants' quarters in all your finery and expect to walk back out with an armful of rags without anyone noticing." The words came out in a rush, cutting through Marian's voice, and Elena shut her mouth with a little gasp of surprise as her cheeks reddened. "P-pardon, my Lady, I didn't mean to . . ."

But Marian could have laughed at the absurdity of it all, conspiring with a servant, planning disguises and jailbreaks, all the while remaining carefully respectful of the barriers of class and birth. "I choose to risk myself," she said finally. "If I'm caught, there's a chance my station will protect me, at least to some extent. I can't ask you to—"

"You didn't ask," Elena said, cutting her off again. This time, she didn't apologize for it. "I offered." When Marian would have argued, her maid straightened, lifting her chin. "I'm not offering because I want to help you, my Lady, though I do. I'm offering because between us, I have the better chance of success. If you need a washwoman's clothes to save Will, I'll get them for you."

The plan came together quickly at that point. Marian would leave a basket by her bed full of linens to be washed, which Elena would bring to the servants' quarters, where she'd add an unwitting washwoman's habit to the pile of laundry, then leave it all at the junction where the servants' hall intersected the stair leading down toward the armory and the jail beyond.

"My Lady," Elena interrupted then, eyeing her curiously. "I won't ask you again to tell me what you're planning, but—forgive me for saying so—you're forgetting that the nobles and the guards aren't the only people you must deceive."

"What do you mean?"

"To you, we all look alike." Her maid lifted her chin again, fingers twisting in the folds of her skirt. "You don't look at us, because we're everywhere, and we're harmless, and we're necessary. But to us . . . my Lady, whatever clothes you wear, you still walk like a noblewoman. Your face is fair, your hands unscarred. You look people in the eye. No servant would dare such a thing. You might fool a guard, you might fool the Sheriff, you might even fool your own father if you dirtied your face and kept your eyes down. But you'd never fool the washwoman actually assigned to scrubbing the floors."

Marian stared at her until Elena began to turn red, the tips of her ears showing pink at the edge of her veil. So much had happened since she'd discovered Elena's connection with the outlaws in Sherwood that she hadn't had the chance to ask how long Elena had been disguising herself to sneak out and see Alan, or to consider the daring and guile of the girl who'd always seemed so quiet and domestic.

Now it was like seeing a sweet kitten throw its head back and give a lion's roar.

Marian hunted for her voice. "What do you suggest?"

"A distraction," Elena replied promptly. "We all have our assigned duties, but when we accompany our masters to a grand manor or a castle like this, we're also expected to share in the household labors. There are bells that summon us if we're needed unexpectedly. Different chimes mean different things. Three sharp rings is a summons for footmen and squires to the stables, for example. Four is for kitchen staff."

Marian had heard the little bells, had always known they were for the servants in some manner—but she'd never paid them much attention. "And you can create a situation that summons even the washwomen from the bottom of the castle? What are you going to do?"

Elena lowered her gaze, demure and servile once more. "If I'm caught," she said gently, "they might interrogate you."

Marian had broken into a gasp of laughter, and the sound of it had so surprised her that she'd dropped heavily onto the edge of the bed, needing all her strength to press both hands against her mouth and stifle herself.

Now, as she stood as near to the long stair as she dared, she wasn't laughing anymore. Elena had vanished some hours before with the basket, and as the shadows in the courtyard lengthened sliver by sliver, Marian's imagination could not stop serving her images of her maid in chains, or at the mercy of the guardsmen, or worst of all: in a heap on the floor, her sweet blue eyes still, staring skyward—

Marian shut her own eyes, leaning her forehead against the cool stone of the window's edge. She'd heard a few of the signal bells chime and listened to the patterns of steps. Three chimes had indeed sent a flurry of young men out to the stables when a hunting party returned from a day's outing. Marian didn't know the meaning of the others. Elena had told her only that she'd recognize the signal when she heard it.

Marian's fingers curled into fists around the edge of the window, as if she might summon a few more moments of patience by bodily preventing herself from running off toward . . .

You couldn't find Elena if you tried, Robin pointed out in her thoughts. *You have no idea where she is.*

That realization broke a cold sweat over Marian's body, and she let go of the window, whirling for the stair.

Then the bell chime sounded again. Marian waited, listening for the pattern. The bell rang long, then short, and then short again, and then started ringing a fourth time—and didn't stop.

The bell kept going, like a tiny version of a church bell's fire warning. The background patter of steps and voices shifted, tugged toward the sound of the bells, and through the roaring in her ears, Marian heard feet running across stone, a distant shout, commotion rising and then fading away, retreating toward the servants' quarters below.

The bell was still ringing, and, shaking herself from her daze, Marian abandoned speculation as to what Elena had done and hurried down the stairs.

The basket was there, exactly where Elena had promised it would be, and when Marian lifted aside a corner of her bed linens, she saw the worn, grease-stained hem of a coarse skirt. With a surge of triumph, Marian glanced around to make sure the hall was deserted, then grabbed up the basket and hurried on her way.

She ducked into one of the empty storerooms she'd found while running from Gisborne her first night in Nottingham and pulled the unknown woman's dress and cap from the basket. She exchanged her soft shift for the rough-spun, unbleached version Elena had provided, and pulled the stiff gray overmantle on with some difficulty. It was far too small for her, but she'd been expecting that—few women had her height.

The dagger she'd brought with her, bound to her thigh, no more showed under the washwoman's dress than it had her own.

She hastened to hide her own clothing in among the linens again, then tucked the basket up against her hip like she'd seen servants do and slipped back into the corridor again. She hadn't gone more than a few paces before she heard the approach of heavy boots, and her pulse quickened. She glued her gaze to the floor and stepped to the side for whoever it was, trying to will herself to be small and unnoticeable.

It was a guard. His steps never changed, and when she finally risked lifting her eyes, all she saw was the back of his chain mail, retreating on down the passageway.

She exhaled, shaky and slow, and hurried down toward the caves.

The guard on duty by the jail's entrance scarcely glanced at her when she passed him. She kept her eyes down and said nothing. The slope of the floor carried any spilled or dripping water down each side of the hall, but when it grew thick and sludgy with grime, it had to be brushed along the channels. A stinking brown edge of slime, and the bucket of wash water, told her where to start.

She began to scrub, pushing the gunk down toward the caves. She longed to hurry toward Will's cell, but she was only a few paces past the guard. While he might not have noticed her arrival, he'd be bound to notice her moving with purpose toward the tunnels beneath the castle.

Her knees began to ache, and her fingers went numb before long. She was sweating, and as her body heat warmed her stolen clothes, they began to smell unpleasantly—Marian didn't know whether it was her own sweat or that of the woman who normally wore this dress, but either way, it mingled with the increasingly rank odor of the jail cells beyond.

Robin, she thought miserably, *what I wouldn't give for you to be here. You'd storm the place with sword and bow in hand, neatly incapacitate the guards, and get Will out in a matter of minutes. It'd be daring and exciting and romantic, and most important, I wouldn't be any part of it.*

Though if she, or anyone else, had stormed the place by force, the guard she'd snuck past would probably be dead. Along with any others who'd heard the commotion and come to assist.

By the time the tunnel curved enough that she was out of sight of the guard, her knuckles were bleeding from scraping against the stone, and her back was screaming a protest. She glanced over her shoulder to check that she was alone, then staggered upright. *You don't see us,* Elena had told her. Marian, flushed with exertion and damp with sweat, had to agree with her maid. She'd seen the woman yesterday, seen enough of her to formulate this plan, but she hadn't really *seen* the work she was doing.

Marian stifled a groan, picked up her basket, and made for the cells.

Will glanced at her and then away when she arrived. Marian had to fight a smile. *You don't see us.* It was not a blindness limited to noblemen. She was a woman in working clothes—she was a servant. She couldn't help him.

"Will," she whispered.

"Wha—Marian?" Will started, and leaped to his feet in surprise.

She put a finger to her lips, glancing back along the tunnel. Then she turned and gathered up the hem of her skirt, pulling it up so she could retrieve the dagger she'd brought. It was an awkward and cumbersome process—if she'd been confronted, there was no way she'd have been able to draw the weapon quickly enough to aid herself—but that wasn't why she'd brought it.

She knelt before the lock and eased the tip of the dagger inside. She had to work by feel, and her work-numbed fingers were clumsy with muscle cramp and swollen joints.

Robin had taught her this. Or maybe she had taught him—they'd learned together, certainly, for none of his weapons masters or history tutors would have shown the future Lord of Locksley how to pick a lock. But as children, they'd played at being highwaymen and heroes alike, and Robin smuggled an old battered chest out of storage to their forest hideout. Sometimes it held the Holy Grail, and they were knights seeking eternal life and prosperity for the land. Sometimes it sheltered an ancient druid's magic talisman. Sometimes it was full of gold they'd stolen from a wealthy trader. At first they'd only pretended to pick its lock, for Robin had not found a key to match it. But one afternoon, Marian had been pretending to open it with a stick as a key, and they'd heard a telltale creak of iron.

The stick had broken, but the next time they played, Robin brought a dirk. And while its point was blunted for practice, it was long and thin. And after a few days of trying and failing—and hurling the box against a tree out of frustration—the lock had clicked open.

It was empty, but they'd whooped in victory, grinning twin grins of triumph.

Marian's eyes burned as she worked, and she tore her thoughts away with ruthless focus.

Will was pacing. She could feel his eyes on her as tangibly as the stone under her bruised knees. The metal grated and whined, sometimes with a clink that made Will's breath catch, but the sound was that of the tumbler dropping back into place. Marian could feel the vibrations of each failure radiating back down along the dagger's hilt.

She wanted to stop and take a break. She'd had visions of sweeping in, picking the lock, and freeing Will in one grandiose gesture—but if she'd stopped to think, she would've known it wouldn't be so easy. She needed to stretch her hands and her legs, walk around to get her blood flowing, take a few deep breaths of the noxious air. Gisborne would likely be gone all day, waiting for the outlaws who would never come, and the guard outside the jail would hardly have reason to check on the prisoner.

But words like "likely" and "hardly" made Marian's skin crawl. And she kept working.

Her eyes were still burning—but with perspiration this time—when another more solid clunk of iron, combined with a shift of the weight on the tip of the dagger, broke Marian's concentration.

She blinked. Hands shaking, she withdrew the dagger and looked at the lock. There was nothing to tell of her success—it sat as squat and dark and cold as ever. She raised her eyes, expecting to see Will's face flooded with excitement and gratitude.

Instead, he looked rather stupefied. He'd stopped pacing at some point and was crouched on the floor behind the grille, eyes on her face.

Self-consciously, Marian swiped a dirty sleeve across her brow. "It's done."

"Mary's tits," Will muttered, still staring.

Marian's cheeks warmed, and she straightened with an effort. "I don't think you're supposed to use language like that in front of a lady. Or in front of anyone, for that matter."

Will swore again, straightening as well, and put a hand out to the door. He had only to shove, and it swung open a hand's width. "You're no Lady," he said finally, pushing it open enough to slip out.

The words ought to have cut at Marian, who'd spent most of her life feeling inadequate as a lady—too tall, too loud, too opinionated, too *much*—but Will spoke them like a compliment, and when he stood next to her, free, he smiled.

Marian smiled back.

"So where do I meet the others?" Will asked, glancing up and down the corridor.

"Others?"

"The others, whoever got you in here. Robin's men."

Marian's pleasure vanished. "Nobody got me in here but me," she replied, stung.

EIGHTEEN

WILL'S SMILE DISAPPEARED. "YOU came alone? No one to deal with the guards, or . . . Marian, what the hell am I supposed to do now? I can't just walk out—half the castle garrison knows my face."

Marian shushed him, glancing back in the direction of the guard. "Wait there." She took up her basket, still feeling wobbly from exertion, and retreated into one of the unoccupied cells. Quickly she changed back into her kirtle, trying to stifle her guilt at the relief of wearing clean, comfortable clothes once more. Then, reemerging, she shoved the pile of rough-spun cloth at Will.

He glanced at the clothes in his hands, then up at her. "What am I meant to do with these?"

"Wear them."

He gave her a startled look that did little to conceal the flash of disgust on his face.

"They're no filthier than what you have on now," Marian

pointed out, patience dwindling—true, they were a bit damp
with sweat, and somehow she'd tracked the hems through the
filth she'd been scrubbing, but Will had been wearing the same
clothes since his arrest that first day in Locksley, and they were
little better than rags.

"But this is a *dress*," Will protested.

Marian's patience snapped. "It's as well you don't grow a very
convincing beard yet."

"But . . ." Will shifted his weight uncomfortably.

Marian sighed. "It's a *disguise*, Will. You can wear a dress, or
you can stay here. See how far you get in your tunic and trousers
and rags before the guards kill you."

In the end, he didn't make a very convincing woman. True,
his whiskers were fair and not very thick, but they were visible—
and his shoulders were too broad, his hips too narrow. And he
was scowling, face flaming, humiliation leaking from his every
pore. Marian bit her lip hard to keep from laughing. She tucked
the fabric up here and there, padding the hips, and pulled the cap
down to shade his too-thick eyebrows.

"Keep your head down," she suggested finally, reminding
herself that the guard hadn't so much as noticed her, much less
inspected her, on her way in. "When you leave, put the basket
on your hip, like so." She demonstrated, and added, "No, thrust
your hip out, like—well, yes, sort of. That's close enough."

"They'll take one look at me and know," Will protested, trying again to jut his hip out, and nearly losing his balance in the
process.

"They won't look at you at all unless you give them a reason.
Take a few breaths, and then go on out. I'll be right behind you
if anything happens. There's a stair not far from here down the
corridor. Go up and use the first door you come to—that will

take you to the stables. Do *not* steal a horse—walk through like you're meant to be there. The pasture gate is always open during the day. Leave that way, hop the fence, and then——"

"Then I'm in Sherwood," Will finished. He turned toward the exit but hesitated. "How will you get out?"

Marian hid a smile. "Through the door. With the guard. I'm a noblewoman. He won't question me—he can't."

"Gisborne can." Will's face was grim, and Marian could not help but wonder what the Sheriff's man had done to him in captivity.

"Gisborne's gone. He's out chasing Robin—in the hollow you described to me yesterday."

Will was moving toward the exit again, but he stopped dead when she spoke, his flushed features going white. "The—the place I described? Marian, I thought that was a ruse, something you'd be using to get Gisborne on your side, I didn't think he'd actually . . ."

Marian blinked, trying to ignore the rising sense of wrongness, the infectious nature of Will's sudden fear. "Why? What is that place?"

"It's where Al—damn it. Friends of mine camp there, down in the hollow, because the light from their fire is shielded in the rocky canyon." Will swore again, dropping the basket.

Marian went cold. "Alan and John," she whispered. "Will—you told Gisborne where Alan and John are hiding?"

"*You* told him!" Will protested. "You had me——" He broke off, covering his face with his hand. "I'm sorry," he said finally. "Marian—thank you. You freed me. But I've got to go after them. Warn them, if it's not too late." He was so agitated, he didn't even think it strange she knew his cohorts by name.

Marian tried to imagine Will, half-starved, disoriented by

the sudden daylight, in a tattered dress, weaponless and on foot, saving Alan and Little John from a dozen of Gisborne's best men. "Will, no. You need to hide, recover your strength. Get out of England if you can—I can get you some money for passage—"

"While Little John and Alan hang?" Will's face was like a sky threatening to burst with rain.

"I'll handle it," Marian said, keeping her voice low and tight.

Will stopped his urgent pacing and looked back at her. "My Lady—"

"Shut up," she snapped. If the guard had come in while she was picking the lock, she might've been able to talk her way out somehow. But there was no help for them if he walked in while they wasted time arguing. "I got in here, I got you out—"

"But you're only one woman, and they're—"

"I'll get Robin to go!" she blurted.

Will took a step back, some of his agitation fading. "Robin?" He swallowed hard. "Then . . . then it was him, that night in the woods?"

Marian could have told him the truth. She could have explained, could have sat through the endless rounds of questions—*but you're a woman, and you handled a sword*—*but you're a girl, and you risked your life*—*but you're nobility, and you helped an outlaw*—and maybe he'd see what she was doing. Or maybe he'd just say, *But you're a woman.*

"Yes," Marian said, feeling empty. "It was Robin. I can get a message to him as soon as you're free, and he can make sure no harm comes to Little John or Alan. Tell me exactly where they are—anything that can help Robin find the spot before Gisborne."

Will's face cleared and then filled with such hope that Marian felt breathless to look at him. "My Lady," he repeated, and reached out to take her hand. The gesture was clumsy as he bowed over it and pressed his lips to her ring, but he did it with such heart that Marian couldn't fault him for his lack of gentility. He described the camp's location in detail, as much as he could.

"Go," she said.

And with one last look at her, Will hitched up the basket against his hip, ducked his head, and went.

Marian listened as she slipped her dagger back into the binding on her leg and adjusted her skirts. Her heart pounded on and on, until she thought it might burst—at any moment she expected to hear shouts and thuds and the scrape of a sword being drawn. But there was only quiet, and the distant sounds of life in the castle, and somewhere behind her, the squeak of a rat.

She took a few moments to work herself up into a state of agitation, and then rushed out into the corridor. The guard was so surprised that he drew his sword halfway, realized the "threat" was a woman, and a *noblewoman* at that, and tried to sheathe it again. She sobbed and wailed about being lost in the caverns and *so* frightened, babbling over the guard's confused questions. He shouted for assistance. Another servant appeared around the corner, saw the situation, and vanished again, presumably to fetch someone capable of dealing with her.

The guard tried to calm her down, and Marian was starting to feel a bit light-headed from all her gasping and carrying on, so she let him. But then he asked, for the fourth or fifth time, "How'd you get yourself down there, m'Lady?"

So, Marian fainted.

At least, she gave a theatrical sigh and let herself drop, anticipating that he'd catch her, and be so preoccupied with carrying her someplace more comfortable that he'd forget that rather vital piece of missing information. Instead, he jumped back in surprise, and Marian hit the floor rather harder than she'd planned. She banged her elbow quite hard on the stone, and all her effort went into keeping herself still and silent, eyes closed, instead of writhing around clutching at her arm.

I can see why you never spent much time in a faint before, Robin remarked. *Everyone is terribly inefficient at solving the problem.*

Servants and guards came and went until, eventually, they found someone high enough in the hierarchy worthy of laying hands on a noblewoman to carry her. She was nearly to her quarters when Elena arrived—Marian recognized her voice, her cry of alarm upon seeing her mistress in an apparent swoon, her agitated footsteps as she hurried on ahead to open up Marian's door and fold back her sheets. She took charge instantly, ordering the footman—for that was who they'd summoned to carry Marian—out of the room immediately.

As soon as the door closed, Marian risked opening one eye. She and her maid were alone.

She rose from the bed, limping a little, for the man had been gripping her legs rather too tightly, and her feet were tingling. Elena turned from the door and uttered another cry, this one of surprise.

"I'm fine," Marian said, forestalling her questions. "And Will's escaped."

Elena grasped at the door handle, the only thing nearby she could use to support herself. "Will?" she echoed. "Will's safe?"

Marian nodded. "I don't know how safe—but he's out of the jail, and if he did as I said, out of the castle by now."

Elena pressed her hands to her mouth, tears tracking down her cheeks and onto her fingers. Then she flew at Marian, stopped, hesitated, and glanced down. Ordinarily she'd stoop, kiss the hem of Marian's dress, clutch at her ankles as she thanked her. But Marian was tired—exhausted, really—and she could not stop yet, not unless she wanted to trade Will's freedom for that of Alan and John. Gisborne was hours ahead of her and could already be on his way back to Nottingham with his prisoners. She was *tired*, and she wanted to be happy Will was free, but she'd spent much of the day scrubbing floors, and everything about their situation was so ridiculous and so far beyond convention that she thought she might cry if Elena fell to her knees.

So she leaned forward and threw her arms around her maid, and drew her close. Elena hugged her back, pressing her face against Marian's shoulder, her arms tight.

"Thank you," Elena whispered.

As if the girl's warmth and solidity were catching, Marian felt a little stronger, a little less tired. She drew back and saw her maid's tear-streaked face split by a smile of such pure relief and joy that Marian found herself smiling back.

I did it, she thought, relief striking as sudden and shocking as a thunderbolt. And like lightning gilding a storm cloud, the realization seemed to illuminate her thoughts, giving them a crystal-clear edge. True, there was more to do. But she'd *done* it. No midnight fumbling, no fleeing for her life from Gisborne's sword.

She laughed, breaking free of Elena's clasp and dropping onto the dressing stool not far away. *A few minutes to rest*, she thought, *and then I'll ride out and look for Alan and John.* Tired? Certainly. Battered? Absolutely. But in this moment, Marian was immortal . . . untouchable. She'd freed a prisoner from the heart of Nottingham Castle, under the noses of the guards, without shedding a single drop of blood or triggering a single alarm.

She'd saved a man's life.

Looking back at her friend—she could not keep thinking of her as her maid now—she saw that her normally immaculate dress was spotted with dark stains, and that the hem on one side was ragged and black.

She blinked. "What did you do?" she asked, rubbing at her bruised elbow now she was free to do so. "As the distraction?"

Elena wiped her tears from her cheeks and smiled again. "I set the kitchen on fire."

NINETEEN

MARIAN'S EXHAUSTION WAS CATCHING up to her, and the familiar gait of her horse's canter kept making her eyes droop.

She'd hoped to encounter Midge in the stables, but instead found an apprentice perhaps five years her junior.

A little walk around the pastures, she'd said, smiling at the boy shyly, doing her best to imitate the sweet, inviting look so many of the other ladies cultivated when speaking to potential suitors. He'd blushed a fierce red, saddled up Jonquille, and strapped up her bundle without asking any questions.

All this time, Marian had thought, as she rode through the gates of Nottingham town, *I could have been getting my way with charm.*

It does come in useful, said Robin's voice, always on the edge of laughter. *I wouldn't have that in my arsenal, if I were there.*

Marian urged Jonquille forward. She had to get far enough into the forest to change, unseen, into Robin's clothes. Then she would gallop on to the hideout Will had described, and get Alan and Little John away before the Sheriff's men could find them.

The afternoon was bright, the sun filtering down through the leaves of the forest canopy. The emerald of summer was shifting to the topaz and carnelian of autumn, and with that shift the voluminous foliage of the forest was withering away. In the height of summer, there were areas of Sherwood where she could have passed within twenty paces of Gisborne's men and they wouldn't have seen her. Now, she had to keep alert, with a sharp eye on her surroundings.

She found a thicket of blackberries to occupy Jonquille— and provide a bit of shelter as she dismounted and changed her clothes. There was no one around, and yet one always felt in Sherwood as if one were being watched. The presence of the blackberry brambles all around her kept her bare skin from prickling quite so much as she changed.

Marian shivered as she pulled the hood of the cloak over her hair and face. It was autumn, indeed.

Gisborne had far too long a head start on her. But he'd be following the river, searching for landmarks that matched Will's vague description, whereas she was pretty sure she knew the spot he meant. She could save valuable time by riding straight there without pausing to search every rocky overhang near the river.

The river bend was a few leagues ahead still, but Jonquille's gait was starting to jolt. She'd held the mare at a canter too long, tiring her. She let her settle down into a trot, gritting her teeth against the bone-jarring bouncing.

When the granite boulders melted out of the distant foliage, Marian left Jonquille to drink at the river's edge and crept forward on foot, senses tingling. She saw no movement, heard no sounds except for the rustle of leaves overhead in the breeze and the distant, multithreaded tapestry of birdsong. She halted at the edge of the hollow, listening intently, but heard nothing out of the ordinary.

Finally she gave up and slipped around the stones, eyes scanning the shady hollow. They had been here, certainly—Alan and Little John. The remains of a fire, or several to judge from the thickness of the ash, dominated the clearing, and they'd rolled up a few half-rotten logs to serve as benches. A pile of apple cores, brown and humming with flies, lay nearby, and by the far edge was a handsome pair of stag's antlers. Marian couldn't help but snort at their foolishness—the antlers were smooth and white and knobbly at the ends, obviously shed at the end of last winter, but a nosy patrol wouldn't necessarily have the wood sense to know that. They'd arrest them on the spot for poaching.

She didn't see the tracks until she'd crossed the hollow to examine the antlers. When she dropped her eyes, she saw that the earth was churned up by hooves, and not those of a single horse. At least half a dozen men had ridden up to the edge of the hollow, and then, Marian realized with a sinking, creeping feeling, ridden off at a gallop. If there had been footprints—if Alan and John had tried to escape—they'd been obliterated by the horses pursuing them.

Marian took off at a run. She didn't bother to whistle for Jonquille—Alan and Little John wouldn't have gotten far chased by horses, and she couldn't risk Gisborne seeing "Robin" riding Lady Marian's dapple gray.

She saw Gisborne's party through the trees, a glinting, sickly metallic tumor in the autumn colors of Sherwood. She crept closer, moving around toward the north where the trees were thicker and older, and provided better cover.

The first she heard of them was a roar of outrage, a bellow that made her halt in her tracks. She'd never heard Gisborne so angry—his was a cold, quiet fury. The shout came again, inter-rupted this time by a resounding, meaty thud. Now that she was close enough to see, she realized the shout hadn't come from Gisborne at all—it had come from Little John.

She'd been dumbfounded by the "little" man's height when they first met, unaccustomed to anyone towering over her. But now, seeing him surrounded by a swarm of the Sheriff's men, she was struck anew. They looked like children in their fathers' war regalia in comparison, with shortened toy swords to match. John was struggling in their grip, stronger than any one of them by far, but not stronger than six. Every so often he landed a blow that sent one reeling back, but there were more men than could gather round him at once, and another would replace his disoriented cohort in seconds.

There was no sign of Alan. Would she find him some dis-tance away, a crossbow bolt between his shoulder blades?

"Down!" a man's voice commanded, and a few of the men fell away. Gisborne strode up, holding John's staff, and swung it in a massive arc at John's head. John grunted and dropped to his knees, his eyes glazed. He'd brought two men down with him, and they scrambled out of the way as Gisborne readied the staff for another blow. Marian, crouching behind an oak, dug her fingers into the leaf mold to stop herself from rushing headlong into the fray.

Her heart was as cold as Gisborne's anger as she watched him drop Little John into the dirt, breathing hard, face grim. Some part of her, Marian realized, felt a strange pity for Gisborne, in obsessive pursuit of a man who didn't exist. But as the man prod-ded John's now unconscious form with an armored boot, Marian could no longer find so much as a glimmer of compassion.

When Gisborne turned, she saw that his face was red, one

eye half-shut with swelling. John had gotten in a few blows of his own before Gisborne felled him.

"Tie his arms and feet." Gisborne's voice was terse and hoarse. "And bring him round if you can, after you've made certain he's bound tight."

Marian could not come any closer or risk being spotted. Unarmed, she had to wait for her opportunity. If one of the men moved away to search for Alan, or to relieve himself, she could ambush him—take his sword and crossbow if she was lucky enough to get one of the bowmen alone. For now, she could only watch.

Gisborne had struck John so hard that at first, they could not even elicit a groan from the man as they slapped at his cheeks, trying to rouse him. Marian thought for a horrible moment that the blow might have killed him, until he did give a little moan, slumping over onto his side as they let him fall.

The forest around them was silent, the birds having fled, and the sounds of the Sheriff's men drowning out the whispering breeze. At least—most of the birds had fled. The *tick-tick-tick* of a robin's alarm call grated against her ears, high overhead. Gisborne must have caught up to John too close to the bird's nest.

But then Marian blinked. It was autumn—the spring's hatchlings had long since fledged, and only the presence of young would keep a territorial robin in the branches when the commotion below had sent the rest of the birds away.

A robin . . . ?

The clicking cry came again, and Marian's head jerked up in time to see something move in the branches above. It was little more than a shadow slipping from a thinner patch of leaves into concealment, but it was enough.

Alan.

Marian glanced round the edge of the oak's trunk once more, checking that she could still see each member of Gisborne's little hunting party, and then started up the tree. Climbing was a skill she'd taught Robin, rather than the other way around. He'd lived his early childhood in town, and when his uncle, the Lord of Locksley before his father, had died, he spent the first year or so falling out of so many trees it was a miracle he'd come through it intact. Marian had—quite ruthlessly—laughed at him.

She made slow progress this time, forced to test each new branch carefully to make sure it wouldn't quiver and wobble, betraying her presence to Gisborne or his men. And then, when she was high enough to see the dark shadow that was Alan, she had to pause to make sure her hood hung low, making it difficult to see.

She kept on the other side of the trunk from Alan, staying close to the bark and easing one eye out to look at him.

"Sard me," breathed the minstrel-turned-outlaw, staring, white-faced. "You do exist."

Marian had never heard that particular swearword spoken before, though she knew what it meant. She wondered what Alan would think if he knew he'd asked a woman to . . . well. She could laugh later, when John was safe.

She nodded, deciding to keep her speech to a minimum. Instead, she pointed at Alan, and then off into the trees, away from where they crouched.

Alan's wonder and shock at seeing a ghost made flesh faded, and his eyebrows drew together. "He's my mate." He spoke in a low voice, clever enough to know that a whisper would carry farther. "I won't leave him."

Marian sighed. In this moment, she could've wished he had a bit more of the heartless outlaw in him, a willingness to turn tail and leave his cohort behind. True, he'd double her manpower—but two unarmed people against a dozen were no more likely to win than one, and he'd make it harder for her to stay hidden. She shifted, looking down at the crowd below. They were still trying to rouse Little John. She could see the big man's muscles twitch, and thought he might be pretending unconsciousness.

Smart, though the deception wouldn't last very long. And Gisborne was getting impatient.

"Why are you here?" Alan asked, keen eyes sweeping over Marian's cloak, tunic, the well-fitted boots. She shifted her weight so she could withdraw the hand in his line of vision—her height gave her the seeming of a man, but she still had a woman's narrow fingers.

"To help." Marian kept her voice as low as she could. With a start, she realized that Alan wasn't unarmed after all. One hand gripped the branch on which he perched, but the other was clenched around his bow. How he'd managed to climb one-handed, Marian could not imagine.

"Why are you hiding your face?" Alan asked suspiciously, starting to lean sideways to get a better look at her, then stopping when she withdrew behind the tree trunk.

"I'm an outlaw." Marian smiled, though she knew Alan wouldn't see it.

"Yes, but *I* know you're Robin of Locksley. Why hide your features from me, unless you are not, in fact, who you claim by your dress and your manner?"

Marian bit her lip. *Minstrels,* she thought sourly. *Too clever by half.* Aloud, she said briefly, "I have my reasons."

Alan eyed her for a long moment, as she eyed his bow. How she could convince him to part with it, she didn't know, but John had teased the man for his poor skill with that weapon—and in Marian's hands, it could begin to even the odds against the Sheriff's men.

"You ought to wear a mask."

Marian's foot slipped, and she caught herself before she could fall against the branch. "What?"

"The hood is all well and good," murmured Alan, "but one quick movement—a duck here, a head butt there—and your game's up."

Marian blinked, secure in the shadow of her hood, not bothering to hide her surprise.

The suggestion made sense. The only masks she'd ever seen were the ornate, stiff plaster objects worn by jesters and thespians, but with some time and planning, she might be able to procure one.

Shifting his weight, Alan drew a small eating knife from his boot and pierced it through the fabric of his tunic, working slowly to avoid a louder sound of tearing cloth. Carefully he cut a strip of gray linen—Marian did not want to think about what color the tunic had started out—from its edge. Working more quickly now, he cut slits in the strip, widening them by unraveling the fabric until he had two holes—eyeholes, Marian realized.

He held the makeshift mask out, sheathing his dagger. "Go on," he said. "I won't look." He sounded like a lad promising not to watch his ladylove at her bath, and gave her a mocking smile.

Marian took the mask and waited until he'd averted his gaze, then retreated behind the trunk so she could fit the fabric to her face and knot the ends tightly behind her head. It wasn't perfect—she couldn't see as much out of the corners of her eyes, but that was already the case with the hood anyway. For once, she was glad she didn't possess a delicate nose and chin and generous full lips—Robin had always said her eyes were her best feature, and behind a mask, no one would see her long lashes. She drew the green wool back over her hair and peered out.

Alan was still looking away—down at John, who had given up his attempt to feign unconsciousness and was glaring mutely at Gisborne as the latter shot question after question at him. When Alan looked up in response to Marian emerging from behind the trunk, his expression was grim.

"Good," he said shortly, nodding at her appearance. "I'm not sure how much longer he has before Gisborne starts removing bits of him."

"I have a plan."

Alan's eyes switched between Marian and the tableau below, the crowd of armored men and Marian's belt, which held no sword. His doubt was clear in his gaze without him having to say a word.

"Did they see you before the two of you fled? Does Gisborne know who you are?"

Alan shook his head. "We heard them approach and fled. But Little John is not so fleet of foot as you might expect."

Marian tried to imagine the big giant of a man sprinting like a deer and shook her amusement off ruthlessly. "So for all Gisborne knows, the man with John was me." She paused. "The idea of the mask—you were an actor at one point, were you not?"

Alan's eyebrows rose in surprise, but he nodded. "As a lad. Before I was skilled enough to make my way as a minstrel."

"Then we will stage a little play."

In low, hushed voices they outlined their plan, and Marian was gratified to see Alan's expression lightening moment by moment. In her mind, it had seemed a fragile idea at best—but now, hearing it aloud and seeing Alan nodding, it felt possible. And, despite her exhaustion, Marian's heart was still flickering with the triumph of freeing Will from under Gisborne's nose.

"You're sure you won't hit John?" Alan asked, reluctantly letting Marian take the bow from him and slip the quiver from his shoulder.

Marian tried not to smile, now that he could likely see her mouth. "You're sure you can move fast enough?"

Alan grinned, but before he could respond, a shout rose above the rumble of voices below. Gisborne had hurled Little John's staff to the ground and thrown his head back, and was turning in a slow circle, scanning the forest around him. "I know you're out there," he bellowed. "In the shadows, hiding like the criminal you are. Robin of—but you are *not* Robin of Locksley. You are Robin of the Hood now, forsaking your right to live free so you can masquerade as nobility. I have your man, Robin—and if you will not show yourself at the sound of my voice, perhaps you will do so at the sound of his scream."

His sword scraped from its sheath. *I will never grow used to that sound,* Marian thought distantly, watching the dappled sunlight glint off the blade's edge. *He has a way of drawing it such that the very scrape of steel is a threat worse than death.*

She looked up and found that Alan had gone—he must have crept away through the branches as Gisborne spoke. *Good.* For their plan to work, he needed to start some distance away, on the opposite side of the clearing. She scanned the treetops, but could not distinguish the rustle of leaves at his passage from that of the wind.

Marian turned and lowered herself so that she could wedge one foot in the crook of a branch and brace the other behind her against the trunk. She tested the draw of the bow and inspected the fletching of the arrows Alan had given her. *I'm sure I won't hit John.* She echoed her promise to Alan in her mind, trying to still the sudden doubts that came crawling over her. An unfamiliar bow, arrows she hadn't fletched herself . . . Marian swallowed, her throat dry as dust.

She waited, watching as Gisborne stalked back and forth before Little John. She had to give Alan as much time to get into position as possible, but at any moment Gisborne might lose patience and harm John.

Harm him more than he already has, Robin corrected her grimly, as John's bruised head drooped toward the ground.

Gisborne waited too, but when there was no answer to his challenge, he turned toward Little John with a mocking tilt of his head. "What say you about loyalty now?" he said, barely loud enough for Marian to hear.

Little John seemed to consider the question, then spat onto the ground at his side.

Marian didn't hesitate a moment longer. She nocked an arrow and drew, not bothering to take a steadying breath first. This was one of the more battered arrows, and it buzzed through the air between two of Gisborne's men and thudded into the earth, making them swear and leap away. The bow still felt strange in her hand, but it was getting easier to shoot with abandon, to dismiss the tangle of fears and worries that made her hands tremble.

She let two more arrows fly, sending them to the men's feet as well. Half a dozen more swords slid out of their sheaths, and every one of the Sheriff's men stood alert now, jumping to their feet, scanning the canopy.

"Good afternoon, gentlemen!" Alan's voice seemed to come from everywhere, genial, almost amused.

Gisborne's eyes shot skyward and he stood turning and turning, confounded in his attempts to locate the source by the fact that the voice and the arrows had come from two different places.

"I am, as you so graciously named me, Robin of the Hood. And you, gents, are trespassing."

Gisborne continued to look around in a slow circle, his black eyes roving across the canopy, devouring every detail with an intensity he'd never shown when he gazed at Marian. "How merry," he said in a low, carrying voice. "I suppose that would make this your forest."

"It is mine," came the voice of Robin of the Hood, bright and cheerful. "That is my stone your crossbowman just kicked, and those are my leaves you tread under your boots."

Marian fingered the fletching of the fourth arrow she'd nocked to the string. Alan was enjoying his role—so much so that she felt a thread of unease tease at the nape of her neck. And it was making the men below nervous. They had the advantage, and yet their unseen quarry was laughing at them, mocking them.

All nervous—except for Gisborne. Gisborne was cool as iron. "This land belongs to the King." The point of his sword moved as he turned, inscribing a deadly circle as Marian watched from above.

"Then perhaps you should be kneeling."

Enough, Marian thought, and let the arrow fly without pausing to think. For a moment, she was herself again, and the arrow flew true. Instead of thudding harmlessly into the ground, this one whistled through the air and pinned the hat from a crossbowman's head to a tree a few paces away, making the man drop to his knees in surprise. Three of the horses reared, and one bolted, sending the rest milling about in confusion and fear.

Alan could not have missed that signal. Her eyes found a rustling of the canopy nearly opposite her around the clearing. Seconds later, a rain of acorns and branches sent those few of Gisborne's men who hadn't started running after their horses in pursuit of shadows. Alan abandoned stealth entirely, his path easily visible in the quivering branches and crashing leaves. When there was no ready branch for him ahead, he dropped to the ground and took off on foot.

Gisborne was already moving, shouting for a few of the men to stay with John. His horse had not bolted, but instead of making for the beast, he was sprinting after Alan. Marian's breath stuck in horror. They'd anticipated that, crippled as he was, he'd go for his horse. And over a short distance, mounting and getting up to speed would waste the valuable seconds that Alan needed to reach the spot he planned to hide. With Gisborne on his heels, he wouldn't be able to hide at all—he'd have to keep running.

Marian drew the bow, arrow at her cheek, eyes fixed on the black figure. She could prevent him from reaching Alan, or Little John, or anyone ever again.

What are you doing?

This time, Robin's voice in her head wasn't laughing.

Marian's eyes widened and then she blinked, muscles freezing. Slowly, achingly slowly, she let the force of the taut bowstring draw her arm forward, her fingers still gripping the base of the nocked arrow. Her knuckles were white by the time she trusted herself to let go without shooting.

She'd been about to kill a man.

A pained yelp from below wedged its way past her horror. She looked down to see that one of the milling horses had knocked down one of Gisborne's remaining men. There were four of them—more than Marian had hoped, but not more than she'd feared.

She shook her head, trying to rid herself of the sight of her arrow trained on Gisborne's back, and made her way silently down the tree.

The rest was laughably easy. While Alan sprinted and sweated and, for all Marian knew, fought, she had only to sneak up behind the smallest of the four remaining men and catch him in a stranglehold, her dagger at his throat.

Marian whispered in her hostage's ear, and in a shaking voice, he ordered the others to drop their weapons. Marian was shaking too, waiting to see if they'd call her bluff, watching the other three men size her up.

Sweat had loosened the knot fixing the mask around her head, and she realized that the sun was on her brow. Her hood had fallen backward—only Alan's mask had saved her from exposure. The grip of the dagger felt slick in her palm.

Then one of the men, a stout, bearded fellow with a hard mouth, slowly stooped and laid his sword down in the leaves. Marian's vision swam as the other two did the same. She inhaled shakily and whispered her next command.

"Un-untie the prisoner," her hostage quavered.

His comrades glanced at one another, and the bearded one eventually nodded, and they went to remove the bindings from Little John. Marian was half-afraid he'd emerge from captivity swinging, and that the resulting melee would break the tentative command she held, but he moved carefully once his hands were free, watching Marian with an unreadable expression.

"Tie them up," said her hostage, on her order in his ear. His fear was turning to chagrin, and when John had finished binding the other guards, he shot her a furious look as the big man led him off to join his fellows.

Marian waited until John had nearly finished with the last man's bonds, then slipped away, moving quietly until she'd put enough distance between them to break into a run. The longer she spent with Alan and John, especially in daylight, the greater the chance she'd be found out as a woman. And after that revelation sank in, it wouldn't be hard for them to realize *which* woman she was.

She ignored the sudden shout of surprise from John, out of sight behind her, as he realized his rescuer had vanished. Ears straining, she listened for sounds of pursuit. She was so focused, so intent on what she could hear, that she only saw the man who leaped out in front of her a fraction of a second before his fist slammed into her stomach.

She staggered back, all the air driven from her lungs. She dropped onto her knees as her assailant leaped back, waiting to see if she'd recover. Her pulse pounded a frantic tattoo against her temples as the rest of her body crumpled to the forest floor. She struggled and tried to gasp, but her lungs wouldn't work, stunned into uselessness by the sudden blow. The world around her grew dim, the green-gold of afternoon fading into a deep, velvety gray twilight.

"Breathe from here." Robin puts his hands on Marian's sides, against her ribs, looking over her shoulder.

"I can't breathe—I'm in this stupid dress!" Marian half draws the bow again, but she's too distracted, too frustrated, and she ends up dropping bow and arrow both into a pile at her feet.

"Ladies at court practice archery," Robin argues, "and they're in much fancier dresses than that one."

Marian scowls at him. "Ladies at court shoot genteel little bows whose arrows wouldn't scratch a squirrel."

Robin's own frustration surges a bit. "You think it'd be easier in a nobleman's tunic? The laces rub at your neck, and the sleeves—"

"Would you like to trade?" Marian's voice drops into that dangerous area, the one Robin knows well—she gets very quiet, right before she yells.

Robin knows better than to answer her.

Then she swears—a word that would've gotten him a boxed ear—and starts taking off her clothes, right there in front of him. Robin freezes, wanting to look around for anyone who might be near, anyone who might have found their combat training yard in the middle of the ripening wheat. But he also doesn't look away.

She tosses her dress in a heap, heedless of everything else—even

Robin—as she stoops and picks up the bow again, the breeze stirring her shift around her legs. This time, when she draws, she's focused, determined, calm. She breathes, and when she looses the arrow, it thuds into the rotted log target so solidly that it spins halfway around and falls off the stump.

Robin barely has time to see before she gives a delighted whoop and whirls, throwing herself at him, bow and all. He staggers back, arms going around her, her hair tickling his face, her sun-warmed skin pressing his cheek.

She's talking about the shot, about how much easier it is without the dress, about how well the breathing technique works, about the fletching on her new arrows, about how much closer to center her arrow was than his—but Robin's only half listening, because in his mind he can hear his mother's voice.

You might want to give the ring to her, someday.

"Marian?"

"You are never outshooting me again," she crows, her face shining. Then her brow furrows. "What?"

Robin's frozen again, mind emptying. "The . . . blade instructor. He's coming tomorrow to teach me more counters."

Her eyebrows lift and she's beaming again. "Meet you here after?"

Robin turns his back as she puts her dress back on again. He stares at the half-ripened wheat until the sunlight makes him dizzy.

TWENTY

"I'M TELLING YOU," WHISPERED a distant voice out of the darkness, "I'm going to look. I want to see who he is."

"And I'm telling you," said another voice, "that you'll get a knock on the head if you try."

Marian recognized the dry humor in that voice, but her mind was so muddled she could not make sense of it. She ached everywhere, and her face itched where it pressed against a carpet of dead leaves.

"And who's going to give me that knock?" said the first man, sounding sullen and incredulous all at once.

Alan—for it had to be the minstrel—laughed. "Maybe he'll give it to you himself. Looks like he's starting to come round."

Marian opened her eyes in time to see Little John mutter something under his breath. He cast a sour look at Alan before turning his attention to Marian. "You awake down there, Robin o' Hood?"

Marian opened her mouth to speak, but the only thing that

emerged was a little groan, and it was with great effort—and pain—that she started to sit up. Her body felt as though it had been bent in half and then dropped off a cliff.

"He took a pretty bad hit," Little John announced, grinning around a fat lip and swollen cheek of his own. "Dropped him like a stone."

"Not everyone is built like a bear," Alan said absently, crouching by Marian and peering at her face. He looked so intent that for a brief second, Marian had a flash of panic—but then she registered the feel of linen on her face and knew her mask was still there.

Marian licked her dry lips, looking from one man to the other, confusion still turning her thoughts to sludge. "Did you—carry me?"

"A ways." John grinned again.

Slung over his shoulder like a sack of flour, Marian thought, grimacing as she experimentally flexed her abdominal muscles. She could not tell which had done more harm, being punched in the gut or being draped carelessly over the giant's shoulders. "Thank you."

"We're not all that far from where we started." Alan spoke quietly, but without any hint of fear. "They've gone."

"How can you be sure?"

"Because they followed me half to Locksley by the time I lost them, that's how."

Marian finished sitting up, propping herself on one arm while making sure her hood was in place with the other. She looked around, blinking at the dim forest for long moments before she realized it wasn't wooziness dimming the landscape— the sun had set.

She started with a muffled cry and began struggling to her feet.

"Whoa," said John, raising both of his large hands in an appeasing gesture. "Calm, Robin. You're with friends."

"I must go," Marian muttered, drawing back and looking wildly about, as if she might spy Jonquille lurking in the twilight nearby. By now, Marian's absence from Nottingham Castle wouldn't just be noticed—it'd be everywhere. Gisborne could already be back, already know Will had escaped, and already know Marian had vanished shortly thereafter. . . .

"Leave him, John," Alan said, as John made a sideways movement to intercept Marian. "He'll fall down in a few steps anyway, and then you can carry him again."

Marian tried to suck in a deep breath, found her lungs still ached, and burst into a fit of coughing. They were right. She was in no shape to go tearing through Sherwood, on foot or on horseback, in the dark. But more important, she'd still have to explain where she'd been if she made it back.

Marian sank back down onto the ground, hunching over until she could rest her head in her hands.

"Easy," Alan said, voice a little gentler. "John spoke the truth. You're with friends."

Marian looked from one man's face to the other, their twin expressions full of triumph. They'd stood up to the Sheriff—his men, anyway—and won.

She knew the feeling well. It was the hot satisfaction that had shot through her when she'd realized she'd freed Will, and it was the warmth creeping over her now. "I'm sorry that Gisborne believed you to be one of my men."

"I'm not." Little John clasped his hands on his lap and grinned. "We were already outlaws. But now we're Robin o' Hood's men."

"Merry men," Alan muttered, sounding a bit sour. "Gisborne

called me 'merry.' How is that meant to be awe-inspiring, in the centuries to come when our tale is told and retold?"

John, undaunted by Alan's dismay, went on. "I've always said Alan and I are still here because we've got each other's backs, don't sell each other out for the bounty. But you—you've got all Nottingham's back."

Marian's eyebrows lowered, and she blinked at him.

Alan saw her hesitation and snorted. "You're already developing a bit of a reputation, Lord . . . ahem."

"Robin will do," she murmured cautiously, still frowning.

"Robin, then." Alan made a sweeping, dramatic gesture. "Come back to his people in their time of greatest need! Unafraid to shed the comforts of his station and live like the lowest of us! Willing to stand against the unjust laws of the land!"

"I haven't done anything," Marian protested, voice a bit faint.

"I beg to differ." The voice came from the darkness, so abruptly that Alan leaped to his feet, a knife appearing in his hand. John swore. Before Marian could react, however, Alan let out a yell and dropped his knife, and threw himself at the shadowy figure.

Marian staggered to her feet before she realized Alan was embracing the man, not attacking him. John let out a whoop, and it wasn't until she heard the newcomer laugh that she recognized him, like the sound had unlocked some distant memory.

Will.

"How'd you get out?" Alan was asking, holding the boy at arm's length and inspecting his features as best he could in the gloom.

"Um," said Will. "I had help."

Alan glanced over at Marian, and for a moment she felt like the two lives she was leading were slamming together, with her caught between them. "Robin?"

It was impossible to see Will's expression from where she was, in that darkness, but he shifted his weight uncomfortably. Marian had only time enough to realize that the truth—that his rescuer was a woman—would embarrass him, and to feel a stab of conflicted sympathy and irritation, before he blurted, "It was Lady *Marian*."

Surprise struck them dumb for a several breaths. Then both Alan and Little John broke into a laugh.

Will dropped into a crouch, letting Marian see some of his features. Then he scowled up at the others. "You wouldn't laugh if you'd seen her do it."

Alan shook his head. "I'm not laughing at you," he said. "Or at her. I'm just—what a pair you two make, taking directions from a noblewoman!" This last was directed at Marian.

Will looked over at her, seeing her as if for the first time. "Your Lady has my thanks."

"She got me a message," Marian said stiffly. "Telling me where to find Alan and Little John, thanks to you."

"Thanks to me," Will echoed sourly, a shadow crossing his features. His eyes fell on John's bruised features, and his expression grew longer.

Pity lapped at Marian's heart. His guilt was as unmistakable as if he had shouted it aloud. "If you hadn't gotten Gisborne out of Nottingham Castle today," she offered, "Marian wouldn't have been able to help you escape."

"It's worth a few bruises to see you free, lad," John added kindly.

Marian could not help but think of her father, probably at

table for supper even now. Would he be afraid for her? If they were home in Edwinstowe, it would not be strange for her to lose track of the time and be late returning to the house. But in Nottingham . . . there were people everywhere, noble and peasant alike, and they'd all notice how long she'd been gone.

She could say she'd been thrown from Jonquille's saddle and struck her head, and had been too disoriented to make her way back to the castle until morning. But even a cursory inspection of her head would show no bruise, and her apparent incompetence would give Gisborne all the reason he needed to curtail her freedoms when it came to leaving Nottingham.

The mental leap required for Gisborne to realize Marian could actually be the man he sought was massive, but it'd take only a tiny step for him to believe she might be *helping* Robin of the Hood. He already suspected she sympathized with him. And only an idiot—which, for all his faults, Gisborne was not— would fail to find suspicion in her unexplained absences.

"Why so pensive, Robin?" Alan's voice cut through her turbulent thoughts, as their attention shifted back from Will.

Marian looked up, scanning the faces of the men around her. "I'm trying to think of my next step," she said truthfully.

"Toward what end?" Alan asked.

"Ensuring no one else takes the blame for my actions. Particularly the three of you." She straightened. "You must leave Nottingham, leave England if you can. All of you."

She'd expected protest, particularly from Alan and Will, neither of whom would want to be parted from Elena. But she hadn't expected the loudest protest to come from Little John.

"To hell with that," he rumbled, in what passed for him as a low voice. It drowned out the others, though, and made Marian's bruised ribs ache.

She frowned, clenching her jaw. "I'm serious. Gisborne will believe you're all working with me, and that paints a target on all of you."

Alan broke in. "You saved our skins. None of us is going to forget that."

"Your skins wouldn't have needed saving if it weren't for me," Marian shot back.

"Will's did. He'd have hanged if they hadn't wanted to interrogate him. And you—well, your Lady—got him out."

Unable to sit still any longer, Marian ignored the pain in her abdomen and began to pace. Night had fallen, and the others were smart enough not to risk a fire in case Gisborne had left patrols to search for them. The canopy overhead wasn't particularly dense here, but charcoal-gray clouds hid the moon. The temperature was falling rapidly, and the movement warmed her aching body. "I can't keep coming to rescue you," she said finally. She knew the words would cut, but just now, she didn't care. Let them resent her—they'd be alive to do so.

"Even if we wanted to leave," said Will, "we've got nothing but our clothes, a few weapons, and whatever food we can forage. Hardly enough to get us to the next shire, much less over the channel."

"I can get you money." With a start, Marian remembered the pearl hairnet she'd stolen from Seild. It was still tucked inside Robin's tunic. She stopped pacing, retrieved the net, and tossed it to Will. "Each of those pearls would fetch enough to get you out of the country. The local merchants can't offer their full worth, but you can get enough supplies to travel, and save a few for passage on a ship."

The men inspected the delicate, pearl-studded net in silence. She couldn't see their faces clearly, but one of them—she thought it was Alan—whistled appreciatively. They didn't ask how she'd come by it.

Alan lifted his face, a pale oval in the dark. "You must need money yourself," he said slowly. "Robin or not, you don't have the wealth of Locksley lands to support you. Not now."

"I'm fine," Marian replied shortly. "Take it."

Will was holding the pearls cupped in both hands, gazing down at them with round eyes that caught the patchy starlight and glittered. It was more wealth than he'd ever touched.

Little John got to his feet, unfolding slowly, continuing to straighten long after Marian thought he'd reached his full height. "Maybe this would get us out of Nottingham," he rumbled slowly. "Maybe out of England altogether. But what then? Outlaws again, only this time foreigners to boot. This is our home. We'll not leave it."

Marian blinked. It was easy to dismiss John as a pile of dense muscle and bone, but she hadn't thought about what they'd do once they escaped. If it were her, she'd find relatives in France, or seek shelter in a convent, which always accepted novices of noble blood. But what recourse did *they* have?

"Don't think because we're outlaws that we're lawless," John went on. "We watch each other. We don't take from people as can't live without what we take. We're loyal to the crown, the true crown. And we'd be loyal to you, if you asked us."

Marian's throat tightened, and with a strangled sound she turned her back. Frustration and emotion both stole her voice, and she didn't want them to see her eyes growing damp. The moon was emerging from the clouds, its light painting the clearing in silver and lavender.

What was she to do with a trio of wanted men? *Wanted,* she thought. *What a joke of a word—they're wanted men because no one wants them.* "I can't ask for your loyalty, because I have nothing with which to reward you for it. I don't need your help."

A rustle of leaves made her glance over her shoulder. Alan was standing next to John now, and had laid a hand on the other man's arm to forestall his protest. The minstrel waited, considering, looking thoughtful in the moonlight. "Why are you here?" he asked finally.

"To help," Marian replied, echoing the explanation she'd given him when they hid in the trees above Gisborne's men. "And I've done so." *And it's over.*

The thought, rather than carrying relief, brought only a strange discomfort, a kind of unease that made her shift her weight from foot to foot.

"These pearls—if we don't use them to flee, they could help. They could feed some of those wretches begging at Nottingham's gates."

Will looked up, his expression torn, but when he glanced from the pearls in his hands to Alan's face, he added, "They could buy pardons for some of the other outlaws here in Sherwood, whose crimes don't yet warrant hanging."

Marian looked between them, turning back around to face them, her thoughts spinning. "They could pay for livestock levies and prevent foreclosure of Locksley lands." *As well as Edwinstowe,* she thought dazedly, remembering the angry helplessness on her father's face when he'd told her of the Prince's plans to raise taxes.

"Probably not all those things from a handful of pearls," Alan admitted. "But nobility travels these roads every day, laden with jewels like these."

Marian's heart was thudding so hard she felt certain the others would hear it. "It could help," she whispered. She was looking at the men, but the faces she saw belonged to the two boys she'd seen as she rode through the crowd of beggars outside Nottingham's gates.

"*We* could help," Little John corrected her gently.

"It's mad." Marian's vision blurred.

"True." Alan grinned. "But these are mad times. And the people are desperate for more than food or coin. Why do you think all Nottingham already knows Will's story of a man returned from the grave to defend and aid his people? I've spent my life as a minstrel. I know when an audience demands a hero."

Marian blinked to clear her eyes, and looked round at the three men, all standing now, all watching her and waiting. They knew she wasn't Robin of Locksley—but none of them had asked her to remove her mask. None of them had asked her real name.

They called her Robin o' Hood. The poor and the hopeless beggars outside Nottingham were not the only ones desperately seeking a hero.

The notion was absurd. But so were the laws draining this land and its people dry. How many more men would be forced from their homes into a life of robbery and danger because they could not afford the taxes demanded of them? How many men would hang before the King returned from the war and set the laws right?

Until that day, there was little anyone—lord or peasant alike—could do.

Except for those who already had nothing to lose.

Except for the outlaws.

Marian had begun this masquerade with only one goal—to save Will. She'd never intended that anyone should mistake her for Robin, only that they not recognize her. And even then, she'd never intended that "Robin" should continue to ride, continue to work, after the immediate danger had passed.

The moonlight was electric, as bright and galvanizing as the light of day, and Marian's whole body was tense with the excitement and fear she dared not betray to the others. She breathed hard, in and out, until she felt she could speak without her voice shaking.

"Dawn," she said. "We'll go to Nottingham, and we'll give out the pearls to the beggars there."

"And when they ask us who to thank for lining their bellies and buying them a place to sleep?" Alan's eyes were sharp.

Marian thought of Robin, his warmth, his generosity, the bond he shared with his people.

"We tell them the truth," Marian said finally. "We tell them it was Robin Hood."

TWENTY-ONE

MARIAN LEFT THE OTHERS to celebrate their newfound determination and went in search of Jonquille. She told them she had preparations to make, and they didn't so much as hesitate. They accepted her word in a way no one ever accepted Marian's.

She was still bubbling with that urgent sense of purpose. It buoyed her through the exhaustion that tried to drag her down. She knew that if she paused, she'd think about the folly of the idea, the ways in which it could never succeed, the sheer arrogance of it. . . .

The hubris of volunteering to be a hero.

Would Robin think such things? she wondered as she followed the river and located the spot she'd left Jonquille. The mare's tracks led upriver, and she traced them idly in the moonlight.

Robin wouldn't have wasted time worrying about the arrogance of the task, because all little boys grew up proclaiming that they'd be heroes someday. But little girls . . .

Little girls are told to be quiet, Marian thought, steps quickening.

And to wait, and to forbear. And to obey. Marian had never been good at any of those things, but she'd *tried*.

She'd wanted to be good at them. She'd had more lectures about expectation than there were stars in the sky. She hadn't needed them, and they weren't what had truly taught her what she was supposed to be—it was every glance, every word, every interaction with servant and lord alike.

The *world* had told her what she was to be. And she'd known all along that she wasn't enough.

She felt it keenly, the fact that she'd never be good at what was expected of her. She'd known it young, too, though she couldn't have articulated then what brought her such childhood agonies of unrest and resentment. She remembered Robin telling her, promising her, that he couldn't ask her to be anything she wasn't, but he couldn't help doing so. His existence had asked it of her—his love demanded it of her. She could not be his wife without striving for the rest of her life toward those narrow goals of gentle obedience and conformity.

She'd never have been enough. He might never have noticed, but it wasn't his disapproval that would've haunted her. It would've been her own.

Robin's death hadn't changed that. Even if she could evade Gisborne's pursuit of her hand, she would be married eventually to someone. She could forsake her father and her lands and enter a convent, but Marian's life would still be one of quiet and obedience. She couldn't change that. Marian's life had been ordained when she was born a girl.

But Robin Hood's life . . .

She found Jonquille dozing by a meadow full of wildflowers and whistled softly to wake her. The flowers growing clustered about the glen were half-closed now, huddled against the autumn night's chill, but Marian paused to breathe in the faint, ghostly echo of their perfume. She stroked Jonquille's nose, fingertips lingering against the warm, velvety skin, and laughed as the horse examined her hand. The agile lips moved past her fingers and explored her palm, searching for the treat Marian usually had for her upon greeting. Jonquille whickered a protest when she found nothing, and Marian moved closer so she could run her hands along the horse's neck.

Robin Hood wasn't just a man, or the ghost of one. He was a hero. A symbol.

Marian stood stroking Jonquille's neck, her movements automatic, her eyes seeing not the moonlit glade but rather flashes of a strange other life. A vision of herself, hooded, armed with her bow, leading Alan and Will and John and a faceless crew of others to take back what the Prince, through the Sheriff, had stolen from this land. The freedom of abandoning her life at Edwinstowe, the relief of never being forced to marry, of never speaking to Gisborne again except in battle.

She'd get a message to her father somehow, so he'd know she was alive. Elena would marry Alan and join their band. They'd set up a permanent camp, deep in the caves or else hidden in the treetops. Someday Marian would reveal her identity, and the weight of what she'd already achieved would be all the men needed to acknowledge her as an equal.

A wet, hot puff of air on her neck shattered the vision, and Marian jumped. Jonquille chuckled at her, horsey lips fluttering, then gusted another grassy sigh in her face.

Marian swiped at her eyes with her sleeve. She might as well have been dreaming, for all the reality the idea had. Every moment she spent with the others risked discovery, and when they found she was a woman, she'd be their nominal leader no longer.

Her father would be heartbroken if Marian went missing, and if her identity under Robin's hood became known, most likely he'd be hanged as a coconspirator. There would be no one after her father to care for Edwinstowe, and the lands would be given to one of the Prince's devotees, like he'd given Locksley to Gisborne.

And Gisborne . . . Gisborne would not rest if Marian simply disappeared. He'd assume it was the work of Robin Hood and commit himself to the man's capture all the more.

Marian hesitated, an idea seeding itself in her mind. She was already too late to get back to Nottingham without raising the alarm of her absence. And in her mind's eye, the storeroom full of grain bound for trade taunted her, sitting behind the walls of stone that separated it from the people gathered in the streets of Nottingham. People who needed it to fill their bellies.

Her lips curved into a smile. She reached for Jonquille's saddlebag and got to work.

By the time she reached the camp where she'd left the others, the sky above the treetops was beginning to lighten. Marian could tell they were awake before she could see them. The intermittent rustle of leaves told her someone was pacing, and the low murmur of voices sounded agitated.

"We have the pearls," Alan was saying. "If he doesn't come back, we do what we said. We give them out at Nottingham's gates. We tell them it's a gift from Robin Hood. And we worry about Robin later. He can take care of himself."

"And if the guards try to stop us?" That was Will, his pacing footsteps halting as he spoke.

"We fight." John's voice was heavy.

Will let out a sharp bark of humorless laughter and started pacing again.

Marian, astride Jonquille, took a long, slow breath and made her way into the camp.

Alan and Will were already standing, backs toward her, but John leaped to his feet and let out an oath that signaled to the others that they had company. They stared, for the figure atop the horse was not the one they'd expected to see.

Marian reached up and self-consciously smoothed a hand over her veil, feeling strangely naked in her lady's attire, faced with the three outlaws, who all gaped at her. The rest of Robin's clothes were in her saddlebag, but the cloak she held draped across her saddle. "Good morning, gentlemen," she said lightly, smiling in sheer relief at not having to strain her voice to the lower tones that—she hoped—sounded more masculine.

"Lady Marian." Will took a step toward her but halted when he saw the thick green cloak. "Robin—is he—"

"Safe and well," she said. "I was about to ride out to look for you when Robin arrived in Nottingham and told me that you were safe. He also told me about your plan this morning. We've made a few additions."

Will's face was flushing with agitation. "But he—for God's sake, my Lady, you can't be here. The danger—if you'd been found by a different band of men—not to mention when the rest of Nottingham wakes to find you missing—"

"Let us accompany you back to the edge of town," Alan suggested, firmly breaking in across Will's stuttering. "We're going that way already, and we'll make certain you're safe."

Marian was torn between anger at their misplaced chivalry and the absurd desire to laugh. Instead she only shook her head. "I know these woods nearly as well as Robin does. And I'm pivotal to his plan."

"If you join us in handing out alms, they'll know you're

sympathetic to Robin, if not outright helping him."

"Not that part of the plan," Marian said patiently. "The pearls aren't enough. They'll feed a few people for a few months, but they're a . . . a statement of mission at best. We need to—"

"We need to think bigger," Will interrupted, striding through the leaves, eyes lighting. "Aim for richer targets . . . maybe use the pearls as bribes, get information about the nobles staying at Nottingham. There's more where these came from."

"Steal from Nottingham?" Little John looked dubious.

"I—" Marian barely got the word out before Alan rounded on John.

"Why not?" asked the minstrel. "That's probably where Robin got the jewels in the first place. Our faces aren't so well known—well, Will's maybe—but we could get in and out of the town without difficulty."

Marian wanted to demand their attention, but if she let herself act too much like "Robin," it'd be all the easier for them to make the connection. Instead she cleared her throat, and then again, and finally raised her voice enough to be heard over the others: "Gentlemen, please listen."

Little John heard her and shushed the others. "Pardon, my Lady. Thank you for bringing us the news that Robin's safe."

Marian held on to her temper with an iron will. "I'm bringing you news of a plan," she said again. "To steal the Sheriff's entire shipment of grain headed for market by month's end."

That, finally, brought silence. All three men went still, wearing such identical expressions of stupefaction that Marian almost laughed. Alan's was the first face to change, growing thoughtful as his surprise faded.

"That's got to be whole wagons full," he said slowly. "I can't imagine the Sheriff allowing three men—four, if Robin somehow has a plan for getting in without getting his neck stretched—to lead an entire caravan through his gates."

"That's because he'll send it to us," Marian replied. "In exchange for a hostage."

Alan's eyes widened, then shadowed, his expression carefully blank. Will and John, however, simply frowned at her. She waited, and when enlightenment failed to dawn on them, Marian dismounted, hauling Jonquille's reins to hang down to the ground and then holding out her hands with a smile. "I'd rather you not tie me very tightly, but I ought to have some marks from bindings by the time I get back to Nottingham."

TWENTY-TWO

THE SUN WAS CLEARING the trees at the horizon when Marian heard the low, distant murmur of surprised voices. Something—or someone—had awakened a few of the beggars camped outside Nottingham's walls.

She'd left the others their instructions—orders from Robin—and made her way west around the wall encircling the town. There was a place where the stones' mortar was crumbling, or had been years ago, when she'd discovered it during another of these meetings of the lands' nobility. With some work, it'd be possible to remove enough of the stones to squeeze through, although that wasn't what Marian intended.

Instead, she'd been removing scattered pieces of stone, at seemingly random intervals up the wall. Using those excavations as footholds, she climbed to the top of the wall and peeked over the other side to make certain she was where she meant to be. A shallow, marshy ditch ran around the inside of the wall, but beyond it was a cluster of slumped, crooked houses, and a narrow lane that would soon be occupied by waking townsfolk going about their days.

Marian dropped back down on the outside of the wall. Her skirts caught on the rough, rocky wall and nearly knocked her off balance, and she swatted at them irritably. At her feet were Robin's cloak and Alan's bow and quiver.

Robin will meet me in the forest, she'd told her men, as they moved, leading the mare, toward Nottingham. *This message tied to Jonquille's bridle will tell them his demands. You three will go to Nottingham as planned, give out the pearls, and tie Jonquille to the gates. By the time a guard comes, you must all be safely away, back under cover in the trees.*

They had protested, all of them, but especially Will. His eyes were passionate as he spoke over Marian, telling her that it was too dangerous for her, that she'd already risked too much in freeing him, that they could use some other ruse. When she'd asked him to provide an alternate plan, though, he'd fallen quiet, merely looking at her with anguish.

She'd kept Alan's bow after he'd promised her he could get another, and one for Will as well, so that they'd have more than Little John's staff should they run into trouble. And then she'd checked that the missive in Jonquille's bridle was secure, reassured her mare as Will approached her warily, and watched as the three set off toward the town. She'd waited until they were out of sight before breaking into a run at an angle, aiming for the western part of the town.

Marian might have to play two roles this morning, if there were any snags in their plan. Now that she stood looking down at her costume, she was restless not with fear, but with anticipation. Robin had triumphed—albeit without much grace in some cases— every time he'd come up against Gisborne and the

Sheriff. Today would be no different, except that instead of just trying desperately to save herself and the small handful of people she could defend, she was taking action against their enemies.

The spot where she stood was still in shadow, but over her shoulder dawn was touching the distant edge of Sherwood Forest with rosy fingers and resurrecting the autumn colors from the leaching darkness. Though she could not see the crowds at the gate, she wasn't all that far away, hidden around the curve of the western wall. The indistinct murmur of far-off conversation had risen and smoothed as more voices joined in, and when one voice rose over the others in a cry of relief and gratitude, Marian knew that the "merry" followers of Robin Hood, as Alan had called them, were continuing their work handing out Lady Seild's pearls.

Moving quickly, Marian tied back her hair and secured her mask. She was wearing her dress, for there was no room in the timing of her plan to change her clothing. But she'd wound her skirts about her thighs and tied them, and once she'd donned the green cloak, she might as well have been wearing men's clothes.

As Robin, she crept back along the wall, one hand against the stones, the other gripping the bow. The grass gave way to mud, and as she rounded the curve, she saw the mud dotted with rickety lean-tos and bedrolls. They were empty, however, and once she caught a glimpse of the crowd, she knew she'd interpreted the sounds correctly. She could not see Alan and Will in the press of people, but she could see Little John's head above the others, grinning broadly and shouting greetings and well-wishes in response to the mixed cries of entreaty and gratitude.

Marian's eyes slid left, and she saw Jonquille by the gates, shifting her weight nervously and watching the crowd. There was no sign yet of the guards, but the commotion would bring them at any moment. *Go,* she shouted silently, gaze shifting back to John's smiling face. *Don't stand there basking, GO!*

But as she grew more and more accustomed to the voices, able to pick out more of the conversation, she realized why they were lingering. Alan was doing most of the talking, telling tales of Robin o' the Hood, the nobleman-turned-outlaw, the legend who'd returned from the grave to help the people in their time of trial.

She heard the murmurs of awe and excitement, and she could not blame them for staying long enough to make sure their message struck home.

Alan had paused, just before they parted ways. At the edge of the forest, he'd gestured to the others and turned toward Marian with a troubled look.

"He's not Robin," he said quietly. "Will says his manner is different, and his voice is not the same. But you, my Lady—you know him. Knew him. Both of them—the man who died in the Holy Land, and the man who now bears his name, who sent you here to us."

Marian's heart pounded, and she knew her face must show some of her tension, for Alan's gaze softened.

"Who is he?"

Marian had known the question would come, though she had hoped they'd wait until after the success of their plot. If they failed, she wouldn't have to explain anything to them. But she'd rehearsed her answer as she made her way back to the camp with Jonquille, saying over and over the words she hoped would put an end to their questions.

"It isn't the same man," she agreed. "He's no man I've ever met before. But this man—this Robin of the Hood—he shares

Robin of Locksley's heart. They're of the same spirit. I feel as if I've known him all my life, the way I knew Robin. I trust him as I'd trust myself." The others were listening, standing some paces away, and Marian had to pause to draw in more breath to keep her voice steady. "I cannot explain it, Alan-a-Dale, any more than I can explain God or the sunrise. But perhaps something of Robin of Locksley's soul is here, as Will believed that first night. Perhaps, though it's not the same body, it is in some way the same person."

Little John had glanced upward, lips moving as if in a silent prayer. Will was watching her speak with an echo of the passion with which he'd pleaded for Marian to stay safe and out of trouble. Alan, though, was gazing not *at* her, but *through* her, as though his eyes were seeing something of that same vision Marian had experienced, imagining the life she could lead as Robin Hood. He blinked, his eyes rimmed in red, and turned away.

"I hope you're right, Lady."

Now, half-concealed in the shadow of the wall, Marian fingered the fletching of the arrows at her hip. If the guards came, and came quickly, she would have to single-handedly buy Robin's men—*her* men—time to escape.

A scrape from the gates jerked her attention away from the seething mass of bodies surrounding her cohorts. The gates started to creak open, but at an outraged whinny of protest from Jonquille, they paused long enough for one bewildered guard to slip through and deal with the horse and get a look at the chaos outside. Marian looked back at the crowd, and this time she could not see John, nor hear Alan's voice. She lifted her eyes and caught a glimpse of a few shadows vanishing into the trees.

The turbulent mass of people pressed in around the gates, stirred up by their excitement—and, for those who'd been lucky enough to receive one of the pearls, their need to find a merchant who would trade for them. The lone guard called out in confusion, and one of his fellows came out to help usher Jonquille in through the gates, which closed again behind them.

Marian let her breath out and then withdrew, squatting by the wall in the dubious shelter of a lean-to that would've done little to protect its occupant from the weather. She leaned her head back against the rock, eyes open and ears tuned, and began to wait.

The guards would have to bring Jonquille to the stables. It would take time for her to be recognized by someone who knew she was Marian's horse. More time to connect the horse's arrival and the lady's disappearance. At some point someone—a stableboy—would notice the message tucked into Jonquille's tack. More time to locate someone capable of reading it.

And then . . . Marian had no way of knowing how long it would take the Sheriff to act on the note's contents. Or *if* he would act. Certainly, on the surface, he could not sacrifice the life of a gentle, well-bred noblewoman to protect his material gains. But the Sheriff had not gathered such power without the use of his wits, and she could not be sure he wouldn't find some way of justifying a refusal to cooperate.

Though nothing he said would justify it to her father.

She tried to put thoughts of him out of her mind. She was safe, and regardless of what transpired, "Robin" would not harm Marian, and she'd eventually return to her father and ease his fears. But her imagination kept summoning images of him, face lined with worry, refusing to eat, refusing to sleep, shouting down the Sheriff himself in a demand to put all his resources into finding his daughter.

Then it would take time to arrange the wagons and their

contents. Three carts, the note had specified, and one driver to each cart. No bags larger than a child. Nowhere for more men to conceal themselves in order to ambush the others once the carts had arrived in Sherwood. No guards driving the carts, but kitchen staff. Untrained and unarmed.

Do as I instruct, the message read, *and no one shall come to any harm. You have my word as a nobleman and as an outlaw. Robin Hood.*

The note described a location that would serve as the first of three waypoints in the forest, designed to mislead pursuers if they should come after the carts. John, Will, and Alan would track their progress and eventually order the three men down from the carts, escorting them some distance back toward Nottingham, where they'd be released to return to the town.

And Marian would be "found," shaken and bruised at the wrists from her bonds, but safe. Robin Hood would never have to show his face.

But that was only if all went as she had planned. If her previous excursions as Robin had taught Marian anything, it was that things *never* went according to plan.

The sun had retreated behind a thickening sheet of gray, and as the day wore on, the sky let fall a thin, cold drizzle of rain. Marian tucked her cloak more closely about her, reminding herself that those unfortunates who had crowded so gleefully around her men at dawn, and who were now scattered about the exterior of the walls, sat in the downpour every time it rained. But it didn't stop her from thinking, longingly and guiltily, of the warmth of the fire in her bedchamber or the chest full of dry underclothes.

The people nearby largely ignored her. The increasingly heavy gray rain had muted the color of her cloak somewhat, and none of them were looking for their grand, legendary hero among the miserable wretches huddled by the walls. The owner of the lean-to she squatted by was a man about her father's age, but thin and wearing a grizzled beard, who gave her a suspicious look when he'd returned to find himself with a neighbor. But when she merely gestured *by all means* to the filthy pallet under the lean-to's shelter, he shrugged and turned his back on her as he curled up in his rags.

A face appeared amid the gray drizzle. It belonged to a girl some distance away, peering around the edge of a woman's skirt. She was young, no more than seven or eight years. Marian could not help but look at her, reminded with a sudden, strange pang of Robin as he'd looked after his mother died. Thin and angry and in a kind of pain that defied comfort or logic.

The girl was staring at her, and too late Marian realized that while most of the people around her weren't looking for their hero among them, children were not so blinded yet by practicality and experience.

So Marian smiled, and when the girl's eyes widened in response, she lifted a finger to press it to her lips. The girl's mouth opened, though Marian could not hear her gasp over the rain. Then she vanished again behind her mother's skirts.

The gates opened, pushed across the mud by a pair of guards at each door. Marian's breath caught, and she gripped her bow, watching. She could hear the creak of wheels and the thump of hooves, but not until the first cart emerged, driven by a boy wearing the spare, worn tunic and leggings of a servant, did Marian take a proper breath again.

Mary's tits, she thought, echoing Will's epithet in her mind with joyful rebellion. *It's working.*

She watched the three carts trundle along, the beggars

melting out of their path ahead of them. The gates stayed open, but that wasn't unusual—the gates of the town opened each morning as a matter of routine. A few of the poor—those with pearls to sell, no doubt—darted inside. The carts moved along, and though Marian's gaze kept darting back toward the gates, no one emerged to follow them.

Movement caught Marian's eye, and she scanned the carts. Every word of her instructions had been followed, to the letter. There were no large bags, no convenient places for soldiers to hide. And yet something nagged at her, something she'd seen out of the corner of her eye that was the tiniest bit . . .

There. The driver of the third cart. There was nothing strange about his appearance—from this distance she could see only dark hair, a nondescript build, a slump in his spine as if of nervous resignation, like that of the other servants driving. But while Marian watched, he took one hand off the reins and slipped it into his tunic. He withdrew something, and with a jolt, Marian realized it was the note from Jonquille's bridle, and that he was scanning the words on it, head bowed.

What kitchen servant knew how to read?

In one movement, Marian launched herself to her feet and nocked an arrow to the bowstring. "I said no guards!" she shouted, voice low and harsh, cutting through the rain and across the scattered conversations among the people between her and the cart.

She spoke without thinking, too intent to fear betraying herself with her voice. The effect was instantaneous and unmistakable—but no one recognized her woman's voice. Instead they saw a man in Robin's green hood, bow drawn. Conversation ceased and people fell back with exclamations of fear and amazement. A few scrambled out of the way, although the path away from Nottingham led downhill, and on the higher ground she could fire at the carts without worry of hitting anyone in between.

She hesitated only a moment, remembering that flash of cold calculation that had led to her nearly shooting Gisborne in the back, and then let the arrow fly. It hummed through the air— distantly, in her own mind, Marian made a note to teach Alan how to properly fletch an arrow so it would fly silently—and struck its target.

The driver fell back with a cry into the sacks of grain as the horse, startled by the sound of the arrow thudding home, skipped up into a trot for a few paces.

The man in the cart sat up, head turned toward the arrow that had whistled past his nose, pierced the paper in his hand, and pinned it to the wood of the cart. Marian was aware of mur- murs of admiration and excitement among the people around her, but she had eyes only for the guard disguised as a servant. He was still staring at the note and the arrow, but then he started to turn in search of the source of the missile, and that was when Marian's heart sank.

It wasn't a guard at all. It was Gisborne, and his dark, biting eyes had gone straight to her.

TWENTY-THREE

FOR A LONG MOMENT they stared at each other across the mud and the huddled watchers. Rain drove the rim of Marian's hood low and plastered Gisborne's hair to his brow. A wind rose sluggishly, etching a curving sheet of water into the air that stretched between them. They were so far apart Marian could not be certain he had heard her voice, and yet she saw his chest rising and falling as he breathed, saw the scarred flesh at his throat move as he swallowed. She saw his eyes burning.

A voice from the crowd, thin and sharp with sullen fury, shouted, "You missed! Kill 'im, Robin!"

Marian whirled to run, slipped in the mud, and fell hard onto her knees. A glance over her shoulder told her that the shout had broken the spell for Gisborne, too—he dove into the sacks of grain and emerged with his sword in his hand, scrambling amid the cargo until he could vault out of the back of the cart. He might walk with a limp, but he could run fleet as a foxhound when he chose—she'd seen him on Alan's heels in the forest.

"Keep driving," he shouted at the other carts. "If they have the lady, you must make the exchange."

Marian scrambled upright and broke into a sprint, dropping the bow and wrenching the quiver free so she could move unimpeded. Her boots slid with every step, and the muscles of her hips and inner thighs screamed with the effort of staying upright.

When she'd been planning for the possibility that she'd need an escape, the section of wall she'd tampered with had seemed dangerously close to the front gates. Now the wall curved ahead of her, stretching on toward the horizon. The mud underfoot gave way to grass, but before she could shift her focus from balance to speed, her boots slid against the wet blades and shot out from under her. She ducked her shoulder, turning on instinct so that she could roll when she hit the ground, and managed to use her momentum to get to her feet again.

But her slip had cost her valuable seconds, and as she reached up to pull her hood down low to hide her hair, a hand shot out of the drizzle and slammed into her shoulder. She skidded backward, breath driven from her lungs as she hit the wall. Her head snapped back and she would've been knocked cold had she not had the knot of hair at the back of her skull to cushion the blow.

Dazed, ears ringing, she forced her eyes to focus in time to see the hand coming at her again. She ducked, and twisted, and grabbed for the arm as it passed her, and threw all her weight against the body the arm was attached to, and sent it into the wall with a sickening thud.

Gisborne reeled back, swinging, but Marian had danced out of his reach. She could have cursed herself, had she the breath for it—all this time she'd counted on the fact that these men, her allies and enemies alike, saw what they expected to see and believed what they knew to be true, and in the space between,

Marian had Robin Hood. But she'd looked straight at Gisborne in that cart, and all she saw was a servant in a faded jerkin.

He looked different in his beige tunic, without the unrelieved black of his usual attire. Marian knew now why he preferred that shade, for his scars were all the more visible above the pale collar of his shirt. Gisborne put a hand to his mouth, and Marian saw a flash of crimson on his fingertips before he spat into the mud at their feet.

His sword lay next to them. She'd been lucky, for had he simply struck with the blade, Marian would be dead now instead of standing poised on the balls of her feet, facing her opponent, watching his blood mingle with the rain as it puddled and began to course down the slope away from Nottingham. The sword was no closer to him than to her.

Gisborne's gaze followed hers, a flick of his eyes only, and he spared breath and focus enough for a twitch of his lips, a wryness that called an answering sense of the absurd from Marian. "You're not that fast." His voice was calm, as calm as if they were speaking over a game of dice, and yet there was an intensity in his face that gave him more life than she'd ever seen in him before.

Go, shouted Robin in her mind. *You stay, you speak to him, and you're playing his game. Abandon your plan, head for Sherwood, and figure out how to bring "Marian" back. Run.*

But Marian felt her own lips twitch. "You don't know me." Experimentally, she shifted her weight with a barely perceptible movement to the right, her eyes on her opponent. Gisborne matched the movement, head tilting left, so that she stayed exactly in the center of his focus.

"You're of noble birth," Gisborne said quietly, watching her. "Disgraced one too many times with the household servants, or else a bastard son banished when you came of age. Either way, you've never belonged. You've never been offered greatness—you've had to create your own. And this is how you've chosen to do it. Stealing trinkets from helpless women and pretending to be the people's savior."

Marian kept her face immobile. The mask was still in place across her eyes, but how much else the hood concealed in this light, she could not know. *I'm no bastard,* she thought. But the rest . . . had she not spent the small hours before dawn telling herself this masquerade was worth it, for a chance at greatness, as Gisborne called it? A chance at being a hero?

She must have revealed something in her face, for Gisborne's lips twisted in grim satisfaction. "I've had plenty of time to think about who you are," he continued. "Not your identity, though I intend to find that out once you're in irons, because I do mean to take you alive. But who you *are* . . . that need to rise, to be acknowledged? I recognize you well, brother."

Rain lashed at her hot cheeks as Marian battled the urge to break the impasse and strike. The smugness, the arrogance of his assumptions—the implication that she was, that she could ever *be* anything like Gisborne . . . her breath came faster.

He's trying to rattle you, said Robin. *Be as cold as he is.*

Marian breathed deep. She wasn't far from the spot where she'd planned to evade potential pursuers, but she'd never make it with Gisborne on her heels. She moved carefully, easing to the side with one step, slowly, showing no threat. "I am not your brother."

"No," Gisborne agreed, his seeming amusement vanishing from his face. He straightened a little, as though put somewhat more at ease by her nonthreatening stance. "But we are kin nonetheless, in this world that judges a man's worth by the color of his blood." He touched his fingertips to his lip again, which he must have bitten when he hit the wall. He huffed a sour laugh and held up his hand as if to show her the watery red trickling down his wrist with the rain—and then he was moving, lunging at her with shocking speed.

Marian dropped to the ground, lashing out with her knee as she moved and sending Gisborne sprawling in the mud. She scrambled back up, slipping and sliding and cursing, and made for the wall. Her fingertips brushed the edge of the stone, and then something wrapped around her throat and hauled her backward, choking.

Gisborne had the edge of her cloak, and with a second heave he flung her down to the ground and rolled on top of her, breath quick and eyes burning.

Still choking, Marian jabbed an elbow into his gut and tried to get purchase on the ground, but Gisborne just grunted and her boots only skidded, and then he was ripping at the mask while she pushed at his face to try to get his weight off her ribs. Robin had never treated her this way, not during their worst fights, and Gisborne was bigger than he. She could not move him, could not breathe, could not stop him. . . .

She groped at the mud and her fingertips brushed something cold and hard. Not a rock. Metal.

Marian tried to gasp for breath and could only gurgle, the hasp of the cloak still digging into her throat, the rest of the wool wound round her body.

"Stop fighting me," snarled Gisborne, the calm cracking for an instant, as quick and bright as lightning. "There's still time for you to show some honor, man."

Honor. Marian could have laughed. These noblemen with their honor, as though honor was a deity greater than God himself, to be worshipped and feared and respected above all else.

Robin spoke of honor, when he told her he was going to fight at the King's side in the Holy Land. Her father spoke of honor too, in his attempts to comfort her after she'd learned of Robin's death. He told her that he'd died with *honor*.

Honor or not, Robin was still dead.

Marian went limp, surprising herself with how easy it was. She thought she'd have to fight every instinct to make herself stop struggling. But the fight drained down, down, out of her hands and her legs and deep into her body, where it nestled, burning and tight and hidden, in the pit of her heart.

Gisborne's grim smile wrestled its way back over the snarl, and he lifted his head. "Good. Now, roll over and—"

Marian jerked her body sideways, taking advantage of the slight laxity in Gisborne's grip, and curled her fingers around the hilt of the muddy sword. So close together, his weight still driving her into the sodden ground, she could not use it like a blade, so she swung its hilt with all her strength into the side of Gisborne's head.

The man went sprawling, and Marian moved.

Her vision was dim with lack of air, and every instinct told her to double over, to claw for breath. But she ran, instead, and made for the wall again. Through the rain she could not see the divots she'd made by chipping away at the stones, and her fingertips scrabbled against the wet limestone until they found one of the handholds. She climbed, her fingers numb with cold, her muscles burning with fatigue. Her whole body was braced, ready for that horrible, suffocating clasp of wet wool and metal when he caught at her cloak again. Any moment, and he'd drag her down off the wall . . .

And then her grasping hands met with air.

Marian blinked rain and sweat out of her eyes and focused

on her palm as it pressed against flat stone. The top of the wall. She pulled herself up, shaking, and looked down. Gisborne was lying in the mud where she'd left him, and for a moment she sat there, one leg still hanging over the edge of the wall.

Had she killed him? Perhaps that terrible moment in Sherwood, when she'd sighted down the shaft of her arrow at his back, was prophecy, not warning.

She ought to be frightened. Horrified, as she'd been in the forest. But her blood was pumping hot and fierce, and the knot of resolve and fight in her heart was unchecked. She looked down, and for a moment, she was *glad*.

Then Gisborne's legs moved, and he groaned and rolled over.

And Marian slipped over the wall, hung down as far as she could on the other side, and dropped down into the marshy trench. Her legs ached with the impact, and she looked around wearily. She saw distant shapes, blurry through the rain, but no one nearby. With an involuntary moan of reaction, she dragged herself up out of the trench, peeling the heavy wool cloak from her shoulders. She'd intended to hide it in the thatch of a house closer to the castle, to be retrieved that night in darkness, but she couldn't risk moving with it now. Gisborne might go after the carts if he was well enough to ride, but Marian thought it was more likely he'd go after Robin Hood. Which meant that Alan and John and Will would be safe, if she could only stay out of Gisborne's grasp.

She went to the nearest hovel, kicked at the mud at the base of its wall until she'd made a dent, and shoved the cloak in against the boards as far as it would go.

In the rain, it looked like a boulder, or an empty burlap sack. She'd come back for it later, if she could. For now—Marian clawed at her face, remembering the mask, and threw it down after the cloak. Shaking hands moved to unbind her skirts from her legs, and after another moment of thought, they pulled the tie from her hair as well. It fell wet and heavy against her neck, for an instant so like the strangling touch of the cloak that she nearly cried out.

She wasted one more breath, pausing, trying to remember if there were any other alterations she had to make to become Lady Marian again. Her mind was blank. She could not think.

So she moved instead, venturing out into the little alley between houses. A figure appeared in front of her and melted away with an intake of breath. Others appeared and vanished, voices crowded at the edge of her consciousness. She wondered what she must look like, and could not imagine.

She stumbled sideways, her shoulder hitting the edge of a house, and she paused, clutching at the wood and plaster, trying to catch her breath. The air felt like fire in her throat, and she could not help the tears that mingled with the rain on her cheeks. *Keep moving*, she ordered herself. Marian had to be "found" so close to Robin's appearance that it would seem like they were both there at once, with no time for one to change into the other.

She shoved herself away from the corner she leaned against, and out into a bigger laneway. But her feet slid again, and this time the muscles in her legs had given up, and when she tried to catch her balance, she fell.

She was braced to hit the ground, too tired to roll or protect herself. Instead she fell into a hard grip, a grip that hauled her upright. A hand brushed her sodden hair from her face, and someone let out a strangled sound of surprise.

She looked up, and in her exhaustion, she let out a muffled scream. The face inches from hers was covered with blood and dirt, rivulets of bloody mud dripping from his chin and from the hair plastered to his head.

The grip relaxed but did not let go. Instead an arm circled her waist. "Easy, easy." Gisborne's voice was thin and remote, but in a strange, dislocated moment of clarity Marian saw the tight features under his calm, the fury in his eyes, the restrained passion in the thinly pressed lips. "I've got you. You're safe."

Marian let him hold her, too stunned and weary to think. He smelled of sweat and rain and grass, exactly as he had moments before when his weight had her pinned to the ground. The hands that brushed mud from her features were gentle now, the same hands that had bruised her shoulder so badly that it hurt when he embraced her.

And when he drew back to gaze at her, looking almost as confused and stunned as she, there was no flicker of recognition. He'd looked into her eyes on the other side of the wall, spoken to her face, lingered over her masked features—and he hadn't known her. And he didn't know her now.

Her exhaustion shifted, something else stirring in her heart. They'd been as close as lovers, grappling there in the mud, and he hadn't seen her. She'd fooled him.

She'd won.

Gisborne's hands, cold and shaking, clasped hers and drew them up to his lips. "You're safe," he said again. "You're safe now."

TWENTY-FOUR

MARIAN SAT AT THE window, wrapped in a woolly dressing gown and an extra shawl, the fire crackling anxiously in the fireplace. Her father, pacing within the limited confines of his chamber, had asked more than once if she wouldn't prefer to sit closer to the hearth, but though she still felt chilled through her bones, she could not tear herself from the window. Her eyes scanned the grassy slope beyond the walls of the town, searching for a prick of warmth in the gray afternoon.

They'd promised to build a bonfire, her men, to signal that all had gone right on their end of the scheme. But the slopes were farther away than Marian had remembered, harder to see than she'd imagined, and if the fire never came, she would have no way of knowing whether it meant they were captured or dead, or that they simply couldn't find any dry wood and get it to catch in the rain.

Marian tried to look as though she were only watching the rain, which had slowed back to a miserly drizzle again, but she suspected her father saw some of the anxiety on her features.

"Tell me again what happened," her father said, his expression wooden.

"I took Jonquille out," Marian said quietly, echoing the story she'd given Gisborne once he'd brought her inside the castle. She hated to lie to her father—he'd done nothing wrong, except possibly, in the eyes of others, indulged her freedoms more than a stricter guardian might have done. "I heard a cry from the forest, and when I went to investigate, they were waiting for me."

"This Robin Hood and his men?" Her father had heard the story already, but he was watching her intently, as if waiting for her to contradict herself.

"Yes." Marian met her father's gaze, ignoring the inexorable pull of the soggy vista beyond the window. "They were very courteous. I wasn't injured."

Her father's eyes crinkled, but not with the laughter that had etched those lines. He frowned, and his lips were thin. "But for rope marks at your wrist and bruises on your throat and—"

Memory made Marian swallow instinctively, and she immediately wished she hadn't. The binding marks were little more than patches of irritated skin and would fade—were already fading, far too soon for believability—by the end of the day. But her neck, where Gisborne had half throttled her with her own cloak . . . those marks were bruises, and they were growing more livid by the hour.

"None of Robin's men meant to hurt me," Marian murmured. *Gisborne did.*

Her father let out a derisive sound, then dropped heavily into an oaken chair by the fire, facing his daughter at the window. "Marian." His voice was gentler now, carrying a hint of appeal. "What really happened?"

Marian opened her mouth, but she was still looking at her father's face, and the warm familiarity of him caught her in a way his interrogation hadn't. The repetitions of *I don't know* and *My memory is fuzzy* died on her lips. She hesitated, fighting the need to shiver despite her extra layers.

Her father waited, and when she didn't speak, he leaned forward in the chair, elbows on his knees, eyebrows raised. "It cannot be coincidence, Marian, that this man masquerading as Robin targeted you. I won't be the only one who comes to that conclusion. If you tell me, I can help."

To her surprise and dismay, Marian felt tears stinging her eyes and blinked hard. She could trust her father when it came to Gisborne and the Sheriff—he would never turn her in or betray her identity.

But if he knew, it would put him in danger. Her father had a reputation as an honorable man, but she could not know how the Sheriff would react if Marian were ever caught and found out. If she were a man, she'd hang for the things she'd done so far, and that would be the end of Robin Hood. As a woman, though, they might well assume that she couldn't have acted alone and that her father must have helped her. Women did hang, but *noblewomen* . . . the people would much more readily find someone else to seek vengeance on. If he knew nothing, there was a chance they would not be able to prove to anyone's satisfaction that he had done wrong.

And if he knew, he would certainly forbid her from going out as Robin again, and keep her so closely under watch that she'd have no hope of a moment's freedom again.

And it had taken only seconds, standing there in Gisborne's arms, shivering with cold and reaction, listening to his uncharacteristic reassurances with that strange triumph coursing through her, to know that she *would* go out as Robin again. As often as she could. And as long as it took to see change.

Marian searched the rainy landscape one more time and then left the window to join her father in the other chair before the fireplace. "I . . . I sought him out." She wove this altered tale effortlessly, so aware of the way her father viewed her that she could match her story to that image without hesitation. "Lady Seild said he was so like Robin that I had to see him. I had to *know*."

Her father's expression softened as she twisted the ruby ring around and around where she wore it now on her finger.

"No one captured me," Marian went on, mentally bracing herself. "I offered to be a hostage when I found out that Robin Hood needed a way to steal that grain from the Sheriff."

Her father's eyes widened with a combination of fear and fury, and for a moment he couldn't speak. Marian searched his face, certain that as the surprise began to die, she'd see a glint of something else—maybe not admiration, but a recognition of some kind.

"Good God, Marian," he said, his voice sounding haggard, his eyes suddenly ten years older. "You offered to . . . Why, in God's name? He isn't Robin, it cannot be loyalty or . . ." He stiffened, his eyebrows shooting up. "Or is that why you . . . It's not *him*, is it?"

Marian paused only for a heartbeat. If she claimed her other self was actually Robert of Locksley, she could be proven a liar. She could hardly be mistaken about the identity of a man she'd grown up with and was promised to marry. The moment someone returned from the war who had known Robin, had seen him die, she'd come under suspicion.

"No," she said softly, fingers tightening around the ring. "But Father . . . the people are suffering because of the Sheriff's taxes.

They're losing their right to work the land, being forced from their homes. Families are being torn apart when they can't pay. Yes, Robin Hood is breaking the law, but the laws are wrong. That grain will go to feed the people of Nottingham now, not line the Sheriff's coffers with gold. This man, whoever he is, he's doing what Robin *would* have done, if he'd come back to us."

Her father gaped at her, and for a moment Marian thought wildly that her rhetoric had convinced him. He shared her convictions, had every bit as much compassion for the suffering of his people. He only needed to see that what Robin Hood was doing was *right*, even if it wasn't lawful.

Then he burst out, "Good God, my girl, Robin would never have acted this way. You claim you loved him, and yet you—" His lips thinned.

Marian's face stung as if she'd been slapped. Eyes burning, she whispered, "And yet I what?"

Her father already regretted his outburst. "You say this madman in the cloak, the masked Robin Hood, wanted by the law and most likely destined to hang when they catch him . . . is like your Robin? Who was by any account an honorable, loyal, devoted Lord? It's like comparing your mother to a—" But there his better sense stopped him, and his lips went thinner still as they pressed together.

Marian's own lips felt tight, anger rising to flush away her weariness. "Robin was a *good* man. He would not have let his people suffer the way Gisborne's prepared to do."

"The way *I'm* doing?" her father retorted, eyes dark.

Marian's jaw clenched. "I cannot accuse anyone of negligence who obeys the law," she said thickly. "But neither can I condemn someone who defies a law that is unjust."

"And who decides what laws are just?" her father exclaimed.

"This unknown brigand who holds my daughter hostage in exchange for a cart of wheat?"

Marian surged to her feet, pacing away from her father. She gazed out the window again at the unrelenting gray scene. There were still tears in her eyes, but she could no longer tell whether they were of grief or passion or anger or sheer exhaustion. "Robin would have understood."

"Robin would have ridden out on that cart beside Gisborne. And would not have rested until this man was hanged."

She'd left the warmth of the fire, and she pulled her wrap more tightly about her shoulders. "Maybe you didn't know him as you thought you did."

"Maybe *you* didn't." Her father's voice was quick and sharp, and when Marian looked over at him in astonishment, his face was grave. This time, there was no remorse there for his harshness, no regret over a hastily inflicted hurt. "Marian, my darling—are you certain you're remembering Robin as he truly was, in life, and not as you imagined him to be?"

Marian's cheeks were hot despite the chill settling back in around her. "Robin was good, and kind, and he never would have—"

"He *was* good." Her father got to his feet and crossed over to the window so that he could take her hands. Marian had not realized she'd balled them into fists until his fingers smoothed them out. "But he was reserved, and careful, and loyal to the crown."

"Yes, when the crown was—"

"Robin didn't *want* to fight in the King's crusade," her father interrupted.

Marian felt as though she might fall, were he not holding her by the hands. "No one wants to fight a war . . . but he was eager to . . ." She trailed off, because her father was shaking his head.

"Loyalty sent him there," he said grimly. "Loyalty to the *crown*, not to the *cause*. Can you see him defying that same crown now, for this? There are other ways to change this land and its laws."

Marian could not speak. Her throat, already inflamed and aching, felt as though it had swollen shut. Her hands in her father's shook. *I know Robin*, she thought fiercely. *I knew him then and I know him still.*

Softly, no stronger than a whisper, Robin's voice said, *Are you sure?*

"Robin *was* a good man," her father repeated. "But this man, this outlaw, is nothing like him. Radical and insurgent and impatient." He paused, and when he went on, his voice was a shade warmer, and he squeezed her hands. "Those qualities sound more like you, my love."

Marian's voice was still choked. "Qualities you despise . . . so much."

Her father's eyes shone, and he gathered her close, his warmth enclosing her in a way the brash heat of the fire couldn't. "Oh, Marian. I love you for those qualities and so many more. I love you and I'm terrified of you."

Marian could only return his embrace, twisting her fingers in the fabric of his tunic as she'd done as a child woken by nightmares or crying from skinned knees. Her cheek rested against his shoulder, her face turned away toward the window. She sniffled, and he tightened his grip.

"We can never tell anyone that you sought this man out," her father said gently into her hair. "Not even our closest friends. And I know you long to do something—your blood compels it of you. You will always be Lady of Edwinstowe and Locksley both, always care for the people of both estates. But promise me, daughter, that you will not speak to Robin Hood again. Come to me if you find yourself tempted."

Marian nodded against his shoulder, forced to pause, drawing in a shaking breath before she could speak. *There are other ways to change this land,* her father had said. His days here at Nottingham were endless stretches of discussion, lengthy and pompous speeches of learned men and landed nobles alike. But he and the other noblemen, dancing attendance upon the Sheriff all day, never saw the faces of the beggars outside Nottingham's gates. They didn't see how blinding was the flare of rekindled hope in the face of someone who'd abandoned it long ago. He didn't *know.*

Her mind roiled, as turbulent as the clouds outside, and she tried to pull her disjointed thoughts together. She'd never before wanted to tell her father what she was doing, but now, ever since that moment in Sherwood when she'd stood with the outlaws and realized what she and they could do for the people of Nottingham, she *wanted* him to know. She *wanted* him to approve. She wanted him to be proud of Robin Hood's deeds, even if he never knew that the face under the outlaw's mask was his daughter's.

She opened her mouth and then stopped abruptly, her eyes on the window. She must have stiffened, for her father lifted his head. "Marian?"

"I promise." She blinked away the last of her tears. They made her vision blur, made it difficult to tell true sight from imagination. "I promise never to speak to Robin Hood again."

Her father's lips pressed together and then relaxed, and he leaned forward to kiss her on the brow.

Marian, heart abruptly light and giddy with relief, glanced back toward the window as he drew her away back toward the hearth. She could not resist checking one last time that what she'd seen through the window was real: a tiny, distant glow of orange blossoming on the slope before Sherwood Forest. The signal fire.

She's different today. Marian's distracted all through their battle games, letting him beat her soundly at swordplay, and when he calls her on it, she turns red.

"I'm not feeling well," she mumbles, driving the point of her practice blade into the leaf litter.

"Right," Robin scoffs, brandishing his sword. "Claim you're feeling faint because I'm winning—just like a girl."

Her face goes redder. "Well, I am a girl. As easy as it might be to forget it."

All Robin's joy at victory drains away, and he lets the tip of the sword fall. She looks different today, too—her lips are redder, her eyes darker, her hair unusually tame and shiny. "I know that," he mumbles.

Marian's eyes close, and she fingers the end of her braid, drawing her shoulders back after a few moments. "If I have to hear one more lecture about what life will be like after I'm married, how I'll be expected to act, what I'll be expected to do . . ."

Robin's hand steals inside the pocket he wears at his waist. His mother's ring settles onto his fingertip as if drawn there by a lode-stone. They've never talked about the fact that everyone expects them to marry—Robin has never had the courage. And on any given day he's not sure which prospect is more frightening: that she'd respond by kissing him, or by killing him.

She paces a few steps away, then turns, regarding Robin with a curious gaze, her darkened lashes lowering a little. "Did you mean it? That day here in Sherwood, when we were children. When you promised you'd never make me be anything, act a certain way."

Robin swallows. "I meant it."

Her eyes change while she watches him—her lashes lift, her gaze softens. Her lips curve, the smile there different from the grin she usually flashes him over their clashed swords. "Then pick up your sword, Locksley."

Robin must suppress the urge to grin wildly, a strange rush of feeling making him want to shout. "As my Lady commands," he answers, with a sweeping bow that makes Marian laugh.

TWENTY-FIVE

NOTTINGHAM CASTLE WAS QUIET the next day, and for several days after. Marian kept to her room at first, conscious of the role she had to play as victim, except for one excursion, late in the night, to retrieve Robin's cloak. But when she made it to the edges of town, the cloak was gone.

She took to walking the corridors of Nottingham Castle, venting her restless energy and learning its twists and turns all the more intimately. She came across Gisborne once and managed to retreat around a corner before he saw her—but she could hear the orders he was giving to the men who stood at his side.

"The Sheriff has decreed it, and no expense spared. The jails must be expanded. We'll need stoneworkers, locksmiths, blacksmiths—we must triple the available cells by fortnight's end."

"Sir," one of Gisborne's men said in a low voice, "I heard that Hood's men were few. Just a handful."

"The cells aren't for them. Go—you have my orders."

Marian peeked around the corner in time to see the first man march off, as Gisborne reached out to take the arm of the second. "In two weeks' time we'll be asked to begin making arrests for failure to pay debts. There's no need to tell the men just yet. But pick a few of the most discreet and start preparing, for the numbers will be staggering, and we'll have to work quickly."

He sent the other man off and then stood motionless for a time, head bowed, cold eyes on the stone floor. Marian's stomach churned, anger and dread both making her feel sick. She fled before Gisborne saw her, and when he called upon her later she could not dismiss the memory.

He'd interviewed her extensively when he first brought her in, but when he visited her the next day he made no mention of it. He'd bowed over her hand, and his eyes had lingered at her throat, which bore a grim necklace of onyx and azurite bruises. He'd asked after her father, and whether she was well, and informed her that the stableman had seen to her horse and that the mare seemed fit and in good spirits.

Marian could not stop thinking about the missing cloak. She knew it could not lead him to her, but a dozen little voices whispered and pointed out different paths to disaster. Someone could have seen the woman hiding the cloak. If the rain didn't wash them away, the mud could have preserved her boot prints leading from the hiding spot to the place where Gisborne had found her. There could be a few shed hairs clinging to the inside of the hood, her exact shade of chestnut, wavy and too long for a man's. . . .

Gisborne gazed at her, a faint frown distorting his features. "You seem well," he said finally.

"I am unhurt," she replied, an undercurrent of pleasure coursing through her. He didn't know after all. She was still winning. "The Sheriff has been keeping you busy."

"Indeed." Gisborne's face showed not a trace of guilt at the idea of arresting otherwise innocent people for failing to pay the Sheriff's ever-increasing taxes.

Marian's heart hardened just a fraction more.

Gisborne cleared his throat. "I hope, my Lady, that soon you will have no cause to fear."

Marian fought the urge to point out that she wasn't afraid—not of Robin Hood, at any rate—and bowed her head. "I know you are doing everything in your power to find him." *And failing.*

Gisborne's frown lessened a degree, though the expression that curved his lips now could not have been called a smile. "I have reason to believe he'll be apprehended soon."

Marian's pleasure vanished, and every ounce of her willpower went to avoiding a telltale flicker of her expression or shift of her weight. Gisborne watched her, but mildly, without the eagle-eyed intensity she'd expect if he suspected her involvement. "Oh?" was all she could think of to say.

"It will take some time yet, but I will catch him, Marian. My Lady." The slip was absentminded. The correction, however, was not. His not-even-a-smile vanished, and his shoulders drew back. Dour, remote, and rigid once more, he inclined his head. "I will be away from the castle for a while. Please forgive my absence."

And he was gone.

Though the castle was quiet, the town below was in a relative uproar. It had taken less than a day for Marian's men—*Robin Hood's men,* she corrected herself—to begin distributing the Sheriff's grain throughout the town. Marian had caught fragments of conversation between guards and officials saying that there were roadblocks, and agents at the markets to detain, and searches, trying to make it impossible for the thief to profit from his ill-gotten gains—but it was a lone monk from one of the local orders who noticed a sudden and puzzling decrease in the crowds begging for food at the church. Gisborne had raged, in that icy way of his, and the guards had torn through the town, but even Gisborne could not tear a piece of bread away from a hungry child, nor arrest a toothless old man for the bowl of porridge in his gnarled hands.

The name of Robin Hood was everywhere: in the jokes told by the guards, in the whispers of the servants, and in the conversations over needlepoint and music in the solar.

Lady Cecile, the youngest daughter of one of the minor visiting nobles, declared that Robin Hood was "just like a knight of Arthur's court," and that he was welcome to *her* jewels anytime.

Marian winced and sucked at her finger where she'd stabbed it with the needle. She kept her eyes down, unable to dismiss from her imagination what Alan might say to that.

Cecile's sister, Tess, who'd always struck Marian as the more practical of the two, shot Cecile a dark look. "He's a traitor and a thief. And anyway, you wouldn't think he was so romantic up close. He lives in the *forest*, Cess—he must smell like a sty."

Marian concentrated on the lopsided periwinkle she was embroidering. *I smell a good deal better than the men who live in luxury, thank you.*

Of all the women except Marian, only one kept silent on the subject, though she was the only one among them with anything of fact to contribute. Seild was playing a lap harp and seemed focused on that task. Her notes never faltered as the other ladies spoke, and indeed she'd offered so little about her encounter with the increasingly infamous Robin Hood that the others seemed to have forgotten it entirely.

She did, however, glance up as conversation drifted away from the outlaw. Her eyes met Marian's, and her fingers struck a sour note. No one noticed, but Seild's lips twitched in a faint, rueful smile.

Cecile wasn't the only one who found the much-embellished tales of Robin Hood romantic.

As midday arrived, and the ladies drifted away to meet their husbands and fathers as the men broke for food and restoration, Seild bade Marian stay behind and dismissed her servant so that they were alone.

"How are you, Marian?" Seild sounded tired, and after a moment, she reached up and lifted the coronet of silver and lace that covered her hair—a replacement for the pearl-adorned net that Robin Hood had stolen. Her fingers combed through the copper braids until her hair hung loose, an intimacy that she'd never shared with Marian before. Seild was always proper, even around other ladies—she never went anywhere with her head uncovered, never spoke a word out of turn.

"I'm well," Marian said, fighting a rising sense of unease and confusion. "A little sick for missing home, perhaps."

Seild flashed her a wan smile. "Edwinstowe is beautiful," she agreed. "I wish I shared your fondness for home."

Her tone was rich with such uncharacteristic bitterness that Marian leaned forward. "What is wrong?"

"Lord Owen has decided that we will leave Nottingham early. In two days' time."

"Because of the hooded man? Because he thinks you may still be in danger?"

Seild's lips twitched, but the expression they formed could not have been called a smile. "He was less concerned with the theft and the danger to me than he was with the possibility that people might notice he was not in my bed at the time."

"I didn't want to ask," Marian murmured.

"It's all right." Seild was inspecting the coronet with a frown, fingertips rubbing at a spot on her scalp. "He prefers the company of women who are too afraid to refuse him."

After the silence stretched a beat too long, Seild looked up and saw the helpless anger in Marian's face. She smiled and closed the distance between them, taking Marian's hand. "Don't fret, dear," she told her, with that oddly maternal air that seemed so strange from a woman only a few years her senior. "I'm quite accustomed to his ways. I wanted to tell you I was leaving, as Lord Owen is keeping it secret until we've gone. And I wanted to warn you."

"Warn me?" Marian gave Seild's fingers a light squeeze, but to her the gesture felt lacking, a feeble echo of Seild's reassurance. She wanted to say more, find words to express the sympathy and the hurt in her own heart for Seild's unhappy marriage, but the trueness of it stuck in her throat.

"There are rumors, Marian." Seild's expression turned grave. "Everyone knows this Robin Hood is not your Robin, but knowledge has little impact on rumor—that he wears his name and mantle makes them think there must be a connection."

Marian started to protest, the words coming more easily now than they ever had before—lying was becoming more natural than speaking truth.

Seild shook her head, silencing Marian far more effectively than had she simply interrupted. "At best, people think you are sympathetic to his cause. At worst . . . they think you might be helping him."

Marian reminded herself that Gisborne had already suffered these same suspicions, and had disproven them to his satisfaction. "Thank you for the warning," she murmured. "I am grateful, truly."

Seild scanned her features, searching, then released her hand. "Two days' time," she said, echoing the time frame carefully. "And Lord Owen intends to travel with a much-reduced escort, so as not to attract attention from the outlaws. He's hoping no one will see him go."

The woman's eyes were intent upon Marian's, and Marian could not think why. She was sad to see her friend go—and sadder still to see her so unhappy in her marriage—but why Seild was running over the details of their departure, she had not an idea.

Seild was watching her face. "So take care you don't share what you know with anyone. Especially not outlaws who might prey upon Lord Owen's cowardice. And *especially* not outlaws who might use his wealth to good purpose."

Marian sat dumbfounded, watching as Seild's lips twitched to the tiniest of smiles. She'd seen realization strike Marian.

"Go, Marian. Speak to your outlaw."

"Seild—" croaked Marian, trying to form the words of a protest. But her mind was already working, already calculating the timing, imagining and discarding plans, counting the wealth of jewels and gold her men could redistribute.

"The people down there are not the only ones starving," Seild whispered, tilting her head toward the slit window that overlooked Nottingham town. "Go."

Marian shook off her confusion and moved forward, bending so that she could kiss Seild's cheek. She said nothing—she did not think Seild wanted gratitude. She slipped out before she could betray anything more to her keen-eyed friend.

Too restless to stay in her room, Marian abandoned the castle and went out to the stables, seeking Jonquille's company. The sky was a clear, uninterrupted blue, the air crisp with wood smoke. The chill had dampened the sharper, more acrid smells that Marian associated with Nottingham and the sheer number of people who lived within its walls so that more delicate odors washed across the courtyard. Someone not far from the castle was brewing cider, the sour, cloying smell of fermentation not unpleasant amid the crowd of other autumn aromas: damp earth, pickling spices, beeswax, hay and horses, bonfire ash, and the ineffable and increasingly pervasive scent of fallen leaves.

Midge was working on Jonquille's tack when Marian strode into the stables. He saw her and straightened, eyes lighting. "Good afternoon, my Lady. I'm glad you came, I was going to have Elena summon you."

"Summon me? Why, is Jonquille hurt?" Marian moved past her father's stable master until she could see her horse for herself. The mare bobbed her head in greeting, and though Marian imagined she saw a spark of resentment in those round, dark eyes for abandoning her at Nottingham's gates, the horse lipped at her hair the way she always did, shifting her weight as she wondered whether they'd be going out for a ride.

"Not at all. But when you went out on Jonquille the other day," Midge said, referring to it without emphasis, as if she were taken hostage on a regular basis, "you had someone else saddle her."

Marian blinked. "You weren't here, and I was only planning on being out for an hour or so." Which was not true—she'd avoided Midge, knowing he might check her saddlebags as he secured them to make sure the load was even, and find Robin's clothes.

Midge only grunted, leaning into the saddle brush. Marian waited, but the man kept working for a time in silence, giving

her little notice. Just as she was about to give up and demand
an explanation, he set the brush aside and stood. He heaved the
saddle up and onto its rack. "Some years ago," he said, almost as
though talking to himself, "you asked me about changing Jonquille's tack so you could shoot better."

Marian watched him work, bemused. She had indeed asked
him about that very issue—when she was nine. She'd wanted a
way to use her legs to steer her horse, freeing her hands for the
bow, so she would not have to dismount or stop her horse to fire.
Time, and familiarity with her horse, had taught her other ways
of managing horse and bow simultaneously—Jonquille now
responded as readily to a nudge of her knee as a tug on her reins.

Midge wiped his oil-stained hands on a rag and then scratched
at his chin, fingernails rasping over his stubbly beard. "Been on
my mind lately. Opens up a whole world of other problems to
solve, you know—where do you keep the bow when you're riding, that sort of thing." His eyes were momentarily distant and
thoughtful. "Any rate, when they brought Jonquille back in, she
only had one saddlebag, and no doubt the thieves had taken
whatever was in it, but you shouldn't have let someone else load
her."

Marian hid a smile. He'd called her down to rebuke her for
letting someone else do his job, however briefly. "It won't happen
again," she assured him.

"I've added some straps here," he said, gesturing to the saddle
and tacitly inviting Marian to come inspect his work, "and here.
So the load can be adjusted more easily. See how it feels."

Marian ran her hands over the freshly shined buckles, which
weren't fastened, and then lifted the flap of one of the bags. A
flash of green wool caught her eye, and she let the flap fall closed
again with a gasp.

Midge, unconcerned, was cleaning off the saddle brush with the rag. "I've got a sister lives here in Nottingham," he said, inspecting the brush with a frown. It was beginning to look a bit worn. "Two little ones. Seems they've had bread, these past few days."

Marian's heart was pounding as if she were still grappling with Gisborne, still expecting him to drag her down off that wall by her cloak. The cloak that now rested, folded neatly, in the saddlebag before her. "What is this?" she asked, her voice sounding cold in her effort to reveal nothing.

Midge replaced the brush and then rolled up his sheath of leatherworking tools, tying off the packet and stowing it. "Jonquille went out that day with a full load, if poorly balanced. She came back empty of rider and load, and you walked back in with Gisborne." He raised his head to look at her. "I think you lost something."

Marian's face was hot, and her throat had closed again. Fear licked at her voice, making it unsteady. "Midge—"

"There's also this." Midge was back at the saddle again, reaching for the stiff leather strap of the stirrup. He shoved the heel of his hand through and pushed up, causing something inside to poke out through the top of the saddle. He grasped it and worked it back and forth, muttering, "It's easier if you're actually astride . . . ah, there."

Marian's mouth fell open, but she found no words with which to speak. It was her bow. Unstrung, it was little more than a long, slender stick, and Midge had fashioned a leather sleeve concealed inside the straps. She'd have to dismount and string the bow if she wanted to use it, but it was not unlike a sword's sheath. It would conceal the fact that she traveled with a weapon, whenever she took Jonquille out.

She could hardly take her eyes from the bow, which Midge must have returned to Edinwstowe to fetch, for she had not brought it with her when she first traveled to Nottingham. She forced herself to lift her gaze and saw the grizzled stable master watching her evenly.

"I think you should make sure I'm the one saddles Jonquille from now on," he said mildly.

Marian could have cried from sheer bewilderment. Of all the people who might have guessed the truth, Midge was the last she would have expected. Gisborne, her father, even Elena, yes, but Midge? He waited, radiating equanimity, leaning on the saddle rack with his hands clasped over his stomach.

"Indeed," she said finally, words failing her. "I'll make certain of it."

Midge flashed her a quick smile and then began bundling the saddle back to its usual rack in storage, giving her a bit of time to recover her balance as he worked. When he returned, she reached out and touched his arm. He stopped. He was a little shorter than she, and he looked up at her, no longer amused, expression grave.

"Her husband died a year ago. My sister's barely clinging. I send her what I can, but—" He shrugged, looking grim. "I'm not sure what kind of starving hurt worse, the kind in their bellies or the kind in their hearts."

Marian licked her lips, thoughts still turbulent. "Thank you," she whispered. "Thank you, Midge."

His lips twisted a bit, and his gravity seeped away. "You know—my Lady, I never much cared for that nickname."

Marian was still trying to reconcile his tacit approval of her actions as Robin with the placid, genial man who'd looked after her for so much of her life. "What is your real name?" she asked, feeling a tiny flicker of shame at having to ask the question of a man she'd known her whole life.

"It's Much, my Lady. You can still call me Midge, I'm used to it. But—well, I figure you're old enough now, might as well tell you who I really am." He started, as though remembering something, and retrieved a bit of fabric dangling from his belt that Marian had taken for another rag. He held it out to her, and as soon as her fingertips touched it, she realized what it was.

"Thank you, Much." Marian met his gaze, slipping Robin Hood's mask inside her kirtle. *Who I really am,* she thought, watching Much go back to work as though nothing strange had happened.

Robin waits, heart pounding, moonlight playing tricks on his eyes. It takes her longer than usual to get ready, but after a few agonizing moments her window swings open and her face appears there, grinning in the darkness.

She makes quick work of her escape, forsaking her window for the arms of the yew tree and then shimmying down until she lands neatly beside him. She's not even out of breath, a fact Robin notices with some consternation.

"Well?" Marian asks, her eyebrows lifting as she eyes him. "What is so urgent it could not wait until morning?"

Robin's hand is in his pocket, fingers clutched around the ring. With an effort, he forces himself to draw it out. He's never been so terrified in his life. "I wanted to give you something."

Intrigued, Marian reaches for his hand and pries his fingers loose from the object—clearly, she's expecting some whimsical token or joke, for when she sees the ring, her eyes widen and her hand falls away. "Your mother's ring?"

Robin stares at her, his mind empty of words. He clears his throat once, twice, then manages, "She wanted my wife to have it."

Her eyes go wider still, until she looks almost as fearful as Robin. She says nothing, but he can see her withdrawing, stiffening. Pulling away.

"I meant what I said," Robin blurts, voice full of feeling. "You'll never have to be someone you're not. Not with me. It's you, Marian, you're the one I want."

She swallows hard, only barely able to lift her eyes from the ring to meet his gaze. Robin can see her thinking, can trace the signs of her racing thoughts in the dart of her eyes, the flutter of her pulse, the tremble of her lips.

"Will we still shoot?" she whispers.

Robin feels his face crack into a smile. "And ride, and fight, and duel, and—"

"Yes," says Marian.

Robin grinds to a halt, blinking. "Yes?"

There's a tiny smile on Marian's face. "The ring, Robin, if you please."

In his haste, he drops the ring, and they search for it together, laughing in the moonlit grass.

TWENTY-SIX

RAIN HAD DAMPENED THE forest, and although the skies had dried again, water still dripped from leaf and twig. Marian longed for activity, to come down from her vantage point and stretch her legs and escape the chill seeping beneath her damp cloak.

A terrible day to travel, said Robin in her ear as she scanned the limits of how far she could see through the thickets and branches. *Perhaps Lord Owen has changed his plans.*

Marian flexed her cold fingers and tried not to let doubt make her question their strategy. It ought to be easy, far easier than getting Little John out of Gisborne's clutches. But she could not afford to let down her guard even for an instant.

Their plan to steal and distribute the grain in Nottingham's storeroom had unfolded exactly as Marian had intended—except for her run-in with Gisborne—and the boys, as Marian had come to think of them, were as excited as she felt. Success was more intoxicating than the strongest wine.

And Nottingham had noticed. There was a current in the air, something of much-longed-for action after a long sleep— even the nobility were a part of it now, though Marian had to admit Seild was hardly indicative of the rest of the nobles. Marian never would have guessed that her friend had such rebellion in her heart. Or that Midge would risk his neck to help another break the law. Or that Elena could be leading a double life too, dressing as a man to pass messages of strategy and battle between her lady and her beloved under Sherwood's canopy.

Perhaps I don't know the people of Nottingham as well as I think I do.

Robin's voice added, quiet and warm: *Perhaps all they needed was someone to show them what they could do.*

A birdcall pierced the quiet, and Marian's attention snapped back into the present. The call was Alan's, from farther up the King's Road. Marian listened, straining, until the call came again, this time with a fluttering tail that rose and fell four times.

Four guards. Marian shifted her grip on her bow, still scanning, though she knew it would be a few moments before the carriage Alan had spotted came into view. That meant five men to fight, including Lord Owen. Six if the carriage driver could wield a sword.

In the distance, a horse neighed a protest of some kind. The sound was brief, but enough to show Marian where to look— and there, emerging around the curve of the road below, was a carriage and its entourage.

The four guards all rode ahead of the carriage, a mistake that made Marian smile as she carefully drew a couple of arrows from her quiver. Her heart was far from easy, for the next bit of their plan rested solely on Will's shoulders, but there was such serenity about the procession beneath her. If the guards had begun the journey wary, they certainly weren't anymore, looking half-asleep on their mounts.

A drab figure slid out of the underbrush alongside the carriage as the guards passed, out of Marian's line of sight—and then just as carefully eased back again, retreating once more into the forest.

Both carriage and horses were still moving along the slight decline, and Marian could not see clearly enough to know if Will had accomplished his task, but she could not afford to wait for someone in the party below to notice something was wrong with the carriage.

Marian moved before sense could stop her.

She sent two arrows thudding into the carriage walls, and as the horses drawing it reared and shied in alarm, she dropped down out of the trees.

Panicked, the horses bolted. Will had cut their traces after all, for the carriage groaned to an unsteady halt, and the four horses that had been drawing it galloped, still hitched together, into the undergrowth.

Two of the guards shouted and wheeled their mounts to go in pursuit of the horses, for they hadn't seen the masked, cloaked figure drop to the forest floor. Marian was reaching for another arrow when a small mountain covered in ferns and sticks suddenly shifted from the ditch beside the road with a roar. Little John felled one of the remaining guards with one sweep of his staff, and by the time the other guard reached for his sword, Marian was standing in front of him, bow drawn, arrow just a breath away from his nose.

"I wouldn't do that," she said lightly.

The guard swallowed, eyes rolling from Marian's masked face to John's, and then toward Will's as he emerged from the undergrowth, flushed and panting. Carefully, he unwrapped his hand from the hilt of his sword.

A bellowing voice from within the carriage was swearing and demanding answers. As John began binding the remaining two guards and the driver, who clearly had no desire to fight anyone, Marian moved quickly to the door of the carriage. She thought about switching bow for sword, but Lord Owen was a noted swordsman, and as long as she stayed beyond the reach of his blade, her bow would serve her better.

"Good afternoon, my Lord," Marian called, deepening her voice and falling back on Alan's flippant attitude. "Your men are down, your carriage is surrounded. For your safety, I recommend you accept defeat with dignity."

Will crept up to open the door, ready to skip back out of the way. Owen was a large man, barrel-chested and well on his way to becoming fat, and when the door opened he was caught with his sword half-tangled in its sheath as he tried to draw it in the confines of the carriage. He froze when he saw Marian's drawn bow, fury mottling his face red and purple.

"Why don't you step out and join us?" Marian suggested. "Sherwood's hospitality is yours, my Lord."

Owen clambered down, snarling as Will sidled up to confiscate the sword from its sheath and the dagger from his other hip. "Robin of the Hood," the Lord said, in a voice like a death sentence.

Over his shoulder Marian caught a glimpse of another face in the shadows of the carriage. "I see you travel with company," said Marian, voice warming as she let the tension in the bow relax a little—she had time to draw it again should he move, and no one could hold it drawn indefinitely. "Do I recognize the lady I met that night in Nottingham Castle?"

Lord Owen's fingers clenched and unclenched. "Only a coward sneaks into a man's chambers while he's absent."

Marian's jaw tightened. "Only a coward leaves his wife alone while he forces himself on his servants."

Owen's mouth fell open as Marian's heart began to pound. From fear, from tension—but mostly from exhilaration. Never had she told someone so directly what she thought of him— never had she truly imagined being free to do so.

"We've no desire to turn Nottingham's wealthy into paupers." Marian smiled beneath the shadow of her hood. "Ordinarily we'd take only a fraction of what you own—but your cowardice demands a larger tithe. Men?"

John had finished with the guards, and together he and Alan began searching through the bags and trunks piled behind the carriage while Owen stood, shaking with fury. Marian heard the clink of coin, and muted exclamations of triumph, and knew her men must have found Owen's coffers.

Marian waited until they were done, not taking her eyes off Lord Owen, who stared back at her like he might incinerate her by willpower alone. Only once John stood at her back, staff in hand, and Alan had nocked an arrow to his bow, did Marian lower her weapon.

"And now, Lord, if you'd be so good as to step aside, I should like to pay my respects to your lady." Marian had no expectation that Owen would do as she said, and instead moved past him while Alan and John kept him at bay.

Seild had not left the carriage. She sat, hands folded in her lap, as demure and calm as if they'd stopped only to rest. Her eyes, though, were alive with excitement and, Marian saw with surprise, enjoyment.

"Good afternoon, Lady," Marian said in Robin's voice, bend- ing into a courtly bow.

Seild inclined her head in response, eyes dancing. "Robin.

You venture into bold territory."

"Only when I am certain to find allies." Marian tilted her head, as if to indicate her men, though for Seild's eyes she smiled, just a little, beneath her hood.

Seild ran a hand over her veil, and Marian saw with some agitation that it was shaking—despite having wanted this, despite having volunteered for it, Seild was still nervous. She did not know Marian, and Marian could not show her who she was.

"You've nothing to fear from me, sweet Lady," Marian said gently. "My quarrel is with the one who owns that small fortune my men have confiscated."

Seild's lifted her eyebrows. "But I too own a fortune. Why have you no quarrel with me?" She leaned forward a little, into the light, which glinted off the gemstones she wore at her throat. In another circumstance Marian might recognize that tactic, for it displayed Seild's décolletage as well as her jewelry.

"That is a beautiful necklace you wear. Too beautiful for the rigors of travel, I should think."

"It was a gift," said Seild, still leaning forward, still watching Marian. "From my Lord husband."

"Ah, then, it is not really your fortune after all, is it? I think your husband would say he owns it still," Marian declared. "Close your eyes, Lady."

Seild gulped a breath but did as Marian requested, allowing her to step up into the carriage and bend over her long enough to release the delicate clasp of the necklace. Marian could see Seild's pulse fluttering rapidly below her ear, and as she drew back, a flush mantled her friend's cheeks. Startled, Marian nearly dropped the necklace—suddenly she could not help but remember one of the other ladies declaring Robin Hood a romantic, dashing figure.

"Thank you, Lady," she said in a low voice, for Seild's ears alone. "The poor of Nottingham will eat tonight." Marian took her hand in order to raise it to her lips. Her heart sang with pity for a woman so starved for affection that a stranger's touch upon her hand could stir her so easily.

But when she lifted her head, Seild's face was pink with pleasure. Her eyes were alive in a way they never had been at Nottingham Castle, and there was a strange satisfaction in the way she sat back, chin raised, poise in her every movement. Marian knew the fire that had stiffened her spine and lit her features, for she'd felt it herself: she'd taken action, and she'd won. Against her husband, against the other lords, against the unfairness of poverty—whatever caused Seild to act, she would be forever changed.

"Thank you, my Lord," she said quietly. "Be well."

Marian withdrew to find Owen's purple face twitching with rage, an anger that suddenly made Marian's heart quail—for while she and her men could vanish safely into the forest, Seild could not.

Marian threw her bow to Alan and drew her sword, advancing upon Owen. "I will not tolerate injustice of any kind," she said quietly, though her voice was as hard as the steel in her hand. "Whether it be the disdain of a government for the welfare of its people or that of a husband for his wife. My men are everywhere. I have the love of Nottingham's people and a reach far longer than that of Gisborne or his Sheriff. If you touch her in anger, I will know about it. And I will return, and this time I will take from you something far more valuable than gold."

Owen's face was still distorted with fury, but Marian saw something else there that quickened her pulse: fear. She could not help the flicker of satisfaction that came with that.

They took great care binding Owen's hands to the carriage, and when Marian made certain the ropes would not budge, they cut the driver free. They gave him instructions to wait half an hour before releasing the others, a time frame Marian knew would drop to mere minutes once they were gone and Owen started shouting orders.

But minutes were all they needed to melt back into the forest that had so utterly masked their ambush.

Marian signaled to the others to continue on back to their camp, sheathing her sword and retrieving her bow from Alan. He hesitated but did as Robin commanded—Marian watched them disappear, then turned to creep back toward the site of their victory.

As expected, the driver had released Owen and the guards, and the Lord was like a sullen bear, snapping at his men to find the horses—and the two guards who'd fled with them. Marian watched as the horses and errant guards were led back, Owen's angry humiliation weighing heavily on her heart. When he turned toward the carriage and shouted unintelligibly, Marian nearly whispered aloud, *Don't go to him.*

But Seild had little choice when faced with a direct order from Owen, and she emerged from the carriage. At this distance, Marian could not hear what she said, though her lifted chin spoke of defiance.

Instinct, some tiny current of premonition, prompted Marian to act even as Owen raised his hand.

The arrow was silent, no telltale whistle to warn of its approach. Its point pierced Owen's hand in the dead center of his palm, causing the man to stagger back and fall with a howl of surprise and pain, clutching his wrist with his good hand.

The guards had all drawn their swords and were scanning

the thickets around them with obvious fear, and the driver of the carriage had retreated into its interior. Only Seild stood unmoved—she'd been braced for the blow. Now she turned to scan the forest, eyes moving right past where Marian lay concealed. She kept scanning until a particularly agonized groan at her feet drew her attention back, and after a moment, she stooped to tend to her wounded husband.

Marian waited until they were underway once more, then slipped away to double back to the campsite.

She'd expected to find the others celebrating—she'd noticed that John had liberated a cask of wine along with the rest of their loot. But she heard only silence as she approached, until she got close enough to hear hushed voices.

One of them belonged to Alan, but the other was young and high, a voice that sounded strangely familiar.

"But there must be a catch," Alan was saying as Marian approached.

"The catch is that they want to reveal who he is," the voice replied.

"If he were to win—and you know he could—they'd be forced to pardon him. It wouldn't matter if they knew who he was, they couldn't arrest him."

"And you think this Robin Hood would be content then? To take his prize and settle back into his life as . . . what? Disgraced nobility? No, he'd go back to this life sooner or later, and the Sheriff would have the advantage of knowing who he was."

Marian was on her feet, ready to melt away into the forest, but the familiarity of that voice stopped her. She stood, poised, heart pounding, until Will appeared from the forest with a cry of welcome. "Come," he said, ushering her unresisting form toward the fire.

Alan was sitting next to the owner of the voice, a boy she'd never seen—who lifted his head when Marian appeared. "You won't guess what's happening in Nottingham. The Sheriff has announced a festival, with an archery contest as the final attraction. And here's the best part: the prize is an arrow fashioned from gold, and a legal pardon of any and all past crimes."

The minstrel was looking at her, and she felt more than saw John's gaze swing toward her as well. But Marian could not spare a moment's notice for them, or for the news. She could not stop looking at Alan's companion, because he—*she*—was no lad at all. It was Elena. And she was staring straight into Marian's eyes, her expression rigid with shock.

TWENTY-SEVEN

"ARE YOU ALL RIGHT, my love?" Alan's hand at the "boy's" arm slid around her shoulders.

Elena had lurched to her feet and was still staring. The mask fooled these men who barely knew her as Marian, and it fooled the average stranger, and it even fooled Gisborne, who saw what he expected to see. But for Elena, who helped her dress and who did her hair and who shared her life, Marian might as well have been standing there naked. She could not meet Elena's eyes, not after that first searing moment of recognition. She kept glancing up and then away.

Alan looked between them. "You've never met Robin. Our fearless leader."

Not so fearless right now, said Robin's voice in her head. He sounded sullen these days, and had ever since he'd told her to run and she'd chosen to face Gisborne instead.

Elena's face was white with shock. Marian forced herself to move and took a breath as she stepped away from the tree at her back. "My Lady," she said, in her low voice, and bowed to her maid as she took her hand.

"I'm no Lady." Elena's voice was thin and strangled, and her hand in Marian's was limp. "Only a maid."

Marian let go of Elena's hand and straightened. "Nevertheless," she said softly.

Alan's grin had hardened a little, brow lowering as he looked between the two of them. "What's going—"

Elena jerked her eyes from Marian's face and spoke smoothly, her shock scattering like a flock of birds taking flight. "I came to bring word of the festival," she announced, glancing around at the others.

"Festival?" asked Will, curiosity all over his face.

"It takes place in a week's time, as the visiting lords prepare to depart Nottingham. I knew Robin would hear of it eventually, but it seemed safest to bring you the news straightaway. I can't stay, though. My—my lady will notice I'm gone."

Elena did not so much as glance at Marian as she spoke.

Marian cleared her throat, making certain her voice would come out low and steady. "I will accompany you back to Nottingham if you wish," she offered, her heart slamming against her rib cage. She had to get Elena alone, talk to her, before she spoke again to Alan—or to the others. "I have business there."

Elena did look at her then, and this time her eyes scanned more than Marian's face. She took in the mask, the cloak, the bow at her side, the sword she wore at her belt. "I made my way here alone in perfect safety," Elena replied finally, with an air that suggested it wasn't the first time she'd had to make this argument.

Alan let out a sigh and let go of Elena entirely, lifting his hands to show his lack of involvement. "Here we go," he muttered.

Elena shot him a dark look, although her gaze was fond, and Alan's eyes as he watched her in return were soft. The girl, whose hair was tucked up under a bycoket cap, turned her keen eyes on Marian. "I do not require an escort."

Marian nearly took a step back, but something about the set of Elena's face stopped her. There was a glint in her blue eyes— she was *teasing* her. Marian straightened, waving a hand toward Jonquille, who stood, reins down, nosing around in the thicket for the last of the year's blackberries. "But my horse can travel much more quickly than you can on foot. You said your lady would miss you."

Elena considered this, or seemed to. "Very well."

Alan twitched and frowned. "Very w—you're accepting?"

Elena smiled at him. "Why not? We're both going to the same place. And my feet are tired."

Alan had no ready response to that, but when he looked back at Marian again, his eyes were harder. This time Marian *did* take a step back—she'd never received a look quite like that from anyone, much less Alan. Marian knew she cut a dashing figure in her tunic and her cloak, the mask that suited her strong features. And that flicker of heat in Alan's gaze—it was jealousy.

"You can't go yet." Will was oblivious to the new tension in the air. "What about the archery contest?"

"It's a trap," Little John's voice rumbled. He remained on his feet, respectful and stiff, hands clasped behind his back. Elena might have been dressed as a boy, but only to fool strangers and avoid attention while she traveled—Robin's gang knew she was a girl.

"But he could win," Will protested. "He *would* win."

"Yes," said John patiently. "And it's a trap."

"Most of Nottingham thinks it's a trap," Elena said, watching

"Robin" curiously, either unaware or unconcerned that the longer she gazed at the band's leader, the darker Alan's face grew. "But they're also almost all certain that Robin will appear to compete anyway. Evidently, it's a matter of honor. The Sheriff said he'd be a coward if he didn't show himself."

Honor. Cowardice. Marian's lip almost curled. "I'll think about it," she said finally. "For now, I must get to town, and you three must make use of the day's earnings, and your beloved must get back to her lady."

Alan was hardly mollified by Marian's choice of words. He drew Elena aside, and while the rest of them talked and pretended not to notice, the two spoke quietly together at the edge of the thicket. Marian tried to concentrate on John and Will, but she could not. The words the couple exchanged were too soft and low to hear, but out of the corner of her eye, Marian saw Alan draw Elena closer and reach up to touch her face.

His fingers slid across her cheek, thumb running along the edge of her lip as it curved into a little smile. They moved together, her smile, his caress, until Marian could not tell whether it was her smile that made him want to touch her, or his touch that made her smile—either way, he tilted his face as though he'd like to kiss her, and her cheeks flushed, and they stood basking in each other.

Marian felt a stab of jealousy so pure and unrelenting that she let out her breath and turned away. Not of Alan, not of Elena, but of both of them. Of what she'd had with Robin, and lost. Of what she'd never have again.

Jonquille was inspecting Elena with interest—her horse had always tolerated her maid, even sought out her attention. Marian let them get reacquainted, but when she would've mounted in preparation for helping Elena up behind her, Alan took Marian's elbow and drew her off a few paces.

"Keep her safe," he said in a low voice.

Marian raised an eyebrow. "I thought she could take care of herself."

"She can," Alan said, weight shifting from foot to foot. "But it doesn't mean I don't worry. She already risks everything every time she comes to see me. I can't tell her not to—I wish I could, sometimes. But I'd be asking her to be someone she's not."

Marian's heart thudded, and she glanced up toward the canopy in what she hoped was an idle way. Her eyes burned tellingly. "You're a rare man then," she said quietly. "Most people cannot help asking those they love to be something different from what they are."

Alan's grip on her elbow tightened a fraction. "I mean it, Robin. Danger follows you like a loyal hound. Don't let it catch her scent."

Marian's eyes fell back to his face. "My oath, Alan." She smiled. "I'll look after her the way I do the rest of you."

Alan snorted but let her go. Marian swung herself into Jonquille's saddle and let Alan help Elena up behind her. There was no pillion pad for riding double, and Marian hoped Elena had fashioned some sort of undergarment for her man's leggings. Her first outing on Jonquille, riding astride without skirts, had taught her that lesson painfully enough.

The others were already discussing the archery contest as they rode out of the clearing—or Will and Little John were. Marian could feel Alan's gaze on her back as she went.

Marian urged Elena to hold on and nudged Jonquille up into a trot. The gait was more uncomfortable with two, but she could not wait—now that they were moving, Marian could barely keep her tongue quiet. Questions and explanations burst half-formed in her mind, and the need to put distance between them and the men took over her good sense.

It wasn't until Jonquille had to skip over a fallen branch that Elena protested. It wasn't a jump so much as a little hop, but when their weight came back down against the horse's back, Elena stiffened and let out a little groan.

Marian reined in her mare, her hands tense and shaky. She dismounted, then reached up to help Elena down, trying to lift her by the waist and instead ending up half dragging the poor girl to the ground.

They stood, holding one another's arms, bemused and breathless. Then, carefully, Elena let go one with one shaking hand and reached up to push Marian's hood back and tug her mask up over her brow.

Marian stood, blinking in the afternoon sun, nose itching with cold and the smell of autumn leaves. Elena's eyes searched hers, grave and as unreadable as her betrothed's. Marian tried to dismiss the strange fear that tingled along her every nerve. Elena was her *servant*. Marian didn't answer to her—it was the other way around. Elena ought to be the one afraid, caught sneaking out to see her beau.

But everything had changed. Elena had become her friend, which meant Marian *did* have to answer to her.

Elena let her breath out audibly, steaming the air, and closed her eyes. Before Marian could digest this reaction, her maid leaned forward and wrapped her arms around Marian. "It was *you*," she whispered. "*You* saved Will, the night Gisborne's men came for him."

Marian's throat was tight, and her mind empty of words.

"You've saved him three times now." Elena drew back. Her eyes were wet. "But the rest—Lady Seild's midnight intruder, the grain from Nottingham, the stories they whisper in town . . . My Lady, how long have you been Robin Hood?"

"Always. I didn't mean to be at first—Will mistook me for Robin, that first night. I wore his cloak so I wouldn't be recognized, and instead . . ."

"Instead you were recognized as him." Elena's eyes were sober and earnest, and Marian found it hard to look at her for more than a moment or two. "And the rest?"

"All me." Marian let the truth fall and straightened as if she'd been bent under a heavy burden. The words that had been so conspicuously absent from her mind a moment ago came rushing up in a torrent. "I didn't intend any of it. But I am Robin Hood now. Oh, Elena, I would have told you, but—"

Her maid's eyebrows rose, and she shook her head. "You'd have been mad to tell me," she countered breathlessly.

Marian's head jerked up. "You're not going to scold me? Tell me I'm being foolish or reckless?"

Elena let go of Marian's arms and tugged at the edge of her tunic to settle it into place. "I don't know if you're being foolish. Probably you are. Probably so am I. But it's done, isn't it? You can no more stop being Robin Hood now than I can stop seeing Alan."

Marian let the air out of her lungs to draw a new breath, dizzy. "To speak about it," she whispered. "To a friend. What it means, you can't know . . ." Her eyes stung, vision blurring.

Elena's expression softened into a tiny smile. "I thought you were in love with him," she admitted. "With Robin Hood. And that's why you were vanishing all the time."

Marian laughed, as giddy as if she'd had too much to drink. "I suppose I am, in a way. In love with *being* Robin Hood. The difference it makes—to speak to men and have them listen to your words. To act in the world, not merely react. To ride out when I choose and be *free*."

Elena gave the horse a sidelong look and tugged awkwardly at her leggings. "I'm sure it made for a theatrical exit, as Alan would say, but I don't much care for riding post, my Lady."

Marian laughed again and reached for Jonquille's reins, then wiped the tears from her eyes. "I was going to suggest we walk the rest of the way." She hesitated and then started forward as she added, cheeks warming, "You have to wear something under the leggings if you're going to ride."

Elena fell into step beside her, and rather than casting a scandalized look at her mistress, she said thoughtfully, "And all that bouncing—I think I was actually glad to have my chest bound up tight."

They walked, leading Jonquille and laughing, and Marian began to realize that there had been iron bands of tension squeezing her ribs and throat that she hadn't known were there. Each step she took with Elena chipped away at that cage, until she tipped her head back in a patch of dappled sunlight and took a deep breath for what felt like the first time in weeks. To speak openly about Robin, about the things she'd done, was like surfacing from a dark, cold pool.

The forest started to thin ahead, where woods gave way to tilled land and eventually the road toward Nottingham's gates. Marian stopped. "I can't go back as Robin. And we probably shouldn't return together."

"I get in and out through the servants' entrances anyway," replied Elena ruefully. "You'd be conspicuous in either costume." She hesitated, her eyes flicking up to meet Marian's. "You mustn't tell them who you are," she whispered.

"Who?"

"The others. Alan and Will and John."

Marian blinked, stung. "I hadn't planned on it." And yet she could feel those iron bonds tightening back up. No, she hadn't planned on it. But as soon as Elena spoke, she'd known she *wanted* to.

Elena's expression was taut and full of sympathy. "To them, I'm Alan's betrothed. They accept me as part of him, I suppose—but not in any real way. I'm not one of them. I never can be. Not like you are."

Robin Hood's mask was still up over her brow, and as her throat tightened, Marian reached up to yank it off. In her haste the mask became tangled in her hair, and she swore, frustration making her fingers clumsy.

Elena stepped toward her and drew her hands away with the firm, gentle touch she'd always used when helping Marian dress. Marian clung to Jonquille's reins and dropped her eyes. How strange they both were, standing in their men's clothing, in the woods, a noblewoman and her maid.

"They respect you. They follow you and admire you. As Robin."

"I know." Marian kept staring at the ground, the patterns of fallen leaves swimming in her vision. Every tiny tug and pull at her hair made the colors dance in her eyes until it seemed the whole clearing was ablaze. "I didn't intend for anyone to find out."

Elena smoothed Marian's hair with a gentle touch and then took her hand so she could slip the mask into it. "I'm glad I know."

Marian lifted her eyes to find Elena smiling at her, her eyes sympathetic and full of admiration all at once. "I'm glad too," Marian said quietly.

Elena offered to help her change, but Marian assured her she could manage the transformation on her own. She watched her maid until she vanished between the trees, thinking of the dress rolled neatly in Jonquille's saddlebag. Elena's choice of words—*either costume*—kept ringing in her ears.

Robin's clothes felt more and more comfortable every time she put them on—but it was still a masquerade. And as Elena had reminded her, one she could not shed even around the men she trusted with her life. But she hadn't gone so far as to think of the clothes she wore every day as a costume—as unreal as her mask and her hood.

Slowly, she pulled the crumpled shift and kirtle and veil from the saddlebags and began to change. Jonquille, reading her heart in that way animals could do, stamped impatiently and nuzzled, confused, at her shoulder. Marian unstrung her bow and painstakingly slid it back into concealment among Jonquille's tack. She smoothed her veil and carefully remounted the mare.

She did trust them with her life, John and Alan and Will. But she couldn't trust them with who she really was.

TWENTY-EIGHT

THE STABLES WERE IN an uproar when she returned to the castle, for Gisborne had returned, and with him a number of men he'd taken along. Their horses were still dull with sweat and dust, and people scurried here and there with arms full of tack and brushes. Midge was nowhere to be seen, and the stable boy who took Jonquille's reins from Marian looked so harried that she knew he wasn't about to waste time investigating the horse's packs. Marian slipped away and headed for her room, hoping to reach safety before anyone could take note of her rumpled clothes or her own layer of sweat and grime.

She passed a few of the guards who now patrolled every corridor of the castle, but they took little notice of her. Her heartbeat quickened as she passed the door to her father's room—she could not quite face another confrontation with him—but it didn't open.

Marian pushed her door open with a visceral sense of relief and leaned against the cool, varnished wood gratefully.

A scrape of leather on stone sent relief scurrying away, and her jaw clenched as she lifted her head. She wasn't alone.

Gisborne stood by her bed, for once lacking the stiff poise he wore like armor. He was half bent over, his hand on her blanket, head turned toward the door. She was too scattered to interpret the flickering display of emotions that crossed his features, and by the time she'd taken a breath and looked again, his face was impassive.

"Forgive me," he said, straightening and settling, like water taking the shape of a vessel, back into his usual rigid posture.

Fear transmuted to anger in her voice, which blurted, "What are you doing in my chambers, Sir Guy?"

The man's eyes slid sideways, his immobile features darkening with a flush that would've shocked Marian had she not been so unsettled. "I came to look for you."

Marian stopped herself before she could look at the tapestry in the corner, the one she'd been admiring when Gisborne had first come to her quarters. Rather than hide her sword in the bed's canopy as she'd done with her cloak, where its rigid weight would leave a telltale shape in the draped fabric, she'd stowed it along the top of the tapestry, where it could not be seen from eye level.

Gisborne interpreted her silence as fury and combed his gloved fingers over his dark hair. "I came to look for you," he repeated. "And when you were nowhere to be found, I . . . I searched your room."

The knowledge of the sword's location pulled at Marian's eyes, and she resisted only by forcing herself to look not at Gisborne's face but at the scar at his jaw and throat, where it vanished underneath the high collar of his tunic. "You searched my room?"

Gisborne turned away, pacing toward the narrow slit of a window. "I have no excuse, my Lady. I can only try to explain. When out on the road, long hours of riding with no conversation or interruption, the mind . . . opens up. An idea came to me, and I could not dismiss it, despite how mad it was. And when I found you absent, I . . . I could not resist it."

Marian had not left the door, her back still pressed against the oaken solidity of it. A bead of sweat worked its way down between her shoulder blades and huddled, itching and distracting, in the small of her back. "What idea?" Her voice sounded as if it belonged to someone else—remote, cool, detached. She sounded like Gisborne.

Gisborne put a hand against one of the stones framing the window, and though his gloves hid the strength of his grip, Marian could see the line of tense muscle shifting in his back. "Robin Hood," he said in a low voice.

Marian leaned hard against the wood at her back. She could not move or speak—she could not even think.

Gisborne's head bowed. "His crimes are all any lady—or lord, for that matter—can speak of, and yet you never speak his name unless I ask you directly. He wears the mantle and the name of your . . . of Robert of Locksley. And you . . . try as you might to seem so, you are not like other ladies."

Absurdly, Marian's mind seized on his last few words, conjuring up images of Elena and Lady Seild. *You don't know ladies,* she thought, but managed to bite the words back. With his head bowed and his back turned, Marian risked a look toward the tapestry. As far as she could tell, it lay undisturbed, but she could not see whether the sword was still there without climbing on the dressing stool.

Gisborne shifted his weight, then finally turned back toward

Marian. "I believe someone inside Nottingham Castle must be helping him. I thought—God help me—I thought it was you. I thought if I searched your chamber I might find evidence of collusion. A letter, perhaps, or some other token that would connect you to him."

Marian forced herself to move, peeling away from the door and taking three steps toward Gisborne. She could not manage a fourth. "You don't trust me."

Gisborne's eyes met hers, lingered for half a breath, and fell. "Forg—" He cut himself off and shook his head. "I will not demand forgiveness. Lady Marian . . . I apologize. I searched and found nothing. I shouldn't have doubted your honesty."

Marian regretted leaving the support of the door at her back. She could not think what to say in response, not least because, looking at Gisborne's stricken features, she felt a flicker of something alien and unsettling: guilt. "You are forgiven nonetheless." Her voice sounded almost gentle.

Gisborne's lashes fell, and for an instant his eyes stayed closed, a sign of relief he could not—or did not bother to—hide. "You are more gracious than I deserve, my Lady." He took a step toward her, then seemed to change his mind. "Would you indulge me further by letting me stay, and talk to you?"

Moving as if controlled by some unseen force, Marian gestured to the chairs before the hearth. The fire was little more than a smoldering heap of embers and ash, for Elena had been gone as long as she, but warmth still radiated from the coals.

Gisborne crossed to one of the chairs but waited for Marian to seat herself before dropping into it. He didn't speak, gloved fingers wrapped around the lower half of his face, elbow on his knee as he stared into the fireplace.

Marian took the opportunity to study him. She rarely looked

long at him, for fear he would somehow see her secret in her eyes. But despite the conflicted shame of deception still knotting her insides, Marian felt strangely emboldened, shielded against suspicion—at least for now—by her near miss.

He looked tired, features darkened by exposure during the last few days. He'd clearly come straight from the stables, for his clothes were travel stained and worn, and he smelled of sweat and horses. His lips were pressed into a tight, unforgiving line, and the scar that pulled at one cheek was less visible surrounded by the dark stubble that had grown while he'd been away.

"Why do you not grow a beard?" Marian heard herself say, the words tumbling out unbidden.

Gisborne lifted his head, taken aback. "My Lady?"

Hot shame warmed her face, and Marian's fingers twisted in her lap. "Your scar. The way you dress, you try to . . . Why not grow a beard to cover it?"

The hand he'd had pressed against his mouth was still half raised and, after a moment's hesitation, moved to rub self-consciously at the patch of uneven red-and-purple skin. Finally, he said, "The beard does not grow from the dead flesh." He paused, and added, "I would have a bald spot."

Marian blinked away her surprise, and as she watched, the man's lips moved. His face was dark with his own embarrassment, but he was smiling. Only a little, but it was there. Marian exhaled, the sound of her breath shaky and loud in the quiet, and found herself smiling back. "I don't really like beards anyway."

Gisborne's lips quivered, and he glanced toward the fire so that she could see only half of his smile.

"How did it happen?" Marian was trying so hard not to let anything slip about herself, or Robin, or her allegiances, that her tongue was running wild on any other subject that came to mind.

"I was wounded," Gisborne said shortly. His smile had vanished. But then the hand over his scar dropped into his lap. "I was taken prisoner," he elaborated, keeping his eyes on the coals. "Saracens are nothing if not skilled at interrogation." Marian could not help but recoil, and Gisborne did not miss it. He watched her for a long moment out of the corner of his eye. "I suppose you think I should have killed myself rather than be taken prisoner. For the sake of honor."

Marian's eyes widened, in spite of herself. "That had not occurred to me," she said truthfully.

Gisborne's eyes unshielded a fraction, but his face had gone cold again. "Then why do you flinch?" When Marian only looked away, he added, "You can speak honestly, Lady."

Marian had never had the footing or the daring to speak to Gisborne so, and she took a breath to keep herself in check. But he was still watching her, and waiting, and she knew he would wait until she spoke. "I was thinking that must have been where you learned those same skills."

His face had gone still and cold again, eyes remote. "You are speaking of the boy, Will." When Marian didn't answer, Gisborne straightened in his chair. "The Saracens poured oil from a jar down my face and tied me over a lamp so that I could feel its heat rising against my skin, and had to hold myself back against the ties or else be burned. When I refused to tell them of the King's plans for battle, they cut the bonds. I was too weak to stop myself falling against the burning lamp."

Marian felt sick, unable to look at Gisborne without also looking at the scar, which did look, now she saw it, like a ribbon of fire had dripped down from his cheekbone and under his collar.

Gisborne remained unmoved. "When you spoke to the boy,

did you see evidence that he had been burned?"

Marian's vision swam, and she looked away, pressing her lips together. She would not cry for someone like Gisborne, but she knew she had to maintain the illusion that she was not wholly averse to the prospect of marrying him. "They really are godless infidels," she whispered.

Leather creaked as Gisborne shifted his weight back in the chair. He was silent so long that Marian looked up, and she found him staring once again into the hearth. But now she could not tell whether he was seeing the ruins of the fire Elena had laid that morning or another scene entirely, burning sand and perfumed oils.

"I have seen Englishmen do worse," Gisborne murmured. He seemed almost unaware of her in that moment, rigid not with proper posture but with memory. But his next words proved he had not forgotten she was there. "It is war, my Lady. There is no God in war. Not on any side."

The words made her stiffen in spite of herself. She would never be accused of overbearing piety, but the sacrilege in his speech plucked at lessons she'd learned from infancy. A coal in the fireplace popped, and she flinched. She hadn't intended to ask Gisborne about his wound in the first place.

Gisborne seemed to sense her discomfort, for he gave a sharp shake of his head as though ridding himself of memory and straightened. "If I should not have told you, my Lady, forgive me."

"I asked," Marian replied.

Gisborne's lips twisted a fraction. "Most people don't." The answer was quick, informal in a way he'd never been with her before.

Emboldened, Marian asked, "Why has this business with

Robin Hood driven you to such distraction?"

Gisborne's eyes darkened again. "Robin Hood is a criminal. I am tasked with keeping order and peace, and he threatens that order."

"But there are other criminals," Marian countered. "There have been before, and will be again. Why—"

"Because he doesn't just break the law," Gisborne blurted, "he makes a mockery of it." He lurched to his feet as though unable to stand the warmth of the fire any longer. He reached the window again and looked out, his jaw clenched in sharp relief. In profile, his hair still damp with sweat and curling over his ears, he looked younger than he did when charging after Robin Hood or when trying, in his inept way, to woo Marian.

"He breaks the law," Gisborne went on, "and the people cheer him for it."

Marian rose cautiously, carefully, but did not quite dare to join him at the window. "Perhaps the laws he breaks are unjust."

Gisborne made a slicing gesture with his hand, dismissing her words. "Just or unjust, the law is absolute. You, Lady, have the luxury of safety here. You've never seen chaos, *true* chaos. Chaos makes no distinction between those of noble birth and those born low—a man with a sword in his gut will die whether he owns the land or works it."

Marian's hands gripped the back of her chair. "You killed people there—in the Holy Land."

"Yes." Gisborne's answer was quick and ready.

"You had to," said Marian, before she could question the urge to comfort her enemy. "You had no choice."

Gisborne shook his head. "I killed because I was ordered to. Not because I had to." His shoulders rose and fell in a long, silent breath, and he turned away from the window to look at her.

"*Order*, my Lady. That is all the certainty there is in this world. Good and evil are questions for philosophers and holy books. I cannot say what God wants of men—but I know what my King demands of me."

A little voice in Marian's mind made itself heard, but it wasn't Robin's. It was her own, defending her actions to her father. *It's what Robin would have wanted.*

Robin, Marian realized, had been increasingly silent in her thoughts.

"Your work these past days," she said quietly. "You told me before you left that you believed Robin Hood would be captured soon. Were you able to do whatever you needed to do to ensure that?"

Gisborne shifted his weight, and only as he began to assume his distance once more did she realize how much he had revealed in speaking to her. "Yes."

"The archery contest?"

Gisborne raised his eyebrows, lip curling. "That is the Sheriff's plan, not mine."

"You are his brother. I thought—"

"We are *not* brothers." Gisborne's voice cracked like a sheet of ice in midwinter. "His father raised me when mine was killed, but we are not brothers. That has always been abundantly clear to me, my Lady. I will never be of noble blood. No matter my title, I will always be a commoner to him."

Marian watched him draw himself up, oddly defiant in his stiff air, the one he assumed to look like the rest of the nobility, the one that sat so poorly on him, like an ill-fitting tunic. "Then you don't believe the archery contest will work?"

Gisborne's eyes were calm and cool again, and he shook his head lightly. "The Sheriff believes that Robin Hood cannot resist the pageantry of it, that he'll be drawn in by talk of honor and cowardice."

"And you don't?"

"Robin Hood is not stupid enough for that." Gisborne spoke the words evenly, but there was an intensity to the set of his mouth. "I know him, Marian. I fought him, I saw his eyes. He will not be trapped by petty accusations of cowardice. He is too clever, and lacks the uncertainty that would give power to words like 'dishonor.'"

Marian's heart had quickened. "You sound almost as if you admire him."

Gisborne's lips twitched, then parted. He stopped before he spoke, however, and focused on Marian's face. "I cannot admire any man who defies the law."

"But you have your own plan." Marian saw Gisborne hesitate at that unspoken question, then added gently, "You needn't tell me, Sir Guy. I would not ask you for your confidence when I don't have your trust."

Gisborne straightened. "You have it, my Lady. I trust you. I swear it. My plan has little to do with Robin Hood, but that we need to move a large amount of goods through Nottingham, and I fear he might interfere."

Marian folded her hands carefully behind her so that she would not betray herself by gripping the chair's back in excitement. "Another shipment of grain?"

"Gold." Gisborne spoke in a low voice, though the oaken door to Marian's room was thick enough to muffle a shout. "The Sheriff hopes to catch Robin Hood with this archery contest, but all I need is for him to be distracted. Revenue is pouring in from across the countryside, and we cannot risk large detachments of guards signaling the value of the wagons as they come in. But if Robin Hood is busy preparing for the contest, then he's unlikely to waste time searching every merchant coming and going for the festival."

Marian felt light-headed and fought to keep her face somber. Gisborne had spoken of the gold coming in during the festival, but not where it would go once the festival was over. What she and the others could do with that amount of wealth . . . all Nottingham would cry out in relief. Those in debt could pay back their taxes from the Sheriff's own personal coffers. She longed to ask for more information, but sense overruled her enthusiasm.

"Brothers or not," she said gently, "the Sheriff's confidence in you is not misplaced."

Gisborne was silent at first, watching her from the window. Then he crossed the room and reached slowly for her hand, giving her ample time to step back or resist. She let him capture her fingers, folding them in his and raising them to his lips. "I hope," he said, voice gruff and stiff, "that when this is over, you will consider my suit, my Lady." His gaze rose from her hand, and she was pinned by the intensity of it, a sudden and startling departure from the emotionless mask he usually wore.

Marian would have stepped back, but for the hands around hers. They were warm, and her mind seized on that detail, struck by the strangeness of it. His manner was so cold—that his skin should be warm, like that of any normal man, seemed impossible.

"I believe you loved Robert of Locksley." More than ever, his stiff manner seemed skin-deep, an ill-fitting tunic settled on his shoulders. A costume. "And I regret asking for your hand so soon after his death. If I wounded you, Lady, then know I intend it to be the last time I cause you pain."

His gaze dropped, and he stooped to brush his lips against the backs of Marian's fingers again. He released her and moved past, and Marian heard the door open and close again as he left. Her body tingled, and surprise kept her pinned to the spot.

It took another loud snap from the glowing embers in the hearth to jar her from her confusion. With an effort, Marian left the chair before her and dragged the dressing stool to the tapestry. Her fingertips explored the top of the tapestry, blood pounding in her ears, until they touched the cold, familiar edge of the blade.

She replaced the dressing stool and let her gaze wander, moving from the window to the chair Gisborne had occupied, and then to the hearth that had so captivated him. She waited for her racing heart to slow now that she'd reassured herself Gisborne had not found the sword in her room, but it only continued to pound, until her very fingertips throbbed with each pulse.

With a sudden, biting need, Marian whirled and went to the washbasin and plunged her hands into its chilly water, scrubbing and scrubbing until she could no longer remember the feel of Gisborne's lips on her skin.

"You can't go!"

Robin has never heard Marian sound so angry, and he's seen her a breath away from murderous rage on more than one occasion.

"I must serve my King," he says softly.

Marian's staring at him like he's gone mad. "But Robin—you'll be gone months, years even, and I . . . what'll I do without you?"

Robin cannot help but smile a little, for all his heart is wrenching itself from his chest. "You've never needed me to be you," he points out. He's practiced—he's good at it now. She never sees how much it costs him to say such things.

Marian dashes her hand across her eyes. "You've made up your mind."

Robin lifts his chin a little, watching her face, but says nothing. Because he cannot lie to her, and the truth is that he doesn't want to go—the war is a mad, foolish enterprise from a King more interested in glory than in the well-being of his own people. The truth is Marian could change his mind. So he cannot let her realize that.

Marian watches him in return, anguish in her every glance and breath. Then, hastily, she's tugging at the ring on her finger until it comes free, and she holds it at arm's length. For a moment Robin is staggered, not understanding, wondering if her temper was so hot that she could really reject him now because of his loyalty to the crown.

"To remember me by," Marian says, holding the ring out again. "While you're there. To remind you to come home and give it back to me."

Her voice breaks on that last word, and, unable to resist a moment longer, Robin closes the distance between them and gathers her into his arms. She holds on to him so fiercely, and her shoulders are shaking.

In this moment Robin can almost pretend that she loves him as he loves her.

She does love him—Robin knows it, can feel it in the tightness of her embrace. But it is a different sort of love, and it always has been. Robin lets her be Marian, and that is what she loves best about him. Perhaps the time apart will change them—perhaps her love will change with distance. Perhaps his service to the King will show her a side of him she's never considered. Perhaps . . .

He presses his cheek to hers and tightens his arms around her. He will love her whether her heart changes toward him or not. They will have years together, a lifetime together. When Robin returns from the Holy Land, he will marry her, and they will live together and love together and she will see what he has always known, that they are destined for each other. Someday, Marian will be ready to love someone. There is no rush. He will wait for her.

They have time.

TWENTY-NINE

WITH GISBORNE BACK IN Nottingham Castle, Marian could not so easily visit Sherwood Forest as Robin Hood. She went once as herself, bearing news from "Robin," who could not come for fear of leading pursuers to his loyal compatriots. She told them of the influx of gold Gisborne had described, and that Robin was working on a plan to steal it after the festival. Every time her lips formed the words "Robin says" or "according to Robin," she felt like a traitor—but whether she was betraying herself or the men who trusted her, she could not tell.

The ambush of Owen and Seild had transformed the band, igniting a sense of purpose that Marian herself could barely control, even as Robin. They robbed another wealthy traveler, and another, perfecting their tactics, until Marian had to tell them to slow down their efforts, for fear the wealthy would stop traveling through Sherwood altogether. The wealth being distributed to the people spread beyond the walls of Nottingham and into the farmhouses and cottages of the surrounding shires.

Together, she and Elena discussed and dismissed idea after idea for how Robin Hood could enter the archery contest without betraying Marian's identity or risking their lives. All Nottingham expected Robin to compete, despite agreeing it was a trap—so bewitching was the spell that the masked figure had cast upon the people that their expectations defied all sense. And though she knew it was vain, and foolish, and dangerous, Marian could not help but want to preserve that spell as long as she could. She would not risk her father's reputation or the lives of her men, but if she could only think how to win the arrow safely . . .

With the last of their secrets exposed, Elena and Marian spent more time than ever together. They didn't speak often of Robin Hood, or of Alan and the others, but they managed to share more pieces of themselves with each other, and as the days passed, Marian could no longer imagine bearing the weight of Robin Hood alone.

Elena told her how she and Alan had met when she was a girl and he a traveling minstrel living off scraps from town to town, always coming back to Locksley when he could. She told Marian of their years-long courtship, that they'd both grown out of childhood trying to create a future for themselves. And that Alan had been caught only because he'd stayed in Sherwood Forest after performing in Locksley so that he could spend one more day with her before moving on to the next town again.

"We only have to hold on until the King returns," Elena said, combing Marian's hair in preparation for a morning with the other ladies in the castle. "Once he pardons Alan, we can be together."

Marian longed to sit and linger in the warmth of contact, the gentle touch of comb on scalp, the fantasy of happily ever after—but she could not help but speak. "What was his crime? His original crime, what he was outlawed for?"

"Poaching," replied Elena. "He had no money for a meal, and wouldn't leave for the next town without saying goodbye to me."

The King's deer, thought Marian, *are the King's deer whether the King is in Jerusalem or Aquitaine.* Aloud, she said, "You think the King will pardon him?"

The comb paused. Voice higher with surprise, Elena said, "Of course he will. When the King returns, everything will change."

Marian fell silent, and when Elena had finished her hair and crowned it with its veil and declared her a vision of loveliness to spark envy in any lady's esteem, Marian thanked her. And if she wasn't as warm in her gratitude as she might have been, or as friendly in her goodbye, she was distracted by the strength of the realization that had taken root in her heart.

Good or evil, she thought, remembering Gisborne's dismissal of philosophy and piety. She could not know what the King would do when he returned. She could not know if he *would* return. She'd always imagined Robin Hood would put away his bow and his mask when the King returned, for there would be no need of him—but she could not know for certain.

Nor was she willing to let Elena and Alan's future hang upon the mercy of an absent King. She would see them wed and safe herself. Robin Hood would see it done.

And Marian had, deep in her mind, still fragile and ephemeral as a spider's web, the beginnings of an idea.

As night blanketed the countryside, Marian left Jonquille in the stables, with Robin's costume safely hidden in her saddlebags. She'd been out to the campsite to make plans with her men and had gathered information not about the archery contest, but the shipment of gold Gisborne had mentioned. There were too many smaller targets to effectively rob them all on the way *into* the festival, but there would be a brief window of opportunity as the gold left Nottingham on its way to Prince John. As on the way into the town, there would be few guards, nothing to attract attention. They'd leave sometime after the festival's end, once the other vendors in town for the event had left, so that Robin would be distracted harrying the vendors and not the shipment of gold, humbly disguised.

She discussed strategies with Alan and John, while Will gazed at her with shining eyes. Not for the first time, she wished he'd been born with a little of his sister's good sense. He watched her with as much worship in his gaze as the lads in town whenever Robin Hood made an appearance, and it made her nervous. Love—even the love of a boy for his hero—made people foolish.

Despite her attempts to keep them on the subject of the gold, the others were more interested in the archery contest than highway robbery. Marian could not stop thinking about it either, though not for the same reasons as the others—they talked about the poetry of it, the idea that Robin Hood meant something now to the people and could not be seen to abandon them even when faced with an obvious trap. But she could not help but think about the other prize offered almost as an after-thought alongside the golden arrow: pardon.

She had left them arguing about the best way to cause a dis-traction in which Robin could escape after winning the contest. Will had proposed winning the contest with one arrow and kill-ing Gisborne with the second. John had countered with an offer to challenge the winner to a public wrestling match, which he'd graciously allow Robin to win, and then escape in the press of the crowd. Alan was explaining all the ways their ideas wouldn't work when Marian slipped away, and an indignant rumble of "Shut up, Alan" followed her as she hurried back toward Nottingham.

She'd left in the late afternoon, but the sun had set by the time she reached the walls of the town. Marian was counting on the darkness to aid her in reentering the castle. She was used to sneaking in and out by now and had discovered more than one inconspicuous route, but this time she intended to bring the cloak and bow with her. The contest was in only a few days' time, and with all the arrivals and departures taking place, she didn't like the idea of leaving her gear in the stables with Jonquille anymore.

Marian climbed up the wall where she'd grappled with Gisborne and then ran lightly along its top. People rarely looked up, she'd discovered, and in the tricky indigo that followed twilight, she was nearly invisible. She'd left a second cloak in a hollow where a stone had fallen away from the wall, and this she slipped on to cover the signature green of Robin's. The bow and quiver she tucked close to her side, and after scanning the alley below to make certain no one was watching, she dropped with a bone-jarring thud to the earth.

Elena had shown her a few of the servants' entrances, and it was through one of these that she crept back into the castle.

The important thing, she thought as she made her way through the castle corridors, was not so much that *Robin* won the contest, but that someone did. The pardon was meant to be a lure as great as the golden arrow itself, in case Robin was not tempted by wealth—Marian thought it likely that Gisborne, and not the Sheriff, had been the one to propose adding a pardon to the prize. Marian knew who she wanted that pardon for, but Alan's skill with the bow was mediocre at best. He could hit his mark more often than not, but only if the target was the size of a deer—or a man—and then it was anyone's guess where his arrow would strike.

It had to be her own hands that drew the bow and released the arrow, if she wanted to be certain of victory. But it must be Alan who received the prize.

A guard stood at the junction of the stair to the corridor that led to Marian's room. He was one of the younger ones, helmet too large for his head and beard too wispy despite his best efforts to compensate for his youth. Marian strode forward, ignoring him as most of the visiting nobility did, and he made no move to stop her. They were all so busy looking for a masked man in a green cloak, and so besieged by unfamiliar visitors, that Marian had more freedom than ever.

She was halfway down the hall when a voice called from the stairwell behind her, "Here—halt a minute, your Lordship."

Marian pretended she hadn't heard the guard's request and hurried her steps.

"Wait—you dropped your . . . uh . . . "

Marian risked a glance over her shoulder and saw that the guard had stooped to retrieve something from the floor. It was no more than a scrap of fabric, but as soon as she saw it, Marian's heart seized.

The mask.

She'd tucked it inside her tunic, but it must have worked its way free as she walked.

The guard was examining it, poking his gloved fingers through the eyeholes. He looked up, and his eyes met Marian's in the same instant that she realized turning over her shoulder had pushed the hood back far enough to show her features.

The moment stretched out, punctuated by the distant, surly

crow of a cockerel in the town, protesting the night. The guard was slack-jawed, wispy beard quivering, and Marian's mind had gone blank. The mask, her identity . . . she needed an explanation, some excuse that would satisfy the guard. Some way out . . .

The guard's eyes dropped, and with a confused oath, he reached for his sword. Marian saw that she'd shifted her grip on her bow, and that she held it ready at her side, not tucked out of sight below her cloak.

The sword scraped against its sheath. Marian moved without thought. Her fingertips searched the coded fletching in the quiver at her hip and found the twist of cord that meant a sharp, mail-piercing tip. The arrow found its way to the string, and she lifted the bow. Her hand was steady, her breath still. And the arrow whispered its familiar quiet song as it flew through the air.

The guard's sword hit the floor with an ear-shattering clang of metal on stone. The force of the arrow's impact had knocked him back against the wall, and he stayed leaning there, mouth open. He stared in open confusion down at his chest, where his chain mail had sprouted an arrow shaft and ivory fletching. His beard trembled. He did not look back at Marian but tried to take a step on quivering legs—and when they gave way, he moaned as he slumped toward the ground.

Marian could not move. She still held the bow at length, feet still braced, fingers still half curled by her cheek where they'd let fly the arrow. She'd brushed her hood with her arm and it had fallen the rest of the way down, and she stood exposed until a voice called out from the stairs. Someone had heard the sword hit the floor, or the guard's cry, or the thud of his body on the stone.

Marian wrenched herself out of stillness and leaned against the wall, reeling and dizzy, before summoning the will to make it the rest of the way to her door as booted feet came pounding up the stairs at the end of the hall.

The bow clattered to the floor once she'd shut the door behind her, and Marian fell back against it, every nerve screaming.

It was not a mortal injury. It had struck nearer the shoulder than the heart. He could live. Flesh wounds could bleed like a death blow. And his fellow guards had been moments away. They'd stop the bleeding. Remove the arrow. Send for a physician.

He'd be fine.

Marian drew a breath, and it made her retch. She doubled over, too stricken to reach the chamber pot, and vomited in the corner, stomach heaving long after it had emptied itself. The sound of bile splattering the floor sounded, in her ringing ears, exactly like the clang of metal on stone.

Marian had missed. She hadn't been aiming for his shoulder. She'd been aiming for his heart.

She'd been trying to kill him.

THIRTY

"HE SAW ME." MARIAN sat, limp, as disconnected from her own body as she'd been the moment Gisborne had told her, all those weeks ago, that Robin was dead.

"I know, my Lady, I know." Elena was bundling soiled rags into a sack, pouring fresh water over the stone where Marian had thrown up, and wiping it a third time. "You had no choice. I know you never wanted to hurt anyone. The servants say they think he'll live."

Marian's heart thundered with relief and terror combined, so profound that she moaned the words that came next: "No—Elena, he saw *me*."

Her maid stopped, lifting her head. "You weren't dressed as Robin?"

Marian's head shifted to the side, and she found she could not hold it upright, and let it fall back against the wall behind her. "He saw me."

Elena watched her from the corner of the room, on her

knees, scrubbing rags and water pitcher beside her. Marian sat opposite on the floor, a blanket wound around her shoulders, hair half escaped from the tie that had held it back. Her maid had found her there, shaking and white as snow, and had taken over without missing a step. She'd stripped both cloaks from her and stowed them and the bow and quiver God knew where—Marian could not remember what she'd done with them, or what had happened between that moment and this one.

Elena went back to work without a word, mopping up the last of the water and stuffing the rags into the sack with the others. Then she rose, her face grave, expression trying to hide the fear Marian could read in her eyes.

"Maybe he won't survive." She sank slowly to the floor at Marian's side.

"I pray to God he lives." Marian closed her eyes and felt the hot sting of tears on raw cheeks. She must have been crying already, because her skin burned where the salt touched.

Elena slipped an arm around Marian and pulled her in close. A few weeks ago Marian would've stiffened at her touch, but now she turned and buried her face in Elena's thin shoulder, curling up as the agony of guilt ripped at her body.

Robin, she called out desperately in her thoughts. *I need you—where are you?*

But his voice in her mind was silent.

How long Marian wept she did not know—but she and Elena were still there on the floor when the door burst open.

Marian lifted her head, but Elena was already on her feet, moving far more quickly. "Sir!" she exclaimed, indignant as she moved to stand between Marian and the door. "My Lady is unwell. You cannot—"

"Unwell?" Gisborne's voice was hoarse. "Is she—is she hurt?" He started toward her.

"My Lord!" Elena, in her haste and distress, moved to intercept him—something no servant, and certainly no female servant, had the right to do. "Please, she is merely ill, you must let her rest, she is not decent—"

Marian saw the flash of Gisborne's eyes over Elena's shoulder. They swept over her form, blanket and dressing gown and all. Then he turned away abruptly, shoulders tight. "I will send the physician—"

"No," croaked Marian. "No physician." She would not shoot a man and then deprive him of care because she could not control her reaction.

Gisborne flinched at the sound of her voice but did not turn. "My Lady," he said quietly. "You heard?"

"I saw." The lie—except it was not a lie, was it?—came more easily than ever, more easily than breath just now. "I heard a sound and looked out and saw him lying there, and blood, and—" Her voice gave out, for she *had* seen what she described, and she saw it even now, transposed over the tableau of Elena and Gisborne at odds in her chamber.

Gisborne exhaled audibly. "You will see to her?" This, Marian assumed, was directed to Elena, who nodded and made a shooing motion.

"She needs rest and prayer and solitude," Elena said firmly.

I need Robin, Marian thought, and the words burned in her mind.

Gisborne said something Marian could not hear and stalked out. Elena stood for a moment, trembling, and then whirled to return to Marian's side. She bathed Marian's face with a cool cloth, combed her hair back from her perspiring face, led her to the hearth. She put a cup of well-watered ale in her hands and told her to drink. Marian, all too eager to let someone else take charge of her, drank. Elena disposed of the soiled rags, built the fire back up, wrapped Marian's ice-cold feet in woolen stockings. She sat beside her and held her hand, and Marian's eyes were closed before she realized that water and ale weren't the only tastes on her tongue—she recognized well the bitter flavor of the draught she'd been given for her terrors all those weeks ago.

She tried to curse Elena, for if the guard survived and named her, she could not be asleep or dulled by drug. She had to ready herself to flee, and warn her father as well, and tell the men in Sherwood to scatter, and find what Elena had done with Robin's gear and dispose of it, and think of somewhere to hide, and . . .

She woke in darkness. The fire was little more than a glow at the foot of her bed, and she heard nothing but her own heart-beat. She must have made some sound, however, because a soft voice came from the darkness at her side, gentle and familiar and warm.

"I'm here, my Lady. The guard sleeps. He has not spoken." A touch smoothed the hair at her temple. "Close your eyes."

Marian closed her eyes.

Morning dawned gray and cold, a veil of rain muting the world outside the castle windows and drowning out the distant sounds of life in the town. Elena forced Marian to eat a few bites of bland porridge and then vanished for a time, disposing of the dishes and, Marian felt sure, listening for more information.

Marian stood by the window, looking out and seeing little. The fingertips of her right hand were raw, for she'd not been wear-ing her archer's glove when she'd used her bow the night before. She toyed with the damaged skin, running her hypersensitive fingers along the cold stone, the rough fabric of her dress, the hot, equally sensitive flesh of her lips.

For all the immediacy of her guilt and grief the night before, she felt as remote and distant as Gisborne himself now. It was as if the woman who had tried to murder a man the night before was someone else altogether. Another identity to add to her collection. The Lady Marian, the outlaw Robin Hood, and the murderer.

Her thoughts were quiet and still, and cold. And Robin's voice was silent.

Have you left me now? Marian demanded, pressing her forehead to the window's pane. *In the moment I need your counsel most?*

She got no answer.

When Elena returned, she didn't waste a moment in pleasantries. The guard still slept, she reported. Which meant he also still lived. Perhaps her maid sensed she didn't want company anymore, for she was gone much of the morning, returning only to give Marian news of the guard, which was always the same. *He still lives. He still sleeps.*

Another servant came to ask if Gisborne could call on her, and she refused. Her father came, and she told him she was ill with monthly humors. Seild tapped at her door and called a hesitant greeting, and when Marian didn't answer, Seild didn't come in.

The rain continued to fall, Marian's heart continued to beat, and the guard still slept.

Sunset brought the day's first change, and it arrived in the form of a man at her door. Elena was there, and opened the door cautiously. On the other side was an emaciated figure in a rough-spun robe, whose shaven pate told of his calling.

"Good evening, Frère," Elena greeted him respectfully. She

did not, however, stand aside to admit him to the room.

"Good evening, child." The monk's eyes moved from Elena to Marian, who sat by the fire, motionless. "I heard the lady was ill and had refused the physician's care. I have not his skill, but I thought I might see if she would consent to what aid I can offer."

Elena glanced at Marian, who rose. She was steady on her feet again, and her hands had stopped shaking. She smiled. "Thank you, Frère. I am well. It was a female complaint, and I am better now."

"In that case," said the monk gently, starting to withdraw, "please excuse my manners. I should return to Tom."

Marian lifted her head, brow furrowing. "Tom?"

The brother paused and turned back, explaining, "I'm sure you've heard, my Lady. A lad was wounded last night here in the castle. He is now gravely ill."

"Tom." Marian echoed the syllable, lips shaping it as if the ordinary, familiar, common name was one she'd never heard before.

"How is he?" Elena asked swiftly.

The monk's thin features drooped. "He survived the night. The physician has done all he can. Now it only remains to wait, and to pray for God's mercy. If the wound begins to heal, he may live. If the wound poisons his blood . . . he will go with God."

Elena closed the door behind him and then looked at Marian, who still hadn't moved away from her chair. "God's mercy," she whispered, leaning against the wood at her back.

Marian closed her eyes, too hollow for tears, but unable to look at her maid's face. She knew what Elena meant. If the guard—if *Tom* died, he'd take Marian's identity to his grave, and she would be safe. Robin Hood would be safe. If God willed it, their problems would be solved.

But the lad, as the brother had called him, would be dead.

Marian would be a murderer.

She'd been seeing him fall, again and again, whenever she closed her eyes. This time, though, she saw not the guard's face, not his wide eyes and wispy beard and stricken features, but the faces of the two boys outside Nottingham, the ones she'd imagined with food in their bellies when she'd stolen the grain from the Sheriff's stores. There was not so much difference between them and the guard who straddled life and death. In a few years, if they were lucky, one of them might find work as a guard at Nottingham Castle.

Marian asked Elena to leave, and then changed her mind and took her hand instead, and then changed her mind again and said she wanted to be alone. Elena squeezed her fingers, her eyes full of understanding, and slipped out.

"Let him live," whispered Marian, drifting once more to the window, watching the rivulets of water meet and split and course down the glazed pane. "Please, God. Have mercy."

THIRTY-ONE

THE RAIN FELL UNTIL the next morning, which dawned as clear and rosy as if a higher power had ordered the weather to turn fair for the festival that would begin that day. The town had transformed itself, every square packed with vendors, the grassy stretches of hillside filled with carts, minstrels, and performers on each corner trying to wheedle a coin out of passersby.

Marian dressed in her finest, a rich indigo that bordered daringly on royal purple. Elena braided her hair into a crown and teased a few strands out from beneath her veil to frame her cheeks. Lady Seild, on seeing Marian's face, drew her into her own chamber in order to ply her with cosmetics, darkening her lips and cheeks.

"You look like an angel of death," Seild muttered, brow furrowed in concentration as she smudged at Marian's lips.

Marian didn't answer.

When Cecile and a handful of others arrived, with the

intention of all going down to the festival, Marian told them she would join them soon. She slipped out of the group and made her way toward the chamber in which the wounded guard lay.

Elena had looked at her sharply the night before, when Marian had asked her to find out where the injured man was being kept. She'd gone without comment, though, and had come back with the location. It wasn't until she'd finished Marian's hair and had stood back to inspect her handiwork that she said anything at all about it.

"Perfect," said Elena. And then, hands falling to her sides, she said, "What will you do?"

Marian looked at her friend, the normally clear blue eyes now hooded with weary dread, the fingers twisted in her skirts, the lips pressed thin—and she knew what Elena meant.

For a moment, Marian felt that frightened stare like a hot blade. "You think I would kill him?"

Elena moved instantly, without another moment of hesitation. She stepped forward and wrapped her arms around Marian, who stood as stiff and unmoved as Gisborne. "Never. I could never think that, my Lady."

Except she had. Marian had seen it in her face. And now, as she passed a pair of guards leaving the barracks to go down to the festival, she thought, *Shouldn't I?*

It still wasn't Robin's voice, but it was as shocking and unreal as if it had been. Her dagger rested in its sheath bound to her thigh, for she never went anywhere now without it. Its blade was narrow—she could drive it through the wound her arrow had already made, and no one would know.

Marian paused, wondering if she was about to throw up again. But the nausea passed, and pressing a hand to her mouth, she moved on.

The room where the wounded guard lay was little better than the cell that had contained Will. It was cleaner, but only slightly—the air still smelled of urine and waste, and another odor the cell had lacked. The smell of decay. Marian stood in the doorway, unwilling to leave the relative light of the corridor for the dank interior of the room, until a voice bade her enter.

"Come in, child." It was the monk, one bony hand extended toward her. Marian had not seen him there in the corner. "He is asleep. You won't disturb him." The monk was seated upon a rough-hewn stool and got laboriously to his feet in order to gesture to it, the only seat in the room.

Marian drew back, shaking her head. "No. I can't. I couldn't. Sit, Frère, please. Sit."

The monk waited a few seconds, studying Marian's face, and then resumed his seat with a little sigh of relief. He wasn't an old man, younger than her father, but he moved with difficulty. When he rested his hands against his thighs, Marian saw that his fingers were gnarled, crooked as if with great effort, like hands clawing for freedom. Or mercy.

He saw her looking and smiled. "A test God has granted me," he said gently. "A wasting illness. Would you believe I was once stout enough to fill that doorway?" He chuckled and leaned his back against the wall behind him.

Marian shifted her weight, uncomfortable but not willing to move her gaze from the holy man to the still form in the bed on the opposite wall. "Why do you laugh?"

"Because it's funny," he replied placidly. "To me, it is."

Marian glanced at the doorway, wishing she could leave the old man to his prayer, but held her ground in spite of herself. "How is he?"

"The wound has soured," said the monk. "But I have seen men live through worse. They tell me Tom has a great will. Perhaps he will live."

"I thought it was up to God." Marian could not help the bitter note in her voice.

"Ah." The monk seemed unfazed by her tone. "But if his will to live sees him through another day, who gave him that will, child?" He didn't seem to expect an answer, for after a brief pause, he went on. "His parents, I suppose, who taught him grace and duty. But who gave his parents strength to see a child through the hardships and pitfalls of life?"

Marian eyed the monk askance as he muttered on. She became aware of a soft sound now that she was still. Breath, shallow. In and out. Faint and fluttering as a butterfly. She took a deep breath, ignoring the sour smell of the air, and looked at the bed.

The wide eyes were closed, and if it hadn't been for the wispy beard, Marian would not have recognized him as the young man she'd faced in the hall two nights earlier. His cheeks were sunken and white except for two spots of color, and his pale brow was beaded with sweat. His lips were cracked like dry mud, and the breath whistled past them in a defiant reminder that the body in the bed still lived.

"God has already spared him once." The monk was speaking again, and when Marian glanced his way, she saw that he was watching her. "The arrow that wounded him was very close to his lungs, where he breathes. If it had been a finger's breadth closer, he would have died there in the corridor."

Marian wondered what she was doing there, why she had come to haunt the man she'd tried to murder. "It doesn't seem to me a merciful act. He's dying, isn't he?"

"Yes." The stool creaked as its occupant leaned forward. "I

don't claim to know the will of God, child. But if He spared this boy only to take him later, I might think perhaps the arrow missed for another reason."

"Another reason?"

"There are two souls hanging upon each breath he draws," said the monk softly.

"It's still murder if he dies now," Marian whispered, staring at the corpselike body breathing laboriously in the bed.

"Aye." The monk sighed. "But if he dies now, perhaps he'll go with the prayers of the one who killed him."

Marian's eyes burned, and she wished she could turn away, but there was nothing in the room to look at, nowhere to rest her blurring eyes except for the man she'd shot and the monk standing vigil as he died.

"Do you think it makes a difference?" Her voice was small, and she knew she was speaking sacrilege, but some part of her knew the monk would not take offense. Or, perhaps, she didn't care.

The monk considered her question, his eyes resting on the still form of the wounded guard. "Would it make a difference if it were you?"

Marian, too, watched the wounded man. *Tom*, she reminded herself. Not "the guard" or "the injured lad." Tom. *Would it make a difference?* she asked herself, or Robin. But no answer came.

The monk said, "Will you say a prayer with me, child?"

Marian pressed her fingers and thumb together, feeling the sting of raw skin, the wound from the bowstring that she hadn't let heal. She took a step backward toward the door. "I'm expected at the festival."

The monk smiled at her. "Go with God."

❧

Autumn was in its fullest, richest regalia, smells and colors permeating every corner of Nottingham town. Laughter and music rang through the laneways. Rickety stages had been erected at either end of the main road up to the castle, though when Marian made her way past only one was in use. It featured a pair of puppeteers performing a much-simplified version of a miracle play. An exquisitely decorated fish made of autumn leaves swallowed up a humbly robed figure, drawing hushed gasps from the assembled crowd of all ages as Marian walked by.

Shouts caught Marian's attention, and she waved away a cluster of sweetmeat vendors as she headed toward the commotion. A wrestling pit had been set up in one of the livestock market pens, and despite the soggy ground after the rain, it was even more popular than the puppet show. Two men—she assumed they were men, she could scarcely see them for the mud that covered them—were staggering around, bare to the waist, trying and mostly failing to get hold of each other. Abruptly one of them rolled, grabbing the legs out from under his opponent, and pinned him down until the fellow cried out and slapped at the mud to be let free.

When the victor stood, Marian nearly swore aloud. Though his height was unmistakable, Marian scarcely would have recognized Little John. He was covered in mud and he had darkened his hair with what looked like ink or soot, turning it unnaturally black. But more startling than that, the bushy beard was gone, revealing a surprisingly well-shaped chin, complete with a little dimple nestled in its center. Marian could see why he'd let the beard grow before—he didn't seem half so fierce without it now, despite the mud streaking his face like war paint.

He started to look her way, but Marian ducked back into the crowd before he could catch his eye. All three of her men were to be here the day of the archery contest, but that wasn't until tomorrow. She had not expected them to twice risk being identified and captured by attending both days of the festival, but she could not blame them for coming, either. Alan would be here somewhere too, no doubt, winkling a few coins out of festivalgoers in exchange for a song. She hoped Will had had better sense, so soon after being face-to-face with Gisborne and his guards in the jail, but she could not help but look for his face among those she passed.

Though it wasn't yet noon, a cluster of people had gathered to dance outside the city gates. Their feet were rapidly turning the grassy slope into a mudslide, but they persisted, despite the fact that Marian saw several people vanish with a yelp only to resurface moments later, muddy and laughing. Marian stared hard at the trio of musicians half-invisible in the crowd, but none of them had Alan's features or bearing.

Shrieks of laughter blended into the wail of a shawm pipe, leaves swirled about on the wind like soaring flames, and the smells from cooking fires mingled with those coming from a nearby spice merchant. Marian twisted her fingers together, skin still stripped raw by the bowstring's cut.

Robin would have loved it.

Where are you? Marian thought, her eyes stinging with tears, her heart aching.

She could not look at the dancers without imagining Robin among them, darting out to grab her hand and pull her in. She could not turn toward the vendors without remembering a May fair two years ago where he'd bought her a beautifully carved wooden pendant. And when a little girl, bedecked with a crown of autumn leaves, beckoned her down to offer her an adornment similar to her own from the basket of bright leaves at her side,

Marian could only shake her head mutely and back away.

"Marian!" Cecile's voice blended with the background chaos, but the use of Marian's name cut through to her ears. "Come, see what we've found!"

Marian dug in her pocket until her fingers found a coin, which she offered to the girl with the wreaths. "Later?" she asked with a smile. The girl snatched the coin, flashed her an answering smile that lacked at least two teeth, and vanished in search of other prey.

Marian made her way toward Cecile, who stood with Tess by a portly man standing guard over a wooden display. The sisters were looking a little bored. Tess was watching the dancing with naked envy, for none of the dancers were nobility, and the idea of her joining in was impossible. Cecile, on the other hand, was watching the musicians. One of them was a younger man, and quite handsome, and quite aware of that fact—he grinned and strutted as he played his tambour. Marian gave him a second inspection, uneasy, making doubly certain it wasn't Alan.

"Look here, Marian." Cecile took her arm and drew her close. "Look at that necklace. Beautiful, isn't it?"

Marian sighed and dutifully inspected the portly merchant's wares, which consisted of a motley assortment of jewelry and hair ornaments. Most of it was poor quality, inlaid with semiprecious stones or cheap glass. The necklace was obvious at a glance. Studded with clear sapphires, woven with silver and gold wire, it was blatantly worth more than his entire collection put together.

And it was familiar.

Marian glanced at Cecile, who was grinning as she asked, "Doesn't it remind you of Seild's?"

"I think hers was not half so lovely," Marian answered, her eyes on the jewels she'd stolen from around her friend's neck.

Her men had moved quickly. Whether they'd sold it to the merchant and distributed the profit, or given it directly to someone in need, she couldn't know.

"A coin, m'Lady?" begged a wheezy voice by her elbow. Marian started and glanced down to find a bent old man there, clutching a stout walking stick that stood taller than he did. "Alms for the poor?"

Marian's hand went automatically to her pocket, and she'd already closed her fingers around a couple of coins when something tickled along the back of her neck—recognition . . . or suspicion.

She looked up and saw that the old man had lifted his head, and that a pair of amused, youthful blue eyes was watching her.

She swallowed her shock and managed a gesture to the other ladies, telling them to go on ahead without her. When they'd turned their backs and had moved out of earshot, Marian drew back with a furious whisper.

"Alan! Why in God's name are you here? And what—how— is that *flour* in your hair?"

The minstrel gave his head a shake, and a bit of white dust sifted out of it. "It works pretty well, don't you find, my Lady?"

Marian stalled for time, sorting through the coins in her palm and trying not to look directly at Alan, who was clearly beyond pleased with his disguise. "You shouldn't be here today. I saw John, too—you're taking a terrible risk."

Alan gestured dismissively, drawing himself up until he remembered he was supposed to be bent with age. "Everyone's looking for Robin Hood," he said airily. "Not his men. And I wasn't fool enough to come as a minstrel, though the good Lord knows they could use me. That man's hopelessly flat." He jerked his chin toward the viol player among the dancers.

Marian glanced over her shoulder and saw Cecile's head turn in her direction. "Be careful, both of you."

"Don't worry yourself, good Lady. Enjoy the festival. Will's here somewhere, too, dressed like a dandy." Alan saw Marian's face and hastened to add, "He only borrowed the clothes from a tailor's stall. He'll give them back."

Marian ran a shaking hand over her face. "I could kill you for being so reckless," she muttered, handing a few coins—the smallest she had—to Alan with a dark look.

Alan crooned a wheezy thank-you and then added with a sidelong grin, "You're spending too much time in our company, Lady. You're starting to sound a little like Robin, you know."

The feast in Nottingham Castle that night was grand, with a pair of spring's piglets glazed and spit-roasted, potatoes rich with butter and gravy, and pheasant stuffed with diced apple. Marian could not find her appetite despite having walked most of the day with the other ladies through the festival. Amid the odors of roasted pork and sweet fruit, she kept catching the scent of something else, something sickly sweet with decay. She knew she was imagining it, but she could not muster much enthusiasm for the feast, for she knew what smell it was. The same smell she'd noticed when she visited the wounded guard that morning.

She joined the other ladies in a few rounds and caroles, and sat with her father when she wasn't dancing. They sat quietly together, and though Marian could not shake the memory of what he'd said about Robin Hood—that he was nothing like her Robin—he reached out occasionally to pat her hand, as if reminding himself that she was there.

Gisborne was nowhere to be seen.

Too busy planning my arrest and execution, she thought, thinking gloomily of the archery contest to take place the next day.

Marian made herself stay until some of the older ladies began to retire, later than she might have wished. Once she was able to slip away, she didn't go straight to her room, but rather headed for the barracks again. They were almost completely empty, with most of the guards either on duty at the feast or joining in the festivities in town. She hesitated outside the door to Tom's room for a time, and only entered after footsteps at the end of the corridor told her someone was approaching who'd see her lingering.

The monk was there, his gaunt features thrown into sharp relief by the flickering light of the lamp on the floor next to his stool. He greeted Marian without surprise, inviting her in for all the world like a highborn Lady welcoming company into her home.

"Is he changed?" Marian asked, half-afraid to look at the body in the bed.

The monk shook his head. "It's been many hours since he last took any water, and he's hot to the touch. But God is merciful, my Lady."

Marian forced herself to the guard's bedside. He looked very much as he'd looked that morning, though the warmth of the lamplight lent his face color, and its dancing flame almost seemed to animate his still features. His lips were pinched tight and there were lines in his brow.

Lines of pain, Marian thought hollowly.

The distant roar of voices that rose in a cheer turned her head toward the window. It was only a slit in the wall, and it had been covered with a piece of sackcloth to keep out ill humors. She lifted it aside and looked out.

Bonfires dotted the slopes, and the streets were alight with torches and lanterns. Distant music floated over the town, punctuated by the occasional voice of a particularly merry reveler.

"A beautiful night," said the monk amicably.

"You don't object to all this?" asked Marian, tilting her head toward the man. "Drunkenness, dancing, gluttony . . ."

The monk chuckled. "They can have their bonfires and their dances. They'll still come round to church in the morning for food and alms."

Marian took one more lingering look at the town, which glowed amber-gold in the crisp autumn air, and then let the cloth fall back over the window. She could not quite bring herself to look at Tom again, and held instead that image of warmth and cheer, and tried to summon some matching warmth from her own soul.

The monk was watching her. "Did you know the lad, child?"

Marian shook her head. She knew the holy man was trying to figure out why she would be so interested in the fate of an unknown guard, whose job it was to stand between danger and nobility like her. But she felt drained of deception in that moment, too listless to lie.

Instead, she drew a slow breath. "May I stay here with you, and pray?"

THIRTY-TWO

MARIAN'S FATHER ESCORTED HER around the festival the next morning, which was as clear and crisp as the first day of celebration had been. The streets were packed with nobility and commonfolk alike, and the crowd was a living thing, buzzing with excitement—the name of Robin Hood was everywhere, each whispered rumor biting at Marian like a stinging fly. The anticipation of seeing the outlaw win today's contest had brought the people to the streets in staggering numbers.

Her father bought her a roasted apple so hot she had to wait to eat it, letting the fragrant steam rise and bathe her face with warmth. The air smelled of last night's bonfires, and Marian wasn't the only sandy-eyed, weary attendee—though she hadn't been out late reveling. The halls had been empty and dark when she finally left the monk by Tom's bedside and made her way back to her own room.

"Sir Guy asked if I might consider staying here at Nottingham for a few days after the festival." Her father spoke without looking at her, his eyes moving idly over the faces of a small crowd that had gathered around a thimblerig game.

"What?" Marian's steps faltered, her heart quickening. "Do you know why?"

Her father's eyebrows rose, but he didn't take his eyes from the plank slung over two barrels, where the game's operator was moving the thimbles back and forth. "Why? Marian, you know why. He's hoping for your promise before we go home."

A little flicker of embarrassment tickled at Marian's throat. "Oh."

The thimbles whirled in rings and figure eights, and Marian had been too scattered by her father's words to catch the moment when the man behind the makeshift table palmed the pea. Though there were certainly some among the more credulous in the crowd who didn't know, Marian felt sure almost all the watchers knew the game was no game at all, but a deliberate trick—and yet all eyes were riveted. They knew it was a lie, but there wasn't one among them who didn't think they could spot the pea.

When the thimbles stopped, a middle-aged man wearing a red beard and a well-made and much-mended tunic stepped up. Her father's lips twitched, and he murmured for Marian's ears, "The pea's in the busker's right sleeve."

When Red-Beard jabbed a thick forefinger toward the middle thimble, the game's operator lifted it with a flourish to reveal the empty wood beneath and took Red-Beard's penny in one movement. He did not lift the other thimbles, gathering them up before anyone could ask where the pea really was, and Marian heard a tinny little rattle as he set the game back up for another round: the sound of the pea falling back into place.

Marian was not immune to the thrill of excitement that

rumbled through the watchers, and she fell into step alongside her father again with reluctance. "How did you know?" she asked, happy to dwell on the subject of the thimblerig huckster rather than Gisborne's request.

Her father tucked her arm through his, settling his hand over hers. "If you watch his face, and not his hands, his intentions are far easier to read. He's not bad, but he still glances up before he makes the change, checking to see if someone's watching."

Marian laughed and hugged her father's arm close. The air was colder than it had been the day before, and when she tried the apple again, it had cooled enough for her to take a bite of the soft, sweet fruit.

"Would you like to stay?"

Marian swallowed the bite of apple and looked askance at her father. He looked much as he always had, lines of humor around his eyes and mouth, a bit more gray at his temples and shot through the rest of the chestnut hair that had once so perfectly matched Marian's own. There was no doubt, had there ever been any question, that she was his daughter—they had the same nose and brow, and the square jaw that had served Marian so well in her disguise as Robin gave her father a distinguished look of strength and determination.

"I don't know," Marian murmured, gaze falling again. There were more opportunities for her to feed information to her men if she remained at Nottingham Castle, more chances at continued victories against the Sheriff. But with most of the visiting nobles departing, the castle's population would be plummeting, and there'd be fewer potential targets for Gisborne's suspicion to fall upon.

"We can decide as we go." Her father patted her hand with a smile. "It is not weakness, Marian, to change one's mind."

Marian halted so abruptly that their linked arms pulled her father halfway round to face her. "Change my—about *Gisborne?*"

Her father's look was mild. "About anything. About Sir Guy. About Robin Hood. About your own Robin. About yourself."

Marian hid her uneasiness by taking another bite of her apple. She could not afford to change her mind about anything, but particularly not Gisborne. He was a cruel toady of the Sheriff's, and a torturer, and so stiff and awkward that she could not stand an hour in his company, much less the prospect of a lifetime.

He was and always would be the enemy of Robin Hood.

"Father," Marian said after swallowing, "did anything come of this trip?" She did not bother to hide the change of subject. Her father never expected subtlety from her. "You and the other lords—were you able to convince the Sheriff that to raise taxes still further would be folly?"

"I don't think we achieved much," her father replied quietly. The lines of laughter set in a look of grim concern. "Taxes will rise. And the more the Sheriff loses to this Robin Hood, the faster they'll do so."

Marian, sickened, had lost interest in the roasted apple. She longed to toss it aside, for the smell now turned her stomach, but her father had been so pleased to hand it to her, as if she were still a child delighted by fairs and festivals and he a doting papa. "Father . . . has no one tried to contact the King? If he knew the suffering of his people, if he could return for a few months . . ."

"You want him to pardon this Robin Hood of yours." Her father sighed. "Marian . . . I know the people seem to think that King Richard would approve of these schemes, but I don't know that the King *would* pardon Robin Hood if he did return."

"But—"

He drew her aside, out of the flow of people walking up and

down the street. Warm fingers touched her chin, prompted her to lift it. "Marian, my dear. No one will ever know you helped him, I swear it on my life. And I don't blame you for it. I might have helped him myself, in your place."

Marian could tell from the timbre of his voice that it wasn't true—but the words were a comfort regardless, and she blinked hard to clear her swimming eyes.

Her father kissed her brow. He had to lift his own head to do so, but she felt like a child again, wrapped in safety and warmth. "Take heart, my dear. We did earn extra time between collection and punishment for debt, and we've established some instances in which failure to pay by the poorest of our people will be forgiven. There will always be more discussions. More opportunities to change."

Discussion.

The word rested cold and uncomfortable in the pit of Marian's stomach. Her jaw ached with the effort of not bursting out with the words she longed to say: that they'd been here all this time *discussing*, and nothing had changed. An entire castle full of lords telling the Sheriff their lands could not bear an increase in taxation had done nothing to help the people. Except for a few instances in which debt would be pardoned.

"May I stroll awhile on my own?" Marian spoke softly, one hand still clutching the stick with her apple.

"Of course. Shall we meet for the archery contest this afternoon?"

Marian glanced upward, surprised to see that the sun was higher than she'd realized. She and her father had been walking for hours. "I don't think I'm going to go," she said carefully.

Her father's eyes widened. "But, my dear, it's archery. How can you, of all people, miss it?"

"Women aren't allowed to participate." Marian let bitterness sharpen her voice, for that rule *was* unfair, and in any other circumstance she would have been wrenchingly disappointed. "I think watching, and knowing I could win if I were allowed to compete, would hold no pleasure for me."

Her father's lips curved, though the smile was as rueful as it was fond. "I cannot think where you learned to be so competitive, my dear. You must have learned it from Robin. Winning isn't the only joy in life."

Robin learned it from me, Marian thought, but she felt an answering smile haunting her lips as she leaned forward to embrace her father and bid him farewell. *And it's joy enough if it will bring happiness to Alan and Elena.*

Pavilions had been erected behind and along either side of the archery range, which had been set up across one of the flatter sections of grass outside Nottingham. A number of vendors and merchants had abandoned the town in order to haunt the temporary lanes and alleys in and among the tents, and if anything the excitement of the crowd had only heightened as the time for the contest approached.

Marian had relied upon Elena to get her costume and her bow from her room to a prearranged spot in a limestone alcove in the rocky outcropping that formed the foundation of the castle. Moving her gear had always been one of the hardest things about being Robin Hood, for a lady did not carry bundles of fabric—and certainly not weapons—about the castle with her. But servants did so all the time, and Elena assured her she'd have no difficulty in doing as Marian had asked.

And though Marian had arrived at the spot a good hour before they'd agreed upon, too nervous to wait, a neatly folded stack of brown wool behind the boulders told her Elena had succeeded. Donning Robin's clothes had once felt like some form of tribute to him—some way to feel closer to him, to keep him alive. Now she felt the way a warrior must feel when he takes up his shield: ready to face whatever fate might bring, and determined to fight to the last if she had to.

Elena had gone white when Marian explained her plan for the contest, but she hadn't objected the way Marian had anticipated she would. Instead she was silent for a long time before she spoke.

"My Lady," she said slowly. "You cannot know how much I'd like . . . how grateful . . . But my Lady—Marian, then—what about the guard? If he dies . . ."

"He won't die," Marian had said, grim.

Elena had stepped closer and put a hand on Marian's arm. "If he dies," she repeated gently, "Robin Hood will be a murderer. The pardon they're offering for winning the contest . . ." She didn't finish the sentence, but she didn't need to.

Marian had looked up, catching her eye. "That pardon is Alan's. If I end up exposed, a pardon won't save me." It was the first time she'd said that aloud, the first time the words had ever formed in her thoughts. But they were true. She'd never survive the disgrace of her blood and her name.

Now, standing outside the pavilion at the end of the archery range, Marian scanned the crowds. Elena would be there somewhere, lost in the sea of spectators. *How agonizing to have to watch,* Marian thought, sliding the smooth, worn leather of the archer's glove covering her fingertips against her palm. *To be helpless in the unfolding of your own fate.*

She was wearing Robin's clothes, but not his cloak—to appear as Robin Hood here would be foolish in the extreme, for there was no guarantee of his safety up to the moment he stepped up to loose his arrows. Her cloak was one of rough-spun brown wool that Elena had procured for her. Neither could she wear a mask this time, for while it would conceal her features, it would also proclaim her identity as the outlaw. Instead she was back to moving carefully through the press of people, ensuring the hood hung low and shadowed her face, checking every time she was jostled that it hadn't slipped back.

A number of other contestants had entered the pavilion similarly cloaked, faces in shadow—the golden arrow was sufficient prize to tempt any entrant, but the pardon had brought more than one outlaw to the town. Watching one bulky fellow with a rough, unshaven face duck through into the pavilion, Marian paused thoughtfully.

Checking out of the corner of her eye that she was unobserved, she stooped to retrieve a handful of dirt from the ground at her feet. She rubbed it in well along her lower cheeks and jaw. At best, it would look like she was sporting a day's growth of beard. At worst, the dirt would hide her fair, clean skin as long as the upper half of her face remained in shadow.

A fanfare sounded, so close by Marian nearly dropped the bow in her hand. She hurried into the pavilion, where a tired-looking official in the uniform of a scribe was making notations on parchment. Marian looked for Alan—Elena had asked to be the one to explain the details to him, sparing Marian the need to sneak out in the night to do so—but in the press of people she could not find him.

"Name?" The scribe didn't look up. Marian would've expected a scribe to be pleased by the prospect of doing his job outdoors for once, here among the people and surrounded by festivities, but the man had an exceedingly sour disposition.

"David," Marian replied, letting her voice crack a little, like a lad's. "David of Doncaster."

"Group four," said the scribe, and waved her away when she would've asked for more information.

Marian had thought the pavilion contained archers as well as spectators trying to identify Robin Hood—but as it turned out, every one of the men crammed into the little space was competing. The notoriety, or the wealth, was too tantalizing for the people of Nottingham and its surrounds to ignore. The contest would proceed in shifts, with the top two archers in each group returning at the end to compete in the final round.

In vain, Marian searched for Alan. She could not risk calling out his name, for he—along with any other outlaws present with an ounce of good sense—would have entered under a pseudonym. In planning their little deception, Marian had anticipated that both she and Alan would be shooting at the same time. But if Alan didn't make it out of his group . . .

The groups were called one by one, and the ranks of competitors thinned each time a new one left to shoot. The murmurs and shouts of the crowd rose and fell, the spectators equally delighted to cheer a good shot as deride a lousy one.

By the time the third group went to compete, Marian was certain Alan must have been in the first few groups, for none of the men left waiting could have been him. Though a few of the men talked and laughed and watched the contest from the edge of the pavilion, most of Marian's fellow archers were quiet and tight-lipped. *Focused,* she thought. *Or else with something to hide.*

She hadn't realized she was distracting herself by observing the others until her group was called. The sound of the herald announcing the fourth and final qualifying round dropped Marian's heart into her boots, every ounce of apprehension or nerves she'd been ignoring suddenly rising to choke her. She joined the rest of the archers as they filed out into the field.

The range stretched ahead of them, the targets standing fifty paces away across the emerald grass. Though the stretch was untouched, the ground at her feet was mud, churned and divoted from the archers before her. At the far end of the range, the straw target had been brightly painted, but the scores of arrows that had already flown had eliminated much of the color. Some of the holes, Marian noted uneasily, were very close to center indeed.

An official lined them up and instructed them to fire one at a time. Each of them had three shots, to allow for mistakes, and the closest arrows would earn their archers spots in the final round. At least half the arrows that flew missed the target entirely. The crowd's halfhearted jeers told Marian that hers wasn't the only group full of poor archers.

She was second to last, and as the archer before her stepped forward and readied himself, Marian considered the target. A few arrows had struck the innermost ring, though none had struck the circle dead center. She could not risk a spectacular shot in this preliminary round—if anyone suspected her of being Robin Hood, they might unmask her before the final contest. But as long as she got one arrow closer than any others had come so far, it wouldn't matter if the archer following her struck a perfect shot. They'd both move on.

Marian was busying her mind with strategy, and so when the crowd erupted in a sudden swell of shouts and cheers, she had to look around to find out why. The archer in front of her was standing stock-still, staring across the stretch, looking at the arrow he'd shot.

It lacked only a thumbnail's width from the center.

Marian choked back an oath. The archer looked so stunned,

Marian felt certain the shot had been a lucky one. But she could no longer afford a safe second. For if the final archer was good—or if he got lucky—he could keep Marian from competing in the last round of shooting.

Marian stepped up to the line, which the officials kept redrawing in the mud. The jeers and shouts of encouragement from the crowd rang in her ears. She still hadn't seen Alan, and though Will and Little John both were meant to be among the lower-class spectators crowding the ground around the pavilions containing nobility, she found she could not turn her head to look.

She inspected her arrows—for the fifth time—and then drove two down into the mud so she could nock one to the bowstring. Marian took a breath, watching the target, waiting for the world to narrow itself, for calm to come.

But it didn't.

The crowds were still shouting, the sun still beating down, the mud still loose under her feet. Marian rolled her shoulders back and shook out each leg. An irritated shout from halfway down the pitch rose above the general uproar: "Get on with it, boy!"

Marian breathed in. *Robin, where are you?* In this moment, she would've given anything for his amused teasing to drown out the din around her.

She breathed out, drew on her next inhale, and loosed the arrow.

It hit, not center, but only a fraction wide of her previous opponent. A rather surprised cheer traveled raggedly around the spectators. The shot might be enough to ensure her a spot in the final round—if she could count on the next archer missing. Squaring herself again, she tried once more to narrow her focus on the target. Archery was as much about will as skill, once the art of it was learned—a clear mind, a focused eye, a steady hand. That was all Marian needed.

But her hand shook as she drew this time, and the arrow went embarrassingly wide.

She stepped back and shook out her legs again, trying to force the tension from her body. For a wild moment, she caught herself longing for the physician's draught, the one that dulled her fears and slowed her pounding heart. It would've been foolish, though, for it would dull her reflexes, too, and she needed her wits. If she could only *calm* herself.

The crowd was a shifting mass that swelled and receded like a ragged, billowing tapestry. The only still spot was the target in the distance, and Marian desperately longed for some other place of quiet to rest her eyes, if only for a moment. Then she realized there was a section of stillness, in the closest pavilion on the left. The Sheriff would be there, no doubt, and perhaps Gisborne and some of his men, hoping to spot and arrest Robin Hood before he could shoot.

Marian wanted to turn her head and look, but to do so would be to allow the sun to fall on part of her face, and she was not so confident in her makeshift stubble as to risk it. But she could imagine Gisborne watching, those cold eyes scanning each archer and mentally comparing him to the "man" he'd fought twice now, and lost to both times. She could picture that stare so easily that she began to feel it, tangibly, a steely line of connection between her and her enemy.

This time, when she retrieved her last arrow from the ground and wiped it clean on her cloak, her hands were steady. It was not so much anger that grounded her as the knowledge that she would never let Gisborne win—for anything other than her victory for Alan and Elena would be his win.

The arrow struck in the exact spot as that of the archer before her. The arrow's natural wobble as it flew meant that the shafts stuck out in different directions, but her arrowhead struck so hard that it knocked the other arrow from its spot, to fall against an uneven cradle of previous arrows below it.

She was dimly aware of the crowd, and of a commotion behind and to her right, where the victors of each round were waiting for the final. The people were shrieking their approval, and the man she'd bested was shouting, held back by a number of the others. Marian ignored him, retreating quietly to let the final man shoot, her heart racing.

The final archer's best shot barely penetrated the third ring of the target.

When Marian joined the others waiting for the final round, she nearly jumped when a hand touched her elbow. She turned to find Alan there, his eyes bright, his face glowing with perspiration. He'd made it, too. She let out a ragged breath and nodded at him, and they parted again. They could not afford more interaction than that, especially not now there were only eight archers left. Each of them would be scrutinized down to the last detail.

The crowd began to hush, and when Marian withdrew back under the shade of the pavilion so that she could look up, she saw that the Sheriff had risen to his feet and was holding up his hand in a bid for silence.

Gisborne wasn't there. Marian felt an odd sense of disconnect—she'd been so sure she'd felt his eyes on her. But when she did catch a glimpse of a man in black, hurrying through the crowd, he came from the direction of the town, and when Marian looked back, she saw Gisborne's horse there, jittery with energy, being held by a nervous servant.

The Sheriff addressed the crowd, making an obligatory sort

of speech about celebration. He was unsuccessful in maintaining silence, as the crowd was antsy, eager for the final round of arrows—and for whatever would come after, if Robin Hood was among the eight competitors, as they all believed he would be.

The Sheriff's voice halted when Gisborne emerged from the crowd to dart up the steps to the platform. Gisborne leaned down a fraction to speak into his master's ear, his own face unreadable at this distance.

She could think of only one thing that would cause him to ride the short way from the castle at such a pace and interrupt the Sheriff's speech. The guard, the wounded man, Tom—he'd awakened. He'd named his killer.

Marian ran her fingertips along the edge of her hood, reassuring herself that it was in place, that she was invisible in her guise as archer. She tore her gaze from Gisborne's indecipherable countenance and watched the Sheriff instead. His features twitched as he listened to Gisborne, mouth stretching to a thin smear of a smile. Then he went on, concluding his empty speech.

The crowd's response was lackluster at best, but for once the Sheriff had no interest in them. He was speaking in a low voice to Gisborne, gesturing one-handed. Marian saw Gisborne's face harden a degree more as he shook his head once, and again. The Sheriff flashed him a grimace and shoved himself to his feet before stepping forward to address the crowd again.

"Good people of Nottingham, one more thing!" There was a faint whisper of discontent from the crowd, which was eager to find out if the contest would devolve into a battle or a grand chase between the guards and the outlaw's men. Hardly discomfited by the lack of command over his audience, the Sheriff continued. "I am sure you have all heard tales by now of the outlaw called Robin Hood."

Silence rent the quilted sound of murmurs and shifting bodies. Nobility and commoner alike gazed up at the Sheriff, with every bit of attention he could've asked for.

He smiled a grim, satisfied smile. "Some of you are here in hopes of seeing him. To turn him in to the law for the reward. Or to venerate him for his so-called kindnesses to the more wretched among you."

Movement to her right nearly caught her off guard, but something in her recognized a scent she knew, a familiar way of moving, some ineffable quality that identified the man who'd taken a step closer to her. Alan was at her side.

"Robin Hood," said the Sheriff, his voice oddly light and musing, as if reciting some monologue rather than addressing his town. "Robin of the Hood. You call him thusly for the cloak he wears and the identity it conceals. But from this day you may call him Hood for another reason."

Marian did not look up. Something had shifted deep in her heart, though she could not have explained how she knew what Gisborne had said to the Sheriff. *Tom,* she thought, numbed to everything but the monk's words echoing in her head. *Go with God.*

"Call him Hood for the hangman's cloth," said the Sheriff, his amiable voice hardening, eyes narrowing as he scanned the assembled archers. "He has killed one of my men. Let it be known here and throughout Nottingham that your hero, your outlaw, your Robin Hood, is a murderer."

THIRTY-THREE

THE SUN RETREATED BEHIND a thin tatter of cloud, like a gentle lady hiding her face behind a filmy veil. Marian watched her shadow against the ground sharpen and soften, rise and fall like breath as the cloud shifted. The blades of grass cast shadows like knives, and then like fingers, and then like memories.

Nearby, archers prepared for the final round. Guards roamed the crowds, warning those who grew too impatient, too brash. Musicians played, vendors shouted, and somewhere a new infant was wailing at the inconvenient, noisy clutter of life.

Marian stood very still. People moved this way and that around her, swirling like little tangles of leaves caught in an eddy of wind. Her fingers were curled round her bow, whose tip rested against the toe of her boot. Her thumb found her leather-bound fingertips and slid across them, slowly, relishing the sensation. The leather had been smoothed when the archer's glove was made, but no leatherworker could match the slick perfection worn by years of the slip of a bowstring again and again and again.

It was solely practical, that glove—unattractive, unassuming, unidentifiable as a glove except to an archer. Two leather thimbles for the fingers, bound to a wristband to keep it in place. *Thimbles,* thought Marian, stroking the leather again, fingers drawing circles on each other. *Round and round they go. . . .*

It had been a perfect moment, standing there with her father, apple in one hand, the other folded under his, watching the thimblerig game. The game everyone knew was a lie—the game you played, because though it was a lie for everyone else, for you it might be different. Because you might spot something others missed.

A hand took Marian's elbow, and she gently raised her head enough to see a familiar face below the lowered rim of her hood.

"We must talk." Alan's expression was grave and urgent. But when Marian lifted her eyes, she saw that some of the flour he'd used to gray his hair still lingered at the top of his brow. How comical he'd looked—and how convincing. The flour seemed more real than the fear that now animated his features, lit his eyes, and tightened his fingers around her arm.

"Rob—" Alan stopped himself and shook her by the arm instead. "How can you be smiling? Wake *up*, man."

Marian hadn't known she was smiling, and when he said the word, the expression fell away. "I'm awake," she said quietly. She stopped looking at the flour in his hair and watched his face instead.

"Take the archery contest," Alan said softly, his gaze light and flitting this way and that, making certain no one was near enough to hear. "Forget me and Elena."

"No." Marian slipped one of her arrows from her quiver to inspect the fletching, nudging a filament of feather back into place with her thumb. "We proceed as planned."

"Sard the plan!" Alan drew a breath and lowered his voice again. "Rob—my friend. Murder. They'll hang you. This pardon—it's for you, not for me."

Marian did not like the shape of the fletching. The angle was off on one of the lines—she could see it, though no measuring device would be exact enough to tell her she was right. It would fly, and it would spin, but it would spin off balance. It'd be a difference akin to the width of a fly's wing, but she could afford no mistakes. She replaced it in the quiver and drew out another.

Alan snatched the arrow from her hands, demanding her attention. "Murder."

Marian resisted the urge to snatch the arrow back. If he hadn't torqued the wooden shaft already, retrieving it would certainly do so. *They were always going to hang me, Alan.* The words were true. They felt true. She'd never spoken them, never dwelled too long on the definition of treason to men like Guy of Gisborne and the Sheriff of Nottingham. But she'd avoided those thoughts for a reason. Then, they might have frightened her into obedience.

And now?

Now Marian reached out to take the arrow back, but she grasped it gently with her fingertips and drew it slowly toward her so that Alan's hand, white-knuckled with its grip, came with it. Marian lifted her head, then ran a fingertip along the edge of her hood. Alan's gaze rose to follow the movement, and Marian was stunned to see that his eyes were wet with tears.

For me? For Robin? For his future? For all three?

She'd nudged the hood back enough so that a man, standing close to her, might see below the shadow it cast on her features. The veil of cloud over the sun thinned, and Alan's fair eyelashes looked like gold as they rose, his pupils dilated, his features stricken as he looked for the first time at the face of Robin Hood.

"They were always going to hang me, Alan," Marian whispered.

His fingers let go of the arrow, and Marian inspected the fletching as she'd done the other. This one was better balanced—this one would fly truest. She drew her hood back into place. She looked up from the arrow to see Alan, who had not moved, who was looking at her with naked and dawning horror, and fear, and anger.

Marian turned away. They were calling for the remaining archers to line up for the final round of the contest, and she slipped away in order to secure a spot near the end of the line.

This time the stretch that lay between her and the distant target held no fear for her. Her heart was as calm as if she were sewing by candlelight, or watching patterns formed by raindrops against a glazed window.

They pulled Alan into the line. He went, unresisting, and stood staring ahead, wit enough remaining to stop him watching Marian as if she were the only one standing there in the broad lawn of Nottingham town.

The first few archers began to shoot. All were skilled but for one, who had either gotten lucky with his first shots or else unlucky in the extreme this round. Perhaps it was the man whose lucky shot had so worried Marian—she could not now remember what his face had looked like, or what colors he'd worn.

The archer before her shot well twice, but the third arrow was badly made, and part of the fletching split against his fingers, and he dropped his weapon, dripping blood from his bow hand and cursing.

Such a deadly thing, a feather, Marian thought, fingering the fletching of her discarded arrow in her quiver under her cloak.

The force and speed with which an arrow left the bow meant that for an instant, the feathered fletching could cut through flesh like a hot blade through rendered fat.

Marian stepped to the line and drew without pause.

Lads in their first growth, men driven to poaching in their declining years, ladies striving to perfect their airs and graces—they all made the same mistake when they first began to learn archery. Marian had done it too. The instinct was to pause with bow drawn, to look then at the target, to adjust the body, the shoulders, the fingers, even the lips, as if an ounce of extra concentration would lend some desperate intent to the arrow's path.

They sought control. They sought it in the jerk of their hand when they tried to pluck the string instead of release it; they sought it in the white-knuckled grip of a bow that would settle in their palm effortlessly if they could but let it; they sought it in the bracing of a dozen different tiny muscles preparing to flinch at the force of the bowstring's release. It had taken Marian years to understand all the cares she wore when she tried to perfect her archery, cares that intruded upon her skill. It had taken her years to realize perfection was the wrong goal.

An experienced archer knew her shot before she drew. Before she put the arrow to the string even, maybe before she ever picked up a bow, back when she was a child, when she first thought to prove she was as skilled as any boy might be.

The soul knew the target. All Marian had to do was welcome the bow to herself, let it become her heart and the arrow her voice, and then step out of the way.

There could not have been more than half a breath before she released the first arrow, yet she could hear a voice, distant, somewhere to the left.

That's him, said the voice. *That's him. I know him, the way he stands, the height of him, how he draws—that's him.*

She could not have said how she heard it above the din of the crowd, how that cold voice, quickened with agitation, came to her ears uncorrupted by those around it. It was as if Gisborne were speaking for her ears alone.

Let me go—in God's name, I would know him anywhere. Let me go, now, before he . . .

The first arrow silenced the crowd when it struck with icy precision. The second, only a breath later, left a resounding thud in the quiet that followed the first. The third splintered the second, so close, its point sheared fletching from shaft and left a fine shower of feathered strands drifting toward the ground.

All landed within seconds of each other. Marian stayed there, bow at arm's length, not lifting her head until the rain of fletching had settled. The leather of the archer's glove was like a kiss on her cheek, warm from the caress of the bowstring.

One voice, a mighty, thundering, bellowing whoop, broke the silence half a heartbeat before the rest of the crowd erupted. Bodies rushed her way, voices screamed approval and awe and delight. The first to reach her was a massive tree of a man, and only when he grasped at her shoulders and pushed her downward did she half realize, half remember that it was Little John, leading the distraction they'd agreed on in advance.

Marian dropped to her knees and let go of her bow, leaving it in the grass under John's feet, and turned. A pair of vermilion leggings stood out among the sea of gray and brown. *Scarlet,* she thought, breath hissing in a giggle that would have betrayed her as a woman in any guise, had she not been so thoroughly drowned out by the roaring crowd. She crawled toward the leggings, and they made way for her, and another pair of arms drew her up.

"No. I won't." Alan was still going through the motions of the plan, fumbling at his neck for the clasp of the undyed cloak he wore. But his hands were shaking, as if agreeing with the words that fell from his lips. "You won, Robin. God, I can't— Marian. *Marian.* It's your neck, your life. Your pardon."

Marian reached out and shoved his hands away so that she could unclasp his cloak herself. Underneath he wore another, thinner cloak—one of rough brown wool. One exactly like hers. "The bow is where I left it. Remember to disguise your voice a little—don't let Gisborne recognize you as the voice of Robin Hood in Sherwood that day. Go. Quick, Alan."

"I won't." Alan was quivering where he stood, eyes full of anguish, expression settling into one of decision. "I won't claim the prize, I'll go to my grave claiming it wasn't me, I'll tell them all who shot those arrows. Those arrows—how did you . . . You can't ask this of me, Robin. Marian. Robin . . . Damn it, I will not let a woman hang, not when I could . . ."

The calm that had seized Marian during her turn at the line, the calm that had possessed her since Gisborne spoke the words that had dimmed the sun, since she'd understood that Tom had died of the wound she'd given him and that she'd murdered a lad whose only sin was that he had done his duty that day—that calm splintered like the shaft of the arrow she'd destroyed with her final shot.

With a muffled roar of effort, Marian struck. Her fist met Alan's cheek with such force that her whole arm went numb. The minstrel dropped like one of the marionettes at the miracle play, like the blow had knocked his soul from him. Marian stooped and seized him by the shoulders. He stirred as she dragged him toward the surging crowd, and he gazed blearily at her, then up at the crowd towering all around them, and then at his own fingertips as he put them to his lips like a child testing a new toy, to look at the blood there.

Marian's shoulders were burning, her back aching, and as soon as she got Alan into the press of the crowd, the jostling people made her lose her grip and nearly sent her sprawling. Red flashed before her, and for a mad, inside-out moment Marian could think only of the berserkers of legend, who were said to turn into bestial warriors at the sight of blood, until their eyes could see nothing but scarlet. . . .

And then Will was there, in his stolen dandy's attire, the crimson tunic and leggings folding down to reach for Alan. "What happened?" he gasped, bewildered.

"No time. Get him in there—easy to say an elbow or a foot found him in this chaos. Go."

Will wasted no more time on questions, pulling Alan with him as he fought back toward the center of the crowd. She could hear Little John shouting somewhere, keeping the crowd stirred up and confused, extending the chaos so that they could make their switch undetected. So that when a form was finally hoisted up out of the crowd up onto someone's shoulders, the face revealed as the hood fell back was Alan's, dazed, bleeding at his lip, but conscious.

And pardoned.

Marian watched from the edge of the pavilion, standing half in its shadow and half in the crisp autumn sun, as a black-clad figure leaped down from the platform opposite with the agility of an athlete of Olympus. *And he thinks me a liar,* she thought, the voice strangely detached. *He puts on a show of limping, as if his scars continue beyond his collar, and yet he runs and leaps like a lad half his age.*

She watched as Gisborne knocked men aside, guard and spectator alike, digging through the masses to their heart. He hauled

Alan back down from the stout fellows who carried him and took him by the shoulders. The crowd fell back at an incoherent shout from Gisborne that wordlessly demanded space, and light.

She watched as Gisborne scanned Alan's face, looked down his body, lifted his hand to feel his thin, delicate fingers, gazed at the elfin point of his chin.

She watched as he spoke, for she was too far away to hear and the crowd was still roaring, but she could see his lips forming the words, and she knew what he was saying.

It's not him.

She watched them. Gisborne, standing alone in the middle of the crowd, a small ring of space around him as if protected from jostling by some ancient spell. Alan, rallying as best he could, wiping the blood from his lips and testing the bruise at his cheek and grinning a flawless grin of victory, a grin so flawless Marian could not see how much it must be costing him.

Marian slipped away.

THIRTY-FOUR

A TAP AT HER door jarred Marian from her contemplation of the bonfires and bobbing torches distorted by the thick pane of her window. She rose, hurrying toward the door, pulse quickening. She had thought Elena would be with Alan, enjoying his company in the open, as herself, sharing in the victory of their new life. The pardon meant he could perform again without fear of being recognized, and that he could marry without tarnishing the reputation of his betrothed, and the golden arrow meant that they'd have all they needed to start a life together. The authorities might suspect Alan was a member of Robin Hood's men, but the pardon granted him immunity from suspicion, and from harassment by Gisborne and his men. He was free, and now so was Elena. She thought they'd be together tonight.

But she could not help a thrill of excitement at the prospect of seeing her friend's face, glowing with happiness, free of its burdens and cares, as light and as transparent as a filmy veil of cloud.

She threw the door open and drew up short. Her father stood on the threshold, head down, feet braced, standing as he often did while listening to someone else speak. He was alone in the corridor, though. Listening, perhaps, to his own inner voices.

When Marian stepped back, he took the unspoken invitation and strode in, steps light and meandering, his expression thoughtful. He headed for the window, and Marian hid a small smile when he went straight for the place she'd been standing moments before. "How was the contest?" she asked, her voice polite, interested.

"He shoots well, this Robin Hood," he said, gazing out across the sea of flame and darkness.

Marian closed the door and went to the fire, which had burned low. She stirred it until the embers glowed, then fed it a fresh block of firewood and watched it while the flames appeared to lick at the offering hungrily. "I thought it was some other man who won," she said lightly. "A minstrel, I heard."

Her father gave a disparaging sound, half laugh, half bark, and then went on as if she hadn't spoken. "If nothing else, today's exploits prove he is not your Robin, for he never shot so well."

Marian shifted her weight, a flicker of defensiveness appearing like a little flame to lick at that bit of criticism. "Robin shot well enough." But the defense fell flat. Marian could not help it—Robin had stopped speaking in her thoughts the night she shot the guard, as if he had known what she hadn't, that the wound would prove mortal. He had abandoned her.

But her father only laughed. "I'm sorry, my dear. He was a fine archer, your Robin."

Marian sat, choosing the chair that partially faced toward the window. As the wood creaked, her father turned and came to join her.

"You know, I used to see you sometimes, when you and he would sneak away together."

Marian's cheeks began to burn. "We weren't sneaking off to . . . to make mischief. We were practicing."

Her father let loose another quick guffaw. "Make mischief," he echoed, shaking his head. "I wasn't born somebody's father, Marian."

Marian looked away, torn between amusement and outright embarrassment, and distracted herself by kneading the fingers of her bow hand into those of her drawing hand, feeling the satisfying stretch of worked muscles.

"Don't fret, daughter. I had no qualms about letting the two of you be."

Marian took a deeper breath, hoping her flush was fading. "You knew Robin. You knew he was honorable. You trusted him."

"I trusted *you*," her father retorted.

Marian, caught off guard, could only watch as he, in turn, watched the fire rising to wrap its arms around the new log.

"The first time I saw you tackle the lad to the ground and sit on his chest, I didn't know whether to be proud or horrified." Her father smiled, still amused, eyes crinkled with that laughter, and gleaming. More than gleaming, Marian realized with confusion—his eyes were wet.

"Father?" Her voice was rickety, uncertain, its foundations crumbling at the sight of his eyes.

He leaned forward abruptly, as if seized by a sudden thought. "Do you remember, for a time you and he had set up an archery range at the edge of the wheat field north of the house? I used to go to that window in my office and look out whenever I heard a shriek of triumph. It was always you doing the yelling."

Marian leaned back in her chair a little, lulled by the warmth of the fire, and of the memories, and of the fact that there was still one man who didn't mind that she was too loud and too tall and too strong. "It's more fun if you yell," she explained. "It makes the victory feel all the more real."

"You were always a good shot." Her father's elbows rested on his knees, his head turned a fraction so he could watch the fire. "But something happened around the time you were . . . oh, thirteen, maybe? I looked out the window and there you were, standing in your underclothes, a shift and nothing else—and before I could so much as rise from my chair in alarm, you loosed an arrow that flew so straight and true, it pierced my heart as surely as it did its target. The way you looked—in a ragged shift, hair every which way, but full of more grace and ease and poise where you stood than the most accomplished lady who ever lived . . ."

Marian wanted to smile, for though her father was kind and caring, he'd never praised her in words that struck her soul so, that warmed her so deeply. But something was changing, the fondness in her father's voice giving way to something else, something she could not name but recognized nonetheless, the way a man recognizes the aggression in the eyes of a feral dog, the way a woman recognizes the sound of her child's voice in a sea of others.

"I could have watched you at your archery for hours," said her father, his gaze upon the fire so distant he might have been a blind man recalling a time when he could see. "I did, over all these years. The way you have at it, artistry and simplicity together, the way you make it a part of you . . ."

He started to raise his head, to look at her, but she caught only a flash of his eyes on hers. Agonized. Grief-stricken. Then he broke, his head dropping into one of his hands, his voice splintering into tiny, spindly shards of itself. "I would recognize the way you shoot anywhere."

And Marian's world broke apart.

When her father raised his head, he looked at her this time without fear of losing control of himself, for he'd left that behind. Tears pooled below his eyes and left shining tracks in the firelight down his cheeks. "Oh, Marian," he breathed. "What have you done?"

She said nothing, her hands clenching tight at her belly, tangled in the fabric of her kirtle, as though her fingers wished they could carve out the offense in her, the part that had led her to this, and offer it up to him like a sacrifice to appease an angry god.

Marian was crying too, but it was her father's tears that frightened her so, frightened her in a way nothing had ever done before. They turned her inside out, they stripped away the years, they left her a little girl trying desperately to seem unafraid of the dark so that her father would think her brave. "Father—oh, Father—what can I do? Tell me what I can do."

His lips creased and trembled. "Tell me it's not true." His hand moved, as if he wanted to reach for her, but fell halfway, the strength draining from him the longer he looked at her, haggard face full of appeal. "Please."

Marian struggled for a breath, and when she blinked, her eyes swam. "Ask me for something else. Anything else."

Her father's face crumpled again, and he buried his face in his hands and gasped the words, "Oh, Marian." He said them over and over, passing his hands over his face.

In the hearth, the fresh log was fresh no more, and the surge of heat that had left Marian so warm and contented faded. It left her colder than before. She hadn't noticed she'd been cold, until she'd stirred the fire. Now she shivered.

Her father lifted his head and passed his hand over his face again, fingers kneading roughly at his cheeks and swiping across his jaw, trying to mold them into shape like clay. His eyes filled again. "I can't protect you."

Marian could not breathe. It was not a warning, nor an apology—his eyes held many things, but what she saw most clearly, what she could not help but see, was pain. Accusation. Betrayal. Not because she'd lied, not because she'd jeopardized their lands and titles, not even because she'd risked her safety. But because she'd stripped from him something so precious he might not survive its loss.

Marian would have said, *I need no one's protection*. She would have said she could take care of herself. She would have leaped to her feet and asked if she had not just proven herself the best archer in the land, if she had not outwitted the Sheriff's best men at every step and gained the love and loyalty of the people. She would have cried out that she had not needed his protection for years, and that she could stand on her own without shame or fear.

And instead her heart broke, and she wept, and she dropped to the floor so she could reach for her father and press her tear-streaked face to the hands that rested at his knees. "I know," she choked out. "I'm sorry."

For a moment, he didn't respond. His hands lay still beneath her cheek, and his knee was hard and unyielding, and his breath became shallow and tight, and remote. Then he bent low and left his own chair so he could draw her into his arms. He laid his cheek against her hair and tucked her under his chin as he'd done when she was small, and he would lift her up to carry her here or there. He could not do so anymore, had not been able to for years, but crumpled on the floor she was a child again, and he held her thus.

He asked her nothing else. He didn't ask how she'd done it or why. He didn't ask who else knew. He didn't ask her whether there were others who followed her, or where she kept her disguise. He did not even ask her to stop being Robin Hood.

Later, when their tears were spent, Marian lay curled up on her side, her back to the glowing embers of the dead fire, head against her father's side. He stroked her hair in that clumsy and familiar way, the way of someone who doesn't understand how to stroke someone's hair but knows it brings comfort.

He said softly, "We'll go home tomorrow. We won't linger for Gisborne. We'll leave tomorrow and be home before dark."

The light was cold and pale when Elena woke her. Marian's father stood in the doorway, grim-faced, so Marian could not ask about Alan, but Elena's eyes glowed. Marian's father sent Elena with Marian's belongings down to the stables, so that when Marian stood ready to mount, she'd had no time to tell her maid what her father knew.

Midge held Jonquille's reins, and Marian looked from him to her maid to her father—they all knew her secret, and yet she was as bound by it as ever, for they could not know of each other's involvement. Her mind was silent, and the pain of that after so long with Robin in her thoughts was like a strangling cloud.

So it was a jolt nearly like that of relief when a familiar, detestable voice called her name.

"Sir Guy," Marian said warmly, turning to greet him with a smile.

He did not return her smile, approaching with swift, long strides, lips pinched with the pain of his bad leg. "I am glad to have reached you before you departed."

"We hope to be in Edwinstowe well before dark." Then Marian added, "I would have come to bid you farewell, but the hour is so early—"

Gisborne brushed her apology aside. "I am sorry to ruin your plans, my Lady."

Marian did not risk turning her head, but she sensed her father behind her, tense. "Sir Guy?"

Gisborne's face was grimmer than her father's had been. "I cannot let you leave Nottingham."

THIRTY-FIVE

HER FATHER PACED BEFORE the fire, wholly abandoning manners and caution, agitation radiating from him as tangibly as the heat from the hearth. "I forbid it," he blurted, furious.

Gisborne's face was impassive. As if in purposeful contrast, he stood motionless, hands folded behind his back, head bowed. He didn't speak, perhaps sensing that Marian's father required no prompting to continue.

"I will not allow my daughter to be used as bait." Her father whirled, soles scraping on the stone. "Catching this man is your duty, Gisborne, not hers. That you would so much as consider placing her in danger for your own vendetta is proof enough that I could never, *ever* consent to a union between you."

Gisborne's face didn't change, his expression as smooth and unyielding as ever. But from where she sat, Marian could see that the knuckles of his hands shone white where they knotted together behind his back. "She will be in no danger, my Lord. You have my word, my most solemn oath, that I will let nothing happen to her."

Marian sat in silence, watching the two men debating her future, without expression.

Her father whirled again, this time upon Gisborne himself. He was so afraid—Marian could see the fear in every step he took, every word he spoke. He sounded angry, but she could see with absolute clarity the terror fueling that anger. "What makes you think this Robin Hood would come for her?"

Marian had to give him the credit he was due, for she had once thought her father had no skill at deception or intrigue, and he did not so much as glance at her when he spoke of Robin Hood.

Gisborne's dark eyes narrowed, and he didn't answer until a loud pop in the fire shattered the quiet. "I feel I have come to understand this man," he said finally. "He believes he is acting rightly, even nobly. If word spread to him that the Lady Marian was being held against her will here in Nottingham Castle, I feel certain his sense of honor would compel him to come for her."

Her father began expostulating again, his protests a dim roar in Marian's ears. She watched Gisborne curiously as he faced down Lord Edwinstowe with the same immovable certainty he'd display to one of his guardsmen. She was as taken aback by Gisborne's plan as her father, but not for the same reasons.

She would have thought Gisborne's own sense of misguided nobility would prevent him from contemplating the idea of using Marian in such a way. The plan was more clever than she'd have thought possible, and cleverer than Gisborne knew. If Marian were under constant guard, Robin Hood could not continue undermining the Sheriff.

Marian thought her father might simply continue shouting until he went hoarse. She could not help but look at Gisborne, whose eyes slid sideways a fraction to meet hers. If he was surprised to find her watching him, he didn't show it—he held her gaze, and after an interminable pause, he lifted one of his eyebrows in silent query.

"I agree." Marian's voice was soft but final.

Her father spluttered to a halt, his tirade cut short by his daughter's soft words. "What?"

Marian got to her feet, lowering her gaze and trying her best to seem as demure and compliant as she could. "I agree with Sir Guy, Father. I agree to stay here and pretend to be his prisoner."

"Marian—" Her father came toward her and halted a step away. "You can't. I mean, I won't let you."

She would have smiled, had Gisborne not been watching them. But she lifted her eyes to scan her father's turbulent expression. "I don't think Robin Hood is as concerned with me as Sir Guy believes he is, but if my staying here will help catch him, then I am duty bound to comply."

Her father shifted from foot to foot, eyes skittering away more than once, as if he wanted to look at Gisborne but kept thinking better of it. "Marian," he said softly. "It's time to go home." The plea in his eyes was so intense, Marian could almost feel it, a dull ache in her heart.

"If nothing else," Marian replied, "perhaps I can prove to my Lord Gisborne that I have no sympathy for Robin Hood. That there is no connection between us."

Her father's expression shifted, though only Marian was close enough to see. Confusion gave way in his creased features, but the understanding that replaced it only strengthened the fear there. He took her hand, grasping her fingers tightly in his.

"Trust me, Father," Marian whispered.

He closed his eyes, hand shaking for a moment where it

gripped hers before he released her. There was a wealth of feeling in his gaze when he looked at her again, but his eyes swung toward Gisborne, and he said nothing else.

Gisborne, who had witnessed the whole exchange, took a step forward and cleared his throat. His chilly expression had eased somewhat, and he regarded Marian with something that seemed almost like warmth, in contrast. Warmth and, perhaps, surprise.

She'd said the words on purpose—*my Lord Gisborne*, as if they were already wed—and he had softened. "I choose to stay, Sir Guy."

Gisborne bowed his head, and Marian thought he was hiding relief. When he raised it again, however, there was nothing to be read there but grim determination. "Very well. While you are here, you must remain isolated. Your father and your servants will return with him today, as planned, to Edwinstowe, with the information that you are being held. No one will know you are not a real prisoner except myself and your father, and we cannot risk anyone else discovering the truth."

"But my maid—" began Marian.

"—is the sister of a man suspected to be part of Robin Hood's band," interrupted Gisborne. "No one, my Lady, except for myself."

Marian could not help but glance at her father, whose face had gone ashen as the furious color drained from his cheeks. "I have to see her, at least, reassure her . . ."

Gisborne flicked his fingers dismissively. "You must see why that is impossible, my Lady. Any reassurance might alert her to the deception, and even if she is entirely innocent, she might unwittingly betray something to someone who is not."

Marian looked again at her father. He did not know of Elena's involvement with Alan, or that Elena knew her identity as

Robin Hood. And Elena did not know her father had recognized her at the archery contest. Her heart ached for Elena, who would fear for her every moment, thinking she truly was a captive in Nottingham Castle. She would assume Gisborne suspected Marian, or worse, that he had learned the truth about Robin Hood.

Gisborne must have interpreted her glances as seeking permission, for he turned to her father as well. "My oath, Lord, that nothing will happen to your daughter. Her safety is my greatest concern."

That Marian did not believe. After she'd said her goodbyes to her father, she stood at the window of her new prison, which was even more comfortably decorated than her old chamber had been. It had been occupied by one of the visiting nobles who had departed following the conclusion of the council meetings. This room had a larger window that overlooked the courtyard, and she watched the tiny toy figurines of her family as they mounted their toy horses and rode away. Gisborne, an equally tiny figure cast in obsidian, stood motionless as he watched them go.

No, she did not believe her safety was chief among Gisborne's cares. She'd seen the fire in his eyes as he grappled with her in Robin Hood's guise. He would stride right past her bleeding, broken body without a second glance if it meant capturing Robin Hood.

She was counting on it.

Gisborne brought her meals several times each day, lavish and steaming straight from the kitchens. He brought her messages from her father and candles by which to read them. He caused several tapestries to be moved into the room and placed alongside the others, banishing the chill of deepening autumn. He even sought to give her what freedom he could within their planned deception.

"I asked that your mare be left in the stables here," he said, lingering inside the door of her chamber as stiffly as if standing at attention. "It has been a few days now, and I think that we might ride together for some fresh air, if you were to go hooded and cloaked—"

"No," Marian interrupted swiftly, barely remembering to keep her voice soft and gentle. The last thing she wanted was to ride with Gisborne in a costume so similar to the one her life hinged upon. "I really am well, Sir Guy."

Gisborne hesitated. It was so uncharacteristic of him that Marian found herself staring in something like amusement, helplessly drawn to his anxious manner. For he had more of the air of a nervous servant than the odious lawman she'd come to know. "You cannot be well, stuck here every hour of the day. I wish there was more I could do." His voice was quiet, and there was regret in his eyes.

No, thought Marian in sudden realization. *Not regret; guilt.*

For so long she had grappled with the fact that Gisborne's interest in her was solely due to her connection with Locksley and her father's lands—for so long she'd had to try to win his trust without having his regard. Now, the realization that she'd at last struck an emotion in him made her feel almost giddy with power.

She was meant to be the captive here, powerless, waiting for a rescuer she knew would never come—and yet Gisborne was the one held against his will, returning to her with excuse after excuse, each moment more a prisoner in this chamber than she'd ever be.

She dropped her eyes and looked up at him through her

lashes, a look she'd learned from Seild when she was a child, a look she'd always dismissed with disgust. She smiled. "You might stay a little and talk," she said, with what she hoped sounded like timidity.

Gisborne stiffened, but Marian held fast. Gisborne could react to the drawing of a sword without a second thought, but a kind word froze him solid. She waited, and eventually he said in a higher voice, "Stay?"

"Here with me." Marian could feel herself blushing, but if Gisborne saw it, he would think it girlish bashfulness, not the effort of deception.

Gisborne shifted his weight with an awkward creak of his leather tunic. He tugged at its hem, straightening his already impeccable attire, and then ran a hand through his hair. He looked so like a lady primping before a glass, but for once Marian did not find it funny so much as oddly sad, in a man of his position and experience. She wondered if a lady had ever invited him in that way to linger and talk with her.

A pang of guilt lanced at Marian's heart. Ruthlessly, she shoved it away. *This is the man who would've cut off Will's hand if I hadn't stopped him. The man who casually threatened to torture John to capture Robin Hood. The man overseeing the expansion of Nottingham's jails, to imprison the destitute until they rot.*

Marian watched Gisborne fidget, and she smiled at him until he dropped his eyes.

"Shall I . . . sit?" he asked, still by the door, as if keeping his escape route close to hand.

"If you want to." Marian abandoned the through-the-lashes gaze and smiled again instead. It had the desired effect—his tense frame relaxed a little, and he came to join her by the fire.

They spoke of little things: Gisborne learning to ride as

a boy; Marian's lack of skill with the needle and the resulting chicken-pillow in her father's study; the smell of autumn as the days grew shorter.

Marian asked if there was not some way to open the glazed pane enclosing the window, that she might enjoy that smell herself a little. Gisborne came the next day himself with tools to scrape free the leaden panes and set them instead into a hinged shutter to allow the window to open and close.

She was standing at that window on the fourth night of her masquerade of incarceration, braced against the chill so that she could lean out. It was large enough to admit her shoulders, and there was a ledge of stone outside it, half the width of her feet. She could not tell if her hips would fit through, but to make the attempt would be folly even if it didn't risk Gisborne arriving to find her missing. The stones in the wall were worn, and while there were places where it had crumbled that might serve as handholds, a fall would surely shatter several bones, if it did not kill her outright.

Still, the window was there.

The tap at her door was not unexpected, but Marian started regardless. She closed the paned shutters, then smoothed the fabric of her kirtle and adjusted the veil over her hair. When she called, Gisborne slipped into her room as comfortably and silently as a cat making itself at home.

He closed the door behind him and then frowned. "I shall bring more tapestries," he remarked in lieu of greeting. "The room is so cold."

Marian chuckled and made her way to her chair at the hearth. "I had the shutters open," she explained truthfully. "That autumn smell, you see."

Gisborne's thin lips relaxed, and he seated himself once she had done the same. "Forgive me for leaving so abruptly after I brought supper. There were rumors of a suspicious figure lingering around the courtyard, and I had hoped to catch the fellow."

"Hoped?" Marian echoed. "Then you didn't find him?"

Gisborne shook his head. "I doubt it was Robin Hood anyway." He leaned forward to grasp one of the logs stacked neatly in the wood bin by the fireplace. The fire crackled with delight as the log dropped into its embers, greedy for the extra fuel.

"What makes you say that?"

He lifted a shoulder, the twist of his lips wry. "I do not think he would be so utterly foolish as to lurk around under the window of his lady when he knows, for I am certain he knows, we are waiting for him."

"Perhaps you give him too much credit." Marian was conscious of a strange sense of pleasure, as if Gisborne's words had been flattery.

"Or not enough." Gisborne leaned back in the chair with a sigh. "Perhaps his wits are stronger than his honor after all. Perhaps he recognized me that day outside Nottingham as I recognized him, and he knows I would not harm you."

"I don't know." Marian drew her feet together and tucked them beneath her chair, demure and ladylike. "You are somewhat of a mystery, Sir Guy. It might take Robin Hood more than a glance to understand you."

Gisborne's eyebrows lifted. "A mystery? How so?"

Marian hesitated, for she herself was not entirely sure what she'd meant by that comment, except as flattery. "Well," she began, "you are the Sheriff's man, and yet you seem often . . . displeased by his actions. You're utterly devoted to your duty and yet you sneer at talk of morality, of right and wrong. You speak of the horrors of war and come home to fight one on your very doorstep against one man with a bow and a hood."

Her voice petered out, and she watched his face with some consternation. Her words held more accusation than she'd intended, and she searched his features for some sign of ire.

But he only watched her in return, his own expression rather searching. "That is what you think of me?"

Marian's eyes slid from his. She'd spent so much time with him in the last few days that she'd almost lost the sense of unease that came of having a man alone with her in her bedchamber. But now the strangeness of it all came rushing back, with all the force of a winter gale, and swept Marian from her chair. She made a show of going to the bedside table for the candles, for indeed night had fallen and the fire's light was shielded by the stone fireplace containing it.

She took her time lighting them, bending over the fire and dipping the wicks into the lapping flames, and then placed them on the dressing stool she'd pulled over to their chairs. Gisborne watched her all the while, and when she looked at him again, she was surprised to find no trace of chill in his eyes, and that the muscles in his face that kept his expression so rigid had relaxed.

So struck was she by the change that she could not help but meet his eyes for a long moment, caught between stool and chair.

"What is it?" he asked, brow furrowing.

"Nothing," she croaked. "The shadows dancing. They trick the eye, make you imagine dark things hidden in corners."

Gisborne's mouth quirked. "You sound more like a man returning from his own war than a lady."

Marian covered her unease with another smile, although it didn't come as easily as it had before. "Who are you to say that being a lady, in itself, is not its own kind of war?"

She only had time to feel a prick of concern that she'd spoken too harshly before Gisborne's face changed altogether, and he ducked his head to lift a hand to his mouth. Astonished, Marian heard him laugh.

"I will grant you that, my Lady. Who am I, indeed?" Gisborne's eyes gleamed. "All right, then—ask me what you will. Though I will admit I find being considered a mystery . . . compelling."

Marian turned that over in her mind, watching him askance. "What is it, between you and the Sheriff?"

Gisborne stiffened, the ease leaving his body as mysteriously as it had come. Marian was hardly easy herself—she'd intended to ask him about Robin Hood, in the hope of learning ways in which to continue confounding her enemy.

"Forgive me," she mumbled, unconsciously echoing the very words that Gisborne so often offered up.

Gisborne cleared his throat. "No, my Lady, I bade you ask me whatever you wanted. I only— It is difficult to speak of the matter. I never do, to anyone."

Marian caught her breath, willing herself to remain still, not lifting her eyes to meet his for fear her gaze might cause him to withdraw.

Leather creaked again, and she heard Gisborne release a pent-up breath with the faintest of sighs. "My father worked for his," he said quietly. "As a weapons master. When I was a boy, there was a great deal of unrest in Nottingham. My father—" Gisborne's voice stopped as abruptly as if a hand had wrapped around his throat.

Marian rose to her feet and crossed to the night table to fetch the ewer of wine that Gisborne brought each day. She poured it into a wooden cup, but when she approached, Gisborne was still gazing at her empty chair. He didn't stir until she touched his arm with her fingertips and then pushed the cup into his hand.

He started at her touch, black eyes flashing briefly before he looked away and took a long swallow. "My father," he went on, "was one of several men who believed that peasants must insist upon their access to justice and to the protection of law, by any means necessary. And those of common blood with access to nobility—those like my father, who worked for nobility—had an obligation to stand up." He bowed his head, the cup dangling between his hands as he rested his elbows on his knees. "I do not believe he would have come to violence, though. He could not be beaten with a sword, but he was the gentlest of men. But I will never know for certain what he would have done."

Marian sat back down in her chair as quietly as she could. "He was found out?"

Gisborne nodded. "The Sheriff at the time, the current one's father, rounded up those involved and had them killed in the square." His chin lifted, pointed toward the shuttered window. "There—where the festival bonfires were lit."

Marian knew she ought to harden her heart against sympathy, that any softening toward her most dangerous opponent could be lethal sometime down the road. And yet she found herself asking, "How old were you?"

Gisborne's eyes flicked up. "I was at that time seven years of age."

Marian tried to swallow the lump in her throat, but her voice still emerged raspy and dry. "And your mother?"

"Died birthing me. I had no siblings." Gisborne leaned close, but Marian's heart only had time to slam once before he stretched out the hand that held the cup. She took it gingerly and brought it to her lips for a sip to wet her dry throat. Gisborne watched, the now-mild eyes almost curious. "The former Sheriff saw in me the skills my father had taught me, of sword and bow, tracking and riding. He took me in, and I grew up alongside his own son."

Marian whispered, "But you have no love for him?"

Gisborne's eyes narrowed, but there was feeling there, buried deep. "He stood and looked on as my father was murdered in front of me." He reached out to reclaim the cup from Marian, and drained it. "I have no love for any of them."

Them, thought Marian. Nobles. People like her. She bought herself a few moments to think by pausing to refill the cup from the ewer. Gisborne had never indulged in drink before, not that she'd ever seen—he drank little with meals and had never appeared red-faced or blurry-eyed from intoxication. Perhaps she could gain something from it, if he were to let down his guard.

He's already let down his guard, she thought, and then buried that guilt deep.

"You seem distressed." Gisborne was watching her.

Marian replaced the ewer with somewhat more force than she'd intended. "I don't understand," she blurted. "You hate them—us—and you hate the Sheriff, but you do as he says and you spend your every waking moment enforcing his will. And you try so hard, so terribly hard, to look like one of them."

Gisborne looked down into the cup, the liquid inside as dark and thick as blood in the firelight. "It is the only way, in this world." His voice was quiet. "My father was a rebel. The men I killed in the Holy Land were rebels. I serve order, my Lady, because that is the only constant I know. I serve the law, not the Sheriff. And I mold myself to fit in amongst our noble lords because that is the route to power."

Marian felt the impact of that word like a slap, and she leaned back, face stinging. "Power? That's your aim in all this?"

Gisborne looked up from the wine, lips shifting to a wry smile. "Do not mistake me, my Lady. Power is a tool like any other. I serve the law, but the law is not always just. Speaking out against the landed nobility would earn me ridicule at best, or at worst a fate to match my father's. The only way of effecting true change is to rise among them, by their own rules, until they cannot deny my right to stand where they do. Until I have my own lands to govern, my own world to shape as I wish it had been when I was a boy, and my father still lived."

Marian looked at him across the pool of firelight, her cheeks hot from the flames, her fingertips numb and tingling. If he had not reclaimed the cup from her, she would have dropped it. "You're not a rebel," she whispered. "You want revolution."

Gisborne's eyes met hers for a long moment, registering her surprise, the warmth in her cheeks, the breathlessness of her voice. Then he glanced down, though he could not in that moment prevent the smile that transformed his face. No little wry twist of his lips, but a true smile that spilled across his features like dawn spreading across the forest. "My Lady," he said in a low voice, "I believe that is the kindest thing you have ever said to me."

Marian could think of nothing to say, so she was forced to dwell in the silence that stretched, beckoning and tempting, between them. She wanted to flee, to think of some carefully worded insult that would drive him away again, to tear open the shutters and let the cold shock her from this strange sympathy.

Use it, said a voice in her mind. Not Robin's. Not her own. Something else entirely. *Use him.*

"Sir Guy . . . you speak of change, of unjust laws, of the hunger and oppression the people of this land face. How—how can you hate Robin Hood so very much, when you are fighting for the same things?"

Gisborne's head snapped up. "The same things?" He barked a short laugh, gripping the cup so tightly Marian feared it would crack in his hands. "Is that how you see it?"

Marian felt her own ire rising in response, and could not entirely keep the heat from her voice. "He wants change as you do—he keeps none of his stolen wealth, he gives it to the people who need it. He's helping them, that grain—"

"That grain was bound for market," Gisborne interrupted. "Do you know why?"

"For coin," Marian replied sullenly.

"Yes." Gisborne's eyes were narrowed, and chilly, but intent. "And do you know where the coin was bound?"

"For the Sheriff's coffers."

"For the King." Gisborne's contradiction was whip-sharp, and it drew Marian up short. "The amount of money it takes to feed an army in a foreign land—you cannot imagine it, Marian. I could not, had I not seen it for myself. Yes, the Sheriff takes his cut, and yes, he lives as comfortably as any man could want. But most of that coin is bound for the east, to feed the men dying at the King's side."

Men like Robin.

Marian swayed. It was as though the chair beneath her had become insubstantial, as if all the muscles in her body had ceased to function. As if, in another breath, she would melt away entirely.

Gisborne, oblivious to her sudden horror, rose restlessly from his chair and leaned against the stone wall above the fireplace, palm flat against the mantel. The other still held the cup, and he sipped at it absently. "Robin Hood is . . . a symptom. People would not rally so to a man who flouts the laws and traditions of a land if that land was not diseased already."

He turned and saw Marian's face, and his own shifted to

reflect some measure of her emotion—though he could not know the reason for it. "For God's sake, Marian," he blurted, "do you think I don't wish I could be their hero? You think I don't wish I could put on a mask and a cloak and give food to those who need it, and see their gratitude and their admiration, feel some return for my service?" He drained the cup again and then, regarding it with sudden anger, he hurled it into the fireplace. The dregs of the wine sizzled and spat, and Gisborne braced himself with both hands against the stone, head down and hidden from Marian.

"Do you think," he said, voice quieter and muffled, "that any man wakes in the morning and decides to take food from the mouths of hungry children?" His shoulders slumped, and the silhouette of his body against the fire cast a monstrous shadow on the walls and ceiling of the chamber that wavered and loomed like a specter. "It's easy to be a hero when you never look beyond your next battle. Only fools believe they know all there is to know."

I believed that.

Marian felt tears on her cheeks, but she still could not move, her body so disconnected from the rest of her that had Gisborne whirled with sword in hand, she could not have lifted a finger to defend herself. His voice was so changed—the informality of it, the heat of emotion, the depth of feeling—she would believe him an impostor, some demon sent to torment her in his stead, except that she had seen, and not recognized until now, so many glimpses of what lay beneath his stony facade that the revelations made more sense than the lie she wanted to cling to.

"I admire him," Gisborne went on, still muffled, head still bowed. "You accused me once of doing so, and I denied it, but I do. And I hate him. Because he does as I wish I could, with utter abandon, and certainty of where he stands betwixt good and evil—he does what I used to dream of doing when I was a boy. I would have worshipped him, but the world is still in ruins, and the King still fights his war, and people from here to the eastern desert still starve."

Marian's arms and legs still refused to obey her, but now they moved of their own accord. She rose from her chair and took three faltering steps toward the fireplace, her own shadow swelling and mingling with Gisborne's on the walls of the chamber as she approached. "He's trying," she said.

Gisborne's eyes were closed tightly, and he seemed not to notice she had drawn near. "If he truly cares for this land, Robin Hood will realize how much he does not know, and *stop* trying."

Numbed, her world upended, Marian breathed, "Maybe he can't." She could not look at Gisborne, the shadows wavering and tilting as he turned toward her. "If he stops now, then maybe he would have always been wrong, and the things he's done . . . If he stops now, he will never be more than a murderer."

Gisborne took her hand. His touch summoned her back into her body, as quick and abrupt as a thunderbolt's strike, and Marian's legs nearly gave way as she was granted control of herself again. Gisborne drew her close, his other hand wrapping around her waist, fingers pressed to the fabric of her dress. He had already torn her world apart—that his touch now made her whole body sing in response was only one more thing that did not make sense.

"Marry me," he said, his dark eyes intent on her face with a strange urgency.

Marian, dazed, whispered, "What?"

Gisborne pulled her in a little more tightly and then released her hand, so that his fingers could nudge aside the veil and touch the soft waves of her hair. He moved so slowly that Marian could have pulled away at any moment, or turned her head, or asked him to stop. She stood utterly still, but for the rise and fall of her chest, and the tremble in her body that made her long to tilt her head into his touch.

"I don't care what you've done," whispered Gisborne, with no trace of the remote, icy calm that he showed to the world. "Who you've helped. Marian—please. As my wife, you'd be under my protection."

She could feel each of his fingers against her back, five individual points of pressure. One moved in the tiniest of caresses, as if memorizing the texture of her dress, or the warmth of the body beneath it.

Use it, said the voice.

This was what she'd wanted all along, after all—her enemy under her spell, an unwitting but devoted ally. Rendered powerless, made easy, another obstacle cleared. Safe.

"I would ask nothing of you," whispered Gisborne. "I know your feelings toward me, Marian. Believe me, you have never tried to hide them. I would know you married me for your people, and your father, and—and for him. I would not touch you unless you wished me to, would not—" He stopped, voice catching and eyes falling. His arm stiffened, as if he was only now realizing that he'd pulled her close, already giving her reason to doubt his promises.

He let her go so abruptly she nearly staggered as he murmured, "I only want you safe, I want . . ."

Marian moved forward, curled her fingers around his arm, and leaned up to stop the torrent of promises and wants.

She had imagined trying to kiss Gisborne before—had dwelled on it in the late hours as she struggled to sleep. Had worried she could not do it, that her hatred would translate to a disgust so visceral that the touch of his lips on hers would be torture. Had argued with herself about whether she could do it, for the sake of Robin Hood, for the sake of winning Gisborne to her side, securing his trust. About whether her pride would let her capitulate to her enemy and give him what he wanted so that she could have her own victories, even if he'd never know they were hers. She'd wondered if it would be as strange as kissing Robin had been, the boy she'd known most of her life.

But now, in this moment—Marian kissed him because she couldn't stop herself.

Her lips met his too strongly, the sudden need for him turning her clumsy. His own mouth was rigid with surprise, and after a second he leaned away, a hand coming up to grasp at her shoulder and hold her off. He drew breath to speak, and she knew he would ask her what she was doing, and she would not be able to answer, for she didn't know herself.

He didn't speak, despite his parted lips and drawn breath. His eyes were like coal, and as they met hers they sparked and caught fire, and the hand gripping her shoulder shifted. He held back a moment longer, eyes falling to her lips—and then he bent his head to kiss her.

His mouth met hers gently at first, but when she leaned close, when her lips parted, when he slipped an arm around her and felt her back arch, he abandoned gentility as utterly as the rest of the facade he'd worn for so many years. His fingers slid into her hair, cradling her head, and his kiss turned hungry. His other hand dropped to grasp her hip, pulling her into him. Marian's hand moved across his chest, over his shoulder, down the arm that wielded his sword, the arm now holding her so possessively. Her touch was not gentle—her hold on him was as tight as his on her, and when her fingers curled, clawlike, to dig into his wrist, he groaned against her mouth, undone.

She might have gloried in her conquest, wondering at how utterly she could affect him—but Marian was gone, and in her place was someone entirely different. A winged being of flame and freedom, unmasked, untempered by expectation and inhibition— something wholly familiar, something she'd been hiding all her life.

In two stumbling steps they moved backward together until he could press her against the wall, his body lean and hard against hers. Her hips moved, tipping up like a beckoning finger, and when he felt her swell toward him he tore his mouth from hers and ducked his head—he kissed her throat, tasted the line of her jaw, breathed into her hair. His breath brushed her ear before he ducked down again, lips trailing across her skin until he could press them into the hollow of her shoulder.

Marian moved as he did, the movement of his body and hers a rising swell she did not try to resist. As he dropped his head, one of her hands came up to cup his cheek—the scarred skin was yielding and warm, indistinguishable from the rest of him but for a soft ridge only her fingertips could find. Gisborne shivered and leaned into her harder, momentarily robbing her of breath.

The hand at her hip dropped a fraction, and Marian's body responded as if they had rehearsed the moment together. He pinned her against the wall and held her there, and she lifted her leg to curl around his. His hand cupped the back of her knee, and as his palm slid up the back of her thigh, she let out a sound.

It was her own raw, unfiltered voice that stopped her, a sudden and visceral reminder that she was not unfettered, that she was not free and unmasked and uninhibited—her voice, and the realization that Gisborne's fingertips were about to graze the leather strip binding her dagger to her thigh.

Marian gasped again and grabbed for Gisborne's wrist to stop him, drawing back against the wall. He felt the change in her instantly and went motionless, breathing hard. They stayed that way, leaning together, her fingers tight around his wrist, his lips still touching her collarbone—until the fire popped, and Marian jumped, and Gisborne stepped back.

They stared at each other, too shaken for propriety or self-consciousness to find its way back and force their gazes away. It had all taken only seconds to unfold, both of them moving together on some unspoken understanding. Marian knew how she must look, her face flushed, lips swollen, eyes as wild and fearful as a deer's in the moment before its hunter lets fly the fatal arrow—she knew, because it was exactly how Gisborne looked.

Shaken, he whispered with an odd quiver of surprise, "I love you."

She said nothing, because he was her enemy, and because she wanted him still, and because he looked so frightened that she could not speak for fear he would bolt—or that she would. She hated him, and she wanted him, and she did not know who she was.

Gisborne was the first to move. He did not try to renew their embrace, or lean toward her again—he only took her hand, drawing it up so he could enfold it in both of his. He kissed her fingers, pressing them close and lingering long enough for Marian to feel the tremor in his lips. Then he bowed his head forward and rested his brow and the bridge of his nose against her skin, and his hand shook as if releasing her was an effort nearly beyond his strength.

She knew what was coming, knew it as if she were about to

say it herself—*Forgive me,* he would murmur, and he would be calm and cold the next time she saw him, and she would remember how she hated him, and the spell, the fragile connection of like souls, would be broken.

But when he spoke, he only said, "Good night, Marian."

She didn't see him go, only heard the door open and close. She stood sagging against the wall as if bound there, as if she really were in a prison cell—and she felt as undone and raw as if it were her torturer who had just departed. Eyes filling, lungs burning, Marian shoved away from the wall and went to the window, where she tore the shutters loose and stood, gasping, in the frigid fall air.

Marian was so disoriented that the cold air felt like a torrent of water, and for a moment it felt as though she could swim through the window, away from the heat at her back. But then something dropped from the shutters, fluttering and falling against her foot. Dizzy, she looked down to find a folded piece of parchment.

Numbly, she bent and picked it up between her fingertips. It crackled anxiously as she unfolded it, and shivered and trembled as she brought it closer to the nearest candle.

It read:

Marian—
Take heart. I'm coming for you.
R.H.

THIRTY-SIX

PANIC SEARED MARIAN'S BODY, as tangible and painful as liquid fire. The note was trembling now in her hand so violently that she could no longer read the words, but she'd read them already, and could not unsee them.

Robin was alive. Robin was coming for her. Robin had been there, had scaled the wall outside her window, had risked his life to bring her a moment of comfort and hope. Robin was alive. Robin was alive, and she'd kissed Gisborne. Robin was alive, and she had given her heart—full of love or loathing, she did not know—to another man.

Robin was alive.

It didn't matter that the letters of the note were not written in his hand. It didn't matter that he never would have signed the initials of Robin Hood and not Robert of Locksley. Truth and logic didn't matter, for panic had seized Marian so suddenly and unyieldingly that she could not think past that single thought that spun on endlessly, cutting her over and over.

Robin was alive.

There was no physician's drug to help her. She'd not needed it, these past weeks, too preoccupied with matters of life and death to fear the shadows in her own mind. And when the room for her imprisonment had been appointed, no one—least of all Marian herself—had thought to ask for it.

She tried to breathe, but she could not remember how to breathe without remembering Robin teaching her, his hands on her ribs as they rose and fell, and then she could not think of anything but Gisborne's arm there, holding her against him. She could only run, but there were guards outside her door, and a castle of guards beyond them, and Gisborne somewhere among them, and she knew, with the kind of certainty that only came with the most irrational of thoughts, that if he saw her face in this moment, he would see all her secrets.

She had to flee. To fly.

Marian had one leg over the sill of the window before she stopped, pulled one breath back toward sanity by the sight of the drop to the courtyard below. She froze. She waited. And then, slowly, shaking, she dragged herself back inside the room.

She picked up the note, which she'd dropped in her rush for the window, and looked at it again.

Alan, she thought, feeling distant and pale within her own mind. *Alan knows how to read and write. He was "Robin" once before, and he knows I am he.*

Elena would have gone to find him and the others as soon as she could get out of the house upon their return to Edwinstowe. Even if the men had not leaped at the prospect of rescuing Marian, Elena would not have let them wait for a Robin Hood who couldn't come. Neither would Alan, now that he knew the truth.

They would come for her, and Gisborne would stop them. And they would die.

Gisborne would kill Robin Hood after all.

Marian carefully leaned down and placed the note in the fireplace, where the remnants of the wooden cup smoldered. She waited to make sure the parchment had turned to ash, and then she went to the night table, where rested a few of the letters Gisborne had brought for her. She picked up one of the pages and folded it until only the blank space showed, and then carefully retrieved a piece of charcoal from the fireplace.

Carefully, her heart a stone, she wrote:

Gisborne—
   I think she would have married you, if not for me.
   —Robin Hood

She placed the note carefully upon her untouched bed, where it could not be missed. She went to the window, took off her shoes, and tossed them to the courtyard far, far below. Before they struck the cobblestones, Marian slipped out the window, finding minute toeholds in the sheer limestone, and began to climb down.

THIRTY-SEVEN

THE HOUR WAS LATE, but not so late that the courtyard was abandoned. Guards prowled the gates and the doors, their numbers greater than they had been during the council meetings. Marian watched them from the shadows as she retrieved her shoes and stamped to bring circulation back to her numbed toes. The castle entrance nearest Marian's window was conspicuously unguarded, as was the south gate. A clever outlaw might see the pattern of surveillance and make for those weak points—but a clever lawman might leave openings to tempt a would-be thief and abductor, lying in wait on the other side.

Gisborne's precautions assumed Robin Hood would attempt to gain access to the castle as he had seemed to do before: by the doors, in disguise. While the usual detachment of guards patrolled the castle perimeter, none of them were looking up. No one had told them to keep an eye on the windows. Gisborne would surely deduce that Robin Hood had climbed the lime-stone wall and stolen Marian away via the window, once he came in the morning to find her missing and the guards at her door still in place. She wouldn't be able to use the window again, that much was certain.

But Marian didn't know if she was coming back.

She kept to the shadows, slinking along the outskirts of the courtyard until she could slip into the stables. Jonquille whickered in recognition as she picked up Marian's scent, and Marian hurried to the mare's side to stroke her nose and quiet her. She waited but heard no footsteps approaching to investigate the sound.

Marian saddled her in darkness, muscles quivering still from her climb. She had no disguise, nothing to protect her should someone spot her riding out, but the guards were focused on detecting someone trying to gain entry to the castle—not someone escaping. She led Jonquille slowly, suppressing the desire to simply mount and break into a gallop. The clipped, sharp tapping of hooves on cobblestone rang like the clanging of a bell in Marian's ears, but when she paused after reaching the gate to the pastures, she could hear no sounds of pursuit.

She mounted, turning Jonquille toward the distant trees. The grasses in the field rippled in the moonlight, fluttering like a delicate veil across the landscape. Her own veil was gone—fallen off during the descent, or else pulled off and discarded while Gisborne was . . .

Marian's heartbeat quickened, and she squeezed at Jonquille's flanks. Without hesitation the horse skipped up into a canter and, when Marian made no effort to hold her there, burst into a loping run. Her galloping hoofbeats drummed in Marian's ears, but it didn't matter now, because she was within reach of the forest.

She plunged beneath Sherwood's dark canopy, scattered with

pools of moonlight where autumn had claimed the leaves overhead. The familiar rhythm of Jonquille's body moving under her
was more effective than any physician's draught could have been,
bringing Marian back to herself step by step. But she didn't slow,
not until a branch whipped by and tore at her ear in a searing
flash. And then it was concern for Jonquille that made Marian
pull the mare back down to a trot.

Sticky warmth dripped down the side of her neck, and
Marian finally told her horse to stop altogether so she could
dismount. She leaned heavily against Jonquille's flank, resting
her forehead on the warm shoulder as she felt at the wound on
her ear. It was bleeding copiously, but the pain was minimal, and
Marian pinched at the rim of her ear until the blood slowed.

She shivered, realizing only now that she had stopped that
she wasn't remotely attired for travel through the forest. She wore
only her shift and kirtle, with no cloak or wrap. She had no food,
no water for her or for Jonquille, and no place to shelter. The air
was cold, and she'd be frozen through if she could not find the
others before the night was over.

Marian put a hand on the nearest saddlebag automatically,
knowing she'd packed nothing, and froze when she felt the
leather give only a little against the bulk of its load. With trembling hands, she lifted the flap and took out the bag's contents,
shaking the fabric until it dangled, inky black in the darkness,
from her hands.

Robin's cloak.

She checked the other bag and found the rest of his clothes,
and a mask as well—not the one she'd lost in the hall the night
she shot the guard, but a new one fashioned of leather and molded
to fit the face. Her face.

Midge? He was the only one Marian could think of with the

skills to make her a mask and know where to put it so she'd find it. But Elena had hidden the rest of Robin's clothes for her, and she couldn't have known about Midge's hiding place among Jonquille's tack.

Unless both servants knew more than they'd admitted. Marian clutched the cloak to her breast, gaze swinging unseeing around the darkened outlines of the trees surrounding her.

Shivering, breath painting pale gray clouds, Marian stripped to the skin and put on Robin's clothes one more time.

One more time.

And then what? Could Robin Hood simply vanish into legend, a murderer and a hero, bound to whichever version of him the people remembered? Or else Marian would be the one to disappear, kidnapped by the infamous outlaw, never to be seen again, leaving Robin of the Hood free to continue his mission.

Robin Hood swung up into Jonquille's saddle, turned toward the King's Road, and set out to find the others.

She'd taught them well, or else they'd taught themselves, for she was nearly on top of their camp before the smell of burning oak and leaves brought her out of her daze. She could not see the fire except for the faintest of glows—they'd dug it so low it was nearly invisible. The scent was so strong that she stopped, reining Jonquille in abruptly enough to make the horse snort a protest.

A shadow leaped up in response to the sound, and Marian grabbed for the dagger she'd sheathed at her belt. Before she could do more, a shout of surprise roused the rest of the men.

"Robin!" It was Little John's voice, hoarse with weariness and cracking with relief. "It's Robin—wake up, fools, Robin's come."

Marian let go the dagger's hilt and slid from Jonquille's

saddle with a thump. She landed on her feet but leaned heavily on her horse, feeling as weak-kneed as she had when Gisborne had first released her from his embrace.

Little John took no notice, a massive looming shadow emerging from the trees to grasp Marian's arm and draw her toward the fire.

Other shapes were stirring, transforming from amorphous shadows to the silhouettes of men as they stood, and when Marian half walked, half slid down the embankment into the glow of the fire, one came rushing toward her.

"Thank God," blurted Will, taking her by the shoulders and squeezing hard. "We've been trying to find you. Robin—they've taken Marian."

His voice was so serious, his eyes so earnest and full of sympathy, that Marian almost burst out laughing. Instead, her gaze swung round until she found Alan, who stood where he'd been huddled by the fire. Though he had no need to hide in the forest now that he was pardoned, he could not have left the others—or Marian, now he knew her secret—for anything. She could see his eyes glittering in the firelight, the angle of the light casting his face in a forbidding mask of deep lines.

"I know," Marian croaked. It always took her a little time to settle into Robin Hood's deeper, hoarser tones, but this time she was simply so parched and weary that her voice was unrecognizable without any effort at all. "That's why I've come."

"Have you a plan to rescue her?" Little John was seeing to Jonquille, loosening her tack and letting her reins hang down to trail on the forest floor.

"She needs no rescue." Marian crept closer to the fire, seeking its warmth as eagerly as she'd sought the cold at her chamber window hours before. "Her imprisonment was a ruse to capture me, and as many of you as came to assist. I came to warn you not to make the attempt."

In her weariness, Marian had not noticed that the three familiar silhouettes of John, Alan, and Will were not the only shadows clustered around the fire. Now, as another shape broke the tableau and rose, Marian bit back an oath.

Elena stood, her arms wrapped tightly around herself, her face nowhere near as impassive as Alan's. "Marian—is she well?"

Marian's breath stuck in her throat, and she could only look at her maid, her friend, attired once more in her boy's clothing, though her cap lay at her feet and her pale hair fell around her shoulders. Her face was haggard and hopeful all at once, concern writ there so plainly it made Marian's heart ache.

No. She's heartbroken, because Robin is truly gone, and because she kissed Gisborne, and because she doesn't know if she ever truly loved anyone in her life, and because she's a murderer.

"She's well." Marian's gaze shifted from Elena to Alan, who remained silent and unmoving. "She got your message."

"And mine, I reckon." The new voice, deep and rumbling, was so unexpected Marian nearly fell back. She blinked, eyes still adjusting to the firelight, and saw the stocky form of Midge, who had not moved from where he sat near the fire.

Will, seeing the astonishment on Marian's face and interpreting it as best he could, laid a hand on her arm. "Be easy, Robin, he's a friend. Alan's lady vouched for him."

Midge finally rose and strode toward Marian, extending a hand. "My name's Much, my Lord. My sword is yours, if you'll have it."

Marian's grip was weak, but Much's made up for it, clasping her forearm in the manner of an old acquaintance and squeezing.

The pressure unfroze Marian's tongue. "Well met, Much," she whispered.

So they did know, Elena and Much—she wondered when they had confided in one another, and how long each had known the other was involved in Marian's double life. For all Marian knew, Much had known of Elena's connection to Alan long before Robin Hood ever made his first appearance.

From Will's unchanged look of admiration, and Little John's hearty cheer as he rejoined them by the fire, Marian could tell Alan had not spoken of what he'd discovered the day of the archery contest.

Marian cleared her throat, eyes scanning the faces of her people. "It's too risky, being together like this—you all ought to be scattered. Gisborne will discover by morning that Marian is— Marian has been freed, and he will send every man he has into these woods to find her, and me. You're too close to Nottingham here."

"We're come to save Marian." Alan finally spoke, his face still impassive. "We could not count on you to save her first. We have no way of summoning you, Robin—for all we knew, you would never come."

Marian met his eyes unflinchingly, bearing the accusation writ there, offering no excuses in return. "All is well," she murmured. "You should all go. To your homes, to hide, wherever you can find that is safe."

"And what will you do?" asked Alan.

Marian blinked, absorbed in the familiar feeling of her lashes brushing the leather edges of her mask. She drew a long, careful breath. "I will disappear."

Alan's jaw tightened, and Elena glanced sideways at him for a moment before reaching for his hand and winding her fingers through his. Will, oblivious to the tension, protested. "But when will we meet again? We need a system, some way of letting each other know when the Sheriff gives up his pursuit and calls Gisborne off, so we know when to start planning our next move."

"There isn't going to be a next move." Alan spoke quietly, watching Marian's face intently, as though he was trying now to see through the mask to the face he knew lay beneath it. "That's what Robin is trying to tell us."

Will spluttered, and Little John gave a rumble of protest as he drew himself up. Marian drew a breath and raised her voice, risking the carrying sound in order to silence the others.

"Alan's right." Her sharp tone cut through the other voices and demanded attention. "Robin Hood has had his time—the risk grows with every move we make. Gisborne is too clever and has too many men at his disposal. That he'll catch us, one or all of us, is inevitable if we continue."

"You can't vanish," Will blurted angrily. "What about us? Alan's pardoned, and he has the arrow to live off with Elena, but John and I are outlaws still. I'd rather die in your service than live like a criminal, stealing food from storerooms already near empty, no purpose but to persist."

"And do you suppose Alan and I would be content to live quietly somewhere, knowing our friends face execution if they're ever caught?" Elena's eyes glowed in the firelight, her grip on Alan's hand tight.

Marian's temper, frayed already beyond snapping, disintegrated into tatters. "What did you think was going to happen?" she demanded. "That we'd continue merrily along, waylaying rich travelers and pulling ever more foolhardy stunts on the Sheriff and his men, until King Richard returns and pardons us all? It was always going to end, and better it ends with our lives intact than at the end of a hangman's rope."

Will opened his mouth to reply, his face so ingenuous that Marian knew her words had gone unheeded.

She threw down her bow, furious beyond what Will deserved, beyond what any of them deserved. She'd put on Robin's cloak that first night so no one would know her, and had discovered a world without the heavy burden of expectation and duty. Now she was as trapped as ever, and all she could think of was Gisborne's voice when he'd told her there were men starving in the Holy Land because Robin Hood had chosen the people of Nottingham over them.

"There is no pardon coming for us," Marian said, sharp and hollow, before Will could speak. "Even if we could continue until the King returns, he won't pardon us."

"You don't know that—"

"Will, *enough.* I do know it. Do you hear? I *know* it. We are traitors, all of us. King or no, if they find us, they will hang us." Marian began to pace, trampling the freshly dug earth by the fireside. "Your best hope, all of you, is to scatter. Go home if you can, and hide if you cannot. Live quietly away from the light, and eventually, one day, the law will forget about Robin Hood, and stop looking for him and his men."

"*Our* best hope," echoed Elena. Her voice held a note of steel in it, a tone Marian had never heard. "What is yours?"

Marian's lips pressed together until she could speak again. "You owe me nothing. None of you. I chose this folly, and the consequences are mine to face. I can bear them." She paused, and had to harden her voice when it would have softened and broken. "But I cannot bear it if those consequences befall the rest of you, too."

The fire crackled, punctuated by the soft sound of Jonquille slurping at a skin of rainwater not far from where John had left her. No one spoke for a few long breaths. Perspiration tickled at Marian's brow beneath her mask, and her ear ached.

Much was holding a cudgel in one hand, and he looked down at it as he shifted his weight, a stick cracking underfoot and drawing everyone's gaze in his direction. When he looked up, he spared not a glance for the others and watched Marian instead. "You did choose this," he said gently. "But I see no bindings. No jailers, loved ones held hostage, no false promises of riches to be gained. Why do you think we are here, if not because we chose it, too?"

Elena's voice was barely audible over the fire. "We're told all our lives what to do. The role we play. Where we fit." She was waiting for Marian's gaze, and held her eyes, lips set. Her gentle maid, with the quick fingers and the soft laugh, flawless with needle and comb and scrub brush, smiled when she saw Marian's face shift with understanding. "You aren't the only one who chafes at being defined by the men who rule us."

To the others, it was a speech about choice and consequence and loyalty, and the rule of nobility. But she spoke to Marian, not Robin Hood. And Marian heard her own heart echoed back to her, and turned away.

"It must end," she mumbled, her face in her hands, thumbs kneading at the leather at her temples.

"Then let it." Little John spoke for the first time since Marian had lost her temper. "Once we've helped the people of Nottingham—once we've made certain they'll last the winter at least—we'll vanish with you, those of us without homes to return to."

Marian's breath exploded in a weary laugh. "As easy as that? Amass enough wealth to give sustenance to all who need it for an entire season, without being caught, quickly enough to vanish before Gisborne's men track us down?"

Little John looked away, rubbing at his chin. His beard was growing back, and his callused hands rasped over the thick stubble like a blade on a whetstone.

"We continue with our smaller thefts," suggested Will, face grave. "Nothing too big, targets scattered across the forest. Too random to track. We can split up, plan each move with care."

Marian turned back but did not resume her pacing. She stared, unseeing, into the fire. "It would take a great many small thefts," she mumbled slowly, thoughts racing. "Or one big one."

"Robin?" Will's voice was uncertain.

Her gaze snapped up. "The gold shipment Gisborne spoke of to Marian."

A hush settled over the circle of faces, each peering back at her. The wind shifted, bringing with it an acrid gust of campfire smoke that made Marian's eyes water.

"It'll be too well guarded," Will said finally, slowly, as if afraid to break the silence.

Marian countered, "We'll be on our home territory, here in Sherwood, where the King's Road passes through. And with Gisborne's attention on the castle, on guarding Marian, he won't be there escorting the shipment."

"Distributing that much gold without being caught—"

"Is a task we can spread out over the entire winter." Marian's eyes swung to find Little John, who fell silent when she interrupted him. "Once we have it, we can lie low until pursuit has stopped, and hand out coin in secret."

"We'll have to fight." Alan's voice was taut, but there was a cautious energy to it as his eyes darted around the circle. "We won't get away with misdirection and trickery—if we hope to capture whole wagons, it'll come to sword and bow one way or another."

Marian thought of the boy, Tom, dead of the arrow she'd made with her own hands and fired from her own bow. She thought of the boys dying in the desert, for a King draining his own land of life and prosperity in order to bring ruin to the infidels. Infidels who were just boys themselves, born of different mothers and sworn to a different god, and dying all the same.

She could not stop any of it. She could not end the King's war or bring him home. She could not feed the starving soldiers on either side, or keep them safe, or bandage their wounds when they fell. She could not save them. She could not save Robin. She could not even save herself.

But she could feed those boys, the ones she'd seen watching her that day at the gates of Nottingham town, who had looked so tired and so hopeful and so very, very young.

This time, when Marian looked around at the faces of her band of outlaws, she saw only reflections of the determination crystallizing in her own heart. Robin's spirit was still silent, and distantly, she wondered if her father had been right all along—that none of this was what Robin would have wanted. If his silence was disapproval, not just of the murder, but of everything. Of Robin Hood.

Perhaps she hadn't known him as she thought she had—he had not truly known her, after all. She had not truly known herself.

Marian buried her unease as deeply as she could. Doubt only slowed the blade or bow, dulled the reflexes—there was no room for it now they'd decided.

"Then this time, we'll fight," she said. "One more mission. Robin Hood's last ride."

THIRTY-EIGHT

GISBORNE HAD NOT TOLD her exactly when the shipment of gold was due to depart Nottingham, only that it would happen sometime after the festival and archery contest had distracted both townspeople and Robin Hood. There was a chance the outlaws had already missed their window, if the procession had departed promptly, but Marian did not think it had. Gisborne had been distracted himself then, occupied not with getting the Sheriff's coffers to the Prince, but with his plan to capture Robin Hood—his plan to use Marian as bait.

They reached the King's Road as dawn snuck hesitantly between the trees, casting its pale rosy curtain across the carpet of fallen leaves. Much was leading Jonquille, and Marian walked at Elena's side. They spoke little, for there was not much to say that could be said in the company of the whole band, but her presence alone was balm, of a sort.

"How is he?" Marian managed to ask, under the cover

provided by John's laughter in response to a particularly raunchy joke from Much.

Elena glanced over her shoulder, where Alan and Will brought up the rear of their little party. "He's angry."

"He must know why you didn't tell him."

Elena's lips twisted. "I'm not the one he's angry at."

"You told me not to tell them," Marian murmured. "You were right."

Elena was saved from replying as Little John began telling a new joke to top Much's in a strident voice. Her maid only glanced at Marian, and then found a smile as she listened to John's tall tale.

They'd gone by way of Edwinstowe. Marian had protested, but her protests were easily overridden—they had between them only one sword, a pair of bows, and the few eating knives the men carried at their belts. Marian could not imagine her father's reaction to the idea of his trusted stableman stealing weapons from Edwinstowe, much less stealing them to help Marian's charade as Robin Hood, but Much waved her concerns away when she drew him aside.

He returned with a bundle of gathered sticks and firewood slung over his back, and when he unbound the cords, half a dozen blades clattered out among the sticks and unstrung bows and quivers.

John had refused a sword, claiming the reach of his staff was greater than that of a blade, and far more familiar in his hand. Elena had picked up one of the swords with surprising ease, after her initial stagger at its weight. She gave it an awkward, experimental swing, and then tossed it back down to the ground.

Marian had heard her and Alan fighting, while they waited for Much to return with the weapons. They'd walked off a ways, but their voices carried in the crisp night air. Elena was as capable as any lad, but she'd never had any training with bow or blade as Marian had. She could not fight, except as anyone could, in desperation, to save her life—in an assault on a caravan, she'd be of no use. Alan did not try to argue for her safety, or for her gentle nature as a woman, or even for the place she held in his heart.

"You'll be in the way," the minstrel said bluntly, voice thick with passion. "God, Elena, do you think I could fight at M— at Robin's side, knowing you were there, without constantly looking over my shoulder to see if you were safe?"

"I can help." Elena's voice was softer than his.

"You don't know how to fight. There's no shame in that, admitting to a thing you don't know."

"Would you tell Marian not to come?"

Marian froze. Little John was at her right, and Will was pacing some distance away, and they could all hear what was being said.

"If *Marian* were the one leading us," Alan said slowly, "I would follow her as I do Robin. She can fight."

"So can I." Elena's voice was hard. "I cannot use a bow or a sword, but don't tell me I can't fight."

"If something happens to you—"

"If something happens to me," Elena interrupted, voice rising, "then it will have already happened to you. Alan, I will not sit quiet and safe in my room in Edwinstowe, waiting to learn from a crier that everyone I love is dead. I'll distract them, spook the horses, call warnings if I see danger the rest of you don't. I won't pretend I can stand next to you, sword in hand. But damned if I will not stand behind you."

Alan did not answer—or, at the least, he did not answer in a way that they could overhear. Silence enclosed them in a tight embrace. Marian glanced aside and saw Little John leaning against a tree. His head was bowed, but enough moonlight filtered through the leaves that she could see he was smiling. His eyes met Marian's and twinkled.

By the time they reached the road at dawn, Marian had managed to give Elena a few lessons in the use of the dagger she wore at her waist. She did not know if it would help, for it took more than a few words and hurried explanations to overwrite the raw instinct that took over when danger threatened. But Elena seemed unconcerned—of all of them, her face was lightest, her step easiest.

Marian felt the weight of the sword at her belt, the curve of the bow on her shoulder, brushed her fingertips against the fletching of the arrows in their quiver at her hip. She swore to herself, silently, that she would see Elena and Alan both safe, if she could do nothing else.

The road bore the scars of repeated travel, the ruts of wagon wheels and the half-moon dents of hoofprints. Marian stooped with Much, examining them. It had rained heavily up until the festival, which meant that the tracks on the road now belonged only to those travelers who had come this way since. The edges of most of the wheel tracks were dry and hard, rounded where they'd sunk easily into fresh mud—but there were some tracks that were little more than crumbled dust, moving in and out of the other tracks.

Those tracks had been left long after the mud had dried. Those tracks had been left that night.

They melted back into the trees and continued on in the direction the wagons had gone, tense and watchful. Twice they passed other travelers, unseen in the shadow of Sherwood Forest. The first time, it was a small group, a family perhaps, travel worn and slow, and moving toward Nottingham town. They traveled on foot, and the band let them pass without speaking.

The second traveler came on horseback, and at the sound of hoofbeats approaching, Marian stiffened and signaled for the others to conceal themselves among the brush. Her heart thudded with certainty that when he rounded the curve of the road, the rider would be astride a big, black horse, and he'd be clad in unrelieved black, and his face would be scarred, and he'd see in an instant straight through the undergrowth to where she hid.

But the horse was a skinny old nag, and her rider a bent man huddled in the warmth of a tattered cloak, and he rode without skill or purpose.

Still, Marian waited until the soft thud of the nag's hooves had faded into silence before she gestured for the others to continue on.

They caught up to the caravan after the sun passed the highest point in its arc. It was not a caravan at all, but a single covered wagon, its contents concealed with coarse burlap siding. The wagon was stopped in a hollow, where the King's Road intersected a sluggish stream that turned the hard-packed earth to mud. It was tilted dangerously to one side, and as Marian and her band gathered in a thicket that overlooked the stream, she realized why it was stopped: one of the wheels was half sunk in the mud, and the horses had been unhitched and left to water themselves at the stream, quivering and exhausted.

"A sliver of luck, at last," whispered Alan at her elbow.

"Maybe." Marian's eyes would not stop moving, though she had counted the number of guards five times with the same result: a trio of crossbowmen stood some distance from each other, scanning the trees with bored but competent efficiency, and half a dozen other men were gathered around the wagon, halfheartedly working to free the wheel. It looked as if they'd been at the task for some time without success, for their actions held less urgency than resignation.

Marian gestured, and the band withdrew enough to crouch down and hold a quick, whispered council of war. Little John and Much would circle around to the north, where the undergrowth was thicker; Will and Alan, with their lighter, slighter forms, would come from the south. Marian and Elena would come along the stream leading Jonquille, and while Elena startled the horses into bolting, Marian would mount and signal the attack, shooting from horseback until she ran out of arrows.

Marian looked at the drawn, tense faces gathered around her and knew she ought to have some stirring speech to hearten them, words about honor and duty and charity, or else a joke to lighten their hearts. But she said only, "Listen to me, all of you. I'm glad to fight at your sides. I'm even gladder to have you fighting at mine. But I want no more death. If you can, spare their lives. And if I order it—if the fight turns sour, and you hear me signal—run."

She saw Will's expression darken, sensed John shifting his weight. She balled her hands into fists, resting them on the ground as she bowed her head, shutting all of them out. "If you ever had any love or loyalty for me, you will *run* if I order you to, understand? I will not fight unless you swear to me, on your honor as my men, that you'll run if I ask you to."

Silence met her demand at first, and she imagined—for she would not lift her head to look at them—her people exchanging glances, silent protests, grimaces of disapproval. But then a gentle voice murmured, "I swear."

Much's hand fell on her shoulder and squeezed. And then other voices joined his, and when Marian lifted her head again, her heart felt a little lighter. She nodded around to each of them, but no one moved.

"Well?" A flicker of fond irritation quickened her voice. "Go, then!"

Little John and Much began making their way down the ridge line, and Will melted into the forest. Alan, close at Elena's side, cast Marian a sidelong look. "'Go, then'?" he echoed, voice dripping with arch disapproval. "That might be the most moving farewell I've ever heard."

"I don't intend that it should be a farewell," Marian retorted.

Alan had Elena's hand in his, though he didn't look at her as he spoke. "No one ever does." He lifted her fingers to his lips for a long moment, and Marian turned away, feeling like an intruder upon something not for her to see.

It was some few minutes later that a gentle touch at her elbow bade her turn back. Alan was gone, and Elena stood with Jonquille's reins in one hand, the other on Marian's arm. She was frightened, and made no effort to hide it, but when Marian caught her eye, she smiled.

"He's afraid," she said softly as she fell into step beside Marian, and they began picking their careful way down the slope to the stream.

"He's not the only one." There was no need for Marian to keep using the lower, rougher voice now that she and Elena were alone, but she found it strangely difficult to stop. The warmth of Robin's cloak, the weight of weaponry, the pressure of the mask on her face, were like an enveloping cocoon. Marian was too deep inside it to be seen—she was only Robin Hood now.

"I mean he's afraid for you." Elena had her eyes on the ground, taking each step with great care to avoid a tumble of leaves or stone that might alert a sentry. "He's angry, but he loves you, too."

Marian drew breath, too astonished to remember she was meant to be quiet, but Elena interrupted swiftly before she could betray herself.

"Not that way," she whispered, amusement warming her voice. "I mean he loved you as Robin Hood. What he means, what he represents. The idea that one man could make a difference . . ." She paused to lead Jonquille around an outcropping of limestone. "It seems such a simple thing, but no one had ever told him that before. No one had ever told any of us that before."

"I don't know that I have made a difference," admitted Marian softly.

They reached the bottom of the gully, and Jonquille paused to lip eagerly at the water in the stream. They were some distance back from the road, out of sight of the other horses, where it would be easier to mask the sounds of their approach.

"I don't know either." Elena reached out and took Marian's arm, halting her when she would have moved forward. "I don't understand enough of the world to know whether you've changed it. But my Lady—Marian—you've changed us. And that's not nothing."

If it had been anyone else, Marian would have turned away, hiding the moisture in her eyes and the reddening of her lips. She would have made some quick retort and moved on. But she bowed her head instead, and hugged her friend, who squeezed her back.

"I don't regret any of it," Elena whispered.

Alan would approve of the poetry in that farewell, Marian thought, emotions in a tangle. Elena let her go after another moment and continued on. They said nothing else to each other, but when they reached the workhorses watering in the stream, Elena pressed Jonquille's reins into Marian's palm. They nodded to one another, and Marian swung up into her saddle.

The others had less distance to cover and would already be in place. The other horses were eyeing Jonquille and the two women with dull curiosity, tails switching idly at imagined flies. Marian waited, listening, but she could hear only the warbling stream and the occasional puff and sigh of a tired horse. No sign that the guards had detected them.

Marian knew if she waited a moment longer, her courage would fail her. Her unease was still there, straining against the prison she'd built around it. Like water behind a dam, little trickles of restless turmoil leaked out to dampen her will. Marian took up her bow and fitted an arrow to the string, and automatically her legs squeezed. Jonquille started forward. A flurry of movement made the horses jolt—Elena was running at them, clapping her hands, splashing the water up. One half reared, and then they were all bolting, herding together for safety.

Another squeeze, and a sharp, low-voiced command, and Jonquille broke into a run after them.

The dam was cracking, shifting. Rather than fading behind the urgency of action, the nagging anxiety in Marian's mind grew stronger as she rode. She kept her eyes on the distant figures of the guards, who were turning to look in confusion toward the source of the commotion.

She spotted one of the crossbowmen reaching for his weapon, and drew. She was still too far away to be sure of her aim, so she avoided risking a fatal shot by loosing the arrow into the ground near his feet. He dropped the crossbow and fell back, but Marian was already turning, looking for the next. If she could take out the bowmen, her band had a chance.

The pent-up pressure of insecurity swelled. Something was wrong, and not only within the tangle of Marian's thoughts.

Some detail she'd missed, some clue she'd been too foolish to see. She fired another arrow, and this one struck one of the guards in the knee, sending him thrashing to the ground.

The clash of swords and the quick, sharp *thwack* of wood on armor beyond her peripheral vision told her that Much and John had joined the fight, but she could not stop to check on them.

The stream melted into the muddy stretch of road ahead, and the horses began to scatter. Three went left, nearly trampling a guard trying to wrestle his sword from its sheath. One had peeled right so sharply that it had swung round behind the rest and was making its way back up the stream. And the fifth . . . the fifth had reached a cluster of guards and reared, startled.

Realization made the next arrow go wide, whistling harmlessly off into the trees on the other side of the road.

Five horses. Not the four required to pull the wagon, or the dozen required to mount all the guards. One extra horse.

It squealed piteously in pain as its legs gave way, and it crashed to the ground, pinning one of the guards. It should not have tried to rear back, for it was far older and skinnier than the others. No more than a nag.

Like the one that passed us this morning, its rider bent and cloaked . . .

The sudden seizing of Marian's muscles made Jonquille bleat alarm and turn, confused by her rider's conflicting signals. She caught a glimpse of John standing a head above the men around him, and she managed to loose an arrow in the direction of another crossbowman who was sighting down his weapon at him. She could not call it off—they were committed, and there'd be no retreat until one side or the other had felled enough of their opponents to clear a path.

They were committed, and it was a trap.

She knew it an instant before the burlap covering the wagon

shifted. She knew before she saw his face who was beneath its concealing folds, along with a handful of additional men, which meant they were outnumbered now more than two to one. She knew before Gisborne's boots hit the ground that either he would die, or she would.

"Go!" she shouted, her voice high and cracking. In the chaos of battle, no one noticed that she sounded like a woman in her urgency—one of the guards screamed a moment later as he fell, bleeding from a shallow gash across his face, and Marian realized that in fear and pain, it was impossible to tell the difference between a man's scream and a woman's. "Run!"

Little John's head swiveled toward her, then ducked away from one of his assailants. Much's familiar form emerged from the tangle of fighting, then vanished again from her sight. She hadn't seen Will or Alan, but there were shouts from beyond the wagon on the other side, and she knew they were there.

"Run, damn it!" she screamed.

Little John responded first, swinging his staff in a mighty arc with a roar that made Jonquille falter. He swept a handful of men aside, shoved Much behind him, and shouted, "Aye, Robin! Retreat!"

Then a blade hissed through the air and Jonquille screamed, her legs giving way beneath her, and Marian was falling.

THIRTY-NINE

MARIAN HIT THE GROUND with a breath-shattering thud. Instinct took over and she rolled as something hit the leaf litter next to her—another body, or a blade, or even Jonquille, she could not tell. Momentum carried her to her feet, and her sword leaped from its sheath into her hand in time to parry a blow that reverberated all the way up to her shoulder.

She parried another blow and then dodged, her attacker moving so quickly she could not find firm footing. Her attacker's face was so transformed by rage that she'd been fighting him for a dozen pounding heartbeats before she recognized Gisborne beneath the mask of fury. She thought she'd seen hatred in that icy stare of his as they grappled outside Nottingham.

But she hadn't seen this.

In the distance she could hear shouts and pounding feet, and somewhere nearby a horse cried out, and near the wagons a yelp of pain rose above the other sounds of battle as something familiar. Whose voice it was she could not tell in her confusion, but that it was an ally, she was certain.

Run, damn you.

She swung hard, with the momentum of her whole body, as Gisborne's next blow came down at her. The force of her parry knocked him back a step, and Marian scrambled back. They stood, panting, tense, staring.

"Go after them," Gisborne bellowed without taking his eyes from his opponent. "Leave Hood to me."

Marian wanted to turn, to seek out the scattered forms of her people fleeing back up the gully. She wanted to call out too, to learn if the cry she'd heard meant one of her allies had fallen. But one movement would bring Gisborne down upon her, and a moment's wasted breath in speech could mean her life.

Gisborne circled, each step as silent and deliberate as a cat's against the padding of leaf litter. Marian turned to keep him in the center of her vision, wishing she could tear the mask from her face. She had not realized how well the cloth mask had absorbed sweat from her brow—the leather did not, and her eyes stung and blurred with perspiration. She kept her breathing slow, for all that she longed to gasp for air.

Gisborne continued to move, one step at a time, round and round. When he spoke again, his voice was harsh and unrecognizable. "Is she alive?"

"Yes."

His face showed little reaction, but the steady pace of his steps faltered and he came to a stop, only the point of his sword weaving slowly with each breath he took.

"There never was any gold, was there?" Marian spoke softly, trusting distance and intensity to disguise her voice. "You told her there was to lure me here."

Gisborne's rage had smoothed, becoming not so much icy

now as molten. "I knew she would pass along the message."

"And taking her prisoner? What purpose in that deception, if you knew what she would do, and that I would be here?"

"There was a chance she hadn't told you." His voice lacked the stiff formality that usually constrained it—he spoke as he had done the previous night, before the fire with Marian, when she had made him laugh and he'd given her his secrets. "There was a chance. I hoped."

The words came without expression, but they struck at Marian's heart as if they'd been flung like spears. *I hoped.*

"But I knew when I went to her this morning and found her gone. You could not have taken her from that room against her will, not her. She would have fought you, and the guards would have heard, and I would have come."

Marian remembered the note she'd written, with words as deadly as the weapon in her hand. She said nothing, ruthlessly forcing herself to watch his body and not his face, to match her movements to his, to be ready for the attack when it came.

"The worst thing," Gisborne said, in a voice like tempered steel, "is that I always knew. Even as I hoped, I knew."

You don't know me at all, screamed Marian, pressing her dry lips together so tightly they cracked, and she tasted blood.

Gisborne watched her. "I always knew she was yours."

The words came before she could stop them. "Marian belongs to no one."

A curve settled along the thin, cruel line of Gisborne's mouth. "On that, Robin of the Hood, we agree."

His sword came down like an elemental force, but Marian saw the shift of his feet and the tension in his arm and she was ready. She dodged and swung her own sword. He was stronger, but she was faster, and she'd grown in confidence and skill since the first night they clashed blades. The night Gisborne first saw Robin Hood.

She saw recognition in his face as they exchanged another blow and parry, and another. They were well matched now, and locked in combat that would come down not to skill or strength or speed but to the force of will.

The sounds of nearby combat and flight had faded away. The groans of wounded men were like the songs of distant insects, faint and fuzzy. Sunlight split and shattered along the edges of their swords when they clashed, punctuated by ragged breath and the scrabble of their boots on the leaves.

Gisborne's style was not so straightforward as Marian had believed. Though he wielded his sword as any Englishman might, folded in and around the downward strokes and heavy blows were smaller, subtler movements. A flick of his wrist here, a quick slash there. They were the movements of a much lighter, smaller blade, and Marian wondered if the style was something he had learned during his time in the Holy Land.

Had Robin fought like this, too, before the end? Or had he died because he wasn't quick enough, had never been quite sharp enough, to learn faster than his opponent?

Marian ducked beneath an unexpected slash and rolled, sweeping out with her sword. She didn't expect her blade to connect, but if he leaped back out of the way, it would buy her time to find her feet again.

Instead steel met steel with a clash that numbed Marian's arm. Gisborne had driven the point of his sword down into the earth, blocking her haphazard swing. She had no defense against the mailed boot that slammed into her chest and sent her sword careening away down the slope.

Vision dim with pain, Marian scrambled to her feet and

ran. Behind her she heard a strangled oath—Gisborne's gambit had worked, but his sword was still stuck in the ground. Marian ignored the agony stabbing her with each breath and focused on speed.

A faint whistle in the air was her only warning before something knocked her sideways. Her momentum made her roll, and she was about to get her feet back under her when something snapped, twiglike, against her body. With that sound came a new pain that blossomed into searing awareness and dragged a scream from Marian's lips.

She got one arm beneath her, lifting herself enough to see Gisborne standing where she'd first fallen, Robin's bow in his hand, still outstretched, his other elbow lifted where he'd released the arrow. The point had broken off when she'd rolled, but when she looked down, a bloody, splintered thing protruded from her chest. He'd shot her in the back, and the force of it had driven the arrow straight through her.

And he had heard her scream.

The bow fell from his nerveless fingers. He staggered, then swayed, then broke into a run. Marian scrambled back, gasping, clutching with one hand at the spot where the arrow shaft protruded as she tried to stop the flow of blood. Gisborne ignored her attempts to escape, grabbing her leg and dragging her back when she would have kicked him.

Her fist met his jaw and he only grunted and pinned her arm beneath his knee, as if the same blow that had knocked Alan unconscious in one hit at the archery contest were of no more consequence than a timid slap. He had one aim, and though Marian tried again to knock his hand away as he reached for her face, he brushed her arm aside.

The leather cord of the mask snapped as he tore it away. In

their struggle, her hood had fallen back and a few tangled locks of her hair had come free of its binding. Gisborne knelt, pinning her at leg and elbow, and looked into her face. His own was so blank he looked like a statue, or one of the miracle play's little marionettes with their painted, still features.

He didn't speak. His eyes met hers, and the look they held was dizzying and familiar, though Marian struggled to understand why. Her thoughts were slow and tangled, and kept seizing upon strange, inconsequential details—the taste of salt and metal on her lips, sweat and blood mingling; the sound of running water, not far from where she lay; the slight, insistent burning of the palm that had gripped her sword, somehow distinct from the liquid agony that poured into her from the hole in her chest.

Gisborne's mouth fell open, and with a moment of sickening clarity she knew where she'd seen the look in his eyes before. They held the same look of world-shattering confusion and surprise the guard's had held that night in Nottingham Castle before he looked down and saw the arrow that had killed him.

His hand appeared again, no longer holding the mask, scarlet gleaming like ruby inlay along his palm. His eyes moved from his hand to her face, and then down to the mess of blood and splintered wood at her chest. He reached for her, fingers instantly slippery with blood, mirroring the motion she'd made when instinctively trying to stop its flow. His mouth moved, working silently, the remote confusion in his face draining away as his eyes searched for answers, flicking this way and that with deepening horror.

Then, punctuated by an unrecognizable cry of effort that rang in Marian's ears, something heavy swung into view and collided with the side of Gisborne's head, knocking him flat.

He had gathered Marian in his arms at some point, for when he fell, he dropped her. The part of the arrow sticking out of her back hit the ground and slid through the wound it had made, the bloody end sticking out of her like the figurehead on the prow of a ship. Marian screamed again and dropped down, down into the dark, cool green of the forest around her.

FORTY

MARIAN KNEW WHERE SHE was before she opened her eyes. Tiny sounds, smells, currents of air that she could not have described had she been asked, but that she'd absorbed in every minute detail over a thousand moments like this one, waking here. The precise give of the mattress beneath her. The scents of meadowsweet and lavender mingling with fletching glue and saddle oil. The light *tap-tap-tap* of the yew tree against her window. The muffled, indistinct sound and vibration of movement and voices below, carried through the floor and the walls and the bed frame and her own body.

Pain came with light as she opened her eyes, and she moaned, vision immediately obscured with tears.

"Easy, easy." The voice was unfamiliar, and a hand, gentle but firm, wrapped around her arm to prevent her from trying to rise. "Lie still, child."

With the pain came memory, fragmented and frightening, flashing swords and heartache and screams. Marian gasped and grabbed for the hand at her arm, though only one of her hands moved, and fresh pain erupted when it did.

"I have to go," she moaned, a ripple of muscle along the side of her body making her shiver with the need for action as pain and blood loss scattered her every effort. "My men—he knows—let me go, I must—"

"You must lie still." The voice sharpened, and only then did Marian think to blink away the tears swimming in her eyes and try to focus. A familiar form took shape, then crystallized. It was the monk, the one who had tended the guard she shot. His amiable features were stern now, set in an expression so ill suited to his genial manner that it broke through Marian's desperation and her breath caught in a laugh.

Mirth vanished as quickly as it had come, and she moaned again. "Jonquille," she managed, eyes flooding again. "I heard her scream—she fell—" A distant part of her knew she ought to be asking after her men, after Elena, after her own wounds, but all she could think of in that moment was her horse, her dearest companion, who hadn't flinched riding into the unfamiliar chaos of battle.

The monk's grip on her arm relaxed a little, and he patted her soothingly, as one might comfort a babe in arms. "Your horse is in the stables below, being tended by the stableman. She is in far better shape than you, child."

Much was alive. Marian took a rattling breath and lay still, trying to collect her scattered wits.

"There you are," murmured the monk.

Marian blinked away the fresh tears, feeling them slide down her temples and into her hair. "Am I dying?"

He patted her arm again and smiled. "I don't claim to know the will of God." The words were so familiar, and his eyes were so sad despite his smile, that memory stirred. They were the same words he'd uttered when she asked whether Tom, the guard she'd shot, the dead man, would survive.

Marian closed her eyes. Lying still eased the pain a little, but more soothing than that, or the familiar surroundings of her own room in her own home, or the monk's presence, was the sudden understanding that she now faced the same fate as the man she'd killed. The relief of it was so profound and abrupt that she almost lost consciousness again, content to let the question of her life be answered by the same power that had decided Tom's.

A sound caught at her, though, before she could slip into darkness. A footstep, light and careful. A gasp. A thin voice, wavering, saying, "Oh God—is she . . . is she . . ."

Marian opened her eyes. Elena, hovering in the doorway of her bedchamber, dropped the armful of fabric she was carrying, rushed into the room, and shoved the monk aside so abruptly that he nearly toppled back off his stool.

Marian could scarcely understand the torrent of words that spilled from her friend's lips and concentrated instead on the warmth of her hands, which had seized Marian's and clung tight. When the flood showed no signs of abating, Marian moved her hand a little and croaked, "Is anyone dead?"

Elena choked on her own words and gulped a breath. She was kneeling at the side of Marian's bed, dressed once more as her maid, not a single mark or scratch on her face. Eyes full of tears, she shook her head and leaned down. "No, my Lady. No, we're all alive. John has a few cuts, and Will broke his foot, but we're all—we're all still here."

Marian turned that over, her thoughts rolling like old honey, thick and slow. "Broke his . . . how?"

Elena's eyebrows lifted, and a tremulous, fleeting smile lit her face. "A horse stepped on him."

Marian tried to laugh, though it sounded to her ears more like a pained grunt. Her eyes moved until she could see the monk again. He sat, hands clasped across his stomach in the habit of someone who had once had a much more ample belly to rest them on, and watched with bemusement.

"Who—how did . . ." Marian could not remember quite how to ask what she needed to know.

"We couldn't take you to the physician in Nottingham," said Elena. "Gisborne would go straight there in search of a wounded Robin Hood. And Frère Tuck was such a comfort when that guard . . ." She bit her lip, and despite her treacle-slow thoughts, Marian knew she'd been about to say "died." Because he hadn't simply died; Marian had killed him.

Frère Tuck regarded her evenly, expression still mild.

"He knows who he's helping?" Marian asked.

"He knows."

Marian groaned and reluctantly pulled her hand from Elena's so that she could try to find purchase on the edge of the bed frame.

"What are you doing?" Elena had half risen from her knees in alarm.

"I have to go," said Marian between clenched teeth.

Frère Tuck, in the background, chuckled. Elena cast him a befuddled look, then put her palm against Marian's brow—a gentle touch, but Marian found she was so weak that it might as well have been an iron chain binding her to the bed.

"You can't leave." Elena smoothed away the hair stuck to Marian's wet forehead. "You're badly hurt, Marian."

Marian tipped her chin and looked down. They'd removed

her tunic, and her shirt, and had cut away the tattered strips of cloth binding her breasts flat. Above the edge of the blankets she could see bandages circling her body, following the curve of her chest, under her arm, around her shoulder. She saw no blood, but the bandages were thick, and every breath brought with it a throb of pain singing down her body.

"I can't stay here." Marian let her head fall, staring up at the wooden rafters. One of them bore a row of scratches, worn by time and obscured by dust. Robin had carved their names there in Greek lettering, though he'd misspelled her name in two places. "Gisborne knows. The physician in Nottingham may be the first place he searches—this house will be the second."

"I know. You'll die if you try to ride, though—Frère Tuck says it's a miracle you survived the trip here in the first place, and that even traveling in a cart could kill you."

"I'd rather die on my own terms than by Gisborne's hand." Marian gasped with the effort of trying to lift one leg and shift it toward the edge of the bed.

"So excited about dying" came the monk's voice, mumbling, as if speaking to himself. He sounded amused.

Elena ignored him. "John and Alan are watching the roads, and Will's in Nottingham watching the stables—we'll know when Gisborne comes for you, and if you cannot walk by then, that is when we'll decide whether to risk moving you or not."

Her voice was so firm that Marian did not dare argue. Meekly, she asked, "Where is my father?"

"On his way back from Nottingham by now." Elena squeezed her hand again. "Word came this morning that Robin had rescued you from Nottingham Castle, that he'd stolen you away without so much as alerting the guard, but he knew . . ." She hesitated, glancing at the monk. "He knew that couldn't be true.

Will was going to tell him what happened before taking up watch on the stables for Gisborne."

"He was the rider," Marian murmured, too weary to keep her eyes open any longer. "The old man on the nag who passed by us."

Elena's hand tightened. "Who?"

"He wore a hooded cloak." Marian's voice sounded dream-like to her own ears, as wispy and insubstantial as a cloud. "And I saw what I wanted to see."

Elena turned to demand explanation from the monk, but Marian was already falling asleep again, dropping this time into a gentler oblivion than the one that had claimed her in Sherwood.

Candlelight flickered against her closed eyelids, and the tree tapped furiously against the window, stirred up by a wind that whistled through the thatch. The hands that cradled hers were so familiar that she was speaking before she'd remembered how to open her eyes.

"You have to run," she rasped, her throat so dry it burned. She raised her eyelids with a monumental effort.

Her father just smiled at her, the same indulgent, amused smile with which he'd always responded to her fancies and whims. He lowered her hand to the bed, keeping it clasped in one of his, and put the other to her brow, soothing. "Go back to sleep, my dear. All is well."

Marian's hand tried to move, but though her father's touch was if anything gentler than Elena's, she had no more success. Frustration bubbled over and strengthened her voice. "Father— you have to leave. Gisborne knows. He'll come. He could be outside now—you cannot delay. If you're here . . . he'll arrest you whether I live or die, whether I'm here or not."

His lined hand patted her hair in that awkward, familiar way. "Let him come," he said gently.

Marian stirred feebly, her body incapable of expressing the urgency she felt. She gave up, tension fleeing and leaving her limp. With a sob, she whispered, "They'll hang you."

Her father smiled his mild smile. "Let them try."

There was no violence or challenge in his tone, no change in the touch at her brow or the clasp of his hand. Resignation hung in the air, but it was not a resignation to death. Marian tried to imagine her father taking up sword or bow against a detachment of guardsmen, defending the door of his home and his daughter upstairs, and she started to cry.

She could not roll onto her side as she wished to do, or curl up—but she could turn her head, and she pillowed her cheek against his hand until she fell asleep again.

She slept, and woke, and slept again. The moon rose. The fire in the hearth crackled. Elena came to change the candles, and Marian listened to her quiet, graceful steps about the chamber, as familiar as the rustle of the branches at her window.

The monk checked her bandages and felt her brow and then knelt, with an audible popping of joints, to whisper an indistinct prayer.

Fog rose from the fields and lingered at Marian's window. A fox cried out for her mate in the night. Marian ran her eyes over her misspelled name etched into the rafters, and breathed, and waited.

And still Gisborne did not come.

The sun rose, and the monk felt for the heat of fever again, and looked pleased before he left. Elena sat by her bed, calmly mending the rents in Robin's tunic, first the neat hole where the arrow had penetrated Marian's back, and then the more ragged gash it tore as it exited her chest. Her father brought his records and sat in the corner, frowning at his taxes.

And Marian raged.

Someone was with her always, no doubt to prevent her from moving. But she did not try again to rise, or insist that she had to leave. Rest had brought sense enough to keep her in her sickbed. But sense did not stop her from wanting to leap up with sword and bow and rush off into the forest. Sense did not lessen the need for action coursing through her veins, swelling with each throb of pain as her heart kept beating.

She slept fitfully, tormented by the intangible shift of memory to dream and back again. She was standing at one end of the corridor in Nottingham Castle, and the guard she'd killed stood at the other. Marian could not move or speak, but as she watched, his chest sprouted feathers like the opening of a morning bloom. She looked up and saw that he wore Gisborne's face, eyes brimming with that same shattered confusion. The corridor seemed to stretch, then snapped taut like a bowstring so they were only a breath apart. Gisborne's lips moved, his expression still surprised and broken, but no sound came out. Still, she heard the words in her mind, a searing brand of revelation: *I love you.*

The sun drooped in the sky, and Marian slept again, and it was dark when she woke. Elena came to tell her that Alan had come while she was asleep—with no sign of pursuit, he'd ridden to Nottingham to see Will and learn that no guards had ridden out, and no word had come that Robin Hood had been captured or identified. He'd spent the day traveling back and forth, but he could discover nothing. And no one could find Gisborne.

Marian woke in the night, so certain that she'd heard a

pounding on the door that she cried out in fear. Her father talked to her until her heart began to calm, and told her stories of his misadventures when he was a boy, and she dreamed softer dreams.

Eventually the monk allowed her to sit up, and Elena helped her to a chair by the window so that she could see out. Her window looked over the fields rather than the road that would bring guards to arrest her, but the sight of the farmers gathering in the last of the year's crops, oblivious to the peril facing their lord and his daughter, was reassuring.

Marian peeped under the bandages once, while Elena was cleaning the ashes from the fireplace and laying a new fire. The wound was a hand's breadth below her collarbone. The hole was small and red and neat, and she stared at it, bemused, until Elena saw and swatted her hand away. Marian could not stop thinking that it looked fake, like Seild had taken rouge and painted the wound as carefully as she would paint her lips.

Another day passed. And still Gisborne did not come.

John abandoned his watch on the road. He and Alan took turns riding to Nottingham and back, expecting to meet Gisborne and his men each time they left Edwinstowe. Each time they saw only the usual travelers and had the same report from Will: nothing.

Marian ventured downstairs. Her arm was strapped to her body by bandages, and each step ached, but the ache grew no worse for the effort. It had been four days. Marian's brow was cool. The fever that had killed Tom had spared her.

Marian's rage at inactivity faded away, and she found herself weeping instead. She hid the tears as best she could from her father and from Elena, although she could not hide them from the holy man. He did not seem to mind them, though.

She wandered, aimless, ghostlike in her own home. A memory came to her. She was walking through Locksley Manor, surrounded by the spectral forms of furniture draped in linen. She had thought then that she might as well be the restless spirit who haunted its halls, for all she felt like flesh and bone.

On the fifth day, Marian was wrapped up in blankets on a chair by the front window when hoofbeats drew her attention. Her heart clenched with fear and relief together. At last, an end to this purgatory of waiting.

But the rider was Will. She was so shocked by his appearance, as haggard and weary as he'd been when she'd visited him in Nottingham's jail, that she could not speak. He entered without knocking, leaning heavily on a crutch at his right and looking around. His eyes fell on Marian and lit a little at the sight of her.

"My Lady," he said, with a little bow. Then his brow furrowed as he absorbed the way she looked, wrapped in blankets against a chill, huddled in the chair, pale as ivory. "Are you ill?"

Marian blinked, too confused to think of an answer until Elena came bustling in from the kitchen, interrupting in a flurry of activity.

"Will!" she cried, rushing to hug her brother, tears of relief in her eyes. "My lady is ill with worry," she said, before Marian could speak, and without looking in her direction. "But what are you doing here? What about Nottingham, and watching for Gisborne, and—"

"Gisborne is there." Will spread his hands a little in helpless gesture. "I never saw him arrive—he must have been there all along. I saw him go to the stables and back, and once I followed him out past the castle grounds to the town, where he prowled along a section of the inner wall before going back into the castle."

Marian glanced between the two siblings and their identical expressions of puzzlement. Elena shook her head, speechless, still not looking at Marian. Will glanced her way, but it was to his sister that he spoke. "Somehow, I don't think it's occurred to the authorities that Marian might be hiding Robin here."

The words fell on Marian's ears like crashing thunder. Elena spoke, and Will replied, and they continued to converse—Marian did not hear. Not until Will had kissed his sister's cheek, bade Marian a polite farewell, and left did Elena finally look at Marian.

"How?" Marian whispered.

"They only saw you briefly, unconscious, bleeding. And Alan is the only one who's visited you."

"But . . . but the mask. Gisborne tore it off."

Elena had crossed the room to her side and leaned against the wall, looking almost as weary and drawn as her brother. "I pulled your hood over your face before the others came."

"They don't know. They think I'm hiding Robin, keeping him safe while he recovers, here in Edwinstowe." Marian put a shaking hand to her head, trying to steady her thoughts. "But to get me from there to here, someone had to carry me, they would have felt . . ." A woman's hips, a woman's waist, a woman's breasts and throat and arms and—Marian could not think.

"Jonquille is no warhorse—she can't easily carry two. Only the lightest of us could go with you. The rest came on foot as they could."

Marian gazed at Elena mutely, lips trembling. It was Elena who had kept her secret, who had gotten her onto Jonquille's back. Elena, the only person other than Marian whose presence the gray mare tolerated, who had spent so many hours at her needlework in the shade by the pasture. Elena, who had held her in the saddle and ridden from the northern edge of Sherwood Forest to Edwinstowe at a gallop fast enough that Marian was still alive when she got there.

"*You* hit him," Marian blurted, astonishment momentarily banishing pain, tingling down to her very fingertips. "You're the one who knocked him out, right before I fainted."

Elena gazed back at her and nodded. "I was hoping I'd killed him," she said calmly. "But Will says he's certain it was Gisborne he saw in Nottingham today. So he lives."

Marian took Elena's hand but was too moved and dumbstruck to do anything but hold it in hers. "I'm glad you didn't kill him," she whispered.

Elena, who had tended Marian in the hours after she'd shot the guard in the corridor at Nottingham Castle, let out a breath and squeezed Marian's hand in acknowledgment.

Marian felt a smile tug at her cracked lips. "I wonder if Alan will ever try to tell you again to stay behind."

FORTY-ONE

MARIAN SAT ON THE ground, leaning sideways against the fence post, watching Jonquille nip lazily at the grass beyond. It hurt still to lean her back against anything hard, but she could move and walk a short way and she could sit in the sun.

A line of reddish brown marked Jonquille's right flank, where a sword had slashed at her. It had healed more quickly than Marian's wound and seemed to irritate the mare more than pain her—her skin would twitch now and then, as if trying to shake off an itching fly. Jonquille sometimes meandered nearer the fence and lowered her head over the top rail and chuckled at Marian's hair.

All is forgiven, Marian thought, watching her horse and fighting the desire to scratch at her bandages. Two of the village boys were working nearby, gathering fruit up in the branches of the apple tree. Marian could hear them talking and laughing, and the occasional thump as an apple fell, disturbed by their climbing, to the ground below.

She watched them for some time before she realized she was being watched herself. It began as a prickle of unease, and she rubbed at the edge of her bandage, restless. The prickle spread, and grew, and when Marian turned to look for Jonquille, she found instead that a man was standing at the corner of the house, half-concealed in the shade cast by the thatched eaves.

He wore a faded tunic of rust brown, and leggings of gray, and might have been one of the Edwinstowe farmers, had she not known his face by heart.

Gisborne saw her recognition but continued to watch her, motionless, for a stretch of frantic heartbeats so quick Marian thought she might faint again. Finally, he moved, pushing away from the wall and coming toward her. His face was as calm and as cold as it had ever been. There was not a crack in the granite, not a twitch in his scarred cheek.

"Good afternoon, Lady Marian." A pause as his eyes traveled down her body, lingering where, hidden by her dress, the bandages held her wounded shoulder together. "You look well."

Her hands had curled to fists in the grass, and her muscles screamed for action—*Run*, they told her. *Run, damn you*. But she couldn't run, injured and weak as she was. He would seize her before she'd be able to stand. She said nothing.

Gisborne's eyebrows rose. "No greeting? Have I offended you in some way, Lady?"

A thud came as one of the boys dropped out of the lower branches, gaze swinging from Marian to the man in peasant garb a few steps away. "Lady?" the lad called, uncertain. "All's well?"

Marian spared him only a glance, her eyes fixed on Gisborne's. His black eyes narrowed a fraction. "Answer him," he suggested softly.

Throat dry, Marian had to clear it twice before she managed,

"All's well. Save me an apple."

The boy grinned and climbed nimbly back up into the tree. Gisborne watched him, his scarred profile betraying nothing to Marian's eyes. Only once the lad had vanished did he move again. He sank into a crouch before Marian, a respectful distance between them. He did not speak, but waited, and watched her, and cut at her with his indifference.

"How did you come without being seen?" she said finally. "I have men watching the road."

Gisborne's head tipped a little as he considered the question, then turned so he could watch Jonquille grazing peacefully some distance away. "Over the past few days, I've come to a realization. What strikes me most about Robin Hood is his arrogance. So certain that his tricks will fool his enemies—a simple cloak as disguise, shortcuts through the trees to avoid patrols on the road—and just as certain that his enemies would never think to use those same tactics against him."

Marian's vision blurred, her urgency and her fear drawing tears to her eyes. She tried to blink them away, but they clung to her lashes, scattering the afternoon sunlight.

Gisborne watched her, unmoved. "I come on behalf of the Sheriff," he said formally, voice rising a little. "I am ordered to make an arrest."

Marian's eyes searched the dark windows of her home but saw no sign of movement. Her fingers tightened until she heard the crackle of ripping grass roots against her knuckles. She summoned all the spirit she could, painfully aware that she had little left to show. "Then make it."

Gisborne inclined his head as though accepting a gracious concession. "If you would be so good as to inform me where she is, I will."

Marian blinked. "She?"

"A woman by the name of Elena Scarlet. She is, as I under-stand it, your maid."

Marian's grip went lax, and she felt the panic rising, heart pounding in her ears. "Elena?" she echoed senselessly.

"She is the sister of Will Scarlet, is she not?" Gisborne spoke respectfully, though his tone invited no contradiction. "Her brother was the first one to tell of Robin Hood and is almost certainly one of his gang of cutthroats. She volunteered to work in the kitchens, a lady's maid offering to do low scullery work, on the day Robin Hood helped her brother escape imprisonment. And, as it turns out, she is betrothed to a man named Alan-a-Dale."

Marian needed a sword, a knife, anything she could use to parry the onslaught of words that cut deeper and deeper each second. She could not think—her shoulder throbbed, and her limbs tingled.

Gisborne's lips moved, but his expression could not have been called a smile. "You seem confused. Although, now I think of it, you didn't attend the archery contest, did you? I worried at the time that you were unwell. Given your love of the bow and arrow, I wouldn't have thought you'd miss it."

"She is only my maid," Marian managed in a sharp, brittle voice.

"She's betrothed to the man who won the contest meant to catch this land's most notorious criminal. I should think the fact that she's your maid is the least remarkable thing about her." Gisborne's black eyes showed nothing but a polite, remote interest. "Or it ought to be."

Marian's lips trembled with the effort of not shouting. The boys nearby were joking with each other once more. Gisborne wore no visible weapon, but she did not doubt he was armed—a dagger in his boot, or tucked up his sleeve. That he had not arrested her, or killed her already, told Marian he wanted something else, something she could not predict. Which meant he would not hesitate to use her people to get it.

"What do you want, Gisborne?" She'd never addressed him so to his face, as a man might, without the trappings of genteel society.

The scarred cheek twitched. "Exactly as I've said. Elena Scarlet. Even if she is innocent, as you claim, she knows something. I intend to learn what it is. The minstrel has his pardon—we cannot touch him. But she has no such protection from the law."

Marian's jaw ached, her teeth grinding. Her eyes flicked toward the apple tree, where one of the boys had hopped down and was reaching up to receive the bushel basket his friend was handing down. She forced her gaze back toward Gisborne's face. "What do I have to do to spare her? Shall I beg?"

Gisborne rose out of his crouch effortlessly. If his old wound pained him, he masked the signs with the ease of long, long practice. His shadow fell across Marian's face, his eyes like obsidian as he gazed down at her with utter indifference. "I want nothing from you, Lady Marian."

The words hit, and she hadn't the strength to hide it. Gisborne's hand moved toward his waist, and Marian flinched, expecting to see the bright spark of sunlight reflected off steel. He paused, watching her reaction—if he enjoyed her fear, he gave no sign of that either. He pulled an object from the pocket hanging from his belt, but it was no weapon.

He loomed over her a moment and then tossed the thing into the dirt beside her. "But I would hear what Robin Hood has to say."

He didn't wait for her response. Turning, he strode away, only the faintest hitch in his step to tell of his limp, and vanished around the corner of the house. Behind her, the boys' laughter began to fade as they carried their baskets back toward the village. Jonquille whickered and took a few steps to a new patch of grass.

Vision still blurred with anger and tears, Marian's fingers curled clumsily around the object Gisborne had tossed at her feet. She knew without looking what it was: the mask of Robin Hood.

FORTY-TWO

MARIAN'S HANDS SHOOK AS she tried to lace her tunic. Fear made her tremble—fear of Elena or her father walking in while she put on Robin's clothes one last time, fear of whether her shoulder could bear the ride to Nottingham, fear of what awaited her if she made it that far. But weakness turned the tremble from a quiver to a quake, doubling the time it took her to dress.

Her bow was gone, whether abandoned in the clearing where Gisborne had shot her or kept as some horrible trophy, she did not know. One of her men had her sword, but even if she knew which of them to ask, she could not risk it. She stood over the dagger, which she'd been keeping beneath her pillow as she waited for Gisborne or his men to come for her, hesitating.

She was going to her death, of that she was certain. She could not fight Gisborne in her condition, much less his entire garrison of guardsmen. She could not draw a bow, and lifting anything heavier than a cup with her right hand made her weak with pain.

No, she would die. Either at Gisborne's hand, now, tonight, or else by the noose, if he meant to take her alive. What she did not know, what made her hesitate, was whether she would try to kill him before they took her.

She ran her fingertips over the dagger's plain sheath. It was hers, not Robin's, one of the few weapons that had not been a gift from him. She could not remember where she'd come by it—she'd owned it long before Robin's family had ever moved to Locksley. She'd had it when she was far too young to be trusted with such a thing. She'd had it for years before her father ever knew of its existence.

Dimly, as if making sense of memories that belonged to someone else, she remembered her mother showing her how to use it. *I pray you never will,* she'd said, running her fingers over Marian's hair. *But now you have a choice.*

Marian's fingertips shook, and she drew away and left the dagger there on her pillow.

She managed the climb out of her window with more difficulty than she'd anticipated, for though she could do it with one arm, she was as weak as a child from the wound and her recovery, and she was sweating by the time her boots touched the grass.

Jonquille greeted her with a soft chuckle of breath, and when Marian climbed onto her bare back—she could not lift the saddle—her horse gave her a curious look from one eye, and then shook herself.

The night was cold, and the sweat on Marian's brow soon grew clammy. Shivering, she held Jonquille to a walk as best she could, biting her lips not to cry out in pain whenever the horse's eager nature made her skip into a jouncing trot.

Overhead the moon was on the wane, drifting in and out from behind wings of mist and fog. The bare branches of Sherwood

Forest stretched up toward the pearly light like skeletal arms, like the bars of a prison. *They can't touch her,* Marian thought, her vision blurring as she watched the branches pass overhead, watched the moon beyond them. *She persists.*

Gisborne had not told her where to find him, but she felt sure someone would see her before she rode through the gates of Nottingham. And when, some leagues out from the town, she came upon a dark figure on horseback, her breath didn't even catch with surprise.

He brought his mount alongside hers, inky black next to Jonquille's dappled gray coat. They didn't speak, and rode in silence for a time, until Gisborne said, "Here."

He turned his horse from the road, heading deeper into the forest. Marian followed. He had moved ahead of her, turning his back. If she had brought her dagger, she could have mustered the strength to throw it. He had not hesitated to shoot her in the back.

Whose arrogance is striking now? she thought grimly.

He reined in his mount when they reached a clearing some distance from the road. He dismounted, taking his time and stroking the black's neck, loosening his girth, murmuring in his ear. The animal's response was not unlike Jonquille's communication with Marian—simple, wordless, but meaningful nonetheless.

He didn't so much as look her way as she dismounted, sliding clumsily from Jonquille's back.

Marian was still shivering, and her body ached from the grueling bareback ride, and the weight of Robin's cloak suddenly seemed heavy enough to drag her to her knees. She wanted to ask Gisborne why he'd brought her here, for she had expected a detachment of guards to emerge from the trees to arrest her on sight and drag her to Nottingham's jails. But she waited.

Gisborne, still stroking his horse's neck, broke the silence. "I serve the law."

Marian took a step, abandoning the support of Jonquille at her side, so she could stand straight in the moonlight. "So you've said."

"Whom do you serve, Marian?"

A dozen answers swarmed into her mind, and she dismissed them all. *Robin of Locksley,* said one voice. *My own heart,* said another. In the silence that followed, she thought with crystal clarity: *I serve everyone.*

Gisborne leaned his head against the horse's neck, looking as if he were embracing darkness itself. "Shall I tell you the answer?" he asked.

"You'll tell me I serve chaos." Marian's voice was taut.

Gisborne's head rose, and she caught the glitter of dark eyes in the scattered, dappled moonlight. "I would have said justice."

Marian's heart was not so hardened as she'd thought. Her arm ached, and pain made it easier for tears to sting her eyes. She breathed sharply, willing them away, willing everything away. She needed nothing but to stand there, straight and tall, unfettered. "Then why are we enemies?"

Gisborne's head dropped again. The horse raised a hoof and stamped, perhaps picking up on intangible cues from his rider's body so close by. "Because the law will never be just. Perhaps it can come close—so close the line is hard to see. But laws are written by men, who are imperfect by nature, and justice belongs to something beyond the power of men."

"I am not a man." Sophistry, Marian knew. But the words came before she could stop herself.

Gisborne turned, and Marian's skin prickled in a wave that swept over her as he looked at her. "A fact that escaped my notice

for far too long." There was something in his voice then, a soft-
ness almost like amusement. Marian realized why he'd brought
her here, in darkness, alone. His control was not so complete as
she had believed when he came to her home with threats and
indifference. He needed the night to hide his face.

"Nevertheless," Gisborne continued, "the law will see you
hanged, man or woman. And so too everyone you love for helping you."

Marian stood still, ignoring the tremble in her knees that
warned her she was weakening, that she was not recovered enough
for this. "You told me you admired Robin Hood. That you and
he were not so different."

"My feelings have no bearing on your fate." Gisborne's voice
was cold again. "Even if I wished to spare you, the well of suspicion you have dug for yourself is too deep. Did you think all this
time the Sheriff was content to simply oversee his council, ignorant and powerless? Every night I reported to him. Every night I
told him my suspicions, the names and families and associates of
the people I believed could lead us to Robin Hood. Every night I
told him—" His voice stopped.

"You told him you suspected me."

Gisborne's silhouette shifted. "He knows what I knew. That
you were connected to Robin Hood by some means, a bond I
could not break. He believes, as I did, that you are . . . intimately
involved with him." He paused for breath. "He does not know
how intimately."

A breeze came and found its way beneath the edge of Marian's hood, running its cool fingers along her clammy skin. She'd
been right. She could have killed Gisborne, had she brought the
dagger and found the right moment. But killing him wouldn't
have saved anyone.

"I thought your duty was to report all to your master."

"Perhaps duty is no longer what drives me." His voice cracked in a quick, bitter laugh. "I am changed, and not for the better."

"If this is not who you wish to be, then turn back." Marian's words were flat, for she could not have taken her own advice— she could not have stopped being Robin Hood for anyone.

"I can't." His voice flared like tinder. "I am changed, Marian. Every move I made, Robin Hood was there ahead of me. Each attempt to catch him took me further from myself—he led me step by step until I found myself using the woman I loved as bait in a trap."

"I consented to the ruse," Marian countered weakly.

"Yes. You made it very easy." His temper, now kindled, was brimming—the anger was like a tangible force trying to push her back.

Marian had to force herself to stand her ground, her own temper rising in response. "Your choices are your own, Gisborne."

His voice, brittle with anger, cracked. "Choices? You've left me precious few of those, Lady."

"You could speak for me." The words felt hollow, for they were bloodless and weak. "For my father."

"It would not matter." His voice was so empty Marian began to doubt she'd ever heard a flicker of warmth in it. "Even if I wanted to spare you now, I could not."

Even if I wanted to, Marian's thoughts echoed in a mocking chorus. She drew herself up again, fighting the desire to crumple and let the earth claim her. "Then why am I here?"

"To answer my questions."

"Ask them, then."

"That day in the forest, when I captured one of your men.

The big one." Gisborne's eyes caught a fragment of moonlight, despite the shadow. "The voice I heard, the voice of Robin Hood, was not yours."

"A decoy," replied Marian. There was no reason to dissemble or mislead him anymore, but she could not resist adding, "A child could have thought of it."

The fragment of light vanished again as a tracery of cloud obscured the moon overhead. "The archery contest," he said, failing to respond to her barb. "It was you, was it not? Your hands held the bow, loosed those arrows. You switched places with the minstrel in the chaos that followed."

Marian caught herself before her knees could buckle out of weariness and pain. "Why are you asking me questions to which you already know the answers?"

Gisborne took a step forward, leaning toward her so that the moonlight, leaking out from behind its concealing cloud, showed a face taut with focus. "How did you do it? Three arrows, only seconds apart, so exactly placed—it's impossible. I thought . . . more archers, hidden in the crowd, closer to the target. But the arrows all struck straight, and shots from the crowd would have flown on an angle." His voice quickened, for all its chilly calm. "No one shoots like that."

Tricks, Marian thought. That was what Gisborne had said when he came to her that afternoon—he'd spoken of Robin Hood's tricks, lies that had deceived him and led him on such a merry chase.

Marian drew her chin up. "I do."

Gisborne shifted his weight, the familiar stiff creak of his leather tunic clashing against the backdrop of singing crickets deep among the trees. "How?"

Marian considered ignoring the question, but some flicker

of pride was left in her tattered spirit, for she could not quite bear the thought of dying while Gisborne believed she'd beaten him by trickery alone.

"Surrender," she whispered. "An archer tries to master his bow, to force the arrow where he wants it to go. He tries with strength and focus and discipline to master it. He uses tougher gloves and stronger bowstrings and stiffer limbs, and restraint." She drew a shaky breath. "But arrows are winged creatures, and will not be restrained. To shoot like that, one must surrender control."

"You? Surrender?" The mockery in his tone did not invite a reply.

The clouds had shifted again, and Gisborne stood in full moonlight. They were some distance apart, but she could see his face as he watched her. If he'd hoped to use darkness to hide himself, he had failed. The pale, silvery light drew her eyes to the contours of his face, and she saw his lips twist, and the scarred cheek twitched. His eyes were hooded. "Was any of it real?"

Marian knew he was not speaking of the archery contest anymore. "Would my answer change anything?"

Gisborne's eyes gleamed. In the treacherous light he looked feverish, as if he'd been the one wounded, and the wound had begun to rot. "Push back your hood."

Marian pushed back her hood, the chill of approaching winter raising the hair on the back of her neck.

"The mask," rasped Gisborne. "Take it off."

Her hands shook so badly she could barely grasp the leather mask to pull it off over her head.

Gisborne's facade cracked, his lips pressing together. His gaze fled from hers, then slunk back again, a cornered animal forced to fight. Marian, her every ounce of effort and will spent keeping herself upright, nearly swayed at the realization that even now, she'd beaten him. He had discovered her secret, would have the satisfaction of killing her or seeing her killed, but he could not look at her face while she wore the costume of Robin Hood without breaking.

He looked very much as he had the day he put the arrow into her shoulder and tried to stop the flow of her blood with his bare hands. But he could not save her then, and he couldn't save himself now, for his expression shattered and he broke away, whirling back toward his horse. The scrape of steel told Marian that he'd strapped a scabbard to the saddle, but the sound didn't prepare her for the uncaring glint of moonlight off the sword's edge. Her breath caught in spite of herself, but she did not move. She would not give him the satisfaction of seeing her flinch at the prospect of death.

He shifted his grip, the tip of the sword bobbing as if with indecision. He hefted it once more, then tossed it toward Marian. She caught it by sheer instinct, feeling its grip in her left palm before she could register that he'd given her the weapon. Only then did she see he wore his sword belt, and that he was reaching for the hilt.

He moved toward her as he drew his sword, halting out of reach of her blade, light on his feet and intent.

"Why?" Marian could not hold the sword in her right hand, and she had never practiced with it in her left. The grip felt as strange and unfamiliar as if she were a novice, but when he made a quick feint, she raised the blade instinctively.

"I want to face you knowing who you are. No masks. No lies. You and me, here in Sherwood Forest, one last time." His answer was light, matching the quick feint of his sword that had made Marian raise hers. "And if you kill me, you have a chance to flee."

"I can't kill you." Marian pressed no attack herself but stood ready to fend off another blow. He was testing her. She could have stood motionless, and he would have halted before the blade touched her—but she could not stop herself from blocking each swing.

"Why not?" Gisborne's voice was low and steady.

"Because you wounded me. I cannot use my arm." This time, when his sword clanged off hers, she stepped forward, sword raised. Frustration prodded her to continue, but she stopped herself—she could not hope to beat him like this, crippled and on the verge of fainting.

Gisborne grinned, an expression so alien on his stiff features that Marian nearly dropped the sword again. "I wounded Robin Hood."

For a wild moment, Marian thought he'd gone mad—that he'd managed to forget what he knew about her, that the woman he loved and his mortal enemy were one and the same. Then he swung again with a grunt of effort, and when his sword glanced off hers, he pressed the attack again, and again, until he'd forced her blade back against her own body. The assault was vicious, and yet restrained—the blade pressed so lightly against her body that it wouldn't have scratched her bare skin, much less cut through the cloak.

"I want you to admit it." His face was inches away, eyes burning. "I want to hear you say it."

Marian could feel his breath upon her face and feel the warmth of his skin so near. Her mind tried to wander, taking advantage of her injury and her exhaustion to conjure a memory of him that quickened her blood and stirred her body.

She fought it, but a flush rose to her cheeks anyway, and the strange mingling of desire and pride and anger gave her strength.

She gave him what he wanted, and whispered, "I am Robin Hood."

Then she leaned into him and drove her knee up into his gut, and struck out with her sword. He dodged her clumsy swing, choking and doubling over, but the ploy had gained her room to maneuver. They circled each other, breathing mist that glowed silver, their horses stamping their uneasiness behind them.

He darted in, beginning a series of blows she recognized from their last battle. She knew what was coming, but her left arm was so untrained she could barely meet each swing. But when the last should have crunched down into her rib cage, it missed instead, and Gisborne staggered with his momentum.

Marian tried to use that moment of imbalance, whirling and swinging the blade, but he blocked it as if he hadn't lost his footing at all.

He pressed the attack again, grim and unyielding despite the glitter of his eyes, and this time she nearly fell from the force of the blows. Fury, or pride, would only carry her so far. The exhaustion and the weakness were waiting for her, and desperation gave her anger an edge. She parried another swing and then raised her sword to bring it down with all the strength she had in one arm. He met it, holding their crossed blades an inch away from his face.

"Why won't you stop toying with me and fight?" she shouted, gasping.

He grimaced and shoved her back before blurting, "Why won't you give up?"

Their swords clashed again—the crickets had gone silent, listening to the staccato of battle, or else frightened off into the shadows. All Marian could hear was the clamor of steel on steel, and her own harsh breathing.

She swung at him, and he blocked—and this time he didn't counter the attack. She swung again, and again, until her hand gave out and the sword clattered against his and fell to the ground. Marian's legs trembled, buckled, and the moon vanished.

"Give up, damn it." Gisborne caught her as she began to fall, his own sword clanging against hers among the leaves.

Her eyes had failed, but she felt him lower her to the ground. He wasted not a moment—as soon as she went limp, she felt his hand at the clasp of Robin's cloak, and the weight of it fell away. His fingers tugged at the laces of her tunic with ruthless efficiency, but when Marian went to push his hand away, in her confusion, she tried to use the wounded arm. Pain erupted across her shoulder, radiating down her arm and through her ribs. Marian moaned and sank into moonless black.

FORTY-THREE

THE SMELL WOKE HER. She was huddled in the corner, face turned to the wall, but she knew without opening her eyes where she was. The stench of human waste and decay assailed her nose, and she tried to curl up more tightly against it.

The limestone walls of the cell were smooth, a natural cave before barred doors had been added to create a prison. She could not tell if it was the same one Will had occupied, although there were comforts in hers that he had not been given. A coarse rug covered the worst of the filth on the stone floor. A lamp burned steadily in the corner. A wineskin and a plate of bread and cold meat rested on a small wooden stool opposite her.

At that sight, realization burst in her mind that she was desperately, ravenously hungry. She scrambled across the rug and tore into the bread, drinking from the wineskin when her throat was too dry to swallow. She had nearly finished the meal, which was generous by any standards, let alone for a prisoner, before her hunger was sated enough for rational thought to return.

There were no windows, so she could not tell how much time had passed. She smelled of horse and sweat, but that told her nothing, since her last memory was of riding to meet Gisborne, and . . .

Her stomach lurched, and Marian's hand went to her throat. The tunic he'd been untying was gone. All her clothes were gone—in their stead she wore a plain, undyed gray woolen kirtle over a coarse-spun shift. Heart thudding, Marian tried to remember those last few moments before she lost consciousness.

Gisborne catching her, lowering her gently to the ground. His hand on the cloak, his fingers at her tunic. But while his manner had been urgent, he was icy calm rather than molten. His anger had fled the moment she began to fall, and he'd shown no sign of the passion he'd displayed the last time he held her.

Marian's fingers twisted in the rough fabric of the dress. He hadn't been trying to undress her—he'd been transforming her from Robin Hood to Marian again. If Gisborne had brought her to her cell as Marian, then he hadn't told the Sheriff yet the depth of her treason. She would hang regardless, whether as Robin Hood or his accomplice, and she could not think why Gisborne had bothered to keep her identity secret.

Perhaps his pride has so overtaken sense that he can't bear anyone knowing his great opponent was a woman.

Marian drank again from the skin, which made her head spin but helped warm her limbs. She was cradling it against her when she realized she'd lifted it with her right arm. Bewildered, she set the wineskin aside and pulled the neck of her dress down.

There was only a single bandage there now, fixed in place by a strap around her shoulder. But when she lifted its edge, the wound underneath was small, clean, edges puckered with new skin.

Distant, fragmented memories hovered just out of reach.

What she'd believed to be dreams suddenly took on new clarity, like shapes emerging out of a fog.

See to her wound, a voice demanded. *Use whatever resources you have, all of them. Try to make her drink.*

But my Lord, another faltered, *if she is bound for the gallows, then—*

Do as I say. Keep her here as long as you can. Drug her if you must, but keep her here. And see to her wound.

Marian had been in captivity for far longer than she'd realized. No wonder she was so ravenous.

A raucous clang and the screech of hinges echoed through the caves, followed by footsteps approaching. Marian crawled to the grille blocking off her cell, curling her fingers through it and trying to press her face close enough to see.

Some part of her must have been expecting Gisborne, for her shoulders sagged when an ordinary guardsman came into view. He glanced into her cell without stopping at first, but then saw her at the grille and halted.

"You're awake." He peered through the gloom, sounding surprised.

"Is my father here?"

The guardsman shrugged and, without another glance, turned back the way he'd come.

"Wait!" Marian tried to reach out to him, but her sleeve got tangled in the grille. "Wait—is he a prisoner also? How long have I been in this cell? What of Gisborne, is he here? Tell him I want to speak to him. Tell me—tell me something, anything, I beg you."

The guard paused. When he glanced back at her, the hardness of his features had cracked a little to reveal a hint of sympathy lurking beneath. "Eat well and drink, Lady, and pray to God if you will," he said finally. "The gallows is nearly finished."

A different guard came to fetch her, hours later, though how many, Marian did not know. He had not the sympathy of the other man, and shoved her roughly across the threshold into the courtyard.

Stiff from captivity and blinded by the sudden light, Marian lost her balance. Her hands were bound, and she could not catch herself, so she went sprawling onto the stones with a jarring thump that sent pain through her shoulder.

Her ears were ringing, roaring, disorientingly loud. She managed to lift her head and focus her eyes, and saw that unfamiliar faces surrounded her, bodies jostling for position, expressions twisted and mouths open. The roaring sharpened, and she realized the sound came not from her own ears but from the crowd.

The guard hauled her back onto her feet, and Marian saw peasants and nobles alike stretched from the castle doors to the distant gates, packed so tightly their shifting forms were like a boiling sea. And at the center of that sea, a ship—a wooden frame, the only constant in the turbulent press of bodies—a floating lifeline with a single rope dangling from its beams.

Hands reached for her as she passed, some grazing face and hips, others grabbing an arm or her hair with painful force. Numb, Marian walked on, propelled by the guard at her back whenever she faltered.

More guards held the crowds at bay, parting them to reveal a set of rudimentary steps up to the wooden platform. Marian climbed them with relief, too eager to find escape from the teeming mass of hands and jeering faces to think beyond those stairs. She reached the top and fell heavily against part of the frame, letting it take her weight.

A voice bellowed for silence, but the din only lessened a

little. That same voice began to speak, but Marian was scanning the crowd. Everywhere she looked there were strangers, and her vision blurred with tears as she searched for any familiar face to steady her. She could not see her father. There were as many women in the crowd as men, but none of them wore Elena's face. When she lifted her head to the balcony that overlooked the castle courtyard, she saw the Sheriff standing there, addressing the crowd, but the other men standing behind him were strangers to her. Gisborne was not there.

The Sheriff's voice was listing her crimes for those who could hear him over the din. Marian could have made out his words if she had focused, but she tilted her head back instead. The sky was gray, the clouds an unrelenting blanket that hid the sun so utterly she could not tell whether it was morning or afternoon. The air hung heavy with damp, so still and thick that Marian could feel it pressing in on her.

She wondered how Robin had died. Whether he had looked up at the sky, too. It would not have been cloudy there, in the dry desert. The air would not have smelled of autumn and bonfires, or been thick with damp.

I miss you, Marian thought, trying to picture Robin's face and finding to her horror that she could not. She could see his eyes, the way they'd crinkle when he laughed. She could imagine his voice, could remember his smell. But she could not picture him whole.

She'd imagined she'd done all this for him. But standing here, the gallows posts at her back, she could not lie to herself any longer. Maybe her father had been right after all—maybe she had never truly known Robin. But she would have had time to know him, if only he had not left her.

I don't know if I loved you. I don't know if I knew you. I don't know if my heart could tell the difference then between the love of being free and the love of being yours.

Marian closed her eyes.

But you were my best friend. And I miss you.

And then a voice came, with such warmth and familiarity that Marian nearly gasped aloud.

You were my best friend too, said Robin.

The noise from the crowd dimmed, as abruptly as if someone had covered Marian's ears. A guard had come forward, and he roughly cut at the bonds around her wrists until they fell to her sides. It was no respite, though—the platform was surrounded by guardsmen, with no escape.

Her gaze dropped, and she saw the Sheriff watching her with keen, unconcealed relish. He was silent, with an air of expectation.

Stupidly, still reeling from hearing Robin's spirit with her again, Marian mumbled, "What did you say?"

"I asked if you had anything to say before you die."

Marian thought, but nothing came. There were dozens of things she wished to say, but she wanted to say them to her father, to Elena, to her men, to Gisborne. She had nothing to say to the man sentencing her to die. "No."

A flicker of annoyance creased the Sheriff's face. "No? I would have thought you'd try to stall as long as possible."

Marian raised her eyes again, watching the sky over the edge of the castle. "If I am to die, my Lord Sheriff, then what does it matter if it is now or a few moments later?"

"Aren't you expecting your Robin Hood to come for you?" The Sheriff was enjoying himself. "To storm in at the last moment in a flurry of arrows and bravery, and sweep you to safety?"

Marian gazed back at him mutely.

"No, you're not." The Sheriff's satisfied smile broadened. "Isn't that strange?"

The crowd was murmuring, milling impatiently, as confused as she'd been moments before. But as she watched the Sheriff, he met her gaze with a cool, cunning gleam in his eye. And she understood.

"I think the reason you aren't trying to stall is that you know he can't come for you. Because you know who he is."

Marian raised her face to the sky again. A solitary raindrop fell from the lowering clouds and broke apart against her lips. She closed her eyes and breathed deeply, and imagined she was in the forest, its dripping canopy overhead, its muffling quiet all around her. Robin was with her again. She would not die alone.

"Robin Hood was wounded a fortnight ago," the Sheriff declared, voice rising. "A single arrow through the shoulder."

A guard came forward and dragged Marian away from the gallows frame. A large hand grabbed the neck of her dress and pulled, the sound of ripping fabric cutting through the collective gasps of shock and confusion that rose from the crowd. Marian staggered but kept her feet by sheer force of will. Dizzy and shivering, she clutched at the torn edges of her dress, the sleeve pooling at her elbow, the neck gaping low over her right shoulder.

Not all present understood the significance of her bandaged shoulder. Realization spread in waves, voices rising and falling, whispered questions and explanations passing from man to woman, parent to child. Tension grew like a creeping mold, and whispers turned to cries, and cries to shouts. In moments the crowd was even louder than it had been before the Sheriff spoke, and pressing in so close that the guards ringing the gallows platform had to draw their weapons to hold the spectators off.

The voices were so many as to be indistinguishable, and yet by some strange trick of echo, Marian distinctly heard someone cry, "Long live Robin Hood!"

The Sheriff had heard it too, and heard that cry begin to spread, taken up by another, and another, until at least a dozen voices chanted the words. He bellowed again for silence, and didn't wait for obedience before he went on.

"Well? What do you say to this? Do you admit it?"

Marian looked up, and it took some time for her to focus on the Sheriff's reddened, angry face. Her lips parted, and she tasted the droplets of rain there before speaking. The crowd hushed, and waited, and watched with upturned faces. Marian murmured, "Long live Robin Hood."

The Sheriff's red face went purple, and he leaned out over the balustrade. "Confess," he shouted. "Confess, and I will spare your father."

The world went still. She no longer heard the crowd, no longer felt the cold on her bare shoulder and throat. Another raindrop fell, and she blinked moisture from her eyes. Intention crystallized, and she drew a shuddering breath.

"I am—"

"Enough!" The voice cracked through the air like shattering stone, and Marian had a strange swell of irritation. *Will they never stop interrupting me?*

The wild thought scattered, though, as she saw someone forcing his way through the press of the crowd. She could see only the black of his hair and the occasional glint of chain mail and dark leather, and in her confusion she did not recognize him until he'd mounted the stairs.

"Enough," Gisborne said, his mask so perfect he seemed made of stone. "Let her go, my Lord."

The Sheriff, his ire fading in favor of confusion, retorted, "It never occurred to you, did it, little brother? That your infamous Robin Hood could be the lady at your side."

Gisborne let out a snort of derision. "You're mad. She's a woman." He looked as he always had, hair raked back from his face, immaculate tunic laced up to his chin, black eyes cold. He carried a bundle under one arm, but the other rested—casually, lightly—on the hilt of the sword at his waist. He did not look at Marian. "Clever, yes, resourceful. But a woman nonetheless."

"Not much of one," the Sheriff sneered. "Look at her— tall and awkward as a lad, no grace or beauty to her. Have you checked, little brother, to see if she really is a woman after all?"

The question was not meant in earnest—her dress torn and gaping, there was no hiding the rounded shoulder, the swell of her breast. The question was a dagger, and it wasn't meant for Marian.

Gisborne gazed coolly back up at the Sheriff. "She is not Robin Hood—that is all that concerns you."

The Sheriff waved a dismissive hand. "Go back to your poachers and cutpurses. You don't know what you're talking about."

"I do know." Gisborne's lips curved. Marian saw it, recognized that twist—humorless but amused, wry and cutting. He lifted the bundle under his arm and then shook it out. Wool cascaded in an emerald green waterfall, and with it a bow and a handful of arrows clattered to the wooden platform. Gisborne let the cloak fall and held up a leather object in his hand for the Sheriff and all Nottingham to see.

He tossed the mask down upon the green pool of the infamous cloak. "I know because I am Robin Hood."

FORTY-FOUR

THE SHERIFF WAS LAUGHING. Marian could neither move nor think. The crowd, confused by the quick-fire twists and turns, milled and shifted. "Of all the ways you have tried to raise yourself above your birth, this is by far the most entertaining."

Gisborne did not return his mirth. He stood absolutely still, ignoring Marian altogether, watching his lord calmly. "It is no jest."

The Sheriff grinned. "So you wrestled yourself, that day outside our walls, in full view of a staring crowd. You clashed swords with yourself in Sherwood, surrounded by your own guardsmen?"

"Decoys. How better to make certain no one would suspect me than to hire someone to appear as Robin Hood while I was there? *A child could have thought of it.*"

The words brought life back to Marian's mind, thawing her frozen body. She caught her breath as the rain began to fall in earnest, pattering against her hair and bare shoulder.

The Sheriff's eyebrows lifted. He was still amused, though impatience quickened his voice. "Every bit of evidence, every story, every connection points to her. Her family. Her servants."

"And who brought you that evidence, my Lord?"

The Sheriff's breath caught, and amusement drained away.

Gisborne pressed his advantage. "Who spun you a story of intrigue and loyalties and gangs of noble outlaws that pointed in every direction but the right one? Who stood to gain most from the disgrace of Edwinstowe but one poised to take ownership of the neighboring lands of Locksley?"

Color flooded the Sheriff's cheeks. His eyes moved from Marian to Gisborne, disbelief and anger mingled together. "What could have possibly driven you to such an insane plot?"

"Justice." Gisborne's smile was thin, his demeanor as gray as the rain falling around him. His gaze moved, not to Marian, but to the rope that hung from the gallows frame. Though his expression never wavered, Marian knew he was seeing a memory unfurl there. This square was where his father had died. "I am of low birth. A commoner. A peasant. You reminded me of that every chance you had. You have always known how I hated you. Does it so surprise you, *brother*, that I should choose my own people over you?"

The Sheriff was not enjoying himself anymore. His face was taut with fury, eyes snapping and spittle flecking the meticulously shaped beard below his lips. "If you are who you say, why come here? Why confess now, after framing such a clever explanation for your crimes?"

"Because of all the wild stories they tell of Robin Hood, one has always been true." Gisborne's hand tightened on the hilt of his sword, but Marian saw a man searching for support, not readying himself to attack. "He's in love with the Lady Marian."

In the silence that followed, Gisborne's steady eyes wavered. They flicked to the side and back, as if he could not quite stop himself trying to look Marian's way. The Sheriff spluttered, the guards shifted uncertainly, looking from one another to their commander on the platform. The crowd watched, breathless and silent, enraptured by the story unfolding before their eyes.

"Enough of this!" The Sheriff slammed his gloved fists down on the balcony rail. "It's all lies—except perhaps that you feel for the wretched woman. This is all some mad attempt to save her. I saw Robin Hood shoot at that contest, and I've seen you fight all my life—you could never have made those shots."

"You've seen what you wished to see," said Gisborne. In one motion he stooped and retrieved Robin's bow from where it lay atop the cloak, and one of the arrows. He braced himself and then paused, and finally his eyes rose to meet Marian's. His scar twitched, and his lips curved. Then he was moving again, and before the crowd had time to catch its collective breath, he spun toward the balcony where the Sheriff stood, drew the arrow back, and fired.

Gasps and screams punctuated the thud of the arrow as it struck. The Sheriff's bulging eyes rolled right, where the shaft of the arrow was quivering gently a hair's breadth away from his head. He clapped a hand to his face, where the arrow's point had scored a red line across his cheek.

"You missed," he howled, fear and pain cracking his voice.

"Robin Hood never misses." Gisborne tossed the bow down again with a clatter.

The Sheriff turned, reaching for the arrow to pull it out of the wall behind him, and saw that it had struck the exact center of his crest on the banner hanging behind him. Enraged, he whirled and slammed his fists on the stone again. "Arrest him. Kill him—now, you damned slackwits!"

The crowd erupted, and the guards ringing the gallows fell into chaos. They did not know whether to obey their Sheriff or protect their commander, and some were overcome by the press of bodies that drew them, flailing and disarmed, into the crowd. That most of the townsfolk were on the side of Robin Hood was obvious—in a single instant, Gisborne had gone from villain to hero, and they would not see him cut down.

Gisborne dropped to his knees in time to avoid one half-hearted swing from the guard who'd dragged Marian out, and then kicked him off the platform. He turned in time to catch Marian as she threw herself at him, suddenly freed from the spell that had pinned her, in astonishment, to the gallows.

"You're mad," she shouted through the rain, shoving him away when he tried to take hold of her. "They'll hang us all now—you could have—"

"For God's sake, Marian, be quiet!" Gisborne dragged her toward him, behind the dubious shelter of the gallows frame. A sword bit into the wood above their heads, showering them with splinters. "If I am guilty, then all I told him about you is suspect. You and your father, and your maid, and her brother—all of you are cleared."

Marian glared at him, breathless, eyes burning. "So I am to watch *you* hang?"

A guard tried to clamber up the side of the platform, and with a grimace of effort, Gisborne bared his teeth and shoved him back into the sea of bodies below. "I have no intention of hanging."

"But—"

He still had a grip on her arm and tugged her close enough

for him to raise his other hand and take hold of her chin. *"Surrender, Marian."*

The word made her stop, her mind stuttering to a halt. Even the raindrops coursing down his face seemed to slow, each carving its own path across his skin. Gisborne's cheek twitched, and before Marian could recover, he pulled her sideways and dropped her neatly and abruptly off the edge of the platform and into the mud.

Steel scraped, and she heard him roar as he got to his feet and began to fight. Marian rolled, narrowly missing being trampled by multiple sets of boots. She was forcing herself to her feet when hands seized her around the waist and pulled her down. The impact of hitting the ground a second time nearly knocked the breath out of her, and when those same hands dragged her backward into the darkness beneath the platform, she swung out wildly, unable to see her assailant.

Her fist met solid flesh with a meaty thump, and somewhere nearby a familiar voice said placidly, "Ow."

Eyes glittered in the darkness, which was cut into slices by knives of light between the boards of the platform. Another voice, equally familiar, said cheerfully, "Ho, Robin."

Marian's capacity for astonishment had been drained. She sat back with a hard thump. "Alan?" she gasped.

"And Will," said a third voice. "They keep accidentally kicking my foot. It *is* broken, lads."

The strips of light flickered wildly as people passed by above. The fighting had intensified, and there was now more than one man on the platform. Marian's eyes began to adjust, and she gazed around at the three silhouettes huddled in the gloom, damp with rain dripping through the boards overhead. One was distinctly larger than the others.

Little John grinned, his teeth visible in the dim light. "You don't punch very hard."

"I was off guard," Marian said weakly. "What . . . how are you . . ."

Alan spoke quickly, words tumbling out one after the other. "It was the only plan we could think of, the only way to get close enough to stop the hanging, and hopefully escape with you in the chaos that ensued. We've been here since dawn, my Lady. Marian. Robin. Christ, what are we to call you, anyway?"

"Shut up, Alan," Little John said mildly. His large bulk moved toward the edge of the platform, the thin gray light bringing him into view as he peered out through the rushing feet all around them.

"Where is Elena?" Marian asked breathlessly.

"Under guard in Edwinstowe Manor, along with your father." Alan's voice was grim. "Safe for now."

Thudding footsteps showered them with rain and mud from the slits above, and Marian caught her breath and scrambled to join Little John in surveying the rush of feet and bodies beyond the edge of the gallows. "They'll hang him—we have to get him out of here."

"It's Gisborne," said Will, voice hard and flat. "Let them hang him."

"He just saved her life. You really do have shit for brains. Pardon my language, Lady." But Alan didn't sound all that sorry. "I hate to point out the obvious, but you're still—your shoulder is not healed. You can't fight like this."

Marian's eyes darted back and forth, trying to make sense of the chaotic tumble of limbs beyond the shelter of the platform overhead. A body fell heavily to the ground nearby, and a pair of dazed eyes met hers from beneath a guard's helm before he was dragged away by a horde of onlookers. She looked up, trying to peer through the boards, but could see nothing but the flash of light and shadow as limbs and bodies moved across the gaps.

She cast about for a plan. Her men were armed, and her first instinct was to commandeer one of their swords, but Alan was right. Her shoulder was better than it had been, and she might be able to hold a sword, but she'd have little strength to swing it or block more than a blow or two. And she wouldn't be able to draw a bow for a long, long time.

Marian gazed back out into the drizzle-shrouded chaos until her eyes focused on one steady, unmoving bit of color. A corner of green dangled over the edge of the platform. She was not weaponless after all. She made a grab for the cloak and dragged it over the edge and into the shadows. As she pulled it over her shoulders, a hand seized her elbow.

Alan's face was close to hers, intent and anxious. "What are you doing?"

Rising certainty curved her lips into a smile. "Being Robin Hood." She squeezed his arm and then darted out into the fray before her men could stop her.

She was instantly knocked over by someone running past, and she barreled into a short, pockmarked man wielding a heavy spindle as a cudgel. He started to swing it and then stopped, gaping. All he could see was the hood—Marian dropped her eyes as fast as she could—but his arms seized her out of the mud and dragged her back onto her feet.

The crowd carried him away before she could say a word of gratitude, but Marian had her balance now, and she wove her way through the rioting mass of people, many of whom saw the cloak and fell back out of her path.

She reached the platform's edge again in time to see Gisborne's sword fly out of his hands, knocked away by a big man in guard's mail. Gisborne flung himself down onto the wood to avoid two more swords, spraying blood onto the planks from a gash in his neck. Horror gave Marian strength, and she launched herself up onto the platform with an inarticulate cry.

Momentum carried her into the big man, who took a step back onto thin air and then toppled off the edge of the gallows with a bleat of consternation. The other two men were recovering their balance and readying to swing again. Marian straightened, and a ragged cheer went through the masses. To them, yet a third Robin Hood—not Marian *or* Gisborne—had appeared, and they could not get enough.

Marian grabbed for Gisborne's arm and dragged him up, ignoring the breathless, wordless protest that escaped him. She glanced toward the balustrade, careful to keep the hood shadowing her face. The Sheriff was staring, eyes bulging, at her and Gisborne side by side. He began shouting, and though Marian could not hear what he said, she could read his utter bewilderment in his features. He'd been *so* certain the Lady Marian was Robin Hood, and then *so* convinced that Gisborne was, that now he had no idea what to do.

She waited a moment longer, making sure the onlookers had seen Gisborne, half-supported by the cloaked figure of Robin Hood, until a crossbow bolt hummed past them.

"Time to go," she shouted into Gisborne's ear, and then shoved him toward the edge of the platform.

FORTY-FIVE

IN A BALLAD, MARIAN would have swung in on a rope, or a conveniently draped banner, and swept him up and carried him off in a single, breathtaking feat of daring. In a ballad, the rescuer would outweigh the rescued by a significant margin and be able to sling the fainting, dainty form over a shoulder.

But Marian could only push Gisborne bodily into the crowd and then jump from the platform herself. She landed with a thud that jarred her breath painfully in her chest, and she groped around until she found Gisborne on his knees, gasping. She had only one good arm, and blood soaked skin and tunic down his side, but together they careened up and into the crowd.

This time the hands that touched her as she passed were those of allies. When her feet slid and skidded against the mud, someone grabbed her elbow and hauled her upright again. When a guard managed to free himself from a cluster of maddened townsfolk and come at them, sword raised, a stout woman in an apron dusted with flour gave a shout and flew at him, along with half a dozen others, knocking him to the ground.

A path, ragged and changing but unmistakable, opened before them, and Marian broke into a run. Gisborne had recovered his breath a little and kept up with her, limping and swearing. They burst free of the crowd, which had condensed around the gallows like a swarm of flies around honey, leaving a gap between them and the edge of the square.

She could not afford to stop, but her steps slowed with uncertainty. They could not outrun the guards forever—as soon as one of them spotted the two figures outside the crowd, they'd be in pursuit. And Gisborne was bleeding heavily, and her muscles were beginning to shake.

"Domina," Gisborne gasped, panting and leaning on Marian's good shoulder.

She was in better shape than he, but not by much. In confusion, she thought for a wild moment that he was praying. "What?"

"My horse, woman, my horse—he's by the gate. He won't have strayed."

"Your—but *Domina* means 'Lady.'"

Gisborne glared at her, one eye starting to swell shut. "I named him when I was six," he retorted. "Would you rather stand here and discuss the issue or finish rescuing me?"

Marian's strength nearly gave out as a quick, astonished ring of laughter burst from her lips. "You named your stallion *Lady*?"

Gisborne's scowl flickered and shifted as he raised his hand to swipe the rain from his face. His eyes glinted, and the thin lips relaxed into the tiniest of curves. He took her arm, and together they put on a fresh burst of speed.

The people of Nottingham spilled out of the square after them, cascading down the streets and into the alleyways. The riot shifted as they ran, violence giving way to mad triumph and spontaneous abandon, though swords still clanged in the distance and a few wild arrows flew into the thatch of the houses on either side of them.

Domina was waiting, whinnying nervously and sidestepping with agitation. Gisborne didn't break stride, putting a foot into the stirrup and using his momentum to launch himself into the saddle. He reached down, and Marian clasped his arm in hers and let him pull her up behind him. The stallion needed no prompting, but Gisborne let out a shout of encouragement anyway as the horse jolted into a gallop.

Wind tore Marian's hood back and whipped at her hair, soaked from the downpour. Holding on to Gisborne with her good arm, she tilted her head to get a look at the wound on his neck. It had sliced through the scarred flesh, but either the skin there was thicker for its scarring or he had more luck than she'd ever known, for it was shallow and clean. Bloody, but not a mortal wound.

Marian leaned forward, lips close to Gisborne's ear, about to shout at him to make for Sherwood Forest, when something shrieked past them and vanished into the field beyond. Marian turned, her hair tangled all about her face, and made out the shapes of half a dozen men on horseback in pursuit. Another crossbow bolt whistled but went high.

Gisborne wasted no more time, leaning hard and pulling Domina left, into the forest. Bare branches whipped past them, and Marian ducked her head down behind Gisborne's shoulder with only the tiniest flicker of guilt at using him as a shield.

Most of the trees had shed their leaves in preparation for winter, and the thickets and briars had withered to skeletal tangles. Sherwood Forest had transformed itself from a realm of lush shadow and hidden places to an empty, barren landscape that offered no hope of losing their pursuers. Beneath them Domina had broken into a lather, head down and snorting hard for breath. Gisborne must have ridden him hard already that day to reach Nottingham—where he had been, or how he had known to come, she did not know.

She dragged her hood back up and glanced again over her shoulder. The guardsmen were gaining on them. Domina was bigger than Jonquille, but exhausted, and carrying two—the horses behind them were fresh, and carrying only one man each. Marian searched her mind, unfurling her mental map of Sherwood Forest, trying to ignore the jolting, shuddering gait long enough to focus.

"North," she shouted, and without hesitation, Gisborne urged Domina in a wide curve to the right.

They galloped on, until abruptly the stallion gave a squeal of protest, faltered, and fell.

Gisborne and Marian were thrown ahead into the leaves, and Marian hit a knobby root that winded her. Gisborne scrambled toward the stallion, who was already staggering back to his feet in the patch of mud that had caused his fall. He stood unsteadily, sides heaving, nostrils flared.

"He can't run anymore," Marian croaked, voice transformed by the blow to her ribs. "If we survive, we'll come back for him."

Gisborne looked from his horse to the riders closing on them and back. His hands were automatically running over the stallion's legs, feeling for swelling that would tell of a broken bone, or blood from some unseen injury. Gisborne's eyes met Marian's over his shoulder and he swore, leaving his horse with a last lingering, agonized glance.

If Marian had not already known her heart, she would have

then. Gisborne pulled her to her feet and they ran. The river was close, Marian knew. There were narrow, winding paths worn by sheep and cattle down the sheer embankment on the river's south side—if they could reach it in time to get a head start, their pursuers would have to dismount to follow them.

A crossbow bolt whizzed by, so close its fletching tore a rent in the side of Marian's cloak. Her breath was failing her, and her legs—she'd been two weeks in bed, more or less, and was weak with inactivity. Gisborne was tiring too, sweat plastering his hair to his temples and pain beginning to shorten his stride. Marian recognized it now: it was never that his limp was affected to lower his opponent's guard—he simply ran despite it, when he had to. She had to assume it hurt a great deal to do so.

Marian looked behind them again and her breath caught in fear. Their pursuers were so close she could see the clouds of breath from their lathered mounts and hear the jangle of chain mail and saddle.

Then a hard body collided with hers and slammed her to the ground.

Gasping, dizzy, half-tangled in Gisborne's limbs, Marian rolled to sit up—and nearly fell, as her hand at her side met empty air. Wheezing, for she'd elbowed him in the ribs on instinct, Gisborne caught her by the cloak and tried to pull her back.

But she'd seen it now, what he had seen while she was watching their pursuers, the reason he'd tackled her. And in fairness, it was the only way he could have stopped her before her momentum carried her over the edge of the cliff.

Far below, the river roiled like a stormy sky. Gisborne's arms were around her, his panting breath hot on her shoulder, and they leaned on each other as they pulled themselves up. Marian held on to him with her good arm, and he anchored her while she leaned out over the edge, searching for one of the little pathways down. But this spot was an overhang, a sheer drop above the river below. There might be a path out of sight upriver or down, but the earth thundered with the drumming of hooves, and they had no more time.

Gisborne turned and curled his hands around her arms. His eyes were transformed, their black depths full and tempting, inviting her to give in and drown there.

"Marian—I meant it." The words were a desperate torrent, flowing around gasps for breath and cracked lips. "I love you. I thought I loved you, and then you kissed me, and I thought then that I loved you, and then I found out who you were, and I hated you and loved you even more—I'd die for you. I'd die with you." He pulled her closer, trying to fold her in his arms.

Marian shoved them away, inching toward the cliff's edge and looking down again. "Can you swim?" Her voice was high and thin with fear, but sharp—sharp enough to pull Gisborne out of the flood of declarations he was spilling.

He stared at her, bewildered, his arms still half-outstretched.

She met his eyes, trying to shore up her own courage. She'd heard him, what he said—she could not dwell in the words now, but they filled her, rose in her, and when they would have over-flowed she found she was a vessel vast enough to keep them safe. "Gisborne!" she shouted, trying to jolt him from his daze. "Can you swim?"

He ducked as a crossbow bolt hummed overhead, and responded instantly: "Yes."

Marian tried to catch her breath, but there wasn't time. "I can't," she whispered, and took a step back toward the edge. Despite the paper-thin sound of her voice, it was not a plea or a lament. It wasn't a surrender—it was a challenge.

His eyes flickered an instant's confusion, then sharpened with dawning realization. "No—wait—" But his hand closed on empty air as Marian whirled away.

Arrows, thought Marian, *are winged creatures.*

She leaped.

FORTY-SIX

WORD OF THE DEATH of Robin Hood spread across
the land like enveloping twilight. The people of Nottingham
huddled together against the shadow of hopes dashed, darkness leaching away the strength they'd found in defending
their champion. Still, here and there, pockets of light flared up
against grief; a lantern lit when a poacher saw a flash of green
among the bare trees of Sherwood Forest. A torch guttered
to life when a rumor began to spread that the coffin buried
beneath the unmarked gravestone was empty, that all they'd
ever found of him was his cloak, tattered and faded by the river
currents. The soft glow of candlelight swelled each time someone whispered, "Robin lives."

The Sheriff had lost his hold over his land. There was little
he could do, for the strength of a people united had far out-
stripped the meager power of unjust law. And yet little would
change, for the Prince would send a replacement eventually, and
that replacement would be tasked with the same assignment, and

coin would continue to bleed out of England on its way to fund the King's war. The new Sheriff would not be so different from the old. The people would continue to suffer.

And the King never would return from his crusade.

But something had shifted that day, when the land rose up in defense of Robin Hood. The people had seen it, and their lords, too. War would come, and war would go, and barons would rise and fall. Eventually, amid the struggle and blood and rebellion, a great charter would take shape and alter forever the unlimited power of kings.

And the story of Robin Hood would rise. No one would ever tell the tale exactly right, for no one person knew the whole truth even before the details began to slide away into the shadows of memory.

But some things about the story would never change. Robin Hood was always quick and fearless, and devoted to his people. He could shoot faster and truer than any man, and was clever enough to outwit his enemies at every turn. He lived and breathed in Sherwood Forest, and made the woods his home, and if ever he was captured, he would always escape.

And his heart, always, belonged to Marian.

The water had hit her like stone, driving out every scrap of thought and self. She wasn't afraid, for the impact had stripped that from her too, and by the time tatters of conscious thought began to form, there was already a certainty in place that held far more power than fear.

Her leap had not been despair, or arrogance. She could not swim, but he could. He had not thought to escape that way, but she had. He would follow her.

Something caught at her throat and pulled her down and

into the river's current. She struggled, clawing at the thick wool cutting into her neck until the cloak's clasp finally broke. Free, drifting, she opened her eyes and peered through the depths in time to see a vague, ghostly cloaked form floating just out of reach. It seemed to hover there against the current for an instant before vanishing into the murky water beyond.

Then an arm caught hold of her trailing skirts, dragged her up, and pulled her into its grasp.

Gisborne dumped her unceremoniously into the mud on the river's bank and collapsed beside her, facedown, chest heaving in great audible gasps. Breathing was agony, and Marian concentrated on persuading her lungs to work again. Eventually a hand touched her arm, and she rolled onto her side, and the hand grabbed her by the waist and pulled her close.

She could not open her eyes, exhaustion weighting her lids. She could only lie there against his shoulder, her icy lips resting at his equally frigid throat. As if the effort of pulling her close had used up the last of his strength, Gisborne's arm lay across her hip like a wet log long after their breathing began to calm.

Cold caught up to Marian before her strength did, and she curled herself more tightly against Gisborne, shivering. His arms finally moved, tightening around her. His body was little warmer than hers, but when he tilted his head and rested his cheek against her brow, she felt a flicker of life.

"You should run." Marian's voice had been reduced to a cracked whisper.

Gisborne said nothing, gave not even a twitch of his body to show he'd heard her.

"The Sheriff might think me innocent now, but he'll want your head for claiming to be . . ." She waited, but still Gisborne didn't speak, or move, or do anything but lie there still and cold as stone. "I have relatives in Aquitaine—I could send money...."

Her voice petered out, and a trickle of alarm shivered down her neck, for Gisborne was still not moving. She dug one elbow into the mud and raised herself, shaking, so that she could look at his face.

His eyes were open, staring skyward with such empty serenity that Marian's heart froze. Then his mouth opened, and he said in a hoarse, ruined voice, "I could kill you right here."

Relief made Marian's elbow slip, and she fell back against him, making him grunt irritably. "It'd make a waste of the trouble you've gone to."

"Good God, Marian, how could you—" He had to stop to cough, but he was too tired to cough, so he just shook, and groaned.

Marian felt her jaw clench. "I knew if I jumped, you would jump."

Gisborne's hand moved to encircle her arm. "If you had waited half a breath longer—"

"You would've told me not to take the risk, that you'd hold them off while I escaped, that at least one of us might live— something like that?"

She lifted her head and saw that he'd abandoned his study of the overcast sky and was glaring at her. "I would've told you how much a fall from that height was going to hurt when you hit the water."

Marian's breath burbled out in a laugh, and she dropped her head against his chest. "It might take them a day, maybe two, to regroup and send men to Edwinstowe. Time enough to rest a little. We'll give you a horse, and food, and—"

Gisborne's arm tightened, squeezing her battered ribs, and the rest of Marian's speech emerged as a breathless squeak. He grinned at that wordless victory, black eyes wicked and gleaming. "I've broken no laws, Marian." He paused, considering. "None the Sheriff can prove, at any rate. At most, I lied to save the woman I love from an unjust sentence. I don't think he can have me killed for that."

Marian's body had begun to warm, but with warmth came sensation, and she noticed a sharp, familiar burning at her shoulder. She squeaked again and gurgled, "Let me go—I think I'm bleeding again."

Gisborne swore, releasing her so abruptly that she slid down into the muck again. He bent over her, peeling away the torn, sodden wool and linen so that he could inspect her shoulder. It was bleeding, but only sluggishly. It would scab once her skin dried. "Forgive me," Gisborne muttered, frowning at the wound.

"For squeezing me, or for shooting me?"

Gisborne's eyes flicked up, the twitch of his cheek acknowledging the point she'd scored. "Take one of each." He smoothed the edge of her wet dress back away from the wound, and as he started to withdraw, Marian caught his wrist with a muted cry of alarm.

"Your hand!" Three of his fingers were swollen and blistered at the first knuckle, where a bowstring would sit. She'd seen such an injury before—she'd *had* such an injury before, more than once, when her enthusiasm for archery practice overtook her good sense.

"How was I to prove I was Robin Hood, if I could not shoot like him?" Gisborne muttered, trying to pull his hand away from her. "What did you think I was doing all that time before I came to arrest you?"

Marian cradled his hand in hers, conscious of heat rising into her face as her breath steamed the air between them. "Planning my death. Swearing revenge. Rallying your men. Leaving me to tortured purgatory for the pure pleasure of it."

"That, too," he acknowledged. He grimaced, and gave up trying to free his hand from her grasp. "I was practicing. For all the good it did."

"That arrow through the Sheriff's crest was beautifully shot," she murmured dreamily, fingertips caressing his palm.

Gisborne muttered darkly, "I was aiming for his head."

Marian found she had breath enough to laugh, and once she began, she could not stop—she laughed until tears rolled down her cheeks, until her breath tangled in her throat, until Gisborne, in rising alarm, sat up and lifted his hand to slap her. Instinct seized her muscles and she sat up too, swatting his hand away before it could connect.

Movement had sobered her, and she wiped her cheeks, searching for breath and watching Gisborne. She let her eyes linger, noticing details in his features she never had before, because she'd never let herself look so closely for fear he would notice the secrets hidden in her own eyes. He had long, sweeping eyelashes that matched his dark hair. They lowered under her scrutiny.

"I don't know what I'll do," he admitted, voice a bit less ragged now. "I don't think the Sheriff can arrest me for treason, but somehow I doubt he will pass along the Prince's dispensation for Locksley's lands and title now. And he may find some way to punish me that I haven't thought of."

Marian, still distracted by the eyelashes, shook herself. She studied him again, head tilted, forcing herself not to get lost in his features. They sat together, Marian leaning against him with knees drawn up, him with his legs outstretched on the other side of her, arms clasped about her.

"As my husband," she said slowly, savoring the words and

making certain she was repeating them as he'd first spoken them, "you'd be under my protection." She had to fight to keep from smiling.

His lashes had flown up, and as she went on, his eyes narrowed and fixed on hers.

"I would ask nothing of you. I know your feelings toward me. . . ." He reached for her as she spoke, and she quickened her quivering voice in an effort to finish before he could stop her. "I would not touch you unless you wished me to, and—"

His kiss was gentle, almost fearful, until Marian turned in his arms and leaned against him, hard. As if her response had broken a dam within him, he seized her and his lips turned fierce and possessive. His touch said what he could not—that he feared he had lost her, that he would not lose her again, that he needed nothing else but her. Marian let her tears fall, and they clung to each other, and surrendered.

He was kissing the tears from her cheeks when he realized she was shivering, and not from his touch. He pulled back and took in her bare shoulder, and the dress clinging to her body, and his eyebrows drew in as he realized her cloak was gone. "What of the outlaw who rescued us?"

Marian tore her eyes away and looked upon the river, swollen and swift with rain, and thought of Robin's ghost as it vanished into the depths. "Drowned," she said softly.

Gisborne said nothing for a time, watching her. Then he took her hand in both of his and raised it to his lips, bowing his head and lingering with all the chivalrous deliberation of a knight out of legend. "Long live Robin Hood."

ACKNOWLEDGMENTS

No book is written in a vacuum. This one is very much a product of the time it was written, but also of the people who helped make it happen.

As always, I'm eternally grateful for my agent, Josh Adams, and the team at Adams literary, as well as Kristen Pettit and the exceedingly clever—and exceedingly patient—team at Harper-Collins.

I owe a huge thank-you to the various experts who helped weigh in on this book. In particular I'd like to thank Elizabeth Kuhl Nevitt for her expertise on the historical time period, Sarah Brown for her assistance with all things horses, Grimm for getting me started on the path of historical archery all those years ago, and Arjun Anand for his insight into costume, armor, and weaponry of the time period.

On that note, I also owe a fairly substantial apology to these experts, because despite their best efforts, this is *not* a historically accurate book, nor was it intended to be. The various parts of the Robin Hood legend originated across centuries, making any story that includes all of them anachronistic by necessity. At a certain point, you just embrace the madness. And to my experts—and my more historically inclined readers—all mistakes are mine. I'm hoping most of them were on purpose, and that you can forgive me taking license in favor of a story!

To my parents and sister, and my extended family of supporters: thank you. I'm sure at some point I'll get the hang of this whole writing thing, and I'll stop stalling two-thirds of the way through every book so I can question my life choices, but I suspect even then I'm still going to need your help. Thank you for all the years you've backed me.

And finally, my biggest thank-you goes to Amie, who never fails to get excited about my stories long after I've given up on them.

I hope you've enjoyed this book—can't wait to see you for the next one!